THOMAS**KELLY**

The**Rackets**

A PLUME BOOK

PLUME
Published by the Penguin Group
Penguin Putnam Inc., 375 Hudson Street,
New York, New York 10014, U.S.A.
Penguin Books Ltd, 80 Strand,
London WC2R 0RL, England
Penguin Books Australia Ltd,
Ringwood, Victoria, Australia
Penguin Books Canada Ltd, 10 Alcorn Avenue,
Toronto, Ontario, Canada M4V 3B2
Penguin Books (N.Z.) Ltd, 182–190 Wairau Road,
Auckland 10, New Zealand

Penguin Books Ltd, Registered Offices:
Harmondsworth, Middlesex, England

Published by Plume, a member of Penguin Putnam Inc.
This is an authorized reprint of a hardcover edition published by Farrar, Straus and Giroux. For information address Farrar, Straus and Giroux, 19 Union Square West, New York, New York 10003.

First Plume Printing, June 2002
10 9 8 7 6 5 4 3 2

 REGISTERED TRADEMARK—MARCA REGISTRADA

The Library of Congress has catalogued the hardcover edition as follows:

Kelly, Thomas.
    The rackets / Thomas Kelly.
    374 p. ; 24 cm.
    ISBN 0-374-17720-1 (hc.)
    ISBN 0-452-28326-4 (pbk.)
    1. Manhattan (New York, N.Y.)—Fiction. 2. Fathers and sons—Fiction.
    3. Organized crime—Fiction. 4. Irish Americans—Fiction. 5. Working class—Fiction.
    6. Racketeering—Fiction. 7. Labor unions—Fiction. 8. Teamsters—Fiction. 9. Inwood
    (Nassau County, N.Y.)—Fiction. I. Title.
    PS3561.E39717 R33 2001
    813'.54—dc21   2001086948

Printed in the United States of America
Original hardcover design by Abby Kagan

More praise for Thomas Kelly and *The Rackets*

"*The Rackets* is the kind of authentic New York novel that will live with you awhile. Actually, this is more than a novel—it is the elevator that raises (or drops) you from Gracie Mansion to the cellars of the city's criminal underworld. The writing is tart as the street talk of the city, and the story moves deep and fast as water from the reservoir."

—Frank McCourt, author of *'Tis*

"Kelly's take on the remnants of New York's rough-and-tumble, trade-union-to-the-bone Irish Americans is dead on the money—their dialogue, their attitudes, their immutable values. *The Rackets* is a terrific read, peopled with characters masterfully drawn by a writer truly in the know."

—Vincent Patrick, author of *The Pope of Greenwich Village*

"You better have big stones—as they say—to write with convincing freshness about New York City and the Mafia it loves without guilt . . . Thomas Kelly does just that in *The Rackets*, his second novel, which, like his first, *Payback*, ably gathers mafiosi, union officials, and the Feds in a large, engaging portrait of street-level New York . . . *The Rackets* feels lived and true . . . One might add that any New York novelist writing about the city rightly fears the opinion of his hometown readers more than that of a national audience. New Yorkers know so much—too much—and require an extra dollop of inside dope to remain happy. They want to see the stuff that only they, as city experts, will appreciate. In this, Kelly doesn't disappoint, either."

—*The New York Times*

THOMAS KELLY worked ten years in construction, graduated from Fordham University and Harvard's John F. Kennedy School of Government, then served as Director of Advance for the mayor of New York. A former Teamster, he writes for *Esquire*. His first novel, *Payback*, has been adapted by David Mamet for a feature film. He lives in New York and Dublin.

For my brothers, Dennis and Kevin

"Every man has his price, what's yours?"
—Jimmy Hoffa

The Rackets

Days like this Jimmy Dolan figured he had the best job in the world. He stood on the side porch of Gracie Mansion and watched as the sun began to rise behind Hell Gate Bridge. The waters of the East and Harlem rivers met in a turbulent swirl imbued with the soft, encroaching light of dawn. A seagull wheeled overhead, then dove for prey in the wake of a police boat. He checked his watch, then sipped his steaming coffee. The liquid warmed him, and absentmindedly he picked a piece of lint off the front of his navy blue suit jacket. Election year in the Apple and he was right in the mix.

Inside the mansion, the kitchen staff was busy preparing breakfast for the civic leaders who would soon be descending on the Mayor's home. Another early-bird shmooze fest. Jimmy pulled a guest list from his inside pocket and saw that Frankie Keefe was among the expected. Politics. He wanted to laugh. It was bad enough he had made the party switch to work for a Republican mayor, and in doing so had sickened his father, but now he was expected to smile at a face he'd rather scald with his coffee. He'd ignore Keefe as much as was possible. No sense letting his father's feud ruin his day.

He glanced through the window. The Mayor was perusing the morning papers and the day's briefing memos. The breakfast was their first event; the last would end with them dragging their tired asses into a black-tie gala at the Waldorf-Astoria sometime around midnight. In between they would ricochet across the city glad-handing, paying homage, debating, and cajoling the craziest array of constituencies on the planet Earth—Koreans, Jews, investment bankers, public employees at a retirement function, a Sikh taxi association, assemblies of the insanely wealthy and the tragically destitute—all while running a city bureaucracy. There was nothing like a mayoral election. He had already worked them all, up to and including the presidential, but nowhere was politicking as intense and relentless as in New York City. There was no escape. You were on the street and the entire city was in your face. Everybody wanted something from you.

As Director of Advance it was Jimmy's job to make sure that, whatever happened each day, the Mayor was not embarrassed. He was to organize, coordinate, troubleshoot, deflect the nuts that turned up, appease the aggrieved, and handle the press, who were always hungry for a fuckup that would make page one. He loved the pace, the action, being out there, thinking on his feet. He loved even the possibility of disaster. The Mayor was not known for his patience.

Jimmy strode over to the sentry booth that looked onto East End Avenue. Chris Williams, of the Mayor's security detail, sat in the high-backed chair with one foot on the counter and leafed through the *Post*. Jimmy pulled the side door open. "Hey, Chris. How's it going?"

The officer looked up and shrugged. His eyes were swollen and tired from working a double shift, his uniform in need of an iron. "What can I tell you? Another hour I'll need toothpicks to keep my eyes open. You still got a line on Rangers tickets?"

Jimmy nodded and picked up the updated guest list for the morning's event. He scanned it quickly: bankers, elected officials, businessmen, labor leaders, lawyers, lobbyists, real estate tycoons. About half the list would have appeared on the previous mayor's watch. Now there were fewer clergy, fewer activists, less melanin, in short less voice for those on the city's margins and more leverage for those who needed it least. He dropped the list. "Looks like we're running a soup kitchen for millionaires today, Willie."

"Yeah, well, the rich get . . . you know."

"Democracy at work."

"That too."

A black Cadillac sedan pulled smoothly to the mouth of the driveway. The driver emerged slowly, straightening as he stood. He was close to six and a half feet tall. Pete Cronin, an ex-Fed whose career, Jimmy knew, had been destroyed by shady associations, booze, and one very sketchy shooting that left a drug lord splattered on a Bronx street corner. He wore a black-and-purple warm-up suit and carried the keys in his hand, twirling them on his finger. He walked slowly around the rear of the car, his alert eyes belying his casual saunter. Cronin appeared to study everything, as if he were assessing its threat potential—a lone female jogger dressed in shorts and a tee shirt despite the March chill, a pair of moneyed dog-walkers bickering along the sidewalk, a sanitation truck rolling to a halt half a block away and disgorging its crew with a screech of air brakes. He looked directly at Jimmy and smirked with recognition. Jimmy felt a jolt of unease. Cronin, with his bulk, his violent history, and his dead eyes, was a very scary guy.

Cronin opened the rear door of the Cadillac for the man who employed him after the government had dropped him. Jimmy watched Frankie Keefe, president of the International Brotherhood of Teamsters Local 383, step out. He stood, in shirtsleeves, wearing a dark tie and suspenders. There was a crispness to his attire and his manner. His very presence seemed to slap the air before him. His black hair was slicked back and he sported a deep tan acquired poolside in Miami. Cronin ducked into the car and retrieved Keefe's suit jacket, holding it up, playing the ass-kissing valet.

Jimmy felt his teeth clench. Over the course of his reign as president of the local, Keefe had quite literally taken food off the Dolan dinner table. And now Jimmy's father was running against Keefe again. It was as futile the third time as the first. But his father was not the go-along-to-get-along type. Everything about Keefe, from his two-thousand-dollar suits to his larcenous ways to his slippery backslapping demeanor made his father more determined to defeat him. Keefe, however, was firmly entrenched and not above using violence to hold on to what he had. This worried Jimmy.

Jimmy turned back toward the mansion.

"Yeah, Chris, I can get you two for Friday's game. Bruins are in town. You want 'em?"

"Sure, yeah, great. I'm off Friday. I'll bring the wife, make up for all the OT, family crap I been missing."

Jimmy checked his watch. "Those guys are early. Tell them breakfast is served at seven. They bitch and moan, tell them there's a diner

5

on Eighty-sixth. Two-fifty for the special, sausage and eggs. Think it even comes with a short OJ."

Officer Williams looked up with mild surprise. They were not usually that strict with VIPs. Jimmy rapped his knuckles on the counter. Williams nodded. "You got it, Jimbo." The two guys in the Caddy were not giving him Rangers tickets.

Jimmy stepped out of the security booth and strode quickly into the mansion. He checked his watch and looked over the schedule. He made a few phone calls to make sure his staff were on top of things. In the public bathroom downstairs he splashed some water in his face. He felt a little embarrassment over leaving Keefe to cool his heels. It was a stupid move, unprofessional. He combed his hair and considered his face. More and more as he got older he was told he favored his father. He'd be thirty a week after the election, and while he and his father certainly had the same dark Irish hair and eyes, Jimmy always felt closer to his mother's side in all other ways, especially temperament. He doubted he'd wage the same fight as his father against Keefe. It wasn't that he didn't agree with his dad; he did, absolutely. He just did not have his father's dogged idealism. Working in politics had cured him of that. He was pragmatic. It was what enabled him to suffer some of the Mayor's more rabid true believers. He'd put his time in till November, then it was off to the private sector and some real money. Adios politics.

He passed the security room. Two cops in suits sat and idly watched the closed-circuit televisions. All was quiet. The schedule would be tight. He traced the arc of the day's events in his mind. The drones in scheduling seemed to have no idea of actual travel time around the city. Jimmy might have to reschedule one of the evening events. Should he piss off the Korean Merchants Association or the conservative Democratic club in South Brooklyn? To hell with the club. They hadn't delivered anything besides complaints since the days before Ebbets Field was wrecked. Still the symbolism was worthwhile, Democratic endorsement of the Republican candidate. Plus the Mayor liked to wear that Brooklyn Dodgers cap on TV. He'd make a decision before lunch. That would be adequate time for a soothing phone call.

The guests seemed to arrive en masse. They were freshly shaved and coiffed, dressed in business suits, and full of good cheer. They moved through the room with purpose, descended on the buffet, filling their plates, sipping coffee, shaking hands, and greeting each other like relatives at a family picnic. A waft of cologne settled over the room. Jimmy pegged the average age at fifty, almost exclusively white, and heavily male. Jimmy shadowed the Mayor as he moved about the room visiting tables. He was quick to step in and jot down a name, accept a business card, attend to the details as the Mayor moved on. Those who did not get the Mayor's ear latched on to Jimmy and the other staff members. Jimmy guided a photographer around, nodding to signal him when to shoot. Get him. And him. The pictures would adorn walls well before election day.

Occasionally, Jimmy'd look up and catch Keefe staring at him from across the room. Jimmy would just turn away and focus on someone else. A chubby assemblywoman from Queens, her hot coffee breath in his face, pleaded for a job for her nephew. The woman was fighting the Mayor over his choice for Schools Chancellor. Yet here she was, lipstick staining her teeth, wearing a too tight skirt, looking for a payoff. Jimmy nodded, did his best to act interested. While he loved the action and the mechanics of his work, he hated this crass mooching that accompanied it. He wanted to say, Get lost. Instead he smiled and said, "We'll see what we can do."

"The kid's my flesh and blood, Jimmy."

"Oh, right, I forgot, your nephew." The high school dropout with two felony arrests, he wanted to add. "Police Commissioner okay?"

"Ha, ha. The Mayor needs my district."

"He's aware of that."

Jimmy maneuvered past her and came upon a group of men in a semicircle listening to his uncle, Pius Dolan, who held a cup of coffee in one hand and gestured with the other. Punchy, as he'd been known since childhood, was large in stature and presence, his full face crowned by a bushel of white hair. His wild eyebrows projected away from his face like awnings for his blue eyes. Punchy had been to a thousand of these breakfasts, a guest of several mayors. He always showed with checks and a smile and supported both parties and all candidates. His wealth flowed from several sources, some murkier than others.

But Jimmy had barely known him as he was growing up. His father and Punchy did not get along, although Jimmy never really heard why. But since he started working in politics he had spent more time with his uncle. Punchy had served as a major fund-raiser on some of the campaigns Jimmy had worked on. His uncle always treated him well and seemed intent on moving beyond the feud with his oldest brother.

"So then the guy says, Dolan, why don't we arrange a conference call and we can sort this whole mess out. So I put my arm around the guy, he stiffens up, he don't like no one touching him, and I says, you know what your problem is, Councilman, you think you can nickel-and-dime your way into this race—well, you want to play with the big boys, you got to ante up!"

The group pulled their affluent heads back and bellowed laughter. Punchy spotted him and waved to him. "Jimmy, hey, kid. Get in here. You all know Jimmy Dolan, best advance man in town. Not just 'cause he's my nephew." Although Jimmy knew the assembled, Punchy introduced him all around as if he were meeting them for the first time. Everyone acknowledged him with great, vacant smiles. Punchy spun him away from the crowd and whispered in his ear. "You gonna come work for me after the election." It was offered as a statement and not a question.

"If I'm lucky."

Punchy shook hands with a passing congressman. "Looking good." Jimmy felt his uncle lean on his shoulder. "Call me today. I got a contract for you."

Jimmy nodded, all the while keeping his eye on the Mayor. Punchy swung away to focus his glow on someone else and Jimmy made a mental note to call him from the field. He liked dealing with the old-school types like Punchy—men and women who understood the value of contracts, the reciprocal nature of politics, the practical worth of the give-and-take. Compromise, the American way. He was curious to see what his uncle needed.

Jimmy knifed through the crowd to catch up with the Mayor. He watched the boss work the room. The man was a natural, and possessed of charm that, unfortunately for his higher political aspirations, eluded the camera altogether. He came across pale and stiff on film. One of his nicknames among the staff was Dead Man Walking. The Mayor turned away from two bankers and was cornered by an upset county leader—upset, Jimmy guessed, about the solid waste management plant the Mayor had forced on his home district. The Mayor put his hand to his chin, head tilted downward, his eyes fixed on the man before him. He affected concern this way for nearly a minute. Jimmy moved closer. The Mayor began to pull his head away; the county leader leaned closer, rising on the balls of his Cole-Haans, the Mayor backed into a corner.

Jimmy saw Sergeant Gleason push away from the near wall, finger his earpiece, and move toward the Mayor. Gleason glanced at Jimmy, who nodded, and held up a hand, to say, I'll get this one. Jimmy stood at the Mayor's side. "Your Honor." Jimmy held up his watch and tapped it solemnly. "The funeral," he said it with delicacy. The Mayor told the county leader, "Jimmy will call by the end of the week. We'll see what we can do." The Mayor took the chance and escaped.

The county leader tugged at Jimmy's sleeve. "Who died?"

Jimmy said, "It's a family thing. Not to worry."

"Oh." The county leader shook his head, as if not convinced, but said, "My sympathies."

Jimmy knew the man would find out about the lie. Jimmy would have to smooth the guy's hurt feelings and convince him to take 200 truckloads of garbage a day.

The crowd started to thin, but many of the guests seemed in no hurry to leave. Jimmy saw the Mayor motion to him. "Funeral?"

"It was the only way to get rid of the guy." Jimmy was more interested in results than in making everyone happy.

"I guess you're right."

Jimmy handed the Mayor the schedule. The Mayor looked past him and his face broke into a wide smile. Jimmy turned as Frankie Keefe walked up and shook the Mayor's hand. Then they embraced and patted each other's backs heartily, like old friends who'd happened upon each other in a foreign city. "Your Honor. You're looking good. Let me tell you something, it's early yet, but me and all the members are behind you one thousand percent, a hundred thousand. You make that other crowd look like a bunch of trash." Keefe turned to Jimmy as if he had just noticed him. "Oh, hey, what we got here? This is the kid whose old man is running against me, again."

The Mayor turned to Jimmy. "Union democracy at work. Nice to see it."

"Yeah, the two of us are in the same boat, way I see it. You and me, Your Honor. Easy elections against nobody candidates."

Jimmy returned Keefe's fake smile. "Good luck." He turned to the Mayor. "I'll see you in Brooklyn."

"Luck ain't got squat to do with it," Keefe said.

Jimmy could not help himself. "Yeah, and in your case neither does merit."

The Mayor pulled back, looked to Jimmy, then back to Keefe, his face forming a question. Jimmy felt the air go all hot around them, the commotion of the gathering fade to a blur. His face flushed and he watched as Keefe's entire carriage tightened and his eyes went dark and hard.

Keefe bared his canines and shook his head. "Just like your old man, huh, a wisecrack remark for everything."

Jimmy tried to lower his voice, but failed. "Least he hasn't ended up like your uncle, dead in prison for stealing from his members."

The Mayor looked at his feet, then sucked breath through his teeth. "Well, that's what an election is for." Keefe and Jimmy ignored him, locked on each other.

Keefe reached up and, before Jimmy could move, pinched his cheek sharply between two fingers. Jimmy stiffened, yelped, then instinctively went to pull away and break Keefe's grip. He pushed, hitting Keefe high on the shoulders. The teamster stumbled backward, tripped over a chair, and fell, his arms grabbing the air like a man going off a ledge. Everyone in attendance stopped speaking, their faces slack with disbelief. The room converged around them as Keefe rose, brushing his slacks as if he had fallen on a job site and not on the Mayor's polished hardwood. Still cameras and video clicked and whirred. Keefe looked about, his surprise draining away to rage.

The Mayor stood speechless. Jimmy looked down at his hands. They looked foreign to him, soft, clean, liked they belonged to someone else. He'd worked a long hard time to get to this mansion, this job, this place in his life, and these hands that had brought him here had somehow betrayed him. He dropped them to his sides. "It was an accident," he muttered. The Mayor's security converged just as Keefe lunged for Jimmy. Jimmy took a step back and wondered if he was going to have to hit the guy again. Two of the Mayor's detectives pulled him away.

Another two held Keefe, who yelled, "I'll eat your fucking lungs! I want him arrested! You fucking punk! Arrest him!" and flailed away.

Sergeant Gleason held Jimmy by the shoulders until they pushed through a doorway into the kitchen. "Easy does it, Jimmy. Easy. It's over." Gleason held up his hands like a traffic cop. "You done? Okay." Gleason laughed.

"Bobby, it was an accident."

"Yeah, Jimmy. Them there is what we call famous last words. Remember how I told you about all those 'attaboys' and how one 'oh fuck' can wipe out a thousand of them? Well, this qualifies as a real giant-size 'oh fuck.' The press is going to love this one. That, Jimmy, was a major-league, big-time screwup. How big, I don't know. This might be a tough one to come back from."

"Come back from?"

"You might be sent down to the farm team. If you're lucky. The Mayor might want to lock you up, just to prove he's impartial."

"Jesus Christ." Jimmy threw his hands up and thought, How the hell did I let that happen?

Tara O'Neil rolled her sector car to a stop at the light and, along with her partner, eyeballed the kid on the corner. He wore a red baseball cap perched sideways on his head, baggy pants that bunched around Timberland boots that would never see the terrain they were designed for, and a blue down jacket. She pegged him as fifteen, maybe sixteen, and thought she knew the young face that was all hard angles. She wondered if she had collared him once, or tossed him. It was getting like that lately, the faces running together, her memory straining under the accumulation of arrests, the stop-and-frisks, the long nights on patrol. Crime was down, way down.

The headlines screamed it and the Mayor bleated it at every opportunity. The swells in the tonier precincts downtown could walk their little dogs without fear of the two-legged animals setting upon them. But Tara knew that here, uptown, where Harlem dovetailed into Washington Heights, it was less clear. There were no new bistros in this neighborhood, no towers plump with million-dollar condos rising above the streets. There were rows of dollar stores, check-cashing places instead of banks, fried chicken joints, and storefront churches. Everybody seemed to dream of getting out. Crime was down because in areas like this the heat was on. The kid glaring at her had probably been tossed more times than he could remember. Just for wearing his hat funny, or his pants baggy, or looking sideways at a cop. The dirty little secret of the NYPD was there were simply too many cops. And not a single politician stupid enough to propose a reduction in force.

Ninety minutes left on her tour. She wanted no part of overtime tonight. She wanted to get off, grab a beer on the way home, and get to bed early for once. She had class in the morning and had not been studying as much as she should. She had begun to cruise. The light changed overhead, setting off a chain of green lights up the avenue. She looked the kid over as they rolled past slowly. He returned her stare with a look that was all contempt, as if every slight he had ever suffered was distilled into it. She kept her face deadpan. She had grown up just a few blocks from here. She understood.

Her partner said something.

"What?"

"This time next week, the Bahamas. Six nights five days, fun in the sun. Bikinis, body shots, poontang city." He tapped his nightstick absently on his thigh. "Going with three guys I went through the academy with."

"You mean six days, five nights."

"Whatever. Two plus two. I went down there three years ago,

hooked up with a different chick every night. Paradise. I was a fucking animal. A gangster of love."

Andrew Martino, rookie. A Long Island kid preoccupied with weight lifting and skirt chasing. She often caught him admiring his biceps on the sly.

"You wearing rubbers, Andy? I mean, all this action you're getting, might be dangerous."

"Yeah, most of the time. I can tell which of them might be a problem, though."

"Oh?"

"Yeah, I got like a sixth sense for it."

"I see. Like you can tell just by looking at them? Like this one might have syphilis, this one might have the virus?"

"Yeah, mostly. Plus how they talk, dress. I mean, she's got like a nose ring or a tattoo, some shit. Maybe don't shave her armpits. That might be a sign of trouble. Actually that armpit thing, I steer a million miles away from that. I hooked up once—we went to her place, I seen she had like more hair there than I did, like she was outta some jungle or France maybe. It was adios muchachos for me. See ya. I mean, if a girl looks normal, I figure I'll be okay. Means she's got some respect for herself."

Tara turned the heater off. When they had first partnered up, Andy had been reluctant to divulge such thoughts. She had subtly encouraged him, as much out of boredom as curiosity. She had quickly tired hearing about sports and what a great future he was going to have on the job. Now she wondered if she should have stuck with the Jets and the Mets and his high school football glories.

"You know what I think, Andy?"

"Nah, what's that?"

"I think you're out of your mind." She turned left, scanning the street. Ugly Jesus, a recently paroled crack dealer came out of a Chinese takeout. Dying of AIDS, he passed down the street like a shadow, his skin sallow in the dirty light. Another casualty of the crack wars, she thought, this one a delayed reaction, just taking his time leaving the world. Tara knew his mother. A nice old woman from Ponce who went to Mass every day to pray for the five children she had already

13

buried. Sometimes she thought she had been in this precinct too long.

Andy laughed. "Hah, you're just jealous."

"Damn, you really do have a sixth sense."

Tara did not hold the fact that he was not too bright against him. He was diligent enough as a cop, and although she sensed he disliked having a female partner, he was deferential and eager to benefit from her experience. In the few tight situations they'd encountered, he had acquitted himself well and with surprising restraint, despite his husky bravado. He was confident enough not to overreact, and had defused some tense scenes with wit. Tara had asked him early on why he had become a cop. He pointed out the twenty-year retirement and his belief that the uniform was, as he put it, a babe magnet. He seemed correct on the latter point. Though she considered him of average looks, women seemed to fall for his muscle-cop act.

She half listened to the radio patter as she drove. It served as background music, a steady stream of directives and chatter that controlled them. Her inner ear was tuned to what was important, to let the rest flow by. Since it was chilly, the jobs were slow. A few pedestrians up from the subway walked along the street, heads tucked down to avoid the sharp wind that came across the island. A stray dog galloped along, then darted across ahead of them, running with its shoulders slunk to the ground. Storefronts, except for the twenty-four-hour bodegas, were gated and dark, their barricades splashed with riotous graffiti. Spanish music filtered down from a higher floor, a conga beat, fast and sexual.

Recently Andy asked her why she had joined the cops. He was surprised that she had left a much-better-paying career in marketing to take the job. Fact was, she was bored to tears selling health-care plans to companies, flying coach to stay in numbing, bland hotels in third-tier cities around the country. Bad food, stupefying conferences, grim jet age travel. Middle-aged, middle-management married guys pawing at her in cheesy hotel cocktail lounges. Toupees, bad suits, wedding bands secreted in jacket pockets, minted breath, weak-assed come-ons. "You must be tired. You been running around in my mind all day." God.

The home office was worse: cubicle life, petty office politics, people edgy and tense because the boss liked to purge every now and then. Little power plays to prove he was the big dick on the block. She used to have nightmares about spending her life there. Becoming as gray and lifeless as an airport hotel room, stewing in regret and resentment, never doing anything more exciting than getting drunk and behaving badly at the company Christmas party. She wondered why she had bothered to bust her ass through four years of college.

When her appointment letter from the PD came, she packed up in the middle of the day and walked out. Now, five years on, she had no regrets about becoming a cop. It provided her with movement, diversity, excitement, and even a type of idealistic reward. She was high on the next sergeants list and was taking classes toward her master's at John Jay. Between work, school, and training for the marathon, she had little time for fun.

"You hear about that new strain of the AIDS virus?" She liked to goof on Andy when things were slow. It was never difficult. Andy was the type of guy who believed girls didn't fart.

"Me? Nah." He shrugged, dropped his hand to his crotch, and adjusted himself. It was something he did constantly.

"They did lab tests. Big study. Seven, eight years long. Say for some reason it attacks mostly normal-looking women."

"What do you mean?"

"Yeah, it was in the *Times* yesterday."

Andy squinted at her. As with a lot of cops, everything about *The New York Times* and its readership made him suspicious. "The *Times*? Right. Liberal horseshit. Do me a favor. Pull over? I need something to drink."

Tara double-parked in front of a bodega on 155th Street. Merengue spilled out of speakers under the store's awning. Andy tugged at the rearview mirror and checked his hair. He pulled his hat on and cocked it sideways, imitating the street fashion. He jumped out and sauntered past the group of teens congregated around the door. They stared at their feet. The guy was too much. At least she had dissuaded him from wearing his lousy cologne to work. The first few tours she had driven through winter city nights with her window down.

She picked up the *Daily News* on the seat beside her and began leafing through it. A picture on page five stopped her short. She took a breath. There was Jimmy Dolan behind the Mayor at an event in Queens. With the election heating up he was often caught on the margins of the Mayor's photo ops. Little intrusions into her life, even from a distance.

And it was always the same when she saw him, or thought of him, before the rational process could take hold and steady her, a spasm of surprise and longing. She guessed it was so much easier to remember all the good times, the laughter and warmth, their lives together, childhood sweethearts, boyfriend and girlfriend. The promises they made and the goofy dreams they had. They were the two kids from the neighborhood who wanted something more; they would conquer the city together. As if there was actually something different about them. But the dickhead decided that life would be easier without her. The end had been ugly but had made it easy to put him out of her mind, to assign him his proper place in her history. She put the paper down as the call came over the radio. Domestic dispute. A bullshit call, she hoped.

She hit the siren once and Andy came out of the bodega. "We got a job. Let's go."

On St. Nicholas they pulled up to the tenement, a five-floor walkup. They entered through the unlocked front door. The lobby was small and poorly lit. The ceiling was painted the same dark institutional brown as the walls. The tile floor was pitted and sticky under her feet as she moved for the stairs. The smell of cat piss hung like Mace in the air.

Tara was training for the marathon and the stairs were easy for her. She took the stairs three at a time, her heartbeat barely rising. Andy trailed behind cursing, sweating out the remnants of a hangover as he moved clumsily up the stairs. Their equipment belts rattled as they ascended, their radios cackled, announcing the law was here. She could feel the tenants behind their peepholes, gathering for a show, wary and excited. On the third-floor landing Tara heard something coming down and stopped. The light was fluorescent, bad green and weak. A dog came hurrying past her, its gray coat slick with blood, but apparently unhurt.

"Shit. Andy, you see that?" She drew her gun. The pistol, a Glock nine millimeter, felt hot in her hand. She waited for Andy to catch up. Shouts rained down from above.

"Yeah." He drew his pistol. His breath was short and sharp. The air in the hallway seemed to change suddenly, more charged now, electric. Tara felt the adrenaline rush, lighting her up, coming on strong. She loved the feeling. They made their way to 5B. The door was ajar. Tara pushed it open wide with her left hand, keeping her pistol raised before her. The door opened into a living room. There was a couch, two faded stuffed chairs, a coffee table, and to the side of the room, a dinette set. Three people occupied the space, none with a visible weapon.

"The fucking cops?" said a fat man who sat on a couch dressed in a tee shirt and boxers bleeding from a chest wound.

At his side a scrawny woman held her right hand on the wound trying to stanch the bright flow of blood. In her left she held a can of Pabst Blue Ribbon beer. Blood was snaking through her fingers and running off her arm, into the fat man's lap. She pointed at Tara with the beer can. "What seems to be the problem here, Officers?"

Tara and Andy exchanged smirks. The man's face had the pallor of the nearly dead, a chalky white with a tinge of blue. His eyes, though, were twitching and alert.

"She's the goddamn problem." An old woman in a tattered housecoat, her hair in curlers, garish lipstick leaving traces on the butt of her cigarette, pointed at the skinny woman on the couch. She too held an open can of Pabst. Her skin was slack and whispery from the years, her eyes bloodshot, her mouth turned down at the corners. She looked like she had not smiled in a very long time. "Don't you die on me, Johnny, don't you fucking die on me," she rasped. "You're all I got, you're all I ever had." She broke into a sustained wet cough.

Tara reholstered her pistol and took a pair of rubber surgical gloves from her back pocket. She called into her radio for an ambulance, then snapped on the gloves. "What happened?" she asked. "Come on, what happened?" No one answered her.

"I ain't gonna die, Mama." The stench of him, of the whole place, was overpowering. Decay. Stink. Filth.

17

A boy, who looked about seven, crept out from a hallway that led to the back of the apartment, rubbing sleep from his eyes. He wore a faded Batman pajama top that was stained and torn under the armpits, and that was all. He surveyed the scene, then without speaking, or registering shock, fear, or dismay at the spectacle before him, turned and went back to his room. Tara looked at the others. No one else had noticed the boy. Not even her partner.

Andy looked like he was witnessing a botched surgery. She knew that before long the disgust would be replaced by the blank stare of disassociation. You build up layers after a while. You learn to laugh, to belittle, to lie to yourself. You get together afterward with other cops and make fun of the people whose lives are beyond despair. "What happened?" Tara asked again.

The younger woman stared back. She shook the can to confirm it was indeed empty. She looked around, like she was trying to locate another.

"Her fucking ex-husband stabbed me. That's what happened." The man wheezed while he spoke, the color coming slowly back to his jowly face.

"That right?"

Over at the table the mother started to rant. "I'll smack her in the chops, that whore. I'll smack her in the chops." She shook her cigarette at the skinny woman. The gray ashes cascaded down her front. "Bringing that scum around here. Is my baby gonna live?"

Tara eased the woman's hand from the wound. She pulled up his blood-soaked shirt. There were two deep punctures in the man's large pale breast, but he was not pumping. The scrawny woman started wiping her bloody hand on the couch.

"My couch! You hoo-er!" The older woman yelled and coughed so violently that Tara thought she might be in danger of some type of seizure.

"He should be okay, ma'am." Tara heard an ambulance keening closer. She moved over to the old woman, figuring she was the only one coherent enough to give a statement.

"He'll be okay. What's your name, ma'am?"

The woman looked up, her wet eyes focusing slowly. "What difference does that make? I've been in this building for forty-nine years. Widow for sixteen." There was resignation in her voice, defeat. Tara wondered what that was like. A little corner of hell right here on earth. "What's my name? How about the bastard that did this to my Johnny?"

"Okay. What's his name?"

"How the hell should I know? Ask the whore." The woman raised her fist, defiant. "I'll smack her in the chops. She pissed on my rug last week." She sank back heavily in the chair.

"Now, now," Andy said.

Tara made her way down the hall to the boy's room. She pushed the door open. The floor was cluttered with toys and clothes, the air flat and lifeless. A velvety claustrophobia. She cracked a window. A baby Jesus night-light shone from a socket. She went over and squatted beside the bed. The boy's breathing was uneven and quick, but his eyes were open.

"Your daddy's going to be okay."

"That's not Daddy. Daddy's in jail."

"Oh. Is that your mommy out there?"

He shook his head no. She scarcely wanted to ask, but she said, "Where's Mommy?"

"Mommy's in heaven. She has the virus."

Tara slid down onto her knees. With the adults there was choice; with kids like this it was just a cruel hand dealt by fate. "What's your name?" She stroked the hair on his head and pushed it away from his face.

"Johnny. Like my uncle."

Let's hope not, Tara thought.

"My name's Tara. Here, I got a present for you." She took a small Police Department pin from her pocket and pinned it to his shirt. "Your own police badge. You like it?"

Johnny sat up, animated. He pulled at the pin to see it better. She patted him on the back. He let out a yelp, and Tara flipped on the overhead light. She gently pulled up Johnny's shirt. There was a series of welts, marks from a lash—maybe an electrical cord—and what looked like cigarette burns. She pulled the shirt down, gently. She felt

19

a rage start to rise in her. Johnny was silent again. He stared at the badge and fingered it.

"Would you like to be a policeman someday?"

A hint of a smile eased across his face, seeming to come from a great distance.

"Can you help me? Who did this to you?"

Silence. His eyes turned down, avoiding hers.

"A good policeman has to tell the truth. Was it Uncle Johnny?"

A slight shake of the head. "Grandma?" Again no.

"The other woman? What's her name?"

"Aunt Mary."

"Aunt Mary?"

This time yes. That skel bitch. Behind her she felt movement. The door opened.

"Let that boy sleep so he can get up for school. You ain't got no business in here." The skinny woman, Mary, stood in the doorway. She had found another beer and she drank deeply from it.

"I'll be right back, Johnny." Tara laid a hand on his head.

"No, she won't. Go to sleep."

Tara walked toward Mary with a smile. "We need to chat. Little girl to girl?" She pulled the door shut behind them. In the hallway she bit the inside of her lip as a reminder not to lose control. She placed her hand on the small of Mary's back and propelled her away from the boy's room. To the left was the bathroom door. She leaned her shoulder into it, knocking it open. She grabbed Mary by her ponytail and jerked her into the bathroom, using her grip to force her to her knees. With her free hand she slapped her across the face, then spun around so she was behind her. The can of beer crashed into the sink and began to empty.

Mary gasped and reached for the can. Tara forced the woman's head down and yanked her right arm up high behind her back till she screamed. She grabbed the other arm and deftly cuffed her, squeezing the cuffs as tight as she could.

"You pig bitch, I got AIDS." Mary turned her head and tried to spit over her shoulder at Tara. She snapped her gray teeth, biting the air in frustration.

Tara fought the urge to punch the skel's face until it was broken, to bang her head off the tub. She took a breath to calm herself. She counted to five. She wanted to even the score for the pain the boy suffered, to show this piece of shit what it felt like to be bullied. She twisted the ponytail until she was lifting the scalp off from her head and drove her knee hard between the bony shoulder blades. The woman let out a sound that was half growl and half whine, a stray dog being whupped. Tara shut her eyes for a minute, whispering easy to herself, trying to ratchet down her anger before she got carried away. She looked around the bathroom. The shower dripped into a tub coated in grime. An overflowing litter box sat under the sink, cat shit spilled all about. There was no toilet paper; instead a stack of torn newspaper lay by the base of the toilet. The paint was faded and peeling. Large sections of wall were exposed where tile was missing. The place was a cell of despair. Tara felt fatigue roll over her; the urge to punish passed.

The paramedics, absorbed in their work, were bloodstained, deft, and professional. The old woman stroked her fat son's clammy head, murmuring some deranged love chant. Andy looked up surprised.

"What's up?"

"Miss Manners here likes to burn little boys with cigarettes."

Andy shook his head like a man who has just learned too much about life. "No fucking joke."

L iam Brady sat flipping through the channels on his new fifty-inch television. Daytime talk shows displayed every type and dimension of freak. He could not believe these people lived on the same planet as he did, let alone in the same country. Queers, transvestites, perverts, liars, connivers, degenerates—all sorts of mutts. People who slept with their best friends' wives, their siblings, their parents, their pets, whatever they could mount. Although he had to admit he occasionally was intrigued by some of the stories. Like the one chick who confessed to having sex with the best man on her wedding day at the church. Wow. He pictured her bent over in the church basement with the fancy dress pushed up around her waist and old trusty, the best man, having at her while the groom was posing for photos with his grandparents a few feet over their heads. Some people. None of them looked normal either. They were all too fat or too skinny, bad skin. They all complained, sitting up there expecting the world to feel sorry for them. Nobody gives a shit, Liam thought. That's why you got so miserable in the first place.

He popped a cherry Coke and scratched his balls. He was sitting in his Jockeys and a guinea tee, his feet propped up on the coffee table. The table was littered with magazines his mom had brought home for him—*Soldier of Fortune, Guns and Ammo, Commando, Shooting Times, Guns and Weapons, Shotgun Times, Revolvers,* and *American Survivors*. He read the ads for mercenaries with some interest. He'd been with the 82nd Airborne in Desert Storm. The Rack. They did a lot of scurrying around in the desert. But after being carpet-bombed in their bunkers for a few weeks the enemy was not much into fighting. The only time they actually got to shoot anyone was one time they encountered a couple dozen stragglers. The Racks kept coming after their sergeant, a big Leroy from Philly, who supposedly knew the language, was yelling at them to stop. They kept shuffling forward, crazy-eyed and weeping, looking like a crew of deranged glueheads, mumbling to a god that had abandoned their stinky asses. It was like watching *Night of the Living Dead*. They probably had no hearing left after all that ordnance dropped on their heads. They did not stop. So the Leroy opened up, and they all did, Liam went through three clips with his 16. Rock and Roll. They kept firing even after the fuckers were all dead and full of holes. They got medals for that one. Regular war heroes. It was like playing army. Nothing felt real in that desert. Every now and then he entertained the idea of heading over to one of those little wars in Africa. Make some money, shoot the shit out of some bony knuckleheads wearing cutoff shorts and sneakers and carrying AK-47s.

He stopped on a show. Guys in their thirties that still live at home. Liam grimaced. He was only twenty-nine, but still. He changed the channel quickly. That was the worst part. He was starting to feel like one of the freaks, especially since the accident. He was certainly living their lifestyle. Lying around the house all day, collecting workers' comp, eating bologna sandwiches and Campbell's soup. It was fine at first until that asshole insurance investigator started following him around. Now he had to carry on with his hunchback routine, shuffle around like a cripple. Which meant he could not go to the gym. He had black belts in tae kwon do and judo and before the accident worked out every day no matter what. He was ready to go back to work months ago, but his shyster lawyer kept insisting with a wink that he was still hurt, that a six-figure settlement was a lock. The lack of activity was making him jumpy.

That and having to put up with his mother all day. He heard her key in the door. Now he'd have to listen to her go on about Al Sharpton or the Dominican rapists and drug addicts moving into the building, or about the Kennedys. She was laid off from the city hospital a week after his case started. The city repaid her eighteen years of scrubbing sick people's asses with a pink slip. She had been so excited about a Republican mayor. Now she was not so sure. Unemployment will do that to you, he knew. Makes you rethink a lot of things.

"Liam, help me with the groceries."

He cursed under his breath. Pushing sixty-five, she was as spunky as ever. But he was afraid to leave her alone. He worried about her getting sick, about her not being able to take care of herself, about her being old and broken-down. It had always been just the two of them. Still, he was just as worried about being one of those loser bachelors who lived with his mother until she died at like a hundred and then he'd be too far gone to ever have a life. But he would not put her in a nursing home like the Jews and the Wasps or hide her in some hell-hole where they'd dope her up and let her sit in her own shit till some lazy slob, making minimum wage, decides to do something about it.

"You'll not believe the prices and the utter lack of professionalism these people demonstrate. It's as if they've no manners at all, none. Not a bit."

"That's what happens, you pay people five bucks an hour."

She ignored that. She plodded around the kitchen. "My gout is acting up. Dr. McCann says I've got to stay off my feet more and stay away from red meat. But now my blood is iron-deficient. I don't have much choice, do I? Besides, I've got to look after you with your back trouble and all."

"Ma, my back is fine." Every day he knocked off at least five hundred push-ups right before her eyes. Yet she simply refused to believe her son would engage in fraud. Not her Liam. He guessed that lying to herself was some form of survival strategy. Like her bedrock belief that his father had met foul play and had not simply walked out on them.

"You say that now, Liam. You'll end up in a wheelchair, God forbid, if you're not careful. Have you gone for your tests?"

Liam sighed. His mother was convinced that combat had traumatized him and that the government had conducted experiments on its own soldiers during the war. "Ma, knock it off. I'm fine. There ain't no Gulf War Syndrome. It's all the media."

"Ach! Shoosh now. You never know at all what that government is up to, never know at all. Just last year Johnny Lyons was butchered in that VA hospital on Kingsbridge Road. And what ever happened to that neighborhood? Your father and I used to go dancing at the Archway on Sundays after the hurling at Gaelic Park, until you had the criminals come in with their crack cocaine and shanty ways, and . . ."

"Lyons, Ma. Mr. Lyons. The VA." His mother had trouble staying on the point.

"Right you are. Killed him dead. Probably because they no longer wanted to pay his medical bills, rest in peace, that poor man. And now Nancy Lyons is left all alone to fend for herself, and what with her diabetes and the one son having a drug problem and the daughter away and married to a hippie in Arizona, of all the godforsaken places on the globe. God knows what they're up to, politicians and bureaucrats. A bunch of rum-dums. I'd put nothing past them."

"Okay, Ma." Liam nodded his head and opened the refrigerator door. He pulled out a cold can of Bud and cracked it open. He pressed the can to his cheek, felt its iciness, then finished it in one long swallow.

His mother made a show of looking up at the wall clock, which was cut in the shape of Ireland. "It's a bit early to be drinking, Liam."

24

"Nah." He crushed the empty can against his forehead. "One won't kill me, Ma."

He went to his room and got dressed. He put on a pair of camouflage pants, work boots, and a sweatshirt. He pulled a Rangers jersey over that. At the front door he took his scally cap off the coatrack. He placed it on his head backward. His mother stepped before him like a fighter cutting off the ring, using her bulk to corner him.

"Where you off to?"

Liam sighed. He placed his hands on her shoulders. She had his fierce blue eyes. "Out."

"That awful man's down there. Sitting all day. The good-for-nothing stool pigeon—it's the sign of a man that can't hold a real job. Snooping around minding someone else's business. I guess he'll never know how it feels to be hurt as bad as yerself. I've never known a man to be injured sitting on his arse spying on a workingman. I bet he's one of those so-called college-educated people. Is that all yer wearing, Liam? It's damp as death out there."

"I'm okay, Mom." He bent and kissed her on the forehead. "Jimmy calls, tell him I'm down Johnny Mac's."

"Liam, you should not be out drinking with that injury of yours."

"Yeah, Ma."

"What about supper? I was going to make a meat loaf. Just the way you like it."

Liam pulled the door shut and bounced down the stairs, then he slowed and bent forward a bit when he hit the lobby. There was the gray sedan with the insurance moron sitting behind the wheel with, Liam knew, a video camera riding shotgun. Liam waved to him and moved his mouth. Fuck you.

When he got to the corner of Broadway and 207th Street he stopped for a minute to enjoy the scene. The sun was dropping over Jersey and the light was orange and fading. A bus screeched to a halt and disgorged people coming from jobs downtown. A herd emerged from the subway stairs and went in all directions. This intersection was the main hub of Inwood, the rocky northern tip of Manhattan Island, a square mile containing 58,000 souls. For Liam, it was and always would be home. He didn't care how many people fled for

Yonkers, or Jersey, or Florida, or the Island, or any other shithole anywhere on the planet. He was going nowhere and was proud of the fact. Rows of six-story buildings ran back down the hill toward the Bronx, all along Broadway and up 207th Street to the park. When he was a kid, he knew someone in almost every one of the buildings. That was not true anymore.

He passed the pizzeria, waved to Frank the Albanian, who was tossing a pie in the oven, and ducked into Johnny Mac's. Inside there was already a thick cloud of smoke and an after-work crowd. When Liam was born there had been forty-nine Irish bars in the neighborhood; when he had his first beer at thirteen there had been about twenty. Now there were maybe five, all populated by a few toothless ghosts, waiting for the afterlife to begin. Only Johnny Mac's had any life to it.

Johnny Mac himself was sitting by the front door. Liam waved a hello. The man, while working as a night watchman on a construction site, had been shot by a gangster and thrown into the Hudson. Miraculously he had survived, then sued his company and promptly bought the old Cavan bar with his settlement. Getting shot in the head was the best thing that could have happened to Johnny Mac. The bullet had left him unable to taste or smell and prone to drool uncontrollably. Otherwise, he was fine. Day and night he could be found sitting just inside the door at the end of the bar. He kept an eagle eye on his bartenders, lest they rob him. He sipped Jameson, and kept a towel nearby.

Liam nodded to the patrons and secured a seat at the other end of the bar. Johnny occasionally took exception to his behavior. But he would not ban him because Liam was the star shortstop on the bar's softball team. Liam put a twenty on the wood in front of him. He craved the release of a good night's drinking. Blotto city was where he wanted to go. The bottles behind the bar danced with reflected light of the sun and the lone television. He was not happy to see Jack Cooke bartending. The guy was tight with the buybacks and acted like his shit didn't stink. The chicks thought the guy was cute, but Liam thought he looked like a girl, always fussing with his hair in the bar mirror. Prick. But Liam was above all that. He asked for a Bud and washed down a few codeines with his first guzzle. He ordered a burger, black on the outside and red on the inside. When it arrived he devoured it swiftly. He went over and played some songs on the juke-box. The Pogues, AC/DC, Metallica, even a little rap. He enjoyed watching the old goats shudder when his songs came on.

He was into his second twenty-dollar bill when the six o'clock news came on. An urgent hush fell upon the bar. A scuffle at the Mayor's house between Jimmy Dolan, mayoral aide, and Frankie Keefe, Teamster boss. A loud whooping went up from the crowd. Keefe had wound up on his ass. Their Jimmy, local boy made good, had put him there. The patrons were exuberant. After all, despite the college degree and the suit and tie, Jimmy was still one of their own.

Liam winced. Even now he thought of Jimmy as his best friend in the world. He knew Jimmy was still a regular guy. He did not know much about politics, but he knew mixing it up with a mobbed-up Teamster boss was a bad idea. He ordered another beer, went over to the pay phone, and dropped a quarter. He dialed Jimmy's number and the machine picked up. After the whine of Jimmy's girlfriend, the beep went on forever. "Hey, witchipoo, tell Jimmy to call his bro shine down the bar."

They replayed the clip at ten. Liam sat brooding with his beer, a darkness settled about him, a shadow gripping his heart. All his little slights and angers, his grudges and gripes were a goulash simmering on an alcohol flame in his belly. His workers' comp check was two days late. He imagined they were fucking with him; his lawyers were probably in on it. He started drinking faster, pounding the cold Buds down, sucking the icy brew into his system, inhaling the fuckers. The bar took on some kind of glow, and clarity came to him. He surveyed the crowd. He counted at least four girls he had fucked and four guys he had knocked out. He wondered what was more enjoyable, the fucking or the sweet feeling he got when he knocked someone into la-la land, and the guy lay at his feet, completely at his mercy. He often took the boot to them for the fun of it.

People waved hello. He did not want to talk to them. They had no idea what it was like. He remembered the looks he used to get when he went shopping for his mother with food stamps. The bastards look-ing down on them like they were some welfare cheats. His mother going up and cleaning the rich assholes' houses in Riverdale after work. His father going out one day for cigarettes and not returning. His mother telling him, he'll be back, he'll be back, like if she said it enough it would come true. They tossed him out of Good Shepherd grammar school, sent him to public school, where they did not give a shit, said he was antisocial.

"Hey! Lemme get another one!"

He thought he had ordered another beer.

"Easy does it, Liam." Jack the bartender was leaning over the bar toward him with a grave air.

"Easy?" Liam smiled, a leer. "I'll show you easy."

"What was that?" Jack asked.

Liam was not ready to leave, and if he decked the prick, he might be barred. "I said thank you."

Jack regarded him for a minute, then snatched another Bud from the ice and slapped it down on the wood.

They all had a glow to them dimming at the edges. Fat merry faces. Faces Liam wanted to break. He looked them over. He was certain he could lay waste to the lot of them in three short minutes. Kick the fuck out of them all. Laugh at his mother. He'd make them pay. They'd all pay. He giggled. Who really gives a shit? Oooo eeee, I am schnockered. He stood on his stool and shouted, "I was born on a mountain, raised in a cage, drinking and fucking is all I crave."

Tara waited with Johnny until Children's Services showed up. She gave Andy the skelly bitch collar because he wanted the OT. Back at the station house, she changed, and as she was getting in her car, a group of her colleagues waved at her and made drinking motions, bringing their hands to their lips and tilting.

She tried to beg off and yelled, "School."

"Come on, just one," came the response.

So much for studying. She felt the backwash from the episode and needed release, a few beers. They started out at the precinct bar and then moved on to Coogan's on 168th Street, where they picked up the pace. It was the type of furious payday drinking a crew of cops enjoyed. It was a way to blow off steam before going home and trying to be normal, like they were accountants or bus drivers or laborers and had not just spent a tour witnessing humans in their lowest moments. Several hours into the night, Tara reluctantly allowed herself to be talked into a nightcap at Johnny Mac's, back in Inwood, land of her ghosts, her life with Jimmy Dolan.

She looked around the bar, a place she knew as well as any other, and ordered the first round. The place was still lively at 3 a.m., which was unusual on a weeknight. It was in Johnny Mac's that she learned about Jimmy and the Teamster. Liam Brady, her old pal, was in there drunk as ten pirates on shore leave. She watched as he stared at her for a full minute, before he recognized her. He moved to where she was standing.

"Tara. Baby. Good to see you back. You hear about Jimmy?"

She shook her head. She was not even sure she wanted to hear about him. Was he getting married? Moving to California? Being promoted to primary ass licker of the Mayor? Jimmy always seemed blessed by good fortune.

"He smacked a guy on TV. That prick Teamster. Right in front of that asshole Mayor and the media freak show."

"What?" She was interested now. She went to the store around the corner and picked up early editions of the papers. Right on the cover of the *Post* was the headline LABOR PAINS and a picture of the Teamster on his ass with Jimmy glaring down at him. The *News* picture was pretty much the same, but the headline roared TEAMSTER SHUFFLE. Jimmy always had a problem with his temper. During the eight years they went together he could run hot and cold. She learned to ignore his outbursts and they would dissolve without something to bounce against.

She showed the pictures to Liam. "Hardly acting like a college boy there, is he?"

"Yeah, I guess you can take the boy out of Inwood, but you can't . . . "

"No shit." Liam waved down the bartender. "Hey, you know this chick?" Liam pointed his head several seats down the bar at a young woman with long red hair.

"That's Brian Donovan's sister. Audra. Moved to Japan, I thought."

"Oh, right her. Changed her hair or something. Thanks for the intelligence, Officer."

"You're not going after that?"

Liam laughed. "Shit. You don't know about her old man?"

"Yeah, Mr. Donovan. Moved to Woodlawn."

"Yeah, he likes to invite her boyfriends in when they come to pick her up."

"So?"

"So? So he sits there in his boxer shorts and his guinea tee cleaning this old military forty-five, thing looks like a cannon. So he goes, 'You seem like a nice young fella. What time you bringing my Audra Catherine home?' This from a guy who did three tours as a Marine recon in Nam and six years for manslaughter. I'll pass. She'll be a virgin till she dies."

"Might be a blessing in disguise. Won't have to put up with assholes." Tara was glad to see Liam. There was a time when the two of them and Jimmy were inseparable. This place was a minefield of memories. Back when it was still the Cavan, they had met here almost nightly to shoot pool or play darts, to catch up on the day's events. Well, the pool table and the dartboard were long gone and so too were the times they had here. It had been more than seven years since Jimmy walked out on her and as much as she tried to bury her feelings for him and move on, she could not. She usually blamed this on the fact that she had not found someone better or at least as good. She felt like she connected to Jimmy on all levels, the way he touched her, the heat of their interaction, the way they challenged each other. They had much in common and understood so much about each other. No one ever made her feel as good as he did. Above all, she knew, no one ever made her laugh the way he did. That's what she missed the most. She realized coming to Johnny Mac's had been a bad idea. She finished her drink.

She frequently met men about whom she liked certain things. But she never seemed to meet ones with the whole combination and was starting to believe it was all about settling for the closest you thought you were going to get. This depressed her mightily. She wondered sometimes about getting back with Jimmy. She knew he was living with some rich bitch on the Upper East Side, always the social climber her Jimmy.

Tara settled at the end of the bar with a group from her precinct and some cops from the Five-Oh up the road in the Bronx. Angela, her old partner, was there and this made her happy. She glanced at her wristwatch. She did not want this to be a late night. Payday could be dangerous. There were always after-hours places for cops to drink. You ended up going home in broad daylight. She liked four-to-twelves because they were good for school, but they were also a big drinking tour. No need for early rising, and bars were still in full swing when the tour ended. She ordered another Amstel and listened to a sergeant from her precinct tell a story she had heard twenty times.

"So how's things?" One of the cops from the Five-Oh was by her side. They had met once or twice over the last several months. He was a toucher, a feeler, a borderline groper, a hand almost always on her elbow or shoulder while they talked. He was attractive enough, and his wedding band did not seem to matter much to him. She had not had sex in a while and was feeling more amorous with the rising level of alcohol in her veins. She looked at the way his neck met his shoulder, a muscular line. She imagined biting it in the throes of a good tumble. She wondered what life would be like if we knew not just what people were saying but what they were thinking. The world would be a very different place. She realized she was quite drunk. She caught a glimpse of a bar photo on the wall. It was of a softball team, a number of summers ago. There she was in the back row between Jimmy and Liam. She looked away. She smiled encouragingly at Officer Touchy Hands.

After Jimmy, she had gone through a period of casual and somewhat random sex in an effort to stamp out all memory of him, to forget his touch. Of course, she had failed. Some lovers were more energetic, or more creative, but in the end it was just pure fucking, devoid of any real emotional connection. She appreciated sex as much as anyone, but the encounters left her feeling sullied. Trying to hurt him, she had only hurt herself. The last year or so, sex was very infrequent. There had been two attempts at relationships that began with cautious promise, but fizzled quickly.

She felt trapped between her desire for intimacy and the realization that what was out there was not enough. She knew some of her friends had settled, married for companionship, more from fear of loneliness than real love. And now they were full of complaint when they got together, settled into marriages rife with low-intensity strife, a kind of romantic trench warfare where all victories and defeats were distressingly marginal.

She would rather be an old spinster camped in front of the TV wearing a housecoat, with a belly full of tranquilizers. She laughed at the thought. Maybe it was time for a one-night stand. A good fuck and adios. The men tended to get more attached than she did. It amazed her how many of them seemed grateful. She turned to the man beside her and squeezed his elbow. She had not heard what he said. "Gotta go to the girls' room. See you in a minute."

She made her way to the bathroom, saying hello to people she used to see almost every day of her life. Some she had not seen in years. Liam waved her over. She gave him a big hug and kissed his cheek.

He grabbed her arm. "You I love, baby. Shoot this prick for me, will ya?" Liam indicated the bartender. Tara could see Jack's patience with Liam was wearing thin. Liam was too frequently out of control. But she felt the need to look out for him. She smiled at Jack and held up a hand as if to say, I'll take care of him. If Jimmy was often blessed by good fortune, Liam was often cursed in life. Tara believed Liam had a good heart, but that things rarely rolled his way. One of the things she admired most about Jimmy was his loyalty to Liam.

"Can I pee first?"

Liam pulled away to look up at her. "Go right ahead. I ain't gonna get in the way of that." He waved toward the rest rooms, then said to Jack, "When she comes back, she's gonna shoot your stupid ass. Bang bang, motherfucker."

In the bathroom she relished a moment's peace. She made up her mind to have one more beer and hit the road. It was late indeed. She lingered a moment and thought about her reaction to the child abuser earlier. It had not been very professional. She stood over the sink and washed her hands with cold water. She stared at herself in the bathroom mirror. The crow's-feet and smile lines were starting to deepen. Her love of the sun was reflected in her face. Her thirtieth birthday was only weeks away. The big three-oh. She considered this. She had always imagined her life would be different by now. There were no paper towels, so she wiped her hands dry on the side of her pants, and realized with a start why she had reacted so violently to the woman. The kid was the same age her son would be if he had lived. She'd learned to regulate the loss, like an IV drip. Some days still, she lost control. She pushed down a well of sadness and headed back to the party, forcing a smile.

When she got back to her stool, Angela was saying, "I had to take a shit, okay? You know, so I'm trying to get into this restaurant and I am working the ho' stroll. So I am all done up like a hooker and this guy is working the door. He takes one look at me and looks like he's gonna punch me before he'll let me into his place. Like I might scare all the customers away. Now, I used to get into it big time. I'm in heels—big stiletto jobs—garter belt, stockings, my ass hanging out, big hair, scary fright-night makeup, super-skank supreme. I look like I'd suck a watermelon through a fire hose for a vial of crack. You know what I'm saying? I try to explain to the guy I'm on the job. In the meantime I ate Thai food for lunch and I'm on fire. I have about twelve seconds before I have a major embarrassment on my hands. I'm talking an explosive situation is developing."

"You didn't tin him?" Tara asked.

"Yeah, well, when I worked that detail I kept my badge and gun in a little purse, right? So I go to get it and I am so pissed off and so about to shit myself that I drop it. I go to pick it up and this moron kicks it toward the street, right? Now I am rip shit, so I go over and I yank out my shield and slap it right across this clown's face, like I'm trying to brand his stupid ass. Problem is, my backup is in the van, they see this, they come running out, figuring I got a beef. I just push past the guy so I can make it to the bathroom. I pretty much have a one-track mind at this point. Well, the guys see this, they come rushing into the place with their guns waving in the air like some Hollywood cop movie. People are screaming. I mean, this is a high-society crowd. I don't care, because by now I'm on the bowl and I am happy."

"What'd they do?"

"Did I mention they cuffed the doorman to the railing out front?"

"No, you left that out."

"That was a little teeny-weeny problem. Turns out he's some Eastern European immigrant, starts screaming about his civil rights, watching too many reruns of *Starsky and Hutch*, wherever the fuck he's from. Luckily he's illegal, so they shut him up pretty quick. Plus the owner is some cop buff, so they kept it quiet enough. I got kicked off the detail. They left the other guys alone. Hey, limp dick, some more shots over here." She waved to the bartender.

Jack the bartender came over. "You're a regular Sister Teresa. This is my lucky night." He took some money from the pile.

"Bite me, bozo."

"You related to Brady over there?"

Angela ignored him and downed her shot. "So anyway, the moral of the story is lay off the Thai food days you work undercover. Hey, Tara, who's the hottie down the bar?"

Tara realized she was referring to Liam. She regarded him for a minute. He was good-looking, though it was somehow not a way she ever considered him. She had known him too long. But he was well built with dark hair and a boyish face that belied his darker side.

"My pal Liam. He likes his girls to dress up in ninja outfits."

"Ninja?" She still seemed intrigued.

Tara laughed. She had heard stories from other girls in the neighborhood. Liam liked to take them camping and sneak around the woods at night. "Yeah, he's a karate man."

"Two of my favorite hobbies are sex and karate."

"Well, Liam's your man then."

Tara watched as Liam refused to let Jack take his empties away. He liked to hoard them for some reason not clear to anyone.

"Brady, come on. I gotta keep the bar clean. I gotta take the bottles. It's my job." Jack drummed his fingers on the bar.

"No, Jack, your job is a wannabe cop. Not for nothing, you hump. You couldn't pass the cop test, so you're a fucking court officer. Let me drink in peace. Get outta here." Liam waved him off.

Jack flushed. "I never took no fucking cop test. Give them up or you gotta go, Brady. Your act is getting old." He squared himself, his hands on his hips.

Tara wondered if she should intervene. "You want 'em, pricko, you want 'em?" Liam stood with an empty bottle in each hand. He readied himself to duck. "Hah? You fucking want them?" Liam smashed one bottle, then the other off his own head, spraying glass and blood about the bar. "Hah! You fucking pussy! You want 'em?"

Liam threw the bottle necks to the floor and was going for two more when Tara stepped in front of him. "All right, Liam, it's me, come on," she whispered to him, and moved him gently out the door. He did not resist her.

"Liam!" Tara pushed him against the wall of the pizza place next to the bar. "Liam. What the hell's wrong with you?"

Liam seemed to see her for the first time. "Tara?" He laughed and hugged her. "I love you, baby. Ah, that Jack's an asshole. He had it coming."

"He had it coming? Yeah, you showed him." She brushed the glass off his shoulder.

The violence was out of him now. He seemed reasonable. She wondered if he even remembered what had just happened. Some of her colleagues came out, concerned, on the job twenty-four/seven. She shooshed them back inside. A gypsy cab pulled to the curb and honked, looking for a fare. Tara waved him on.

"What's wrong with you?"

"Wrong? Nothing's wrong." He started to pace back and forth. "Nothing's wrong with me." He stopped and looked past her. His face darkened, pulled all tight with fury. She turned to look, and there was a man standing at the open door of a plain gray sedan pointing a video camera at them. "That's what's fucking wrong with me!" He pushed past her. The man ducked into the car. Liam started pounding on the roof with his fists, furiously, the sound like a war drum in the late-night quiet. The man with the camera laughed mockingly, then he started the engine and pulled away. "Blow me!" Liam screamed at the receding taillights.

Tara did not want him going back in the bar. "Come on. I'll walk you home."

"Home? I don't want to go home. I need another beer."

"Yeah. I know, Liam. Come on." As they walked down the hill toward Nagle Avenue, Tara breathed deep the crisp air. The streets were dark and quiet. The buildings seemed denser than she remembered, squatter; the sky seemed more remote. It had the walled-in feeling of some kind of encampment, and if you were to leave you had to sneak away under cover of night. She'd gotten out seven years ago. It did not seem possible that so much time had passed. She considered the fact that Liam would never leave here. No matter what, he would stay and cling to what had shaped him. Tara did not know whether this was a good thing or bad. She only knew that it made her sad.

They sat at the kitchen table sipping cans of beer. The Ireland clock said 4:30, and Tara groaned in anticipation of a rough day ahead. She poured some peroxide over the cut on Liam's temple, brushing his hair away from the wound. "Looks like you could use a stitch or two."

"Negative that. I'm sick of doctors. Fake doctors, real doctors, assholes, all of them. I'm sick of them. Doctors and fucking lawyers."

"It's gonna leave a nasty scar." They spoke quietly in order not to wake Mrs. Brady.

Liam grabbed her arm. "Tara, you're beautiful. Jimmy's an asshole. I mean, don't get me wrong, he's my best friend in the world, but he's an asshole for leaving you."

Yes, Tara thought. Liam might be crazy, but he was right about that.

At dawn she awoke in Liam's bed staring up at a poster of a woman in a commando bikini who caressed some type of assault weapon and affected a dangerous look. Tara looked to her side. Her bra was wrapped around Liam's head and his belt was unbuckled. Otherwise they were still fully clothed. This afforded her some measure of ease. Gee, second base. She laughed. Still she needed to get hold of herself. She saw her pistol lying on the nightstand beside them. Not good. "I am a disgrace to the uniform." She laughed uneasily in the dawn light.

Liam woke up and clamped a hand over her mouth. "Shh! My mother." Which made her laugh. She was twenty-nine years old, for godsakes.

Jimmy Dolan woke up convinced that he had not knocked down Frankie Keefe in front of the Mayor and the media and, by extension, the whole world. He rolled on his side and touched the dent in the pillow where Susan's head had been. Weak light was filtering through the window, and the steady hum of traffic reverberated up from Second Avenue. It was after ten. He had not slept so late in almost a year.

Yesterday had gone from bad to worse. Every stop they made, the focus was his tussle with Keefe. The Mayor cutting a ribbon on a new day-care center in the South Bronx; "Mr. Mayor, can you tell us what happened this morning?" The Mayor announcing a fifty-million-dollar welfare-to-jobs program; "Your Honor, does this mean you've lost the Teamsters endorsement?" The Mayor comforting the parents of a California woman who was tossed in front of a downtown A train at rush hour; same thing. Jimmy Dolan, Jimmy Dolan. "Does he have a criminal record?" They loved turning the crime-fighting thing around on the Mayor.

The laser focus of the media was on Jimmy and it burned mightily. Jimmy Dolan, ace politico, had lost his temper, had knocked a VIP on his ass for all of them to record. Not just any VIP, but Frankie Keefe, shadowy figure of the underworld. The press was euphoric. By noon it was too much. Kirk Ingram, the Mayor's chief of staff, had beeped him. They were in a church in Midwood, Brooklyn, and when Jimmy called Ingram back, he was told to make himself scarce. The Mayor ignored him, did not even acknowledge his muttered goodbye. Jimmy went out the back door and melted into the subway, caught a matinee. He called Susan from O'Hanlon's. She was the deputy press secretary at City Hall, and she told him that she would be working late. He heard distance in her voice, reproach. What the fuck, he thought. The other guy started it, he began to say, then stopped himself. That might sound all right on a playground, but he was supposed to be a professional now. He'd reverted to the street, and now he was going to pay.

He had watched the six o'clock news, the ten, and eleven, NY 1. It was a slow news day, so he was the lead. He had gotten the papers after midnight and there he was, the *Post* and the *News*, on page one. Even the *Times* ran it on the first page; at least it was below the fold. He was getting more ink than a schoolyard sniper. All the papers had more or less the same photo. It was just after Keefe had hit the ground and he was standing above the Teamster, his arms still outstretched, his lips pulled together tight, a grim look of retribution on his face. No way you would think it was an accident from that shot. What really grabbed his attention was Keefe's face. He was sitting, still recoiling from the shove, his arms belatedly rising in an attempt to protect himself. There was something unexpected in the eyes of Frankie Keefe. Fear. Jimmy figured it was an optical illusion.

Now he made a pot of coffee and checked the answering machine. There was a message from his father and several from friends. Then Chickie: "That was dumb, kid. No, make that double dumb. Call me." Even Chickie Donohue, his political mentor, had always cautioned him to mind his p's and q's, the importance of professionalism, how not to live down to people's expectations of an Irish construction worker. He drank a cup of coffee and showered, letting the water burn the alcohol haze out of him, then turned off the hot and braced himself with pure cold water. He wondered how badly he had hurt his career. He had spent almost a decade working toward this job. Years of colleges part-time to finish his degree while working construction full-time, getting involved in politics through the unions and scratching his way up. Now, it was eight months to the election, and he was out. How much would knocking that asshole Keefe down cost him? One hot flash of stupidity. He knew the stories of careers ruined by similar screwups. Charlie Orr, an advance man on the Clinton campaign, had punched out a co-worker at an after-work party. Last Jimmy heard he was handling complaints at the DMV. Still, if

38

Keefe had not provoked him. Jesus, he needed to stop making excuses. Accident or not, if he had walked away, it never would have happened.

He moved naked into the bedroom and dressed in a navy blue suit with a maroon tie. He had a noon appointment with Kirk Ingram at campaign headquarters. Ingram was a buddy of the Mayor's from back when they were prosecutors together. A dark and brooding type who completed the Mayor's innermost circle of two. The man was humorless to the point of rigor mortis. Jimmy sipped coffee and picked up a note that was laid in the center of the kitchen table. It said, "We need to talk. S."

Susan had never left him a note before. He had been living with her for the last six months in an apartment owned by her father, the real estate mogul. He was an old contributor to the Mayor. Jimmy never felt totally comfortable living there, but he figured it was a good place to hang his hat until the election was over and he would get his own place again. Convenience. Kind of like their relationship. Neither of them spent more than six or seven hours a night here anyway, and as the campaign heated up, not much time with each other either. Maybe he had misinterpreted her distance of late.

As he rode down, he checked his tie in the elevator mirror, patted his hair. His palms were sweaty. He was not looking forward to this meeting. He checked the mail, and Ramon the doorman came up. "Yo, Rocky Jimmy, man." He bobbed and threw out a right hand. "You sissy-slapped that guy."

He countered the doorman's right with a side step and weave. Jimmy looked at a handful of bills, all with Susan's name, and stuffed them back in the mailbox. "Yeah, Ramon. I should've kept on hitting him."

"They gonna fire your ass."

"Probably."

"That Mayor's one ugly creature feature. How big is that man's head up close in person?"

"*Muy grande.*"

"Yeah, well, *buena suerte.*"

"I don't think there's enough luck in all New York to bail me out on this one."

Ingram made him wait forty minutes. The Mayor was keen on symbolism, the weighted gesture, and a firmly designed pecking order. He sat in a chair, hands folded across his lap. His temper had gotten the best of him many times in his youth; a spasm would come over him and he would act or react as he saw it, without thinking. He would strike out and regret it a moment later. The impulse to strike back was overwhelming. His two older brothers took turns lumping him up when they were kids. He learned to absorb punishment, but he never gave in without a fight. He came to hate bullies. As he got older, he made a concerted effort to avoid such behavior and thought he had mastered it. It was out of character. Most of the time he was a pretty happy-go-lucky guy. He wondered where it came from. His father was the opposite, rational to the point of exasperation. Maybe it was one of those genetic traits that skipped a generation or two.

He tried to engage Ingram's assistant in small talk, but she busied herself on the phone and avoided eye contact with him. He rubbed a spot on his shoe. The hardest adjustment he had to make working in the white-collar world was the lack of physical threat and how it kept people from being assholes without a real reason. At first, he had been shocked by this. In construction, if you gave someone too much grief, you might catch a shovel off the side of the head. There was much less bullshit in that world. He remembered one super who had strutted too much, who had been fond of deriding the men. Two bricklayers dangled him by his ankles from the forty-fourth floor of a construction site until he blubbered for mercy.

In politics, so many of the men strutted around, abusing their staffs, bellowing, acting like tough guys, secure in the knowledge that there would be no consequence. They berated at will. Jimmy knew that in the white-collar world he had entered, the greatest taboo was getting physical and he had done just that. He could not keep his hands to himself. The fact that Keefe deserved that and more was meaningless. He knew his reputation was changed forever. Oh, the guy that smacked that Teamster? What a head case.

As he sat, the what-have-you-done-for-me-lately brigade made their way in and out of Ingram's office. It was deal-making time. They were lining up support, doling out promises. There was an election coming. There was always an election coming. Jimmy knew most of them, a few Council members from Brooklyn, a black minister from

Queens, the head of the Bar and Restaurant Owners Association, a lawyer for the PBA who trailed the reek of scotch. They would nod, maybe say hello, but even ones he knew well kept their distance, as if he was some kind of talisman that could only bring them bad luck. Like teammates leaving an injured player alone on the field. Occasionally, as he was walking one out, Ingram would come to the door and cast a cold glance at him, like an anthropologist studying a lesser species, then turn and lead another functionary into his office.

Finally, after escorting a roly-poly congressman to the door with a warm goodbye and reassuring pat on the shoulder, Ingram said, "Dolan," and tilted his close-cropped head into his office. Jimmy followed. Ingram sat at his desk and indicated a chair for Jimmy to sit in. The chief of staff sat silently as if he were weighing a grave decision. Ingram pursed his lips and made an A-frame with his long, pale fingers. There were rumors that he was gay, but as if to deflect them, Ingram affected a steely machismo and was known for his intractability.

Jimmy wanted to say something, to break the uncomfortable silence, but looked about the office instead. There was the faint hint of cologne in the air mingled with stale tobacco smoke. The man was known to enjoy a Cuban cigar occasionally. His office was decorated in a Republican pachyderm theme, pictures, paintings, bric-a-brac, campaign posters. Jimmy felt all the elephants were mocking his predicament. His comeuppance for jumping parties to further his career. He was an interloper, a traitor, and now he was to pay the price. There were also a number of pictures of Ingram with failed Republican presidential candidates. Men who had passed into political oblivion, victims of their own outsized ambition.

Ingram got to the point. He slid a letter across and said, "We're sorry, Dolan, but you made your own bed with this one. We have an image to protect. We've convinced Mr. Keefe not to press charges. When the smoke clears, we'll try to place you in one of the agencies."

Jimmy picked up the paper. It was his letter of resignation. So that was it. One half a fuckup and he's gone. Jimmy put it down again. He felt the urge to make a gesture, to say something decisive, a thick-headed response to his own defeat. Something to go down in political lore. He decided no.

"Let me just ask. I've been working with you every day for what, two years almost?"

"That's right."

"I ever miss a day?"

"Not that I can think of."

"I ever come in late?"

"No."

"I ever screw up, blow a site, let the Mayor get ambushed on some issue?"

Ingram twirled a key ring on his index finger and looked past Jimmy when he spoke. "This is not about your ability or your diligence. You might be the best advance man I've ever worked with. You chose to get involved in something. You should have been smarter. What is, on the bottom line, your job all about?"

Jimmy shook his head. He knew where this was going.

"There you go. If I could do something for you, I would."

Jimmy leaned over and signed his resignation. "Who's going to take my job?"

Ingram looked long at him as if considering whether or not he was entitled to this information. "Greg Rubin."

"Greg Rubin? You're joking." Jimmy had been forced to bring Rubin on board several months ago. Rubin Senior was a millionaire fund-raiser and an old friend of the Mayor. Greg was twenty-five, born and raised on the Upper East Side, had attended the Dalton School and Dartmouth, a nice Jewish boy who aspired mightily to Waspdom. As an advance man he was next to useless.

"You're joking." He said again. This was an affront to professionalism.

"I don't joke."

"Yeah, I know, everybody can see that. But let me tell you about little Greggy, the daddy's boy." Jimmy told himself to shut up, but his mouth kept going. "The first job he worked for me? We were doing a church in the Heights, Washington Heights. We're driving up Broadway, and as soon as we pass Columbia the guy is visibly agitated; you know, like his knees are knocking a bit. Now, by 125th Street he was actually shaking, he's looking around like he expects to become the victim of a car jacking or a stray bullet. Me, I don't know what to think of this. I mean, for all I know the guy's got like a condition or some shit." He noticed Ingram wince. "Now, at 145th Street, he turns to me and says, get this, 'Are we still in Manhattan?'"

Jimmy stood and stared at Ingram. Ingram stared back. "Don't you get it?" Jimmy slapped the desk, capsizing a coffee cup filled with pens. "He's from Manhattan. It's an island. We are driving up Broadway. We didn't go over a bridge or through a tunnel. He was born and raised two miles from the spot and he doesn't know if we're still in Manhattan."

Ingram finally answered. "Greg Rubin is loyal to the Mayor. Renee has your paycheck." Then he rose. "You really need to think about growing up a bit."

"The fuck that mean?" But Ingram was gone through the side door of his office. Jimmy's tenure with the Mayor was over. He marched through the mass of cubicles, acknowledging the sheepish looks from his former colleagues. He must have been louder than he realized. Hah, what the hell. It was the only bright spot of his morning. On the elevator reality set in. What was he going to do now? He had eight hundred dollars to his name.

He came into the street, lunchtime, midtown. The office drones, out for their brief respite from the fluorescence, hurtled past him, overtaking tourists caught in the crush. But even the out-of-towners had direction, places to see, a monument, a museum, a famed café. Jimmy Dolan moved along with nowhere he needed to be. So he took his time and walked home along Central Park back to the apartment that was not his. He changed, leaving his suit piled on the floor. Then he put on jeans and a tee shirt and left a message for his father.

Frankie Keefe felt his head fill with hot blood. There he was, on every front lawn in the neighborhood, getting pushed around by some college boy faggot son of Mike Dolan. A Gannett suburban rag had picked the story up from the tabloids.

He was standing in the kitchen of his home drinking fresh-squeezed orange juice. He had just run four miles through the streets of Chappaqua followed by Cronin in the Caddy. Here he was recognized as a civic leader. He gave to the March of Dimes and the Elder Hospital, sponsored a Little League team, went to St. Alphonsus for late Mass every Sunday. No one here questioned his associations, at least not publicly. He had been tempted to snatch the papers one by one this morning. He thought the brisk run would cool him off, would ease the anger, but no. He wanted the kid dead. It was that simple. He wanted the whole family dead. He would petition Tommy Magic to whack the two of them, tie them together, and bury them alive.

He dressed in preparation for meeting with his brother-in-law, that fat son of a bitch, Tommy Magic. While conniving his way up the New York Teamster food chain, Keefe had screwed his friends and enemies with equal relish, always managing to avoid culpability. He took pride in this. But the shrewdest move he had made yet was marrying Magic's sister. He pulled on his socks and looked at a scuff on his shoe. He opened his drawer and pulled out a shine rag, spit on it, and worked the mark out of the supple leather.

It was not an entirely loveless marriage. He felt for her, maybe more pity than love, treated her kindly, gave her whatever she wanted, indulged her, even stuck his cock in her once or twice a month. She did not seem unhappy with the arrangement as far as he could tell. She spent half the year sitting by the pool in Miami with her fat girlfriends, trying to decide what fancy restaurant they were going to waste their husbands' money in that night, what fad diets they were going to take up in the morning. They shopped and complained about life.

He thought about his kids, off in colleges. He was afraid his son was a bit of a fruit, what with his long hair and earrings. Not just one, like the fruits and hippie faggots used to wear when he was younger, but two, like a woman, one in each ear. Kid wanted to be a writer, for Christ sake. Carried around books of poetry, a notebook and pen, was always jotting things down. He'd take the kid out for dinner to Peter Luger's, the kid would order salad just to break his balls. Or they might ride up to the country house in the Catskills and the kid would just stare at him and jot things down as he spoke. Felt like he was the father of a court reporter. Kid was soft and pudgy, almost girlish. He never once had to do a day's work, which, at first, Keefe was proud of. Now he realized he'd probably made a mistake. His daughter kept dropping out of college and going back. What was the name of the band she followed? It used to be that Grateful Dead. What the fuck kind of name was that for musicians? When the slob that ran the show died, he had asked his daughter if she thought the guy was actually grateful now that he was really dead. She had called him a fascist pig and went on about the Teamsters beating up farm workers or some crap.

Kids needed to work their own lives out. He provided, paid their bills, gave them a little extra for spending money. Even so, growing up in the South Bronx, he had despised kids like them. He used to take the subway down to the Upper East side and coldcock rich people. Someone looked like he was in the chips, he'd ask them the time and kapow! fuck you, right there on Park Avenue. Christ, he was a sick ticket in those days.

He banged out a quick fifty push-ups. Shot his cuffs, slicked his hair back with brilliantine. Splashed some cologne on his chest, armpits, neck. He fondled his cock, felt its heft. He was lucky to have a nice piece of meat, like a good-size kielbasa, nine, ten inches of it. Imagine being a poor bastard with a little schwanz. God forbid. He could count on a good fuck with Lorene later on. Nice tits, not too bright; perfect. One thing he never liked in a woman was talking. Most of them seemed to have some biological need to do so. A word quota they needed to meet or they would go up in flames by the end of the day. One of the reasons he married his wife, besides her brother, was that she did not say much.

He studied his face in the mirror, affected the agreeable dipshit face he used around Tommy Magic, then turned to a scowl: "Listen, you fat old guinea." One day. He was dark Irish, actually got a nice tan. Many people believed he was actually Italian but had changed his name like some of them did to hide what they were, like boxers in the old days. He kept up his tan, going to the salon during the winter when he could not make it to Florida. He'd hate to be one of those red-faced micks, always looking like someone just threw a pot of hot water on him. But his bloodlines meant nothing to him. He was American, through and through. U-S-A. He used the Irish shtick when he needed to. In truth, he was embarrassed by some of these clowns. They'd been in America far longer than his people had, since the potato famine, for Christ sake, a hundred and fifty years. Still they get all weepy with the bagpipes and fuck the Brits, all that goofy crap. Best thing ever happened to them was getting chased out of Ireland. The way he saw it they should thank the English. Most of them would be on some hill wearing rubber boots caked with sheep shit, if they could even afford the boots. He'd probably be a farmer with black teeth and big hairy ears. He'd gone over once and the weather was lousy, the food worse. Everything that breathed smoked. What good was all that fresh air if every time you went inside you were in a cloud of smoke? Thank God his people left. Decent golf, though, he'd give them that.

His crow's-feet were more pronounced, his brow was starting to deepen, but his eyes were bright and alert, his hair still pure black. Not a trace of gray. Christ, he was still a good-looking man. He took care of himself. Ate right, worked out like a teenager, did not smoke, drank in moderation. Most guys his age could pass for his father. He let loose with a loud fart and wiped a speck of shaving cream from his ear.

"Marie, honey, I'm ready."

Every weekend he and his wife made the journey for a day of food and goombah bullshit. He followed his wife out to the car. As he was climbing in, Bill Mulrow, his Wall Street prick neighbor, waved hello with his copy of that morning's paper. Keefe grunted and slid behind the wheel. He was not used to dealing with embarrassment. He made his way down from Westchester, through the resurgent Bronx, and crossed the Throgs Neck Bridge. With a heavy foot, he made it to Howard Beach in thirty-seven minutes.

Keefe pulled into the driveway of Tommy Magic's house. It was a dull two-story ranch on a block of Cape Cods populated by firemen, construction workers, mailmen, and various other peasants. Magic was overly concerned with downplaying his wealth. The lawn was well kept and a row of perennials bordered the walk on either side. But the house was in need of a fresh coat of paint and the driveway was pocked and cracked like a hillbilly highway. That was one thing he had over the rotten fuck. Keefe lived a nice life. There was a plushness to it. He afforded himself luxuries that were beyond his imagination when he was young. World travel, fine food, opulent comforts. Magic, on the other hand, lived like a low-rung civil servant. It was all a sign of the decline of the guineas anyway. Just the fact that this was the boss now. In the old days, Tommy Magic would have been one of two things, a killer or a gofer.

Since the demise of John Tuzio, the market had gone south. Feds seemed to be everywhere. Stool pigeons, once the rarest of birds, were a thriving species. Tommy Magic saw betrayal everywhere and had amended his ways. Tuzio had died in prison, alone and racked by madness, betrayed by his right hand. His sanity seeped from him in that cold concrete cell. He lasted less than three years. Keefe shuddered thinking about that. But none of that could touch him. He had built up elaborate insurance policies for himself over the years. He played many sides against each other, and was a lot smarter than these goofs he had to do business with.

Magic's wife, Ruthie, that frail and demented shrew, greeted them at the door. She wore a faded flower-print dress that reached nearly to her bony ankles. There was a crooked line of black hair visible above her lip and she was slightly walleyed. They exchanged hugs and kisses, goombah hellos, hearty, yet false. Marie proffered the cake she had picked up earlier. In the living room there was the boss, the godfather, the good fella king, dressed like a Guatemalan gardener. His moonlike face, pitted and scarred by poisonous hormones and a tortured youth, sported a tiny piece of bloody toilet paper where he'd nicked himself. He reeked powerfully of cheap cologne. As usual, he wore glasses tinted a shade of piss yellow. Christ, Keefe thought, this guy is a discredit to his race.

"Hey, Frankie, come check out the garden."

Magic conducted almost all his business out of doors, head bent mumbling through his fingers. What a fucking life. Keefe followed the shuffling wide behind of Magic through the kitchen. The room smelled of sautéing garlic, onion, tomato, and spices, of meat baking and sea creatures stewing. It made Keefe's mouth water in anticipation. They stepped out into a postage-stamp backyard.

Magic went right to the point, said, "You got an election?"

"No problem, guy's a Bolshevik," Keefe replied. "A dreamer, nobody takes him with more than a grain or two of salt." In truth he was starting to worry about Dolan. His spies told him the guy was actually enjoying a groundswell of support.

Magic picked up a bag that reeked powerfully. He dumped the contents, a pile of fish offal, into a garbage can. "I get this from Billy Spiro, down the Fulton market. Nice fertilizer. Plus, I always get a little extra for the agents."

"Agents?"

"I seen on the TV, *America's Most Wanted*. These government guys, they look through your garbage. For evidence. It's legal. I give them a little something nice to dig through."

Magic tossed the bag aside and half of a rotten cod flopped on his grass. He snatched it and flipped it over the fence into his neighbor's yard. "Donkey Irish 'lectrican. Local 3. Fuck him too."

Christ, Keefe thought. The guy was always waging wars.

Magic selected a type of garden tool, then waved it at Keefe. "Your election. A grain or two?"

There were times when Keefe pondered smacking Tommy Magic to his knees right in his own backyard, rubbing his face in the dirt of his quaint little garden. Maybe piss on his head, help the tomatoes grow.

"Tommy, it's me talking here. Not to worry."

"I don't like the fact you can't take care of your own situation. It makes me nervous. You know what happens when I get nervous."

Keefe nodded, felt his stomach start to flutter. It was not a question. When Magic got nervous, people got dead.

"Come on. It looks good, union democracy at work. Guy will get maybe ten percent of the vote."

"Ten percent, huh? We can't afford to lose you, Frankie. We can't afford it. More important, you can't."

By now Teamster Local 383 was the most profitable and consistent endeavor in Magic's empire. Keefe controlled delivery to half the construction sites in the New York area and personally handed the man a hundred thousand dollars a month in cold cash from shakedowns on job sites. Keefe knew that losing his election would not be healthy. Brother-in-law or no, father of Magic's sister's kids or no, business was business with the Magic man. He wanted to raise the issue of that Dolan kid, but you had to be careful raising things like that. The guy could get touchy. Besides, he was not so sure he wanted Magic involved, after all. The guy was likely to start whacking everyone in sight. Keefe felt his own ire ease a bit. He'd get through the election, then the kid could disappear on his way to school.

Magic was on his hands and knees now massaging the soil with his thick ropey forearms. He had surprisingly long fingers for a man of his build. They were pale in the black spring earth. Keefe had a vision of Magic smoothing over his own shallow grave with those same fingers. There were rumors of a body or two right there beneath them, nurturing Magic's tomatoes and zucchini, his eggplant and spicy peppers. He thought of skeletons and rotted flesh, a twisted rictus grin of the dead. He toed a rock that Magic had displaced. No matter how hard he tried to control it, the guy made him nervous.

"I never use gloves. I like to feel the earth." He picked up a loamy handful and considered it. "You can never start too early, Frankie. The soil, this earth, it needs special attention. You want things to come forth from it later on, you got to treat it nice now. It's like an investment."

A bead of sweat had formed across the top of Magic's nose. He looked up at Keefe. He wiped the sweat with the back of his left hand. "That Irish truck make the rounds?"

Keefe nodded yes, but he was amazed. Magic, through a combination of his own shrewdness and misfortune on the part of others who were in cages or graves, was the head of a family, yet he was asking about a single truckload of corned beef that had been hijacked just in time to sell the meat at a discount to Irish gin mills for St. Patrick's Day. The guy could be so fucking nickel-and-dime it was almost comical.

"Of course, Tommy. Sure."

49

"Makes your people happy, no?"

Magic's emphasis was on your people, as in: not my people. Keefe bit his tongue and fought a suicidal impulse to kick the old dago in the ribs. The prick just could not help rubbing it in. He watched Magic stand and brush his hands together, knocking off loose black clumps of earth. Pots rattled in the house. He heard a faucet turned on, then off. A jet plane came loud and low on its approach to Kennedy. They both looked up and followed its trajectory. Magic's wife called out that dinner was ready. The sun came out from behind a cloud bank and splashed them with harsh light.

Magic handed Keefe tools. "Here, I gotta wash up. Put these in the shed for me."

Keefe took the tools. The dirt offended him. He spent his life getting away from making a living dirty. Still, he smiled, a pleasant peon smile to keep the fat man happy. He looked over to the shed. He hunched his shoulders slightly, a nod of subservience, the grateful, obedient lackey. He had no problem playing the role for the asshole. He took an envelope out of his jacket. Magic snatched it like a starving urchin grabbing an apple off a cart and shoved it down the front of his shirt.

"I love this garden. Remind me, I'll put aside some of my peppers for you and Marie. Now, what the fuck was that in my morning papers yesterday?"

Keefe knew it was coming. "Sure, Tommy. Ah, listen, that."

"Yeah, that."

"It was more an accident. Fucking kid. I tripped more than anything."

A darkness the color of an old bruise crawled across Magic's face, his lips tightened. He took off his glasses, something he did for emphasis. "An accident? Some kid smacks you like a jamoke, and you tell me it's an accident. You should've smacked him back, is what you should've done. I got every type of degenerate fucking immigrant crook circling around waiting for the G to shove me aside, so they can plunder what the fuck is mine, and you get slapped like a girl for the whole world to see."

Keefe blanched. "Tommy, I'll take care of it. Teach the little prick some manners."

"Is that right? You think 'cause you go to that fucking gymnasium and look in the mirror half a day you're some kinda tough guy? You make me fucking laugh. You just keep bringing me my fucking money like a nice mick, keep your hands off of my sister, and we'll all be happy."

"Tommy." Keefe was put off by the sharpness of Magic's response. He had not expected a reprimand.

"You what? All of a sudden you're gonna start taking care of your own work? I been cleaning up after you for years. Now you got the balls to make me look like a fucking gavone for all the newspapers, the fucking television. The kid just happens to be the son of the guy you got an election with. You believe in coincidence?" He put his glasses back on.

Keefe did not know what to say.

"Well, I don't." Magic stared at him in silence.

Keefe shrugged. He wished he had the balls to put this fat bastard in the ground. God only knew what the lunatic might do now. Magic leaned forward, and with his finger pushing one nostril closed, snorted a line of snot out of his other. Keefe had to look away.

"Now let's eat, huh? I'm starving. Put those fucking tools away."

"Yeah, Tommy, sure." Keefe shot the finger at Magic's turned back. One of these frickin' days.

Tommy Magic watched his brother-in-law pull out of the driveway and turned back to the kitchen for another piece of cake. He knew it was time to make a bold move. One of his bookmakers was slapped around in the middle of Queens Boulevard by some Colombian. The Russians were nosing around all over, and now this Dolan kid pisses on his number one earner for the whole wide world to see. He couldn't pick up a paper without a story in it about how they were finished. Nobody was taking them seriously anymore. Maybe it was time to do away with some of the old rules, make a statement, take some action on this kid, or his old man. Do it off the record, keep Keefe wondering what happened.

Lately Tommy Magic was having a recurring dream of being buried alive. Feds, friends, capos, and victims, they all passed the shovel around laughing. He would scream and curse and try to claw his way out, but the dirt got heavier and heavier until everything went black. He would wake up in a cold sweat unable to catch his breath.

RICO was choking them all. The law had changed everything. All the government needed was a few rats. Evidence meant nothing. Every move he made was scrutinized. He watched his wife clean the dishes. There was a tightness to her now, like any minute a spring would snap and she would be gone. They'd had her to those head doctors a few times. Once, after some asshole FBI guy had followed her into the supermarket, she had cried for three days straight. They gave her pills for it, and now she lived on the things. He was feeling more and more claustrophobic, hounded and hunted. He scaled back his direct involvement to a point where he was not sure of his level of control anymore. Outside was the usual sedan with the agents. Their presence on his street was as certain as the rising of the sun. He was not going out without a fight. Maybe back in the day the rules meant something. Well, the other side changed the fucking rules. He scarfed down the last of the cake and washed it down with black coffee. We'll see who's running this town.

U p on the dais the Cardinal was droning on about charity and forgiveness, the brotherhood of man, and, of course, the sanctity of the unborn. Punchy Dolan drank the remainder of his sixth, or maybe his eighth, Jameson and fidgeted in his seat. His hemorrhoids were acting up again, like a blowtorch on his rectum. He had hoped the spirits would cool the pain. He considered the occupants of his table. Ten in all, most, like himself, were thickening white men with red faces and a fair amount of money, except for the two junior associates from his firm. They sat dully regarding their mineral waters, looking as if they were being forced to endure an obscure tribal ritual. Kids today, Punchy thought as he shook his empty rocks glass.

The rest were the sons or grandsons of workingmen. The immigrant cops and firefighters and laborers and longshoremen and tradesmen who had built the city and fought in this country's wars. Most had even toiled some in their youth, but that would be hard to tell this March night. Many had been street kids—some star athletes in high school, some soldiers and sailors before heading to college on the GI bill. They used their hustle and street smarts to carve a place for themselves in the city's hierarchy, breaking their families' long line of peasantry.

Now they sat here at the Sheraton in black tie and feigned thrall to the man with the hat, his eminence. Punchy Dolan had not been to church, save for weddings and funerals, since the early sixties, when he was twelve and bounced out of Good Shepherd's altar boys for running a minor gambling ring among his fellow fresh-faced acolytes, a little sports book that the priests objected to.

The room was packed with an assortment of luminaries. The Mayor and Governor shared a table with two United States senators and the HUD Secretary. Punchy noticed Frankie Keefe, who had recently buffed the floor of Gracie Mansion with his ass, muttering into the ear of an actor who had been killed at least a dozen times while playing mobsters on the big screen. Life meets art, Punchy thought. His nephew Jimmy had better watch his back. He did enjoy seeing the arrogant prick on his keister. But the kid had worked hard to get where he was. Tough break blowing it because of a skel like Keefe. He wondered if he could help Jimmy out of this one.

Bernie Shanahan was nodding off to his left, his head pressing his several chins out to the sides like pink pincushions. Bernie the Bank. A kid from Jerome Avenue who had traded his way up the social ladder. Fordham Prep, Yale. Harvard MBA. The Rent Guidelines Board, the City Charter Commission, a brief tenure running the MTA. Now he was on a half dozen boards and was the number two man at the number one bank in the city. While Punchy's ascent had been far less formal, it was no less spectacular. But now, on this night, the specter of an even more spectacular plummet was gnawing on his consciousness. He forced it away. No time for panic.

Punchy needed to get out of there. He needed air. He needed a drinking buddy. He needed the warm escape of a night on the town, bar stories and laughter. He nudged Bernie. Shanahan came to with a start. "Wha?" A bit of spittle rolled down his chin. People cast censorious glances in their direction. Punchy nodded and smiled, nodded and smiled some more, thinking, Up yours, you uptight hypocritical pricks. He leaned into Shanahan's ear. "Bernie, I got to get the hell out of here. Whadda you say we hit Rosie's for a brewski? Just a quick cold one."

Bernie waved his butter knife at Punchy like he was a magician with a wand trying to make an elephant disappear. "No way. Early meetings."

Punchy started to goad him, but Bernie turned toward the Cardinal and leaned all the way forward in his chair, showing Punchy the back of his perfectly coiffed hair. Punchy might have persisted, but there was the little matter of the four-car pileup the last time they ducked out of one of these snoozers. And a DWI for Bernie the Bank. Not to mention an angry wife, humiliated children, local media coverage, and glee in the eyes of his Westchester neighbors. He'd let Bernie the Bank slide this time.

Punchy excused himself with a whisper, muttered "bathroom," and made tracks for the door. The night crystallized with promise the moment his tasseled loafers hit the sidewalk. He was a man on a mission. On Seventh Avenue there was a line of tourists huddled behind the doormen, who, costumed in bright top hat and tails, looked like attendants at some fanciful court. Their jaded expressions contrasted sharply with those of the wide-eyed tourists. Many of them looked like they expected to be set upon at any moment by a teen wolf pack out of a nearby ghetto. Not under this mayor, you rubes. They obviously did not read the crime statistics, Punchy thought. He stood up straight and adjusted the jacket of his tuxedo, realigned his bow tie. He ran his fingers through his gray hair. White, he liked to call it.

Inside Rosie's there was a nice crowd. Strains of Sinatra from the jukebox, dark, deeply oiled wood and brass railings. The assembled imbibers were a mix of white and blue collars, accountants and cops, lawyers and electricians. Punchy found himself readily at home. This was his kind of crowd. He made his way to the bar, caught the eye of one of the Irish bartenders, and waved him over. The bartender leaned in so he could hear over the din. Punchy ordered a Jameson on the rocks, paid for it, then tipped the bartender a crisp twenty-dollar bill. "Keep an eye on me, young man. I don't like to go thirsty."

Punchy regarded his whiskey. He lifted it to his lips, admired its amber glow, sniffed the contents, then sipped it as if it was holy water. He put the glass down gently on the bar. There was a basketball game on TV. He glanced briefly, noticed the score. He had several thousand dollars riding on a Knicks victory. It was midway through the fourth quarter and the hometown boys seemed to have the game in hand. This soothed him. He waved the bartender down.

"Another, sir. And would you be so kind as to pour a drink for these girls." Punchy indicated the two women to his left. He noted that one was wearing a sweater from RIT. "I believe they may be from Rochester. I have a good friend and business associate from Rochester. Frank, Frank Shattuck. Frankie the Hillbilly, Frank the Tailor. He's a man of many names, aka's. Do you know him? Makes a beautiful suit."

The one closest to him was short. She craned her neck up and Punchy found himself looking straight down her nostrils, which flared when she replied, "We're women, not girls, and we're from Astoria, you fat, old asshole."

Punchy snorted. He felt unjustly persecuted, set upon. Can't a man be a gentleman? He figured the two twerps at his table back in the Sheraton were responsible for this kind of attack. Men lacked backbone these days. "Asshole?" he retorted. "Fat? Old? Me? Why, you titless witch. You're nothing fifty feet of twine and a little cheap whiskey couldn't tame." He fought the compulsion to toss his drink.

The women, executing a duet of scoffing, scowling, and sputtering, wheeled away and were swallowed by the drunken crowd. Good, more room for me, Punchy thought, and squared himself at the bar. "Fucking lesbians," he muttered. He nodded to an acquaintance whose name was lost to him. Somebody with the plumbers union. No electricians.

Punchy looked up at the Knicks game. They were suddenly eight points down with fifty-three seconds to play. What the hell had happened? The night seemed to take on a sinister tinge. He stood and gripped the bar with both hands until his knuckles were white. He pushed back from the bar and knocked into a waitress ferrying a tray of drinks, jettisoning the entire load into the air.

"I'm sorry, sir, but you're gonna have to go." The bartender had materialized at his elbow.

Whoa. "Sir? It's me, Punchy." He felt the ground shift beneath him, a head rush.

"Easy now, out you go."

"You must be mistaken. I'm Punchy Dolan."

Now there was a second barman at his other elbow, more insistent. Punchy contemplated a stand, demands to see the owner. This can't be happening. He'd been drinking here for years. Before these bar boys by his sides were born. He backed out of the saloon onto Seventh Avenue. A cold spring rain had begun to fall. This seemed to focus him. People hurried past him, heads ducked against the rain. Hell, it was not too late to reclaim the night. He was tired of that dump anyway.

He caterwauled up and down the avenues of midtown. He jammed fifty-dollar bills into the tattered cups of startled homeless people. He ducked into gin mills and bought rounds for the house and sang Irish songs at the top of his lungs. "Danny Boy," "A Nation Once Again," "The West Is Awake," "Molly Malone."

When the city that never sleeps was almost nodding off, Punchy was struck with a brilliant idea: the Old Neighborhood. He was standing in the middle of Second Avenue pissing out the night's accumulation of toxins. He finished, zipped, then flagged a cab. At first the Sikh driver was hesitant to travel so far uptown, but Punchy dropped a crisp hundred-dollar bill over the seat and the man nodded like one of those little big-headed dolls you used to see in the rear windows of cars. "Coin of the realm, hey, boy? Solves all woes."

He made the man stop at a bodega for a six-pack. He nursed beers on the ride up the FDR and sang Irish songs softly to himself. He tried hard to keep uncomfortable thoughts at bay. But cruising up the highway, the windows down, a chill East River wind in his face, he briefly realized that his world was starting to fold in on him. Though he had accumulated several million, owned a house in East Hampton, a condo in the Trump Tower, British, French, and Bavarian cars, and two boats, his was a fortune built on bluster and bullshit, not to mention connections with unsavory types. He was going broke fast. Three, soon to be four ex-wives were part of the problem. But it was bigger than that, much bigger. He'd lost his touch. He seemed caught in a vortex, all good fortune beyond him.

"Hey, driver. You know Inwood? Are you familiar with it?"

The driver looked at him in the mirror and shrugged. He seemed tired beyond caring.

Punchy slugged down a beer as the cab turned off on Dyckman Street. "I grew up here. I'm from here. Ah, what the fuck do you know. I lived here till I went to Nam. You got any idea over that, Mr. Singh Singh? How you like being named after the Big House?" Punchy directed him to the corner he grew up on. He lavished another C note on the driver and waved him off. The cab executed a three-point turn, and as the driver accelerated, he flipped Punchy the bird.

"Figures." He stood in the chill air of late night and savored the memories. This was his corner. Punchy Dolan. Nobody could touch him here. He whupped them all. He went out the undisputed king of his block. He'd won two Golden Gloves championships before getting jammed up on burglary and assault raps. Much to his mother's horror. Vietnam or Sing Sing, said the judge. Easy choice that one. He needed space, light, an opportunity to scam. Southeast Asia provided all three. Thirty-three years ago. He turned that phrase around on his tongue. Thirty-three damn years. He occasionally stretched the truth about his war years. He was no hero. He was in rear supply, where he made his first small fortune. Was a REMF, a rear-echelon motherfucker, as the grunts were fond of calling them. Then it was home.

He got in with a few guys down in the financial district, studied night and day while working his way up, all of which led to a legendary run on Wall Street. He took a fierce beating in the crash of '87, but had rebounded nicely, thanks to a few shady deals he went in on. All the while he dabbled in politics, which kept him wired into the power structure of the city. It started out simple enough. He'd have his firm buy tables at dinners and this led to honorary finance positions where he used his connections to other firms, unions, and politicos to build support for candidates. Everybody loves the guy who brings in the cash.

He owned a saloon on the East Side which was really a front for shadowy silent partners. Much of his money came from serving as front man for a pension fund scheme that quietly siphoned millions in fees and commissions from the coffers of Keefe's Teamster local and a few others. He reconciled this with the fact that members' money was never touched. It was all about skimming from the margins, dealing in kickbacks, making money off the float between when funds are collected and when they need to be reported. It was barely illegal. Bloodless white-collar crime. More or less. At least this is what he told himself.

He routinely associated with men whose names would greatly alarm state officials. Over the years he'd lost himself in most of the garden-variety vices: women, food, booze, a four-year run with the cocaine. Thank God he'd gotten beyond that. Now the gambling. That was still a problem. He was, no doubt about it, a degenerate gambler. Owned by associates of Tommy Magic. No question, the guinea bastards held a certain amount of sway over him.

He noticed a group of Hispanic kids on the opposite corner. They drank from cans wrapped in brown-paper bags. They sat sipping wordlessly, staring at him. He nursed his beers, placing the empties back in his paper bag. He thought about his parents and began to feel sorry for himself. They never seemed to catch a break. His father took a heart attack and died while driving a city bus that ended up inside a pizzeria on Fordham Road. Passengers screaming and bleeding. A jolt of mayhem on a quiet afternoon. Punchy had eleven months in-country by then. He shipped out for the funeral and finished his time at Dix. Two days later Tet started, and his base was overrun, taking heavy casualties. It was as if his father checked out to keep him alive. His mother never really bounced back from that. She went old country, wearing black and going off to church every day. They never got her out of Inwood. She died twenty years to the day that his father had. To the day. Punchy saw dark and heavy symbolism in that.

He popped a new beer, nodded at the Spanish kids, and walked unsteadily around the block to reclaim his perch. He remembered the early wars with the Puerto Ricans. This part of Inwood started going quick then. It had always been poor, but the new immigrants brought a deeper level of desperation with them. Knives were introduced to the fray, zip guns. Punchy and his cohorts considered this most cowardly.

The night was cooling; a fine mist began to fall, lending a sheen to the cars that lined the street. The streetlights all wore halos. He sat on his old stoop, a scarred and plump steelhead. He noticed, without concern, that the little banditos had come around the corner as well.

He replayed old scenes in his head. They did not have a pot to piss in, but they had things of far greater value, he realized now. There was life here, a great bustling, striving, immigrant community. His siblings. He was the second youngest. Followed in the New World only by his sister Immaculata. Pius and Immaculata. His brothers, Mike and Pat and Raymond, had all been born on the other side. Two others had died shortly after birth. His mother was so terrified of the God that had claimed her children that she moved to America and saddled her Yank-born kids with ridiculously religious names as if this might ward off the cruelty of a remote deity.

He used to wait out here for his father to finish his bus run. When his father, lunch pail in hand, rounded the corner, he would run to greet him. His father would smell of tobacco and diesel, sometimes beer from the bar. His mother would be upstairs cooking, boiling a hunk of meat and some stiff vegetables. He would ride his father's thick shoulders up the stairs into a warm and stuffed apartment where eight of them lived in four rooms.

With his boyhood friends there were quick, cold swims in the fierce currents of the Spuyten Duyvil, stickball games on bubbling asphalt, furtive rustlings of virginal garments, admonishments from priests, slaps from thick-necked cops. Life was an inch from your nose then, every day was an adventure. We were never going to die. Never, he thought. He crushed an empty beer can.

He turned back and looked at the door, marred now by graffiti. He noticed the number, 347, and looked out at the street. Wait a minute. He had lived in 345. He stood, confused. How could he have been mistaken? He staggered down the steps, dropping his bag of beer. He backed away, staring at the building. "What the hell?" His house was the last in a row of identical walk-ups. It was gone?

He stared in shock at a rubble-scattered lot. There were chunks of broken wall, bricks, mesh fencing, shattered wine bottles, a rotted mattress, the remnants of a bonfire, blackened planks, half of a toilet seat, used condoms. What the Jesus? A great wail of despair came over him. He walked to the next building and peered drunkenly at the number: 349.

This was it: 347 then 349. No 345. His boyhood home was gone. Demolished.

He tried to remember the last trip he'd made up here; it was not that long ago. Every couple of months he'd make his way here in the wee hours, drunk. And now this. Ruin. He felt something tear loose, his bearings knocked off-kilter. This place was a link to his past. He had considered buying the building on several maudlin drunken nights, to preserve it as some kind of shrine. But now it was too late. "No" was all he could manage.

"Yo, fancy man." His bandito friends had formed a half-circle around him. Sneaky fuckers. They stared unspeaking, regarding him as if he were some exotic specimen, a species far from its natural habitat. Punchy felt no danger, for he was too deep in the booze and somewhat bewildered. He picked out the one who might be the leader. He wore a Florida Marlins cap, and a scar ran across his right cheek, ugly and jagged. The scar reflected the urine-yellow streetlight.

"Fancy fat muthafucka." Chuckles all around.

Punchy was glad he amused them.

"Lend us some money, fancy man." More chuckles. A guffaw or two.

"We pay you back."

"Hey, chump, you know Trump?"

60

"As a matter of fact, I do."

Punchy felt a jolt of whiskey bravado surge through his brain. His boyhood home was gone and these little bastards were to blame. He held them personally responsible for the blight that was here, the bars on the windows, the graffiti, the poverty-reeking despair of the place. What had they done to his Inwood? They had turned him into a fucking refugee. He brandished his last beer can. "I'll litter the gutter with you, you fucking carpetbaggers. This is my corner. You hear me? I kicked your fathers' asses, I'll kick your asses too."

They stopped laughing then. They were not even smiling. They looked to scarface. Punchy figured the best defense was a swift offense. He made as if to turn away and then spun and threw his best sucker punch at the bandito.

Somehow, he missed. He stumbled past him and tried to right himself, to regain footing and balance, to steady his world. But they were on him then, and he paid for the decades of aging, of thickening, of the deterioration of his reflexes. He paid for the softness that had enveloped him. He was too old and slow an animal. He went down among the gleeful shouts of the predators he and his friends had once been. The blows rained upon him, found his face, his ribs, the back of his fat thighs, his exposed and ample flank. The sickening thuds seemed to come from a great distance. And then darkness.

In those first half-conscious seconds before Punchy opened his eyes, he wondered how the hell he got home. He opened his left eye first and was staring at the tail end of a '74 Nova. Oh. He was not home, not home at all. He rolled over on his side and opened his other eye. A sour sun was just cresting over the Bronx. He reached for his wallet. It was not there. Neither were his pants. Or his jacket. Or his shirt, tie, or cummerbund. Pius Dolan lay naked except for his boxers and a pair of black socks—in the Old Neighborhood. He managed to sit upright. He felt the lumps on his head, the tenderness in his ribs. He belched, then rolled on his side and vomited weakly, the poison easing its way into the gutter. The wages of sin. He sat back up. Okay, genius, now what? Up and down the block people were emerging for the day's work. Punchy thankfully was hidden between the cars.

A patrol car pulled up. Two cops sat staring at him, trying, he imagined, not to laugh.

He waved, still woozy from the booze and the beating. "I'm Punchy Dolan. I grew up here."

At the station house he refused medical treatment. They gave him a blanket and told him to call someone. He thought for a minute, then figured he had no choice but to call Mike. It had been a while. But it was his brother, for godsakes, and he was just up the road. Plus he needed to tell him about the building. He looked around the station house. What kind of people come through here? A man with one eye sat next to him with blood trickling out of his nose, muttering something about the Pope stealing his VCR. A fat woman in a bright purple dress tried to dissuade four kids, all of whom looked about six, from knocking over a Coke machine. She turned to Punchy and said, "They little muthafuckas. Just like they fathers."

It was change of tours and Punchy provided the officers with much amusement. Apparently someone had recognized him as a mover and shaker. A photographer was trying to talk his way past the desk sergeant, saying he was from the *Post*. Punchy pulled the blanket up and buried his head like a turtle going into its shell. They stuck him in one of the holding cells across from the night tour's bounty. There was a stutterer, a toothless fellow with a goiter the size and shape of an avocado hanging behind his ear, a man in dire need of narcotics, and a howler. Had there been a full moon? It was right about then that Punchy considered never drinking again.

His brother shepherded him to the car. Punchy ignored his look of triumphant amusement. He considered his brother terminally jealous of his success in life. "Back up to the house. I got to show you something."

Mike sat at the wheel, his Teamster cap pulled low over his eyes. Before starting the car, he gave Punchy and his blanket a long once-over. "Costume ball? Some downtown fashion thing I missed in the *Times*?"

"Go ahead. Ha fucking ha, Mikey."

Mike chuckled and dropped the Buick's gearshift into reverse. The brakes let out a wail when Mike stopped to turn around.

"Time for an upgrade, Mike. Or you waiting for classic-car status to kick in?"

"Least I buy American. So where does a guy go about getting an outfit like that, Punchy? Saks? Maybe what, the Lord and Taylor? Barneys?"

"Buy American. You're living in the year this bucket of bolts rolled off the line. Globalization, Mike. A whole new century."

They turned off Dyckman Street and pulled over at the empty lot. It was more depressing in daylight. "You believe this? They knocked it down."

"Like you said, whole new century. 'Bout time. The thing was a rattrap when we was kids."

Punchy shook his head. "You have no sense of tradition. Hang on." He opened the door and limped over to the lot. He picked up two bricks and climbed back in the car. "Here, one for you, and one for me. A piece of our heritage."

Mike looked at him. He took the brick and flipped it onto the back seat. "I don't need a brick to tell me where I'm from. I still live here. What happened with Jimmy and Keefe?"

"That. Jesus, Mike, tell the truth I don't know. By the time I figured what had happened they had pulled your kid out of the room. I didn't get a chance to talk to him. Your favorite Teamster was not too happy. That I can tell you."

"How's something like that play itself out down there?"

Down there. It was like he was referring to South America. His brother did not get around much.

"Not the kind of thing they like to see. I mean, I know it's how men settle things all over the world, what with us being beasts at heart. But not in Gracie Mansion. Not nowadays."

Mike drove in silence for a minute. Traffic was brisk, the sun high. Punchy turned on the radio to snap the quiet. Vinny from Bayside lambasted the latest Jets trade in an angry outer-borough snarl. Punchy needed noise in his life. He sometimes figured he must have gotten the extra talking gene his brother missed out on. The guy could go a week on about a word a day.

"He gonna get jammed up?"

"Not arrested. I doubt that. I'll lay heavy that he's down the road, though. This mayor, you know his crime fighter thing. Not the kinda guy wants to be seen playing favorites, something like this. He cuts his losses, 'cause with him loyalty is a one-way street. Running in his direction."

More silence. "You do anything on this?"

Punchy knew that had to hurt. His brother was not the kind to ask for favors. Some donkey pride bullshit he had thankfully missed out on. Punchy had helped pay for Jimmy's college and grad school and he knew that burned Mike up. It had seemed natural for him to help out. Childless, Punchy was glad to pay for Jimmy. He would have gone for the whole nut in a heartbeat, but the kid wanted to work his way through. He was, after all, his father's son.

"Honest? I don't know. Can't save that job, maybe we can get him put somewhere else. A good spot in one of the agencies. I got a guy in Sanitation, another in Housing. Let the kid ride it out." Punchy had to be careful. Frankie Keefe was someone he did a lot of business with. He did not want to piss off the animals.

Mike shook his head. "What he gets, hanging around with that crowd."

Punchy wondered what he meant by that. Republicans? They pulled up to his building.

"You expect him to sit up there for thirty-five years and retire on a civil service pension? The kid's a comer, Mike, he's smart, he got himself a good education, and he can handle himself. It's a rare combination. You should be proud of him."

"Get out. I got things to do."

Punchy slid over and opened the door. "You know, only in an Irish family can the guy who goes out and hustles, makes his way in the world—becomes a millionaire—only in an Irish family can he be the black sheep. It ain't my fault you stayed in Inwood, Mike. And it ain't Jimmy's neither. Thanks for the lift."

He started to get out of the car, but Mike grabbed his arm. Punchy looked down at the hand, then back into his brother's eyes.

"You know, your problem is that you think staying true to what you are means you're a failure. I don't have a problem with who I am. All your money, you're still getting picked up off the street like a rum-dum."

Punchy yanked his arm away. He got out of the car, leaned in, and said, "Always. You always gotta be the Mother Superior, the moral authority on everything. Least I know how to live, Mikey. Like I said, thanks for the ride."

Mike just nodded. As the car pulled away, Punchy passed into his building pulling the blanket around him like a basket-case escapee out of Bellevue. Doormen stood with shit-eating grins. "Don't gloat," Punchy said. "It'll cost you come Christmastime."

It was not until later, after he'd quaffed a few stiff drinks and he went to shower and shave, that he noticed that the little guttersnipes, to add insult to injury, had shaved off his right eyebrow.

Mike Dolan had to chuckle as he watched his brother scurry into the side entrance of Trump Tower wrapped in a blanket. Mr. Big Shot High Finance. Not today, not remotely. Punchy looked like a peasant woman from the steppes. Until this morning, he had not heard from him in six months. Typical Punchy. He was a brother when he needed something. Mike pulled away and fought his way through tough midtown traffic.

He and Jimmy had played phone tag for the last two days. Mike had been painting a bookcase, half listening to the television as he worked, when he heard the announcer say, "Scuffle mars mayoral campaign," and turned to see Jimmy standing over Keefe. He had laughed, then checked himself. It was something he had wanted to see for years. Keefe knocked on his thieving ass. But he did not believe in violence. Keefe was a man who settled grudges quickly and violently. A knot of fear had formed in his stomach.

He stopped at the corner of Fifty-seventh and Eighth Avenue. A man on Rollerblades passed in front of him wearing only a pair of tight tiger-striped shorts. Two elderly women pulled granny carts laden with groceries, straining from the loads. The light changed and he sped for the West Side Highway past tenements being remade as cramped, high-rent housing. He steered with his hands on his lap and dialed in a country station. Hank Williams sang of love and incarceration.

He had been pushing hard on Keefe with the election. Keefe, convinced of his own invulnerability, had more or less been ignoring him. Not so the last two days. As he made his rounds, Keefe's goons harassed him. Every job he visited he was hassled about leaflet distribution, was met with hard stares and epithets. A hulking presence in his face.

The traffic was light up the West Side. The sun dazzled off the river. A large three-masted sailboat rode a stiff breeze beneath the silver-gray span of the George Washington Bridge. He parked on Seaman Avenue and walked down to Good Shepherd Church. He removed his Teamsters hat and made the sign of the cross as he stepped into the vestibule of the church. The heavy wooden doors closed behind him with a soft thud and the street noise disappeared. Silence enveloped him. He made his way to the candles and lit an offering for the soul of his dead wife, then one each for his mother, father, and his dead brothers. The first two had died in Ireland as babies and were the catalyst for his family's emigration to New York. His mother held the guilt of the children's passing to her last day, as if it were her fault. A deep sadness that might last a week would come over her like some weed and choke her until she pulled herself free of it. There were too many living children, too much toil, too many demands on her time and her hands. She raised six children.

His brother Raymond had died in the line of duty after stumbling on a bank robbery. He was a rookie cop. The year was 1965. Mike thought of Pius. Every time he looked at him he saw Raymond. The two of them, three years apart, looked more alike than any twins he had ever met. Even with all the weight he had gained, Punchy still favored Ray. He wondered why he was often so tough on his brother. For years he had resolved to make the effort to get closer, but he always put it off.

He knelt for a while in prayer, then just sat, taking in the vastness of this place. He had baptized all his children here, saw two of them married here, had sat while the priest swung the censer over his wife's coffin. After the car accident that claimed her life he had an impulse to pull away from the Church, to blame his loss on an uncaring, cruel God. Instead, over the years, he found himself coming here more often, not so much for Mass, but to light candles or pray, and most important, just to sit and reflect, to enjoy the peace.

After a while he stood, made the sign of the cross again, and went back down the aisle and then through the door. Broadway was starting to quicken with rush-hour scramble. He crossed the avenue to Johnny Mac's just as Last Stand Larry Sweeney pulled up on his bicycle. Sweeney's ride looked like the one the Wicked Witch used in *The Wizard of Oz*. Flying from a dowel taped upright from his handlebar was the flag of the 7th Cavalry Regiment. As the neighborhood change had accelerated, with the Dominican population tripling in a couple of decades, Sweeney had come to identify more and more with the plight of Custer on that arid hill over a century before. He had even taken to growing his graying hair, or what was left of it, long. It flowed out from beneath a crusty New York Giants baseball cap. He had a weak chin and fierce blue eyes, the doughy splotched skin of a heavy beer drinker, and the stooped carriage of a man two decades older. He narrowed his eyes.

"You wasting your time praying again, Dolan?"

"Somebody has to say nice things about you, Larry."

"Me?" Last Stand looked up and down the length of Broadway. "Look around you, Dolan. It's too late for prayers. The end, as they say, is nigh."

"Yeah, right. Let's grab a stool, then. No better place to meet the Apocalypse."

"After you." Last Stand held the door open wide and they both entered the bar.

Seamus, the bartender, greeted Mike with a handshake. He nodded wearily at Sweeney. "Hey, Mike, how's Jimmy? That mayor's a hump anyways. Kid's better off not associating with that crowd. Guy's a ball-breaking bully, you ask me." The bartender placed a cup of coffee in front of him.

"Yeah. I guess." Last Stand had spied one of his K of C cohorts at the far end of the bar and slid down a few stools. Mike was not much in the mood for the man's doom and gloom. He had his own problems to sort out. Before Sweeney's Custer obsession his nickname had been Black Cloud.

"No shit." Seamus stepped to the side so a Mexican bar back could dump a bucket of ice on the bottled beer. He leaned on the bar. "I'll tell you what, though, Mike, he's a good kid. I mean, look, he's doing all right for himself, high-profile suit-and-tie job and all, but he comes in here it's like he never left, you know. He always had a nice attitude, Jimmy. Not like some of these brainless wonders I got to deal with. Never gives you any 'big shot, I'm with the Mayor crap,' either. Nice attitude." Seamus spun a swizzle stick in his mouth while he talked, his eyes constantly moving, even though the bar was slow. The man did not miss a movement. "Speaking of elections, how's your thing going?"

Mike shrugged. "Good, you know. It's picking up now. Making up flyers, calling guys."

"Yeah? That's a rough bunch, I hear. Why dontcha get the kid to help you with the campaign. That's his business, right?"

Mike had thought about that before. Now, after the incident with Keefe, it would be a big problem. He would love to have Jimmy work with him. They used to spend a lot more time together when Jimmy was younger. But the last few years he seemed to see Jimmy less and less. The kid was out on his own and Mike was glad about that. Still, he was afraid their relationship was going to end up like the one he had with his father, one where it was too late by the time they realized they'd lost each other. It was so easy to let things slip away. Like him and Punchy. Then all you're left with is could-haves and should-haves and the dull ache of guilt and regret.

"You get too slick on these guys they get suspicious. They hate politicians on principle, and I don't blame them for that. Old-fashioned works best. I try to get by some of the jobs, shake hands. Same thing outside the union meetings. Eye to eye."

"I hear you. I'm surprised that guy ain't been run out of the union by the Feds. As crooked as they come. I follow that in the papers, talk to guys come in here. I mean, if there is a cleanup going on, then come on, this is the guy that should be gone."

"Not half as surprised as I am. Last ten years four, five hundred guys have been kicked out. Maybe five were actually as bad as this guy."

"Some system. Like guys I know from the Javits and the fish market. The government comes in and says, oh, this is a Cosa Nostra thing, they clean house. All those guys, maybe five assholes, but hundreds lose their livelihood. In the end there ain't a single indictment. Talk about throwing out the baby with the bathwater. You imagine they did that to some Wall Street company?"

"Never happen, Shamey. You know how much the government has spent out of the Teamster treasury?"

"I can imagine."

"Seventy million dollars. That's dues money from the rank and file. They come in: Hey, we're here to save you. Then they bankrupt the union in a way no boatload of gangsters ever could have. I'll tell you what. They gotta be pretty selective in who they're tossing out, if a guy like Keefe, who's the worst of the bad, a true degenerate, is still sitting there."

"Unbelievable."

"Believe you me, I was the happiest guy in the world when they first come in. I figured it was the end of a lot of bad things. Now I'm not so sure. Starting to look a lot like two evils to me. And I'm wondering which is the lesser."

Seamus wheeled and moved down the bar to refill drinks. Sinatra came on the jukebox. Mike thought about his kids. The two older boys gone to the suburbs. Patrick a city cop who transferred to Suffolk County a few years ago. Now he was living in one of those developments built on an old potato field with an uptight wife who cared more about things than people. She had Patrick up to his ears in debt insisting on a new car every other year, Club Med every winter, overpriced furniture. It never stopped. He knew the kid never would have left the city if the choice was his to make. Kevin, a city firefighter, seemed to be the most content. Four-bedroom house in Rockland County, three sweet kids, and a nurse for a wife who had a great sense of humor. His daughter Meghan was happy and living in Jersey, although he thought she had married too young. She was always a great student but never went beyond high school. He thought that was a big mistake. But her husband was an accountant who took nice care of her. She made a point of stopping by weekly with the kids and a casserole. She had her mother's Old World values.

He made a series of interlocking rings on the bar with his coffee mug. He took out a pen and laid it on the dark wood. Jimmy was certainly the brightest of his children, the most gifted. Anything he tried, he made look easy. He was always the ringleader, always able to charm his way out of a tight spot. He was the kind of person people instinctively liked and trusted. Mike realized that came from the boy's mother. Mike had been a little rough with the older boys and tried to make amends by being easy on Jimmy. He often wondered if maybe he had screwed his other kids up somehow with the discipline. He was only trying to raise them right, so they would have their heads on straight.

His election worried him. He took a pencil and, on the back of a bar napkin, scratched a list of business agents he thought might back him openly. Then listed those solid in Keefe's camp. Three for, twelve against. Maybe he should lay off, drop out, take it easy, spend more time with his grandchildren. But he knew he wanted one last shot at that SOB Keefe. The man was everything in life he despised. Keefe was a leech who got fat off the blood of his membership, took payoffs for sweetheart deals with contractors, doled out big jobs to friends and relatives, played fast and loose with the benefit plans, and used threats and muscle to subdue opposition. To Mike there was nothing more despicable than a crooked union leader. Any boss or any union-busting lawyer was a better grade of human. With Keefe it was hereditary. His uncle had been a crook too and Mike had waged battles against him before he went to prison to die. Mike had always kept the ugly side from the family. Twice the elder Keefe's thugs had beaten him so badly he ended up hospitalized. He created the fiction of an auto accident and a mugging. His wife and kids, he was confident, believed him.

The bar door opened and light spilled in, bright but without warmth. Spring was just days away. A crew of transit workers came in laughing and took the last of the barstools, heavy key rings jangling as they settled in. The Sinatra CD snagged and hiccuped until Seamus hit the reject button. Mike waved a fly away and ordered a chicken sandwich.

The membership was scared of Keefe and rightfully so. Mike did not blame them. You bitched about things, you found yourself out of work. And while actual violence was not common, it was very much a possibility. Nobody forgot the pictures of Sean Reilly, a dissident who had shot his mouth off once too often. He had been set aflame and hacked to death. The *Post* had run them on page three.

Mike had tried to take action. Last year he had visited the corruption officers at the International in Washington. They had received him warmly, assured him that their aims were the same, praised him for his courage. He went home and waited. And waited. He called Washington every few weeks. They never returned his calls. After eighteen months, he decided to run one last time.

He piled pickles on his sandwich and chewed it slowly. He wondered how badly Jimmy's screwup was going to play out. He had always kept his family out of things. Now Jimmy had knocked Keefe on his ass, involving himself. Secretly, he was proud of his kid. Proud, and very worried.

Seamus came down, brandishing the coffeepot. "No, thanks, Shame. I'll be bouncing off the walls."

Jimmy let himself into his old building on Seaman Avenue. The lobby was wide and grandly tiled. The air was cool and lacking the usual stink of close living. A faux-crystal chandelier hung above and lit the room brightly. Straight ahead was an elevator and on either side were staircases that switchbacked their way up to the top floor. Like most of the buildings in the area, it had been built during the go-go twenties to entice the emerging middle class out of the tenements downtown. While much of the neighborhood was falling into disrepair, the buildings along this block still retained much of their Art Deco grandeur. The old Irish and Jewish families on this street were slower to leave and yuppies with some means, young couples with children, were moving in. Jimmy's father kept the building spotless and well maintained.

Halfway across the lobby he was stopped by Mrs. McMartin. She had come down to retrieve the mail. She greeted Jimmy as if he still lived in the building and they met every day. In her hand was the day's pile of junk flyers and notices, many of them written in Spanish. "You believe how late the mail comes these days? You remember, right? Used to be here nine in the morning. Now you're lucky to get it by five at night. I guess nothing's what it used to be." She wore an old green dress that Jimmy would swear was the same one she'd worn when he was in about the third grade. Her hair was in curlers and covered by a net, as if she was getting ready to go out. But Jimmy knew that outside of church and the grocery, she had not been anywhere in a very long time. Her face was smooth and seemed remarkably untouched by time and heartache.

"It's nice to see you Jimmy. Real nice. But what the heck are you doing smacking people at the Mayor's house? You were raised better than that."

Mr. McMartin had gone to Korea as a newlywed and ended up as a POW. The Communists treated him poorly. He went away a sweet, fresh neighborhood kid and came home with a bad stutter and a vicious whiskey habit. His wife pretended nothing had happened. Their quarrels were loud and legendary. Secrets were hard to keep in those old apartment buildings. Even sighs of resignation and disappointment were heard through the walls. Mr. McMartin had died when Jimmy was eight. Their children were living down South and out West, came home only rarely.

She grabbed Jimmy's arm. "Everything okay, Jimmy?" Her eyes were kind, neighborly, a warm pale blue. He had always been her favorite Dolan.

"Yes, Mrs. McMartin. No problem. Everything's good." He smiled winningly, that old Dolan charm. He was not in the mood for these forced pleasantries.

She shook her head, raised a penciled eyebrow, and leaned toward him. Her breath was redolent of Lipton tea and lemon, faint tobacco.

72

"That fella's a louse. He's got that look about him. You be careful."
She spoke softly yet her words were stern. He watched her shuffle onto
the elevator in her worn fuzzy slippers. As the door was closing, she
said, "Take care of your father."

Jimmy took the stairs to the third floor. He had grown up in the
building, in a three-bedroom apartment. His father had been the superintendent for many years and was trusted implicitly by the land-
lord, an elderly and fair Jewish man who lived in West Palm Beach.
The free rent accompanying the super's duties and the couple hundred a week with it had kept the Dolans housed and fed during his father's frequent spells of unemployment resulting from his runs against
the Keefe regime.

On the door of the apartment were two decals. One was of the
family crest and the other was from the Irish-American Teamsters.
The old doormat that was so worn you could hardly read the welcome
on it. It was made of some thick brown brushlike material and had
been outside the apartment since he was a child. He remembered the
way his mother would take it and hang it out the window and smack it
so all the dust would fly out into the courtyard in the back. He remembered coming home from school and finding his father's work
boots in the hall by the door, a light cake of cement around the edge
of the soles, dust secure in the creases of the worn, cracked leather.
His father would have the boots resoled several times before finally
buying new ones.

Jimmy also remembered long stretches when the boots were not
there. When his father had trouble finding work because Keefe had
blacklisted him. The mood in the house was different in those times.
Most of the light and happiness were sucked out of the place. Jimmy,
even as a kid, could feel the change in the air, the tension, the fights
over money bleeding through the walls. The boots came to symbolize
happiness. There were trips to the Catskills or Rockaway, dinners at the
pizza place, McDonald's, the steak house up on Broadway in the Bronx.
His brothers used to call the lean times meat-loaf mode. Leftovers.
Jimmy knew his desire to make a good living was born in those days; he
wanted to be able to have what he wanted, not just what he needed.

Jimmy stood and perused the bookshelves that lined the living-room walls. His father had a ninth-grade education but was better-read than anyone he had ever met at college. Heavy tomes of labor history. Biographies of all the heroes. James Connolly, Eugene Debs, Mike Quill, John Lewis, Mother Jones, George Meaney, Jimmy Hoffa, the Roosevelts, the Kennedys. His father also loved history and novels, the sprawling works of Dos Passos and Dickens and Steinbeck, Melville, Conrad, and those dense Russian novels Jimmy found impenetrable. His father received a fair amount of ribbing for his leanings in the local bars. Some of them called him Red Mike. "I'm not a Communist," he'd reply calmly, "I'm a trade unionist. What's good for the workingman is good for America." Some were even appalled by his politics. The Irish tended more to conservative politics once they started to do well in the New World. They were of the belief that success was predicated on their willingness to join the mainstream no matter what the cost.

His father's ideals seemed noble but distant to Jimmy. It irked him that so many people had so much more than he did. He was determined to change all that. His father was incapable of understanding this need. When Jimmy was a kid he went to bed many nights listening to the muffled sounds of fighting over one thing and one thing only—money. He wanted none of that. His kids would have protection from that kind of ugliness.

He wandered into his parents' room and opened his mother's old closet. Shit. His father had promised he was going to get rid of her clothes, still all hung in a row. Dresses, hats she wore to church, her shoes. The reek of mothballs was overpowering. Maybe he expected her to walk through the door someday, like nothing happened. Just been away, don't mind me. This was the kind of thing that made him really worry about his father. It had been almost fifteen years since she was killed. Jimmy heard his father's key in the lock.

Quill, an old mutt his father had kept from being put down, went to the door. His father entered, a stack of leaflets in his hand. He dropped his keys on the hallway table.

"Jimmy?"

"Yeah, Dad."

His father had a way of staring before he spoke as if he were trying to determine the direction and tone of the conversation, a seriousness that seemed of a different generation entirely. He did this now, then walked over to him and hugged him. Jimmy smelled the bar smoke on him. His father pointed to a copy of the *News* face up on the table. "Nice going."

Jimmy shrugged. "Yeah, believe it or not, it was an accident. But I guess if it was gonna happen, I should've punched him out. Made it worthwhile."

His father gave him a quizzical look. "You thirsty? Come in the kitchen."

Jimmy sat in the kitchen while his father took two bottles of beer from the refrigerator, opened them, and placed them on the table. He then bent over to retrieve the dog's water dish, filled it, and placed it back down. Finished, he sat across from his son and took a sip of beer. He regarded Jimmy again. Jimmy shifted in his seat. He was embarrassed at causing a problem and all the attention it received. The light was from the west now, slicing over the trees of Inwood Hill Park, through the kitchen window, backlighting his father. Mike twirled the bottle by its neck. Though he was closing on sixty, his shoulders were still thick with muscle, and while his face was lined from working in the sun, his skin still looked soft, youthful.

"They shit-can you yet?"

"Yeah."

His father stood and took off his heavy flannel shirt. Underneath, he wore an athletic shirt that exposed muscle, scar tissue, and three blue smudges of faded tattoo.

"You realize what we're dealing with here?"

Jimmy was not yet particularly worried about anything besides being out of work. He knew what Keefe was about and was grateful for his father's choice of pronouns. The old man had a quiet toughness Jimmy envied. He had always gotten by on bluster. When things really got rough Jimmy always considered running as a healthy and viable option. His father never did. He was slower to commit, but when he did, he was relentless.

"You think it's gonna be a problem? I mean, if he kept his hands to himself, none of this would have happened, Dad."

"You hear what you're saying?"

"The guy's been after you for years, Dad. Fuck him."

"Shhh. Not in the house." His father glanced back toward the bedroom. It was as if his mother was still there to be offended. There had been ironclad laws about such things in Jimmy's youth. If he so much as muttered a curse under his breath, he got a whack.

"Come on, Dad." It depressed him and worried him to think of the old man living with the specter of his mother. For a second he thought of Tara. Their mothers had died four months apart. It was grief that had welded them together with a fierceness that only shared misery could. He'd found a way to ruin that.

His father swept some imaginary crumbs off the table. "I'm not so sure you understand how these guys play the game, Jimmy. This isn't like some political thing where they scheme to vote you out or make you look bad, embarrass you in front of your high-society pals."

"Dad, I spent ten years humping concrete to get here. I wasn't born in a monkey suit. Remember, you were the guy urged me to get the degree, get out of the business."

"Well, then you know what Keefe is capable of."

"You worried about him coming after you? Or me?"

"I think the one thing going in our favor is it's too public, too high-profile. Too much press on the thing. Keefe does not make his own decisions. He needs to take a crap, he asks certain people's permission. Those people don't like things messy, don't like attention. All the same, keep your eyes open."

Jimmy nodded. "How's your campaign?"

"Good."

"You need help, I'm out of work."

"You're too big-time for me. Besides, you might want to stay off of Keefe's radar screen for a while. Maybe you can be one of those unpaid consultants you see on CNN."

"I got time now." Jimmy wanted to let his father know he was in a tight spot. He just couldn't come out and say it. "You sure you don't want me to help on the campaign?"

"I don't think pissing Keefe off any more than he is already is such a bright idea. These guys play for keeps."

76

"We'll make him lose it. I'll show up and heckle him, tell him I'm gonna kick his ass for exploiting the workingman. We'll see who's high society."

His father's face flushed. "You kick Pete Cronin's ass too? The rest of his goon squad and half the mob?"

The hard tone in his father's voice sobered him.

"I was only joking. Jesus."

"You need to take life a little more seriously sometimes, Jimmy. It might do you some good."

Jimmy could not help laughing. When he was a kid his father had admonished him often with "Goddamnit, Jimmy, the trouble with you is you just don't give a crap." Now he stood up. "Life's too short for all that serious stuff, Pops. You want to go shoot some pool? I got nothing but time. You beat me, I'll be more serious. I promise."

His father shook his head. "You'll learn. What are you going to do for work?"

"I got a few things lined up, here and there," Jimmy lied.

"You should maybe call your uncle."

Jimmy said, "I will, Pops. I have a few good options besides him." He knew the fact that his uncle had helped pay for his school did not sit well with his father. It was something his father wished he could have helped out with.

"You do, ask him about his eyebrow."

"His eyebrow."

"Yeah." His father got up and put the bottles in the sink, indicating it was all he had to say on the matter.

As they walked toward the door, Jimmy put his arm around his father's shoulder. "Hey, Dad, we need to talk about Mommy's things."

His father picked up his Teamster hat and said, "Yeah, we probably do."

Cronin pretended to listen as Frankie Keefe whined on about his brother-in-law. He caught snatches, and understood it to be his usual spiel, that Tommy Magic was a "fat greedy fuck." That was the gist of it. He turned into Keefe's driveway and nodded his head when Keefe, getting out, told him to be back at 6 a.m., and to go make the rounds. The man was like a broken record, and the few times he said anything new, or worth hearing, it jumped out at Cronin like a car alarm in a graveyard. So when he muttered about Dolan getting "straightened out," Cronin sat up and listened. But that was it. Keefe slammed the door.

He backed out of the driveway and tapped his horn twice, then made his way out of Westchester County and down to the West Side of Manhattan. He parked beside a fire hydrant on Eleventh Avenue at Thirty-ninth Street and watched the storefront contractor's office until the man he needed to see arrived. Cronin looked at his watch, then up the block. There was Angelo Murphy, right on time. Cronin flipped his Dion and the Belmonts tape over, waited five minutes, then followed him in.

Murphy was out front by the secretaries, leaning over one who looked to be right out of high school, young enough to be Murphy's granddaughter. She wore a hard, salon-bought tan and displayed deep cleavage. Murphy's belly strained against his shirt. He had the distended nose and weak eyes of a man who needs a couple belts of whiskey an hour to get through the day. His hair was sparse and he compensated by growing it long on one side and draping it over the top of his head, like the Mayor. His dual heritage was reflected precisely in his name. Depending on which group he was with, he referred to himself as either half Irish and half ashamed or half Italian and half ashamed. He was one of dozens of contractors who paid kickbacks to Frankie Keefe each month for various work rule concessions. The contractors paid happily. Murphy had been around.

"Hey, Pete." Murphy straightened and a shimmer of relief passed over the girl's face. "Keep up the good work, sweetheart." He patted her on the shoulder, his pudgy fingers lingering a moment, tracing a line on her skin. Angelo Murphy was the type of guy who needed to touch people. Cronin walked up to him and shook his outstretched hand. Angelo made a show of stepping aside and offering Cronin the path to his office. "After you, my man."

Cronin stiffened when Murphy put his hand on his back as if to guide him. Murphy dropped the hand to his side. They walked through the outer office, where there were three desks, all occupied by attractive young women, girls from Bayside and Bay Ridge putting up with Murphy because he paid well and was more or less harmless. They deflected him like they might a drunk at a wedding reception.

They entered Murphy's office. "Pete, nice of you to stop by. Short notice and such."

Angelo Murphy sat in his high-backed leather chair. There was a plaque on his desk that read THE BUCK STOPS HERE. On the wall behind him were a dozen or so framed photographs of Murphy with various local politicos and minor entertainment talent. Cronin noticed that at least several of the politicos had since been incarcerated, one had committed suicide a decade ago, and one Cronin himself had help dump into the trunk of a Lincoln Town Car headed for very long-term parking at JFK. All the pictures were signed: "To my good friend Angelo."

For a brief time in the eighties Angelo Murphy had made some serious money. It owed little to his expertise or hard-nosed business sense and much to the fact that construction was booming and Murphy had the right underworld connections to secure bids. He was in the club, the select group in tight with the Cosa Nostra. Most of his money he had sunk into real estate right before the crash. The office reflected his poor judgment. It was musty and smelled like maybe someone had recently pissed on the rug. But business was picking up all over town, and Murphy had hung around long enough so that he too was about to see better times. Cronin knew all about a large contract he had just been awarded.

Murphy spun on his chair, his side to Cronin, and said, "Things are going good, these days, Pete, but I got to say I'm not too happy about the extra. I mean, I got bids out, maybe a few things break. But I don't understand why the juice goes up. I mean, you guys are cutting into my margin."

Cronin stared at him, thinking, The balls on this little gnome. The way things worked, Murphy had a third of his drivers off the books and was paying them half what he should be. And now he had the audacity to complain. It was one of several scams Keefe ran. It was Cronin's job to make the rounds and collect a monthly fee from contractors like Murphy who paid for the privilege of a cheaper workforce. Of course, the extra was Cronin's doing. He had been assessing his own tax on selected contractors he did not like. Just building a little rainy-day fund. This was not something he wanted to get around.

"I'd like to sit down with Frankie, make my case. No offense, Pete, but I been around the block a lotta years and I don't usually go through no driver. No offense."

Cronin stared hard at the side of Murphy's jowly mug. He willed him to turn and face him. Murphy turned slowly and Cronin gave him his look; all dead eyes and mouth turned down at the corners, a real fuck-you face he often used to powerful effect. He leaned forward just a bit, so his large frame threw a shadow over the contractor. He saw fear in Murphy's eyes and this pleased him. Murphy took an envelope and handed it over to him. Cronin took it and did not say a thing. He just stared at the little weasel, let him stew in his own fear. He was a firm believer in his mother's favorite axiom, "Actions speak louder than words." So he reached over and grabbed Murphy by his comb-over, grabbed a big chunk of it, and ripped upward, yanking it right out of his head. Murphy screamed. Cronin dropped the scalp like a dead rodent on the desk before him and wiped his hand on his trouser leg.

"That looks a lot better," he said in a thick whisper.

Murphy dove under his desk, crawling for sanctuary, whimpering, wishing he had kept his mouth shut. Cronin knew that was the last time the man would complain about anything.

On his way through the office all the women stared up at Cronin. He smiled widely and doffed an imaginary hat. "Good day, ladies."

Back in his car he checked his watch. He was right on time. He dropped his car off at his apartment and took the subway uptown.

Cronin ordered four hot dogs with mustard and onions and crossed Seventy-second Street to Needle Park. Settling on a park bench, he devoured each frank in two bites, then washed them down with a syrupy orange drink. This was one of his favorite meals in New York, maybe the world. He checked his shirtfront for mustard or onion stains, then brushed the crumbs from his lap. He crumbled the napkins and paper plates into a ball and pitched them into a wire-mesh trash can.

A woman sat next to him and placed a large shopping bag between her feet. She reached in and took out a hunk of stale bread and proceeded to break it into small pieces with her bony, deathlike fingers. She looked old beyond time and worry, just a lonely woman whose peers were all dead and gone by now. She only had her birds, Cronin imagined, her birds and the blurring remembrances of a life lived. Even so, this woman appeared to be fairly spry for her years. A body blessed by genetics but cursed by the failings of others, her strength condemning her to solitary confinement. She brought to mind his own mother, whom he had not seen in many years. They exchanged cards at Christmas and birthdays, little polite missives you might get from an old college friend or a second cousin. He left all the family shit to his siblings.

The woman scattered the crumbs about her in a half-moon pattern. The first pigeons, fattened and scarred, landed and strutted back and forth for a few seconds, spinning to look as if they were checking for signs of ambush, then started to feed hungrily. The flock descended from the few sparse trees and the cornices of the old bank building. They were dirty animals, Cronin thought, rats with wings. As a kid, in Washington Heights, he would go on his roof with a pellet rifle and kill a couple dozen at a time, the birds tottering, stunned by the projectiles, before falling dead to the courtyards along St. Nicholas Avenue. They were swarming at his feet now. The bugged-out eyes and the beaks programmed to peck. He fought an urge to kick one of them.

Cronin took out a toothpick and began to clean the hot-dog meat from between his teeth. As kids, he and his buddies would slide the air rifles into the sleeves of their fathers' pea coats or army jackets and head to the park. Squirrels, crows, more pigeons, the occasional skunk or raccoon, thick rats, stray cats, city wildlife, urban vermin. They were stealth hunters. He was always the best shot, the truest eye, and he amassed the highest body count, sixty-six in one day. He guessed that was how it all started.

The woman reached down into her bag. Cronin noticed a jagged scar along the back of her hand and wondered about its origin. Scars told a lot about a life. The woman rummaged a bit, her secret stash. She pulled out a battered paperback and spread it open on her lap. Cronin strained to make out the title. *The Murderer Next Door.* He fought down a flash of something, paranoia. Coincidence. With a capital C. The pigeons had picked the path clean, and most were leaving. The weaker ones wandered around, hopeful of another windfall. The woman, wrapped in her gray coat, was not obliging. She was absorbed now, her head down, her knees firmly clasping the bag, poring over the book as if it might lead her to buried treasure.

Cronin spotted Roth as he emerged from the IRT station. He wore a wool porkpie hat pulled down to his brow and a long trench coat. Cronin stifled a smile. Roth was dressed for the part. He carried a folded-up *Times* under his arm and was opening a package of Twizzlers. He looked as if he were on the way to a Cold War rendezvous. The light changed and he moved along with the crowd crossing Broadway. He was six and a half feet tall, one of the few men Cronin worked with who was taller than he was, although he outweighed Roth by a good seventy pounds. Ichabod Crane they used to call him. Ichy for short. His Adam's apple was the size of a baseball.

Cronin watched Roth enter an apartment building next to a Mexican restaurant. He watched to see that no one was tailing Roth, then followed him into the building. The smell of greasy fried meat was thick in the air. He used a key to open the door and made his way up to the third-floor landing. He let himself into the apartment and passed through a hallway into the small, sparsely furnished living room. There, Roth was sitting on the edge of the table looking out the window. Without turning he said, "*Panic in Needle Park.* Hard to believe this was Needle Park."

It was not hard for Cronin. He remembered the seventies all too well. He was a city cop then. Before the yuppies, before gentrification and the boutiqueing of Amsterdam Avenue. There was the fiscal crisis, the blackout, the gang violence, the scorched earth of the early drug wars, rampant corruption.

Roth seemed to read his mind. "Those were simpler days, no? The bad guys were a lot easier to keep tabs on. Not so diverse. We'll end up spending half our budgets on translators and language schools."

Cronin was not sure of Roth's age but he knew it was shy of fifty. His carriage was of a much older man. He attached gravity to his language, remembered things he was too young to know about. A man who reveled in the shadows. He was a true believer, a patriot who had never dodged a bullet for his beliefs. In Cronin's mind this made him more than slightly dangerous.

"This Dolan. Keefe is important. He may be unsavory, but we need to keep him there. What do they say? He's an asshole, but he's our asshole."

Cronin wondered who Roth might define as they. Lately, Cronin had started to worry about the security of his position. Roth was his contact, and if push came to shove, they would admit he was a contract player, maybe bail him out on something noncapital. At least that had always been the deal. Even though he had been shit-canned by the Bureau, he had never stopped working for the government. Most of his colleagues and superiors were sympathetic, knowing he had been burned at the stake of lousy politics. But Roth he wondered about.

Roth was the head of a group that was established during the Reagan era, a time of smaller government except for intelligence and law enforcement. Wonder years for spooks of all stripes. They were supposed to monitor unions, present criminal opportunities, compromise leadership in order to legitimize federal takeovers of organized labor. Kind of an ABSCAM program writ large. It had become an entity of its own, and in New York, Labor City, Frankie Keefe was its prized asset.

"It's safe to assume Dolan's agenda is not in line with ours."

"I'd be surprised. He's got principles."

Roth regarded him. "Let's not confuse the issue. Principles can be overrated. Held to false esteem."

Cronin wanted to laugh at the irony of it all. The government and Keefe wanting the same thing. One Mike Dolan was fast becoming an unpopular guy. Keefe had brilliantly played both sides of the fence for years. As a top-echelon informer he fed Roth friends and enemies alike to keep himself in power. All the while he was Tommy Magic's number one moneymaker. That was obvious to Roth, but it didn't matter, because Roth was more than willing to turn a blind eye to Keefe's rackets as long as he produced. And as far as the local cops were concerned, Keefe, with Roth as his rabbi, was untouchable. American Justice.

"We need to dissuade Dolan."

"Dissuade." Cronin knew that meant it was time for him to get physical, to intimidate Dolan into dropping out of the race. It was mighty convenient for the government to have men like him at its disposal. Easy to keep its hands clean. He was beginning to tire of violence. Maybe he was getting soft.

"Aren't we counting the votes?"

"We is a relative term. It is a lot easier to fix an election before it happens than after."

Cronin knew Roth had some experience in this. Ichy had spent time in Third World flash points before taking over the labor rackets task force. The skinny man had some State Department shenanigans under his belt.

"You should know you have a great deal of leeway on this one."

"Leeway. Roger that," Cronin said.

Roth pulled on his coat. As he reached the door, he turned and said, "What do we know about Dolan's kid?"

Cronin shrugged his shoulders. "Used to work for the Mayor, and he's not high on Keefe's list of favorite people, after their little tango the other day."

Roth stroked his Adam's apple as if he was plotting something. "I see," he said, and was gone.

Cronin, just to be sure, waited twenty minutes before leaving. He was in the mood to stretch his legs, so he headed west. Soon he found himself walking past the Transit Workers headquarters on Sixty-third Street. His father had been a charter member of that union back in the dismal days of the Depression when the subways were privately owned and the workers were treated with a harshness few Americans today might grasp. His father, a man with few words for his offspring, was fond of the stories. If you wanted to work, it was twelve hours a day, seven days a week for take-home pay of about thirty dollars. Mention the word "union" and you were gone, lucky not to catch a sap behind the ear. No wonder he was a committed Communist, a German Jew who gave up his religion for the masses. He even changed the family name from Kronenberg to crush his past. He and some of his pals had banded with the Irish farm boys, most veterans of various Hibernian wars, to grab hold of much that moved in this city. He married a sister of one, an enforcer for the union.

Cronin made his way back to Broadway and descended onto an IRT platform that had changed little since its opening in 1904. His father had played out his days as a conductor on this line, a bitter and defeated old man, a victim of the Red baiting after the war. He stood in the front car as he used to when he was a child on the rare day his father would let him ride along. He thrilled at the rush of the tunnel, the light and shadows, the speed. He was a boy then and proud of his father in a way he would never be again.

Tara O'Neil folded herself at the waist and grabbed her toes. She enjoyed stretching before a run, took the occasional yoga class, was committed to flexibility. She spread a towel on the oak floor of her living room and brought her knees to her chest, then twisted her trunk from side to side. Her apartment in Stuyvesant Town was roomy and spare. A couch, a bed, an old and worn dining table of heavy hardwood, a desk that held her computer, no more than the essentials. She abhorred clutter.

As her back loosened, she thought about Jimmy Dolan. Her trip back to Johnny Mac's, the incident with Liam, Jimmy's face on the news, all this led her to focus on him whether she wanted to or not. She pulled on her running shoes and tied the laces. She was pounding out thirty-five miles a week, three days on, one day off, but had missed several runs because of work. She was eager to get back on the road, craved the endorphin rush, the rhythm, the clarity that came to her when she was running.

She drank two glasses of water, washing down a vitamin pill. Since moving downtown, she found herself going back to Inwood less and less. It was not a conscious decision. Most of her girlfriends had moved out, which was part of it. But the place was tainted for her, held too many bad scenes, and was certainly not the Inwood of her youth. Her generation had mostly abandoned the place for the green lawns of the suburbs, some north to the gentler parts of the Bronx. The older generation was dying off, and each trip back she learned someone else was gone. It was as if only a sketch of her home remained, an outline, and within a few years there would be nothing left but the brick buildings where they had lived, populated by strangers from other places. It was her own private ghost town.

Jimmy, that asshole. There were nights when she lay awake and felt sorry for herself, sorry for both of them, sorry for all that never was to be. She remembered the night he left. The moment she needed him most. She had missed her period, and, after six weeks, was praying for blood. She could hardly sleep or eat, was abruptly faced with the big questions of life. She had never known such confusion. Jimmy did not even want to talk about it; he just insisted on an abortion. He explained to her in rational and measured ways all the reasons a child was a bad idea. They were too young, too poor, not married, not ready; it was not fair to bring a baby into this. Each one made eminent sense, but when she was not swayed, the rational deteriorated into a hot and angry fight. Every slight and hurt they had inflicted on each other was served up loud and hateful until he simply turned and walked out.

It was as if he had disappeared. She waited a week, then went to the clinic herself. She was too ashamed to even tell her friends. The social worker soothed her, provided wise and informed counsel, sent her home to ponder her options. She considered seeing Father Keith, but did not. She returned to the clinic, steeled herself. Jimmy was right; he had to be. She let them put her on the gurney, her ankles in stirrups, her legs spread, the doctor poised for work. Then she panicked, started kicking at the nurse. She could not do it. She left the clinic. Jimmy had his life to live, but she had hers too. She decided she wanted the baby, regardless. She never regretted the choice. Not even later, when she miscarried at six months.

Back then she considered Jimmy Dolan a coward. But in the seven years that followed, she softened a bit. She wondered if he thought of it at all, if he too lay awake some nights and pondered what might have been. She guessed he felt more relief than anything else, the bullet dodged, the chains of wife and child too young eluded. Losing the baby devastated her. She shut Jimmy out of her life for a year afterward, had shut out everyone. She would wander the streets in a daze, ride the subway going wherever it took her. That year was lost to her, a black hole of sorrow from which she could summon no detail, no memory.

She pulled her blond hair back into a thick ponytail and secured it with an elastic. She strapped on a fanny pack, in which she had her off-duty piece, a five-shot .38 caliber, and her ID. She left the apartment, took the stairs down to the lobby, ran over to the FDR, and crossed the footbridge to the park. The night was clear and crisp. Tugboats whispered up the black expanse of the East River. The wind came from offshore and brought with it the cloying sweetness of the Domino Sugar plant over in Williamsburg, Brooklyn.

She ran. She thought about the beaten boy, Johnny, from the other night. When they passed him off to Children's Services, his face was heavy with betrayal. As bad as he'd had it at home, he was at home; now he was being plunged into the unknown. Even at his age he could sense what that meant. She determined to check up on him, to see that he didn't get lost in the system. She picked up speed, passing beneath the span of the Williamsburg Bridge. Rounding a bend, she came upon two junkies in full narcotic swoon. They were bent at the waist, arms against their sides. One was a woman, whose long hair brushed the ground. They were held up by some incalculable, poppy juice physics.

Around another curve a dazzling view lay before her. There was the Manhattan Bridge, beyond it the Brooklyn Bridge, and the financial district skyline, ablaze with the red light of a magnificent sunset. In the distance, rising from New York Harbor, the Statue of Liberty stood against the sky, its torch upraised. She remembered her grandmother's telling the story of passing through the harbor on the deck of a ship when she was seven and the thrill the statue provided, how much it meant to them. Whenever Tara saw the statue she thought of her grandmother as a girl, at the gateway of the New World, full of wonder and fear.

She decided then to make a long run of it and head for Brooklyn. She had no problem running alone after dark. She always kept to the middle of the path, which was fairly well lit. She was fit and armed. She made her way down to the Brooklyn Bridge. On the boardwalk there were only a few pedestrians; beneath her on the roadways the traffic was light and fast. She ascended to the peak of the span and stopped for a moment to stretch some more. The East River swirled beneath her, its tricky and lethal currents etched on its surface. She had a relative who was killed sinking the caissons into the muck of the riverbed, and she felt proprietary about the structure, as if somehow her family was in this link between two boroughs. She followed the decline of the bridge into downtown Brooklyn, then turned around and, with her muscles rich with blood, retraced her steps at the same vigorous pace.

Liam walked down Sherman Avenue bouncing a tennis ball he had found on the subway platform, a duffel bag over his shoulder. Ralphie Fernandez, his neighbor's kid, was sitting on the hood of his car. "Ralphie. My main man. What's the story?"

"You said you were gonna take me to the Bronx Zoo."

"I did?"

"Yep."

"All right then. We'll go on Saturday. Make sure it's okay with your moms."

The lobby smelled of old meals and cat piss. Mrs. Ramirez in 1B had at least a dozen of the creatures; Mrs. Fisher in 1D had six. He often had to hold his breath until the third floor to keep from puking. Liam entered his apartment and went into his bedroom, where he took four Glock nine millimeters from his gym bag and hid them under his bed. His mother often insisted on cleaning his room. He returned to the living room, where she was sleeping quietly on his chair in front of the television, her mouth hanging open, like the stupid or the dead. He fought the urge to lean over and nudge it shut. An infomercial was blaring from the TV. A pair of tan but nearly forgotten sitcom stars gestured enthusiastically, hawking a New Age vitamin pill they guaranteed would make the user feel like a kid again. Liam stood for a minute wishing it could be that easy for his mother. There were clips of the aging stars, jogging, biking, and playing tennis. Liam scoffed. It wasn't no friggin pill you needed; it was a country-club membership and a ton of leisure time. He clicked off the TV and got a blanket from the closet. He pulled it over his mother and kissed her lightly on the forehead.

He went to bed and lay in the quasi darkness of a city night. He thought of calling Tara to apologize for making a move on her. A dog barked on the street; a car alarm went off. He hoped Jimmy did not find out he had hit on his old girlfriend. Jimmy was about the only friend he had left. He pulled the pillow over his head to block out the wail of the alarm. Going back to humping concrete had actually been fun. Tomorrow he was going to make a little side money. Worn by the day's toil, he was soon gone.

Liam woke at 5:50, ten minutes before his alarm was to go off. He stood stretching and felt a heaviness in his shoulders, his legs sore. It was a good feeling. He had been idle all winter collecting workers' comp. He had called the union and was working the following morning. He liked hard physical labor. The way it made the day pass, his sleep heavy. The sense of accomplishment. There were a few dozen buildings around the island of Manhattan he could point to and say, I built that place. He knew they would be there long after he was gone. Someday, if he ever had kids, he would drive around and show them where he had labored. This is what I do for a living. Not like the yuppie assholes who lived in and worked in the places he built. He almost felt sorry for those people. He could not imagine working in an office, that dead air. Wearing a suit and tie, uptight and pasty-faced like life was one big Catholic school.

He opened the refrigerator and drank deeply from a half gallon of orange juice. He ate a chocolate-flavored protein bar. He went over to the window and looked upon the predawn quiet of upper Broadway. No people, no cars moving—stillness. No merengue music. The Dominicans had pretty much taken over the neighborhood. He got along all right with them. At least, they did not think they were better than him, like so many of the Irish assholes still left.

He dressed for work in dungarees and several layers of cotton tee shirts covered by an old sweatshirt and laced up his construction boots. He retrieved the bag of guns, wrapping each pistol in a sheet of newspaper. He bounded down the steps out onto the street. He turned left, headed for the A at 207th Street, last stop on the line as dawn was coming to his island. A few people were coming out of their buildings, the odd car started for the trip to work. The air was crisp, but held the promise of warmth. A police cruiser came by, the cops leaning away from each other up against respective doors, fatigued from a night tour.

He bought a token from the silent, disinterested clerk, a fat black man who looked as if he had counted out too much of somebody else's money. Liam rarely paid but it was not a good day to jump the turnstile, not with his cargo. He remembered Pat Donnelan, a cop from the neighborhood, who grabbed some mook for fare beating. It turned out the criminal mastermind was wanted for a murder rap in North Carolina and was carrying twenty-five grand in a gym bag. Liam had a hard time believing somebody could be so stupid. The clerk was eating a bagel, working change with one hand. Liam thanked the man. When he did not respond, Liam added, "You piece of shit."

On the train he picked up a discarded *Daily News* and read, checking the Rangers box score first: 6–0 loss to Detroit. Disgusting. The car filled up as it went south. Most of the riders were not white and all were dressed for labor. They kept to themselves and read papers in languages undecipherable to him. Different people, same dreams. An old Chinese woman pulled a granny cart through the car and, while playing with a glowing yo-yo, chanted, "Battery, one dollar. Battery, one dollar." No one paid her any mind. Liam wondered about traveling ten thousand miles to sell Duracells on the A train. He got off at Fifty-ninth Street.

At this station the Wall Street crowd waited to pounce on the day, dressed in their suits, carrying briefcases. The faces were drawn tight, indicating stomach trouble, rising blood pressure, unhealthy ambitions. Man, he hated these people. He shouldered his way through them, daring anyone to give him shit about it. He'd love to ruin their day.

He made his way up the stairs to Columbus Circle. Sunlight was slanting low through the towers to the east. He walked in and out of shadow, in and out of warmth. He entered the tavern directly across from the job site, a thirty-eight-story condo, prices starting at a million two, Liam had heard. Unreal. Shit boxes in the sky, contractor cutting corners at every turn. By the look of the walls going up Liam figured you'd be able to hear someone fart from three doors down. A million two. Morons. The concrete gang would be topping off at the end of the week.

A blue haze lay over the bar, cigarette smoke unmoving, heavy. A dozen or so serious drinkers, priming themselves for a day's work, sat among cops and maintenance guys coming off midnight shifts. Liam recognized Joe Flood from the neighborhood at the front of the bar. Flood sat drinking with another man who might be related to him. Same thick neck and fists. Same type of flinty Irish faces that had been inspiring blubbery confessions in New York for more than a century.

Liam stopped. "Hey Flood. What's with the suit? DT now?"

"Yeah, hey, Liam. Three months I got the shield." He turned to his partner. "Hey, Liam, this is my buddy, Sergeant McCabe."

The man said, "My name is Brian. How you doing? Nice to meet you."

Joe Flood said, "Me and Liam grew up together. He was my brother Sean's age."

McCabe laughed. "Another Inwood guy? My condolences."

"Ah, bullshit. He's a Queens guy, Liam. Explains everything."

Liam laughed. He noticed his customer down the end of the bar watching them carefully.

"Where you living now?"

"Pearly White River. Still in Inwood?"

"Yeah."

"Christ," Flood said. "You speaking Spanish?"

"Sí, sí." Liam laughed. These guys who'd left talking shit about his neighborhood bothered him. He let it slide. "Sean's coming home from the Marines, I heard."

"Yeah, going in the fire academy. A home run, far as he's concerned. What about you, still with the Laborers?"

"That's it, Joey boy. God's work."

"Better you than me. Drinking?" Flood indicated drinks and cash money on the bar in front of him.

"Not this time of day. I like my booze at night. Let me get you guys one, though." He waved the bartender over. "Do me a favor. Get these guys one on me. Thanks. Take care, man." He patted Flood on the shoulder. "Tell Sean to call when he gets back, the fucking guy."

Liam proceeded to the end of the bar and sat next to one of his co-workers from the site. The man was in his mid-twenties and wore a hooded sweatshirt. He had his hard hat on the bar in front of him. His hair was cut short; a gold chain spilled out from his neck. On the crook of his left thumb and forefinger there was a crudely tattooed cross. When Liam sat down, he said, "Friends of yours?"

"One guy's from the neighborhood, coupla years older, grew up with his brother."

"New York's finest."

Liam did not like the guy's tone. "Yeah. I remember when he used to eat a bag of mushrooms and try to shoot down 747s from his rooftop with his old man's service revolver."

"You got what I wanted?" The guy trying to sound like a tough guy.

"Didn't I say I would?"

Man sipped his morning beer. "How much?"

"Four a piece, times four. That's sixteen. My math's still like it was in Catholic school. Same price I said it was all along."

"I can only do three."

Liam snapped his head around to look at him. "You gotta be fucking kidding me here."

"What can I say? Guy backed out, last-minute kind of deal."

"Ah, now, that really sucks, 'cause I'm gonna have to eat the other one, for fuck sake. People I get these from don't like somebody yanking their fucking chain."

"Hey. We never shook on nothing."

"Shook?" Liam could not believe what he was hearing. He reached down and took one of the guns from the gym bag and slid it into the inside pocket of his work jacket. He fought the urge to kneecap the idiot. "Next fucking time? Do your shopping somewhere else."

"Hey, I'm sorry. That's how it goes." He used his foot to slide the gym bag closer to his barstool. He reached inside his sweatshirt and pulled out an envelope, looked down toward the DTs, then slid it across in front of Liam, who took it and turned to walk away.

Liam crossed the street to the job site trying to keep his anger in check. A group of men waited by the construction elevator holding cups of coffee, their eyes heavy with the night. Liam opted for the stairs, climbing briskly to the ninth-floor setback to catch the elevator up to thirty-six, where he would be working that day. He took off his coat and placed it in the gang box along with his *Daily News*. He walked over to the Porta-John with the envelope. He squatted.

The walls were festooned with wild proclamations of sexual escapades with the superintendent's wife. There were even several well-crafted depictions of these purported acts. Liam opened the unsealed envelope and pulled out the pile of crisp hundreds, bubble-headed Ben Franklins. He counted once and clenched his teeth. He counted twice, he counted a third time—there were only ten hundreds. The guy had shorted him. He punched the door. He folded the money in half and placed it in his pocket and dropped the empty envelope in the hole. He left the shitter and went over to his crew. Down below, the concrete trucks were arriving, rumbling in the early Manhattan morning.

He could not let this guy slide. The concrete was hoisted up onto the deck in a large metal bucket. Liam was on a shovel and stood with three other concrete workers as one of their colleagues steadied the bucket and let the concrete flow. Liam bent to the task and shoveled furiously, imagining the asshole's face receiving the strikes from his shovel. He worked at a harder pace than usual, the blood pumping through his muscles as he powered his way through the material. The Laborer next to him stood and laughed. "Jesus, what the fuck you eat for breakfast?" Liam ignored him and worked on, his rage focused and pure.

There was a lull while they waited for more concrete. The finishers, Portuguese men in their fifties with large, hard bellies, worked floats across the fresh gray concrete. Liam watched them work, their grace of movement, which belied their physical appearance. There was a deftness to them, and Liam knew that the casual observer would think their task a simple one. Until he tried it. The men were sweating now as the air warmed. Liam thought about the asshole who robbed him. He could not believe the balls on the guy. He knew what he had to do. His stomach started flopping. Crazy adrenaline energy ran up his legs, made him warm and cold at the same time.

At lunch break he went down to the seventh floor and saw the guy take off his tool belt and head for the john. Liam selected a short-cut two-by-four about three feet long. He hefted it. Its weight felt good. He walked casually over to the Porta-John and waited. He turned to survey the site. Most of the men were scurrying for the exits and a half hour away from work. When no one was looking, he pushed the fiberglass toilet box over backward. It landed with a bang that echoed around the site. He heard a scream from inside and then "What the fuck!! I'll fucking kill you!"

The asshole popped out of the shit box like a gunner coming out of a tank. He was dripping crap and piss and toilet paper, his face all twisted up, surely the unhappiest minute of his life. Liam stifled a laugh, said, "Douche bag," and smiled. The guy, his Carhartt jacket twisted around him, lunged at Liam, but it was too late. Liam brought the club down hard like a battle-ax, snapping the guy's right collarbone with it. He screamed, and Liam, stepping in, punched him hard in the jaw, a crisp left hook that knocked him sideways until he was lying half in and half out of the Porta-John. The man was unconscious. Liam looked around. The few workers left on the floor averted their gaze. The guy taking the beating was known as a ball breaker. It was not their beef. Liam was going to take the man's wallet but did not want to touch him with all that crap all over him. Instead, he kicked him once hard in the side, laughed, and went to lunch feeling a whole lot better about things.

Jimmy spent the night at his father's, and in the morning drank coffee as the A train hurtled him downtown. He and Susan had fought the day before, one of their regularly scheduled blowups that were the result, he felt, of her moodiness. As usual, he could not pin down what started it, but it ended up with her launching into a diatribe about his lack (according to her) of professionalism. Jimmy had retaliated by storming out. It was not the first time. The entire scene was part of the rhythm of their relationship. At least it wasn't boring.

He stopped at the market and picked up some veal scaloppine. He'd get a bottle of wine, clean the place, and have her favorite meal waiting for her when she got home. It had always worked before. She'd be fine. Or so he thought. It pissed him off that she did not back him over the Keefe incident. You should have known better, was her mantra. I do know better. She was all embarrassed by his fall from grace. The woman was gung ho about the Mayor.

As he walked into the lobby, Ramon stood at the doorman's station with a shit-eating grin. "Yo, Jimmy, I got bad news for you."

Jimmy laughed and walked past him to the elevators. Ramon had gone to Good Shepherd grammar school two years behind Jimmy. While they had never said a word to each other in Inwood, here they felt a bond. Ramon stepped in front of him. "Nah, Jimmy, I'm serious. Come on." He nodded with his head to a supply room behind the desk. Jimmy followed him. Ramon opened the door with a flourish and said, "You been eighty-sixed, Jimbo. That bitch was all sorts of indignant. Said we let you up she was gonna have our jobs and shit. Me, personally, I'd love to see that snotty bitch work my job for one hour only. So's I can take my turn looking down my nose at her ass for a change a paces."

Jimmy stared at the boxes and a pile of his suits still on the hangers. Ramon handed him a note. "Sorry, bro, but I read it by mistake." Jimmy ignored his smirk.

So they had argued. What the hell was going on with his life?

He read the note. It was on her personal stationery, lightly perfumed. Jesus. It was to the point. "I think you need help. I can't do this anymore." Ah, bullshit. What is she, nuts? "She here?"

"Bro, I can't let you go up. Changed the locks. Got her poppy with her. Says shit about a restraining order, the five-oh. Don't do it. You ask me, she ain't worf it."

"Come on, Ramon, you went to Good Shepherd. It's worth."

"Yeah, well, speaking of Good Shepherd, I guess I'll be seeing you up on Broadway, Jimmy. You come by for some beers, we're still homeys. I don't mind you couldn't make it down here, the Big Town, Bright Lights. I'll have my mom cook you some cuchifritos, welcome you back." Ramon laughed and laughed.

Jimmy read the note again. Was this some kind of joke? He went out to the street and picked up a pay phone. He dialed her number, looking up at the terrace of her apartment sixteen stories above the sidewalk. She answered the phone on the first ring.

"Hey, Susan. What's up?"

Silence.

"Susan?"

"I think you should try therapy." Click.

Therapy? Jimmy dialed again. Susan's father answered.

"You better listen to me good, fella." The voice was all heavy and full of heat, the father defending his little girl. "You stay away from my daughter or you'll rue the day you crossed paths with me, buster." Click.

Jimmy stared at the receiver. A man dressed in a full-length yellow raincoat and sandals asked him for change. He hung up and handed the man a dollar bill, thinking, What in the hell did I do to deserve this? Her father had had a hard-on for him since day one. Somehow Jimmy Dolan was not good enough for his precious offspring. This, from a slumlord. He considered barging past Ramon, making a scene. Slapping her goofy old man in his tightwad face. He thought better of it. He started for the door and his belongings, then stopped and went back to the phone.

"Let me talk to her, she's an adult, for Christ sake."

"Don't push me, fella." Click.

Jimmy wondered how often a twenty-seven-year-old woman used her father to help her break up with someone. He dialed once more. "Are you people fucking nuts?"

"I've got powerful friends, you little animal."

"Are you threatening me? You toothless old chiseler. Where do you get off?" He beat Pops to the hang-up this time. He stood for a minute, calming himself. He looked around like maybe someone might jump out and tell him it was all a practical joke.

He started loading his things into the taxi as the driver sat on his ass, eating something out of a greasy paper bag. Ramon did not stop giggling, but at least helped out. Jimmy shoved his last box into the back seat and climbed in after it. "I see you uptown, Jaime." Ramon slammed the door shut.

"Where now, please?"

Jimmy looked at the driver. "Inwood."

The driver looked over his shoulder, uncertain.

"Just drive north. Drive until you hit water and that's it. The top of the island. Last stop. Inwood."

M ike Dolan sat in the back row of the Marc Ballroom and listened to Frankie Keefe congratulate himself on being a champion of the workingman. What a load of baloney. The room was filled with five hundred Teamsters who were violating the city anti-smoking ordinance with vigor. The men sat and shifted in their seats; others lined the side and back walls. They wore thick flannel shirts, black satin Teamster jackets, bored faces. Mike nodded to the handful of men who dared to support him openly.

Keefe was a lousy speaker, jumping from praise for himself to stifling details about the ongoing contract negotiations. When he asked for comment from the floor there were outbreaks of applause and hoorahs from his favorite ass kissers and leg breakers. Of course there was no rancor, no dissent. Keefe controlled hiring and could easily black-list a man. Even Harry the Hat, a crotchety Teamster whose dissident rants were legendary, was silent. He sat on his hands and whistled a lost song through broken teeth.

Keefe glanced at his watch throughout, like he had somewhere better to be. Mike knew his only hope was the first secret ballot in the history of the union. It was one obvious benefit of government con-trol. Even Keefe was forced to go along. Keefe moved what little busi-ness there was along swiftly. When a motion was made to accept a change in health-care plans, Harry the Hat finally roused himself. Keefe identified him.

"Why can't we see what this means for us? Who approved this plan?"

Shouts of "Commie!" rang about the hall.

"I'd rather be a Red than a rat! Why can't these changes be put to the full membership for a vote?"

"I thank Brother Hat for his remarks."

"I want a vote!"

"On to other business," called the secretary-treasurer.

Several hulking drivers went and stood in front of the Hat, forming a wall of flesh and muscle. The Hat shrieked on for a few more sec-onds to no avail. The sound was lost in all the beef before him. Fi-nally, he quieted and sat back on his hands.

Keefe went on. "Now I want to say something here that I probably shouldn't, 'cause nothing's signed. And this might be unusual, but be-tween you me and the wall over there, I got a guarantee on this from the contractors." He knocked his knuckles on the lectern. "Just to show the kind of work your negotiating committee is doing on behalf of the membership, we got—and this is only part of what the final contract will be—we got a two-dollar-an-hour jump in your annuity accounts." Keefe held up his hands as if he had just multiplied fishes and loaves. A murmur rolled over the crowd and applause broke out. "That's right," he shouted. "Two bucks more."

Mike sat stunned. There was only one more meeting before the election, and the contract was not to be signed until after it was over. So Keefe could be boldface lying, and it did not matter. He was buying off his members, and there was nothing Mike could do about it. It was just another advantage of incumbency.

After a time Keefe waved off the applause. "Now there are people who have never so much as held a steady job." Heads turned to Mike. "They might tell you how much better they can do. Well, I, me and my executive board, have been bringing home the bacon for a lot of years, my brothers. That you can take to the bank. And as we all know, a bird in the hand is worth more than a whole lot of bullshit coming from some troublemaker."

More applause, shouts. A distinct "Fuck Mike Dolan!"

Mike felt the weight of hatred hit him. He stood and went outside. The Union Square Greenmarket was bustling. Tourists, serious shoppers, and neighborhood people out for a stroll wandered through, picking up vegetables and bread, cheeses, fish from upstate rivers, flowers and herbs, wines from Long Island. He watched three young women, tall and slender almost to the point of poor health, pass by. The trio wore rings through their noses. All these people lived in a different world, sharing this same small island.

There was just a hint of new green against the winter black of the denuded trees, the stirring of spring. Despite Keefe's attempt to buy off the members, Mike felt a bit of optimism for the first time in months. It was eight weeks till election and he was beginning to think he was making some progress. He placed his gym bag down on the sidewalk against the building and took out of it piles of his campaign literature. The leaflet was simple, direct, and laid out his platform. Accountability, Fairness, Better Wages and Benefits. It featured one picture: Keefe and Tommy Magic in a smiling embrace.

Teamsters started to pile out of the ballroom. He passed out leaflets trying to gauge the level of support by looking into their eyes. Some were cold and sullen, others angry. But a fair number were quietly encouraging and accepted a leaflet. Quite a few actually winked as they passed. He figured many of them would be emboldened by the secret ballot. When that was announced he had been ecstatic, but now he wondered if it would make any difference at all. Harry the Hat came out, snatched a leaflet, and said. "I hope you beat that bastard's ass good, Dolan. But I doubt you will. I'd watch myself, I was you. Those fuckers are killers. Stone killers."

"Thank you, Harry. You really know how to cheer a guy up."

Mike looked up to see a phalanx of overfed Teamsters coming toward him. Keefe, surrounded by his personal goon squad, moved along like a feudal lord. He was dressed in his usual two-thousand-dollar suit and tie, a sharp overcoat. His entourage was dressed for labor, except for his bodyguard Cronin, who wore a blue blazer and gray slacks and looked on his way to a country-club cocktail hour. Keefe, all twisted grins and ill-gotten confidence, told an anecdote as they leaned toward him, footmen to a prince. The Greenmarket strollers regarded the Teamsters with curiosity. When Keefe saw Mike, he stopped and glared. "Dolan." He laughed a cold sound like a rock rolling across the hood of a car. One of his sidekicks said, "That piece of shit. You want me to straighten him out, Frankie?"

"Nah. He's not worth the trouble, Timmy. Hey, where's that punk kid of yours, Dolan?"

Mike smiled warily. "Hey, Frankie, this is between you and me, man to man. Why don't you leave the kid out of it." He watched the muscles around Keefe's eyes twitch, his jaw clench. Keefe was bold when backed up. Mike thrust a leaflet toward his opponent. "Here, it might be nice to read some truth for a change."

Cronin shouldered his way between them and snatched the leaflet, tearing it from Mike's hands. He glanced at the picture of Keefe and the fat mafioso. "You some kind of wiseass, pal?" He crumbled it into a ball and bounced it off Mike's chest. Mike stood his ground. Keefe leaned toward him and hissed, "When this election is over, you and that kid are gonna see that I'm through playing nice."

Mike nodded. Keefe and his entourage pushed past him, the mass of muscle moving down the sidewalk. Mike sucked in a breath. He watched a squad car that had been parked on the corner roll up and stop. He had called a guy from the neighborhood, Jack Minogue, who was captain of the local precinct, and asked him to have a cop or two handy in case trouble broke out. Mike was surprised to see that Jack had come himself.

"Thanks, Jack. Nice to see you."

"These days, Mike, with this prick downtown, I couldn't risk sending any kids over here. They got wind of it they'd send them to work traffic in Staten Island, the vindictive bastard."

"Well, I appreciate you keeping an eye out."

Minogue watched a few stragglers come out of the ballroom and shoot dirty looks at them. "You ever consider retiring? Just admitting defeat? There is honor in that, you know. What's the song? 'Know when to fold 'em.'"

Mike looked to the distance, at the retreating Keefe, then back at Minogue. "Every day, Jackie, every damn day."

Tara and Andy were assigned to plainclothes detail. Quality of life. Crack down on urinaters and public imbibers of alcohol, pot smokers, kids with boom boxes, and various other violators of the civil order. It was easy collars and OT. She hoped to go in with some friends on a shore house for the coming summer.

They left the precinct in an unmarked car. The streets were crowded, alive on this first warm night since October. Everyone looked tired and drawn from a winter spent without enough nutrients, fresh air, or sunlight. Music spilled out of the open doors of bars, the sounds of intoxication and merriment. Calls were coming in steady; drunken brawls, noise complaints, a cardiac arrest on 156th Street. A Jeep pulled up beside them at the light, blasting music so loud it seemed the metal was pulsing with sound.

Tara rolled down her window, and the driver, wearing a fedora over a blue bandanna, smiled at her. She flashed her badge and mouthed, "Turn it off." The smile was gone as if he'd been slapped.

Andy pulled over in front of a bodega. "I'm gonna get a bottle of water. You want?"

"I'm good, thanks."

She watched him get out of the car. A half dozen kids passed, jeans hanging off their asses, baseball hats at a variety of angles except frontward, carrying bottles wrapped in paper bags. The radio crackled with calls. She felt a twinge of anxiety as if something was about to happen. A man came out of a building a few doors up the block. He wore shorts and a hooded sweatshirt and carried a basketball under one arm. He stared at her for a second, then bounced the ball down his stoop and turned to walk in the direction of Broadway. The feeling passed, and she reminded herself to get Knicks tickets for her father's birthday. She leaned her head back against the seat. She had run six miles before work and was feeling alert and rested. Then she heard the shots.

It was very clearly the pop, pop, pop of a pistol coming from the bodega. For a second, everything stopped, and there was a sharp stillness around her. She took a breath and felt almost high from the adrenal rush. "Holy shit." She picked up the mike and, with a calm she did not feel, said, "Shots fired. 1-9-8 St. Nick. Storefront. 10-13, 10-13." Then she was out of the car and moving, all animal instinct propelling her, lucid and purposeful.

She pulled her pistol and moved toward the gunfire with her badge hanging from her neck. She went through the door, pushing it wide open, and dropped to a crouch, swinging the pistol before her in a wide arc. Andy was lying on his back. There was blood pooling beneath him and his breath was ragged and fast. His scared eyes rolled up toward the counter. A warning. She spun away from the door as a man stood and shot where she had just crouched an instant before. She felt the whistle of the bullets, the air hot with their passing. She came up firing and pulled off three quick shots. They caught the perp high in the chest, each bullet propelling him half a step backward, his body jerky from the impact, like a puppet whose strings are being yanked without reason. His face went from rage to confusion to blankness. As he collapsed upon himself he squeezed off a parting shot, his last act in this world. The bullet caught Tara square in her left breast, knocking her back against the shelves. She landed on her ass on the dirty floor, and cans of cat food rained down on her. She could not breathe. She started to panic. It felt as if her lungs were being squeezed in a vise. As she fought for air, she felt she might die. She rolled onto her side and stared at a cat-food label. She wondered if this was the last thing she was going to see in this life. Her head rang from the shots. She needed oxygen. The place smelled of cordite and blood and shit and fear. She looked up to see another gunman staring wide-eyed at her through a display case. He looked to be no more than a schoolkid. She watched his eyes go from hunted to hunter.

The perp vaulted the counter and stood over Andy with something like mirth on his face. He pointed his gun at Andy's head. Tara took a bite of air, sat up, and started shooting. The gunman fell straight down on top of Andy in a heap. She wanted to scream from the pain but still could not get enough air, she sucked in as much as she could, filling her bruised lungs. Feeling came back into her legs and arms. She wiggled her toes, was able to feel parts of herself, locate the pain and move past it. She realized she was wearing her bulletproof vest. She belly-crawled over to the second shooter. He was weeping. The blood was squirting out of him, almost comically red, it was so bright and full of fleeting life. His face was turning a color it would only be this one time.

"I don't want to die. I don't want to die. Help me, help me." Blood bubbles dripped down his chin. He gurgled when he spoke, blood filling his lungs.

Tara pulled in more air. She put the pistol to his temple and said, "Let me see your fucking hands!"

"Help me."

She felt the trigger finger, was aware of herself fully. She pressed the pistol harder, digging into the flesh of his skull. She looked down at Andy and figured he must be dead. She thought, I should kill this person. Instead, she lifted her pistol and smacked it over his head until he shut up. She pushed him off her partner. She tried to steady herself on all fours to gain purchase, but slipped in all the blood, her face smacking hard on the floor. She righted herself and raised Andy's head and held it in her lap. His eyes were wide with fear and he was trying to speak, but no words came together. "Ssssshh." She tried to wipe the blood off his face, but there was too much of it, rivers of it, lakes of it. She never thought there could be so much of it. Andy was breathing weakly. She could not tell where he had been hit. She realized he was not wearing his vest. "Oh Jesus, Andy. Jesus Jesus Jesus."

All she could do was hold him and wait for help in the awful silence of the dead and the dying.

In the ambulance, she drifted in and out of consciousness. They had pulled off her shirt and vest, leaving her bare-chested until a fellow officer draped his jacket over her. She had seen the blood, heard them talking about a wound on her neck, apparently from a ricochet or bullet fragments. She listened to mad radio chatter, felt the welling of excitement, the significance of the event congealing in the close rocking space of the speeding ambulance. A paramedic stroked her hair and whispered that she would be fine. She felt cold and then hot and cold and then hot. Finally, fully alert, she began to understand what had happened, that somehow the job would never be the same again. One of the cops from her precinct knelt by her side. He smiled and she reached and grabbed his arm, looking to steady her world.

Jimmy sat at the bar in Johnny Mac's sipping bad coffee and trying to keep the past at bay. It wasn't easy. The bar was the focal point of his life in Inwood, of his relationship with Tara. He had called the hospital that morning and was told that only immediate family would be allowed to visit Tara until the afternoon. He considered that he would not feel comfortable going alone and this troubled him. He wished that, after all they had been through, they could be friends once again.

Jack leaned over the bar and nodded down the end. "You hear about Last Stand Sweeney?"

Jimmy looked at the neighborhood fixture. "No."

"He went on another One Man March."

"He don't want any company?"

"Couldn't find anybody stupid enough."

"What's he marching about now?"

"Says that he believes in the old saying all politics is local, and since we palefaces are the minority here now, that we should be getting the special treatment. Wants some of the affirmative action. Now, our Dominican neighbors, they just kind of watch him and laugh. He's got a sign that says 'no justice no peace,' a bullhorn. A regular albino Al Sharpton. Some kid dropped a water balloon filled with piss on his head. He wants to file a civil rights suit."

Jimmy laughed. He had called a friend at City Hall and gotten an update on Tara's condition from a cop on the detail whom he was friendly with. Stable. Her wounds were superficial and she appeared to be recovering swiftly. Still, he was anxious to see her.

He stood and took off his jacket, thinking about the way things had ended for them. He had been freaked when she said she was pregnant; the news hit him like a gavel between the eyes. As much as he thought he was opposed to it, he lobbied for an abortion, which he saw as a second chance, a reprieve; they would have kids later on. When she wavered, he blew up. What a selfish asshole he had been. There were days when he yearned to turn back the clock, to right the wrongs. He had lied to himself for years, but now, fast approaching thirty, his pretense was wearing thin. He knew the level of hurt he had inflicted on her, carried it with him. He might have a dream, wake in the night, reaching for her. Or it might hit him walking down the street or over a beer with his friends, a spasm of guilt and regret. He had fucked up royally.

It was midafternoon and the place was slow. Outside the weather had soured and cold showers were slanting across Broadway, borne by occasional gusts. Patrons entered and shook water off themselves like dogs emerging from a pond. Jimmy was into his third cup of coffee. The caffeine was making him a little edgy, so he pushed it away and ordered a glass of ginger ale.

"Hittin' it heavy, huh, Jimmy?"

"Things to do, Jackie, things to do."

"Tara?"

"Yeah."

"Too bad about that. Good kid. TV says she's gonna be fine, though."

"Let's hope."

He checked the wall clock. Three-thirty. Liam should be on his way home from work. He looked out the window and watched life pass on Broadway. Inwood. He couldn't believe he was back. By seventeen he and Tara were inseparable, were pals as well as lovers. She was one of the few girls the guys did not object to having around since she could hold her own always, whether they were shooting hoops, drinking, or cracking wise. They stood exactly the same height, five feet eleven and a half inches. She had none of the coyness of a teenage girl in the face of testosterone. At the same time, she was easily the best-looking girl in the neighborhood.

"You seen Liam?"

Jack wiped the bar down and shook his head. "You been away a lot. I gotta say, your pal Liam has gone overboard. I mean, I gotta be honest. I don't doubt for a minute he's gonna end up doing something like driving around a truck full of fertilizer and fuel oil and unleashing some horror based on all the voices in his head. Or maybe he climbs on a roof and rat-a-tat-tat, there goes a whole lotta people's afternoons. 'Cause, Jimmy, I ain't shitting you, the guy is more than three-quarters the way down a slippery slope. And he ain't got no brakes."

"Sounds like the old Liam."

"Jimmy, this fucking guy, I'm telling you, he spends like what, seventy percent of his time lying in wait, about five percent actually pouncing, and the rest of his time sorting through the wreckage. I mean, the guy's got a hard-on for me over something I did in grammar school. I mean, we're going back to the Carter administration, for fuck sake, and I got no idea what his beef is. Maybe I stepped on his foot. I can't remember last month. But he's out to get me, busts my balls every time he's in here. You hear what he did downtown?"

Jimmy looked up at Jack. He was not interested in his diatribe against Liam but he had little choice but to listen. Jack had his knee up on a cooler behind the bar and was leaning over the wood toward him. "He starts seeing this girl he met running in the park. She's some secretary down on Wall Street, good-looking girl, one of these big investment banks. So she opens up to Liam about how her boss, some vice president down there, is always giving her a load of grief, yelling at her when he wants to, your typical telephone tough guy, asshole boss. So Liam hears this, figures he's into this chick now, he's gonna show her how much he cares, you know, prove his love. This is after, maybe, you know, all of three or four dates. He borrows a maintenance uniform from Billy Boardman, the guys with the 32 B-J service employees, sneaks into the building like he's there to mop a floor or some shit, goes into the boss's office right about the close of day, shuts the door, and starts choking the guy with his tie, slapping him around like he's a bad third grader, makes the guy swear he's never gonna be mean to this chick again."

Jimmy laughed.

"It's really not that funny. Chick lost her job, of course, but she was too freaked out to give Liam up to the cops." Jack went down the line to refill some drinks. When he came back, he straightened the front of his shirt and pulled on his pant legs. "All this, and the guy is still on probation for punching out that bouncer down the Village."

Jimmy was glad the bar was slow. He did not need to deal with any bullshit over losing his job and crawling back uptown. He had not yet told his father he was back to stay. He had come up with the fiction of Susan having family in town. He had made a few calls, started to put together a résumé, but so far there was no interest expressed in his services. None. Zero. He was getting worried. He was nearly broke. He considered the humiliation of moving home, of possibly going back on a concrete shovel. He turned his hands over, palms up, and looked at the softness of them. He used to have three rows of calluses like ridges of broken hills rising from the contours of his hands. Now they might be mistaken for the hands of a computer geek.

The door opened. Liam Brady burst into the bar dressed in dirty work clothes. He surveyed the entire place, his eyes going over each patron. He looked back over his shoulder as if to check that no one had followed him. Liam lived his life on some level of alert that Jimmy did not quite grasp. Liam had made enough enemies over the years with his quick fists to be worried about vengeance seekers, but Jimmy thought he took it too far. He was at least mildly paranoid, in a clinical sense.

When his eyes found Jimmy, Liam smiled and came down the bar, passing the line of old-timers hunched over their whiskeys and regrets. He walked on the balls of his feet with his shoulders rolling forward. His fists, as always, were clenched at his sides.

"Hey, you new around here?"

Jimmy laughed.

"There's all sorts of yuppies moving in these days. Yuppies and Dominicans. You don't look like a Domo, so I have to figure you're a yuppie. Got one of those office jobs? Suit and tie?"

"I'm out of work, actually." He figured Liam had every right to bust his balls. There were some unreturned phone calls, a bit of distance since he had left the neighborhood. "What's up, Liam?"

"Alls you know, I might be dead. That might be up. Think how guilty you'd feel, you miss my funeral."

"Come on, Liam. It was that job. I had three days off last year."

"Yeah, well, I was talking to Tara the other day. We both agreed we forgot what you looked like."

Jimmy liked the idea that Tara was even talking about him. "Come on, Liam, how about when you were in the army?"

"I was in a fucking *war*, Jimmy. You been downtown New York."

"All right. Guilty as charged. So it's been a few months."

"St. Paddy's day. Two weeks, it'll be a year."

Time flies, Jimmy thought. A year? "Okay. You want a beer, or what? For old times' sake."

Liam sat down. "I'll have a cold one. I been working all day. You might remember what that was like, cupcake. Working a pussy racket like politics."

"Nah, you prick, I can't recall."

"How bad is she?"

"She's going to be okay," Jimmy said.

"Says her vest saved her."

"Yeah, thank God. So, she hooked up with anyone?"

"You got some pair of balls. You having second thoughts? Little late for that, bro."

Jimmy nodded. That was part of it. He also did not want to bump into anyone at the hospital. Jimmy laughed uneasily. He knew Liam was busting his balls, but still. It was about what he deserved.

"Actually, we been thinking about calling you. We're engaged."

"You got a lot in common. Guns and all."

"Relax, Jimbo. Not that I can see. She's too good for most guys. Including you. Hey, cock jockey, get us some beers."

Jack rolled his eyes at Jimmy as if to prove his point. He shook his head and went and got the drinks. Liam sucked down two beers in quick succession, a man trying to slake a bad thirst. "Five hundred and fifty yards today," he said to validate the vigor of his thirst.

Jimmy sipped his own beer. Sure enough, Liam's hands were thick with muscle, cracked and callused, the kind of calluses that will never go away, and were lined with dirt and scars and peppered with dozens of nicks. Jimmy considered his own soft hands again and missed the life. He had spent years working construction while going to school at night. After he finished his master's degree, he swore he would never go back to hard labor. But things were in some ways easier working construction. You woke with the sun, took the train downtown, and sold your back for a good union wage. At the end of the day there were so many yards of concrete poured, a real sense of what was done. He slept better in those days.

Liam was his oldest friend, and although they had drifted apart, there were bonds that transcend all such considerations. He was closer to Liam than to his brothers or sister. He realized he needed to stay in touch more. After a few beers, Liam eased up on him.

"I need to clean up, 'fore we head over there. Come on, Mom's been asking about you."

Jimmy picked up the tab and left a five for Jack the bartender. As they walked down to Liam's place, Jimmy felt loose from the beer. They passed three storefront *botánicas* displaying tropical interpretations of saints. All three had been Irish bars. Liam did not pay them any notice. Jimmy realized the changes were far less stark to those who still lived here.

Jimmy sat on the living-room couch flipping through a *Soldier of Fortune* magazine when Mrs. Brady came in from shopping and greeted him warmly. "Nice to see you back home, James." She offered him some tea. He declined. She stood and looked suspiciously out the window, up toward the sky.

"Jimmy, you're a big one for the books. Have you ever come across anything about this ozone layer?"

"No, Mrs. Brady. Don't know much about that except you're supposed to not use aerosol deodorant cans."

She spoke with her back to him. "There's a big hole up there somewhere. They say it's going to wipe out life on the planet. Everything. Gone. Dead. Life as we know it. We'll all be staggering around gaping like fish left on a riverbank before we go. Not a bit of oxygen left for any of us."

Jimmy nodded. "That don't sound so great."

Liam called him from the bedroom. Jimmy sat on a stuffed chair in Liam's room and glanced at the books on his nightstand. There were a couple of gun magazines and a paperback, #63 of the Mack Bolan Executioners series. He noticed a thick hardcover that looked like it was from an antique bookstore. He picked it up and read the faded title along the spine. *On the Origin of Species,* by Darwin. Jimmy raised his eyebrows and placed the book down. Liam buttoned his shirt and ducked into his closet. When he turned back, he held a pistol that looked to weigh about twenty pounds. "Check this shit out."

Jimmy took it from him and hefted it. The pistol was surprisingly light. Liam had many gun club buddies.

"Desert Eagle. Fucking Israelis know their ordnance."

"Great." Jimmy was not fond of weapons. He'd carried a gun for a while back in high school when race relations were going poorly and had almost used it once to settle an argument. He later tossed it into the waters of the Spuyten Duyvil. He handed the weapon back to Liam.

As they were walking out, Mrs. Brady called, "Bring Jimmy back for supper. It'll be ready at six. It's nice to see you."

"Yeah, Ma, we'll be back."

They hopped into Liam's pickup. He piloted the truck like a West Texas cowboy trying to run down an errant mustang. Jimmy kept his knuckles white and hard on the dash as they crossed into the Bronx. He figured Liam had the only vehicle registered in the county of New York with a gun rack. They pulled up to the hospital and Jimmy heaved a sigh of relief. "Next time, we take the subway."

"Don't be such a wuss."

Inside Jacobi Hospital there was still the attendant commotion of a cop shooting. Reporters hung around, police brass came in and out, the Mayor's people regarded Jimmy with suspicion. There was a buzz in the room that said, Big story here. This was where his mother had been pronounced dead, he realized with a start, wondering at his level of distraction that he did not remember until he walked into the place. He had gathered here with his family for that tragedy half his lifetime ago. The place seemed not to have changed at all, the same heavy scent of antiseptic, masking death that no priestly absolutions could obliterate. He could not begin to fathom how anyone might work in a place like this.

He bought some flowers in the gift shop. As he walked along, he fought a desire to turn and flee from this place, this idiot errand. They would bump into each other and talk through a stone wall of recrimination, of restraint for the benefit of others. He had no place in her life. What was he doing here? Still, he entered the elevator beside Liam. They shared the ride with two interns in green scrubs and a bearded man who wore an expensive camera and press credentials around his neck. They passed the cop at the door and stepped into the room.

Tara was sitting up in bed wearing a deep blue hospital gown. Her hair was golden and pulled back in a ponytail. Jimmy felt his breath stuck in his throat. She smiled at him, something real and warm. It felt good. The room smelled like a florist, there were so many flowers and a dozen or more stuffed animals. Tara looked drained. There was a livid bruise on her cheek, a bandage on her neck.

"Liam." Jimmy wished she had acknowledged him first.

"Jimmy." Her lips were thick and bordered with smile lines that were like parentheses. Her eyes seemed even greener than usual, brighter.

"How you guys doing?"

"Forget about us, Tara." Liam sat on the edge of her bed.

They shared a bond, combat veterans now. Liam had been shot once in a bar fight, the bullet passing through his arm. Jimmy felt a stab of jealousy. He knew this was foolish. He wanted them to be as they once had been, the three musketeers. Tara looked up at him. There was some distance in her eyes, a hard-earned coolness.

"Hey, Jimmy, nice job. Who would have thought we'd make headlines in the same week. And I get to be the hero and you're the villain."

"Liam's turn now." The floral smell was cloying. Again he thought of his mother laid out, dead.

"Nah, you don't want to see the kind of headlines I might make. Mayhem, chaos. I know what I'm capable of, and it ain't pretty. Here, I brought you something." Liam pulled a folded piece of paper from his back pocket. Jimmy leaned over as he unfolded it and spread it on the bed. It was a sharp rendering of Tara, gun blazing, as two perps fell under her fusillade. She was portrayed as willowy and full of righteous fire. The two robbers looked feral, and were already in their death throes. "An artist's rendition."

"Thanks, Liam. I like it."

Jimmy had to admit the guy always could draw. He handed Tara the flowers. "Here. I grew them myself."

"That'll be the day."

"You gonna get your shield?" Liam asked.

"That's the rumor. I go from zero to hero because of two skels and bad timing. What about you, Jimmy? You're a free agent, is what I hear."

"I'm gonna hook him back up with the concrete local, if he can make it without crying. Think he can?" Liam laughed.

"I doubt it. He's soft now, all that time kissing the Mayor's ass. Look where that got him."

"Hey, hey, hey. I didn't come here to be abused. I came bearing goodwill and flowers."

"Oh, so sorry. I guess we are supposed to feel sorry for you now. I mean, I've only been shot. But you've been fired, God forbid."

"How did this get to be about him?" Liam asked.

"Maybe I should wait outside. You two can hold hands and catch up."

"Tara, you should have seen the look on his face walking down to my apartment from Johnny Mac's. Like he was expecting to get jumped."

"Jumped? More like a voodoo curse from one of those Santería joints springing up on every corner. What, this some kind of tag team? I can find someone else to visit, bring flowers."

"Don't be such a baby. Sit." She patted the bed beside her and Jimmy sat down. Even wan from gunfire and bruised up, she was beautiful. He felt heat coming off her body and caught the smell of her. He missed that as much as anything. He was relieved that she had not tossed him out.

Punchy stood naked in the living room of his million-dollar condo, tossing darts at a wall adorned with blown-up glossies of his four ex-wives. Over the pictures he had written in thick black letters: "The Four Horsewomen of the Apocalypse." He pulled the darts out of the wall, thinking, What kind of asshole gets married four times? Especially, what kind of Irish Catholic asshole gets married four times? He had met Norman Mailer one night at Gracie Mansion, and as they drank cheap wine, they commiserated. He remembered thinking Norman did the right thing stabbing that one broad; the rest probably fell in line after that.

Truth was, he never so much as raised his voice to any of them. Granted, he occasionally left work and ended up taking a flight to someplace like Rio or Singapore after the bars on Second Avenue closed. Phoning them from some nineteenth-century phone in a Third World airport. He was a man of impulses, among them gluttony and self-abuse. He was the first to admit that. But he was, he knew, also a sucker for love. He was a firm believer in the double standard. Coming off one of his epic binges he gave the wives pretty much what they wanted, as much to salve his own remorse as to quiet their complaints. He also believed his money would last forever and that he could always make more.

His so-called business partners were all circling, waiting for him to show weakness. Then they would surely pounce. His creditors too. Hail-fellows-well-met. Right, until you could no longer pick up the tab. The ass whupping those little Mongolians gave him up in Inwood had sobered him up a bit. He was wearing an eye patch to cover his missing eyebrow. He had tried a pencil first, but looked frighteningly like his Aunt Agnes, rest her soul. Problem was, the eye patch screwed up his depth perception. First day he spent knocking things over, bumping into walls. Cursing the fuckers. "I had punks like you for breakfast."

He had been ducking his lawyers and accountants for days. He had to face them, to swallow the bad news. He was on the verge of bankruptcy. The word would soon be out. His phone calls would no longer be returned and all his fine friends would drop him. But far worse, he was in the clutches of Frankie Keefe and his dago cohorts. The Corsican cocksuckers. They would bleed him dry.

Maybe he could try to explain this situation to his more legit business associates. Gee, fellas, I'd like to pay you, but see, I'm about to get my head cracked like a melon. They'd assume he was joking, what with story after story in the press about the demise of the so-called Mafia. Just that morning he read a lengthy piece in *U.S. News & World Report* asserting that made members of a certain crime family were reduced to knocking off bodegas in Queens to finance their gaudy wardrobes. He wished they had interviewed him on the subject.

He thought for a minute about his nephew Jimmy. Good thing the kid was finished with his schooling. He was no longer in a position to be much of a benefactor. Maybe if the kid was going to CUNY he'd be able to spring for textbooks. He wanted to help the kid get a new job, but he had to be very careful. He did not need to piss off Frankie Keefe. He had enough trouble already.

He took off his eye patch and padded down the long hallway to his enormous bathroom. He turned on the water and dropped some Mr. Bubble into the torrent. He went back to his study and poured himself a Jameson over ice. He was scaling back his consumption to several tastes a day, eating his greens, popping vitamins. He sipped from the drink and looked out over the East River, up north to Inwood. Several tugs pulled barges downriver. Pleasure craft bounced in their wake.

He used to think it was all about having this or that, owning things, material well-being. Whoever has the most toys wins. He even had a tee shirt somewhere that said that very thing. There were days now he wished he had never left Good Shepherd.

But what a fucking ride it's been. He needed to hold it together, to come up with a plan. He had not scaled these heights merely to tumble back down to the gutter. He was not going to let the vultures pick him clean. He needed to calm himself, inject some discipline into his slothful existence, steel himself. He went back to the bathroom and shut off the water. He studied himself in the mirror. Staring back was a jowly affront to the human ideal. How the hell did the old Punchy get to be such a fat guy? He sucked in his gut. It was stupendous, a monument to gluttony. The type of midsection a medieval lord would put on display to demonstrate his prowess. At least his shoulders, arms, and thighs were still fairly well muscled.

He stepped into the scalding hot water. It was time for an exercise regimen, some clean hard living until things settled themselves. On the bright, as his father used to say. He lowered his massive ass into the tub, sinking way down into it, his blood roiling with the heat. Settled, he closed his eyes. A little respite before he faced down his lawyers and their tales of woe.

Keefe and Cronin drove towards the city. "Stop at Punchy's," Keefe said. Every time he met with Tommy Magic he felt a need to find someone to dump a little shit on, to pass the abuse down the food chain. Cronin parked the car on Second Avenue and they went into Punchy's. There was a nice crowd for a Sunday evening. There was a Knicks game on and most of the patrons were mesmerized by the event. Keefe never cared for sports, especially ones where ninety-eight percent of the players were noncaucasian. He strutted the length of the bar acknowledging nods and hellos from the patrons. They were mostly regulars and they all knew he was really the owner, not that bloated blowhard Dolan. He called the bartender down. "Get the house a round on me." He made a motion with his head. "Fat boy here?"

"Nah, Frank. Ain't seen him all day. He called, though. He's at home."

"Is that right?" Keefe cracked his knuckles and left the bar without paying for the round he had ordered.

Just when Punchy thought his day could not get any worse, he picked up his intercom phone. "Mr. Keefe to see you."

"Ah, shit. Send him up." He got out of his robe and pulled on a pair of slacks and a polo shirt. The last person he wanted to see was Frankie Keefe. He pulled open the door and presented the Teamster and his gorilla with his best salesman's smile.

"Frankie, how the hell are you?"

"Not bad, Paunchy. Make me a drink. What happened to your eye? Somebody smack you one?"

Paunchy. Guy's a laugh and a half. "Nah. Got some shit in it the other day, scratched up the cornea. No big deal."

Punchy watched as Keefe picked up his mail and leafed through it. He decided against complaining about it. The less he said to the guy, the better. Keefe took the drink and sat on the couch. Cronin, dressed like his boss in a goofy warm-up suit, stayed by the counter as if awaiting a command.

"You sure got some nice view outta here, Paunchy. Not bad for a mick from the Bronx."

"I'm from Inwood."

"Yeah, same fucking thing. Still a mick."

"Takes one to know one."

Keefe sprang from the couch and stabbed a finger at him. "Let me tell you something. I'm American. Red, white, and fucking blue—bucko."

"Got you, Frank. Frank the Yank."

"Fucking A. Good." The Teamster rolled his shoulders up to his ears, then placed his drink down on the coffee table. He smoothed his fingers through his oily black hair. "Your brother is giving me a hard time. Which is not something new, but now that kid of his, the son. That little bit of jism that made it past his mother's thighs. What kind of animals are you people raising?"

Punchy, unfortunately, laughed.

Keefe looked as if he'd been slapped. "Funny? What, you think I like the taste of shit? Hah? Paunchy. You think I sit around and wait

116

for people to make me look like a fucking dingbat?" Keefe paced while he spoke, gesticulating, chopping the air with his hands. His eyes sparkled with dark psychosis. A mad monk lecturing.

Punchy made a lame attempt at dousing his ire. Why the hell did he answer his intercom? "Jesus, Frank. We're barely related, tell the truth. I mean, I ain't been close with Mike since we were kids. I see him at weddings and funerals, if that. You know how the Irish can be. I know more about my doorman's life than I do about my brother's." Punchy thought it was not a great exaggeration. He did not like being between Keefe and his brother. He felt bad enough about helping Keefe squeeze his racket money out of the union's benefit funds.

Frankie suddenly stopped all his jerking and ticking and dropped his voice a few decibels. "Well, let me fill you in. Your prick brother is running against me, challenging me, saying all sorts of very bad things about me. He's making me out to be a liar and a thief, a rat bastard."

Punchy wanted to say, Yeah, so? He did not.

"As for his kid." Keefe sucked air in through his nose. "You were right there—in the very room—Gracie fucking Mansion, no less, when the little college girl had the balls to attack me. You know how I feel about that? Can you begin to imagine what that means to me? You got any idea how pissed off I am? You fat fuck?"

"Frankie, there's no need for that kind of talk. And come on, the kid didn't mean to knock you down. You're letting all that media bullshit get to you."

"Get to me? In my position perception is nine-tenths of the truth. I look like an asshole, like I can be smacked around by any jack-off that comes down the pike, I may as well fold up my tent and go home. You hear me?"

Punchy sighed, nodded.

"You listen to me good, I mean real fucking good. You talk to that brother of yours. You convince him to drop out of that election. 'Cause he don't, there's a lot a people, heavy, heavy people, that are gonna be very unhappy because of him and his bullshit. Let me make my point clear. I'm holding you personally, responsibly, liable. You know what that means?"

Punchy's day had turned to shit. His brother was burdened by ideals, a man who still clung to notions of good and evil, and who thought gray areas were the result of moral and intellectual sloth. Now he was in charge of getting a crusader to disavow his cause. Fat chance, that.

"Frank, like I said, we ain't been close since we were kids."

"That's your problem, not mine. Give me some money, I'm a little short."

"Ah, come on, Frank. I don't have anything laying around." Punchy suddenly yearned for his street-corner days. Back then, he would have snapped this little wannabe guinea gangster over his knee. Success could really be a mixed bag.

"You had plenty to blow on the Knicks last night."

"Yeah, don't I know it."

He peeled a couple hundreds off his roll and handed them to Keefe, who snatched them and snapped his fingers. "More."

Punchy curled his fingers into a fist and squeezed off a grin. "More?"

Keefe snapped his fingers again and looked out over Manhattan. Punchy peeled off two more crisp Ben Franklins and laid them in Keefe's manicured palm. He kept pressing his teeth together, working that false smile. It's only money, he chanted in his head. It's only money. He looked over at Cronin. Two hundred and fifty pounds of human fuck-you regarded him with amusement. Punchy considered that nothing would make Cronin happier than him slapping Keefe. Then Cronin would get to enjoy his afternoon. By breaking lots of little bones and a few big ones.

Keefe pocketed his plunder and before passing out the door said, "Mark my words, fat man. And let it be known. I am officially on the warpath."

Punchy poured himself three fingers of Jameson and sucked it down like medicine. Just another day in the big town.

T ommy Magic muscled his ten-year-old Buick into Manhattan while sucking on an overripe plum. He steered with his left hand and wiped the juice from his chin with his sleeve. It was a high and bright March morning, and he was preoccupied with Frankie Keefe and the Teamster local. Turning up Allen Street, he cut off a livery cab and answered the driver's angry Cantonese outburst with a deft cross-body toss of the plum pit. Bull's-eye. The slope went ballistic. He lost him by running the light at Houston Street.

His guy who kept an eye on the union had come by to say that Keefe's opponent had a shot at winning the thing. A long shot, to be sure, but still a shot. Tommy Magic figured he had two choices. He could sit back and let the chips fall where they might or he could eliminate the competition. He'd lost the convention center and the fish market to this bald nut of a mayor, half his bookmaking to Russians and Spaniards, and, to add insult to injury, a large part of private sanitation to suits from Dallas, of all fucking places. He had some guys nibbling around Wall Street trying to muscle in on penny stocks and some kind of financial wizardry he did not understand. He was reluctantly moving more into drugs. But that was a crowded field and heavily policed. Rats were everywhere. Stand-up guys were as extinct as woolly mammoths.

He slowed for traffic and was right in front of the Russian joint on Ninth Street. A half dozen of the Commie fucks were assembled on the sidewalk in their warm-up suits. All with the hard eyes. They looked him over and smirked. Magic squeezed the wheel and felt his aorta kick open a notch. Not ten years ago, these pricks would be genuflecting, he drove by. Matter of fact, they wouldn't even be on the island of Manhattan. Now they sat, fattening on his territory. He stomped the gas pedal like it was a cockroach and sped away.

He parked in the lot around the corner from his pastry shop and walked along, deep in thought. The streets were crowded. The bright day was encouraging walks. He was wondering what to do about the Teamster thing when he bumped hard into someone. He pulled back with a start and looked up to see a teenager, his face all twisted with insult, little sparse hairs, the making of a mustache, a slight scar underneath one eye, a gold tooth in front. "Yo! Yo, wuz up, you old faggot!" The kid held his arms up, hands wide apart, fingers splayed, like he was readying a slap. "Bitch ass punk."

Magic was stunned. He felt a snap in his chest like a coil breaking, and wondered if he was taking a heart attack right then and there. He started to tremble, a mixture of fear and rage sluicing through his veins. His lips quivered and he was unable to respond. He glanced about and saw people pausing to gawk, to take in the spectacle, a New York story in the shaping. He imagined them at home later, you won't believe what I saw today. He muttered, Sorry, and pushed past the kid. "Punk ass muthafucka. Bitch!" The kid yelled.

Enough. Magic spun and grabbed him by his throat and, squeezing as hard as he could, smashed the kid's head off the brick wall of an old church, three quick smacks, till the kid went limp and he felt hot blood run onto his hands. He let the punk drop and moved for his store.

The sun seemed to dazzle; the fumes choked him. He was aware of smells, the rot of a Dumpster, fresh dog shit, the stale medicinal breath of the old people he passed, the body odor of the spiked crowd, the unbathed. He felt a shimmer of terror as his chest tightened further. He believed for a moment that he was going to die. He saw in the garish faces of those he passed the leering images of his victims. They were gathering, as in his dream, to mock him, to show that they would indeed laugh last. He lurched through the door of his shop, the air conditioning hitting him like a dose of amphetamine. All faces turned as one to watch him brought down. He staggered, pale and shaken, into the back room and sat down.

Mary was over him, all concern, "What's a matter? Should I call the 911?"

"No," he squawked. He was not going to die at the feet of some cop. "Water." Mary brought him the drink. He gulped it down and laid his head on the cool wood of the table. He signaled for another glass and rose to drink it. After a while, his heart stilled, his veins cleared themselves of the juices that his glands had secreted. Before him was a copy of that day's *Post* with the hump of a mayor proclaiming the mob was through in his town. The man inspired in him a murderous revulsion. That sanctimonious prick. He was sick and tired of being hounded, watched, bugged, followed.

He thought of the kid, his tormentor. Talking like that, he must've been Puerto Rican. For that matter it could be worse; the kid might have been one of his own. In the old days, he would have taken the kid up on a roof, ripped his tongue out with a pair of pliers, then tossed him to his death like a rabid dog. The old days. He was tired of sitting on his ass and watching things disappear, the old ways die, the old order crumble. And now his Teamster local was under attack. It was time to make some noise. First things first. He told Mary to call Bobby Marino. He was one of the few young guys Magic still trusted. The kid arrived ten minutes later, muscled up and eager to please.

"Hey, Tommy." Little Bobby Marino stood in the doorway dressed from head to toe in black, his cheek muscles twitching. A dog about to be fed bloody meat.

Magic sat him down and whispered in his ear. The spic prick he left on the sidewalk was going to spend the rest off his life tongueless. He watched Little Bobby Marino head for the street. The kid knew how to hurt people bad. What the kid did not know was that Magic had put Big Bobby Marino in the trunk of a Coupe de Ville, which was than compacted down to the size of a bread box in Perth Amboy, New Jersey. A fucking bread box.

He signaled for a cup of black coffee. He looked over the store, a pastry shop he had taken over from his uncle, although he could not bake a roll if his life depended on it. As the caffeine coursed through his blood, he knew exactly how he would fix the Teamster situation. He replayed the scene from the street in his head and smiled, remembering how good it felt to hurt someone. A real sense of satisfaction. Of accomplishment.

Mary brought his second coffee. She smoothed the front of her apron and presented him with a girlish smile.

"Hey, sweetheart, dontcha run over to the Korean's and pick me up a coupla of those nice plums."

"Sure, Tommy. Anything else?"

"Yeah, get me the lotto. Play 1-6-8, straight and boxed. A pound a piece."

"Feeling lucky?"

"Top of the world, Mary. Top of the world."

Tara awoke from a deep, druggy slumber to find herself still in the hospital. Daylight was just breaking outside her window, a rosy and promising dawn. She had dreamt of open fields, of a childhood trip to the rocky coast of Ireland. But here she was. The hospital was quiet. She was alone at last and enjoyed the solitude, the eye of the storm. She pulled herself upright and winced from the pain. She turned on the light by her bed, opened her robe, and examined her breast in the mirror. It was bruised darkly and swollen. A large contusion from the force of the heavy-caliber bullet. Thank God for the vest. She touched the welt gingerly. She was still groggy from sleep and the pills they'd given her the night before.

She lay back down on her bed and thought about her mother. She had died when Tara was fifteen. It started with a lump in her breast. Six months later she was dead. She remembered her siblings. All much older, they had moved out, had families of their own. It was just Tara and parents. Her father cracked under the horror of terminal illness. He would disappear, hit the bars along Broadway, try to sneak in late at night. He left his wife alone with the pain. Tara would lock him out of the apartment and increase her mother's Demerol drip. Tara thought somebody had to hold him accountable. He had not had a drink since the day his wife died. It was like some twisted penance he offered up on the altar of his failings. As of late, they were friends again, she and her father.

Her mother, aunt, and grandmother had all died young from cancer. She felt sometimes it was lurking inside her, that her body would inevitably betray her as it had so many of the women in her family.

She thought of Jimmy's visit. It had been good to see him and she appreciated that he came by, but she could not help harassing him a bit. She wondered at his motive. Probably just doing the right thing. He was looking more and more like his dad. They were the type of men who got better-looking as they aged. His father had been by some time after Jimmy with flowers and well-wishes. He had always been nice to her, their relationship warm. She guessed when things settled a bit she would call Jimmy and thank him for coming by. But that was all she wanted from him. The past was the past.

She pressed for the nurse. A minute later, he entered the room holding a clipboard.

"What can I do for you, Officer? I'm Hank." Hank, heavyset and bearded, was too bright and smiling for the hour.

"I want to see my partner."

"No can do. He was transferred to St. Vincent's for surgery. Everything went fine. He's in recovery. He's going to be okay. Can I get you anything else? You want the papers? You're quite the sensation."

She closed her eyes and the gunfight played before her like a silent movie in Technicolor. Heat and light and muzzle flash, rivers of blood.

"What happened to the perps?" Everyone had been silent on that question.

The nurse looked at a spot a foot above her head. "One DOA, one died during surgery."

She felt numb. She was not sad or vindictive or glad. She remembered the one being so young, remembered how he looked as he left this life. She imagined a mother grieving, wondering what went wrong. "You can hold up on the papers. Thanks." Hank left and she lay trying to conceive of herself as a killer, a taker of life. It still felt unreal. She knew the ritual would begin. The department had mechanisms in place to deal with shootings. A priest would be by to help her spiritually. Then the investigation, an inquiry into the incident. The department would aspire to make as much cold sense as they could out of a hot instant in time. She thought long and hard, went over the sequence again and again in her head, played the tape back and forth, sideways. After a time she felt sure that she had done what was right.

Her father was late. She watched him enter the lobby and look about with some agitation. In the moment before he noticed her she took his measure. He looked older than he ever had, his thirty-three years on a Con Ed road crew had finally ambushed him. He seemed to have lost a couple inches off his six-foot-four frame. His shoulders drooped forward and he appeared in need of rest. He wore his old army fatigue jacket, dungarees, and a pair of running shoes. His hair, now completely gray, could use a combing. She remembered how he had looked when she was a girl. Handsome and erect, always tanned from working outdoors, thick ropes of muscles along his arms, a wide smile on his face. He always had an air of invulnerability that she thought transcended a daughter's awe of a father. She called to him and he turned and walked toward her. She rose from the wheelchair they had insisted she use and into her father's embrace. It was something he had never before done in public.

As they drove away from the hospital, he asked, "How you feeling?"

"Sore. But good, okay. How's work?"

"Work's work. Three more years, it's over. Then a condo in Florida—all goes well."

"You'll hate Florida."

"Yeah, you're probably right. But at least I won't freeze my ass off."

"Hot and miserable is better than cold and miserable?"

"I hope so. Won't know until I try. Gets too hot I'll come stay with you summers. You okay?"

"Dad, I'm okay. Just a little sore."

"You bein' shot, I bet you're a little sore. Maybe you should get a transfer, some inside work. I know the policy. You get shot, you get your pick, right? Take something down at Police Plaza, work for the bosses. I'll talk to my cousin, Tony Garvey—he runs the LBA. Him and my old pal Billy Bighead Gibbons. They'll hook you up."

She turned so her back was against the door. She stared at her father as they pulled onto Harlem River Drive. A gypsy cab sliced across traffic in front of them. Her father merely raised his hand, a gesture of resignation. When he was younger, he was in a constant state of road rage behind the wheel. Back in those days he would be apoplectic by now, the vein in his forehead throbbing like a steam hose about to burst. "Dad, I like working on the street."

"Sweetie, maybe before you did, but this is going to make things different. You should take some time off, see what you think, reevaluate your situation. You never been shot before. God knows how you'll react after something like this."

"I took this job so I wouldn't rot in some office."

"You don't have to argue with me, Tara. All I'm saying is take some time. Do yourself a favor? You done your time on the street. I don't think you have anything to prove here."

"I'm not arguing with you." Tara drew a breath and looked out at the East River. The light was high and bright; the skyscrapers of Queens, all two of them, stood against an improbably blue sky. They looked alien rising above the flat industrial landscape, jarring the horizon. She was not so sure she would be okay on the street, but she was determined to get back out as soon as possible and find out. She did not want to dwell on her wounds, to milk disability, abuse sick time. She refused to take any more pain medication; she poured both prescriptions down the toilet before leaving the hospital. She was not sure how she felt about the shooting. First, it was the adrenaline, then shock. They had her doped up, numb, the narcotics obliterating her response to the incident. Her clearest recall was of the leer on the face of the perp. She wrestled with the fact that she had killed two people. She had pointed her pistol at two human beings and pulled the trigger, had sent grains of hot lead into the flesh of two teenagers. As she rode along with her father, those two kids were about to be buried beneath six feet of dirt. Footnotes in a violent city's history. She had trouble focusing on her father.

"What?"

"I said take your time, take the sick leave. It's unlimited for a reason. You're no good to yourself or anyone if you're not ready."

She nodded, unable to summon the energy to argue with him.

Her father pulled off at the Fifteenth Street exit. They caught the light, and as they waited, a man with skin so dark it looked blue pushed a hot-dog cart down Avenue C. Two yuppies dressed in matching tights and turquoise Lycra jackets came out of Stuyvesant Town and started jogging toward the riverfront park. Her father eased the car through traffic. He parked next to her building and carried her bag for her. Her medication was wearing thin and she felt the tenderness in her ribs, a sharp ache, less dull by the minute. They turned the corner and walked into a phalanx of cameras waiting outside her apartment, reporters, the media in full heat. A couple of uniformed cops kept them at bay.

Apparently the shooting was taking on political overtones. The dead youths' families had held a press conference, complete with keening mothers and a racial adviser who claimed to represent the aggrieved underclass slaughtered at the hands of a bigoted Police Department. Junior high school pictures of the dead were printed. Friends went on record claiming the boys were good kids who were going to go to college, were never in trouble. The faces were angelic. No one had a picture of what the one looked like when he was pointing the gun at her. A smirk, like Die, bitch.

She kept her head down and let her father lead her through the mob. The reporters shouted at her, seeking comment. They pressed in, taking oxygen and space. She felt a flush of vertigo and leaned on her father's shoulder. He was stern and forceful and pushed his way through the melee. She appreciated his presence, his love and concern. She looked up and saw faces framed in many windows. Her neighbors taking in the spectacle. Microphones poked through at her, hands held mini cassette players that whirred, picking up all sound. The reporters' words were lost to her. There was no syntax, only garble. She caught a glimpse of herself in the lens of a moving camera. She looked stricken. Finally, they were inside her vestibule and the glass doors closed behind her like a vacuum seal. She turned to see two uniforms converge and block the entrance, a mob of faces hungry for the story. She followed her father's back toward the elevator, seeking the refuge of her apartment.

A t 2:45 Cronin left the bar and crossed through Columbus Circle to the corner of Broadway and Sixty-third Street. He chased a homeless man off a bench with a five-dollar bill. The wind had changed again and the clouds were gone. Golden sunlight played across the windshields of the cars snaking down Broadway. He pulled off his coat and folded it across his lap. March in New York. He lit another cigarette, cursing his lack of resolve.

Cronin checked his watch and looked up as a man crossed from the west side of Broadway and wandered out into traffic. The man was neatly dressed in pressed slacks and a sport coat, button-down shirt. It was as if he had left his office for soup and a sandwich and something had gone terribly wrong on the way back to work. He staggered down the middle of the street, a small hunting knife in one hand, his swollen cock in the other. Here we go. Daylight in the Big Apple. The man was shouting about killing all the bitches. Cronin could hear the car-door locks slam down like a pack of firecrackers going off in the distance. Horns blared, cars swerved. The man pressed on, his eyes wide with some invisible horror. Though he was in the middle of the street, pedestrians pushed up against the sides of buildings in an attempt to create distance. No one stared. They stole lateral glances and scurried on, not wanting to become the focus of his derangement. Cronin watched a street vendor reach down and grab the end of a club, his eye roving for a place to run. The light turned red, but nobody heeded it. Just then a patrol car pulled into the intersection and two cops leapt out.

They each held a hand out in front of them and shouted for the man to stop and drop his weapon. One of the cops produced his billy club; the other unbuckled his holster, his hand firmly on the pistol grip. Now, emboldened by the police presence, a crowd assembled.

Cronin stood and backed into a break between two buildings. He had no interest in catching a stray bullet. The cops separated. The one with the nightstick moved to the side, the other drew his pistol and backed up. The man slowed, then stopped, confusion on his contorted face. The cop with the club moved quickly, striking the man hard behind the knee. The man yelped and went down, and the other cop produced a can of pepper spray and squirted him until he dropped the knife and began clawing at his eyes. They pinned him face down and cuffed him roughly. Sirens were closing in on them from all directions. The cops kneeled on either side of the man, holding him down. The man was still screaming incoherently. The cops were young and black, and looked embarrassed.

Cronin walked back to curbside. A woman came up next to him. She was maybe fifty, but fighting it, dressed in a sharp beige pant suit and clutching a Gucci handbag firmly to her side. She had the look of a woman who snapped her fingers while giving orders. She put her hand to her mouth and said, "Oh, my." Cronin watched her face pucker with alarm. "What are they doing to that poor man?" He could tell by the assured way that she carried herself and the cultured look that she was a New Yorker. But she had that flat accent of a small, wealthy percentage of New Yorkers. He had always marveled at that. How some people grew up on the same small island he did but sounded like they were from somewhere very far away.

She repeated, "What are they doing to that poor man?" She turned her head from side to side as if to elicit support. People ignored her, enjoying the show now. The cuffed man was trying to buck the cops off his back. He started screaming, "Rodney King! Rodney King!" The cops smiled. The woman fixed her attention on Cronin. "Are we going to let this happen?"

Cronin took a last drag from his cigarette. Looked her up and down. Civic concern for the underclass, a luxury the rich could afford. "Yeah, he's getting what he deserved. Beat it, dingbat." He gave her a wide smile. She flinched as if he'd smacked her and backed away, her mouth a silent O, but her eyes darkened and turned hard. Cronin imagined she'd take the lash to him if she had half a chance.

After the man was hauled off, the flow of the street resumed. The last two cop cars roared off as a large black Oldsmobile pulled to the curb. The passenger window hummed down as the car stopped. A man in his forties sat behind the wheel. He wore sunglasses and had what they called dark good Mediterranean looks. His features were thick and hinted at danger, Hollywood's current idea of a tough guy.

"Little po-lice action?"

"Yeah, some misunderstood . . . what do they call them these days, mentally challenged African Americans?" Cronin said.

"Crazy niggers."

"Well, this one went bonkers with his prick in his hand."

"True they got big long johnsons?"

"Not this guy."

"Jeez, what a pity. What the fuck's the point of being black then?"

"Come here a second." Cronin nodded away from the car.

The man came out of the car and walked over to join him on the sidewalk.

"I know, call me paranoid, but you just never know these days." Cronin patted him on the chest and ran a hand along the small of his back. "Business."

"Hey, no problemo. I don't blame you. Seems everybody's a rat these days."

"You know our guy. My favorite ball breaker?"

"Yeah. Same one you pointed out?"

"Yeah." Cronin nodded and said, "Message needs delivering."

"Same way, like the other guy?" The man put his hands in the pockets of his coat. He looked casually up and down Broadway.

"Seems to work." Cronin reached for another cigarette and stopped himself.

"I'll say. Today?"

"Yeah. Today would be very good."

"Gonna miss my shift."

"I figured." Cronin leaned into the car and dropped a package on the front seat. He straightened. "It's in there, the envelope. How's the acting?"

"Don't ask, please."

"Forget I did."

"This work today, for you, is about all the performing I make any scratch on. Need a lift?" He indicated his car.

"No, no. I'm good."

"Take care."

"Ring me later."

"No problemo."

Cronin watched him rejoin the flow of downtown traffic. It was time to rattle Mike Dolan's cage. See what a little persuasion did to the man.

Last Stand Larry Sweeney, screwed to his barstool at Johnny Mac's, was holding forth. "What I want to know is, how the fuck the Dominicans get to be minorities? I mean, these are your descendants of the Conquistadors, quite possibly, no, make that definitely, the most bloodthirsty sons a bitches to ever come down the pike, killing and maiming the Aztecs and whatnot. They get to the New World there's twenty-five million Aztecs; ten years later they're down to a million. Genocide! Then they get lazy for a few generations, I guess all that killing might sap your energy, then they move to El Norte, by which I'm referring to Inwood, right here, and now they're eligible for all sorts of handouts financed at taxpayers' expense. I mean, come on. It just ain't right."

Mike Dolan thought the worst thing that had happened was cable TV. Sweeney, who had not read anything besides the *Post* in thirty years, spent much of his time watching the Discovery Channel, the History Channel, A&E. He half absorbed things and became a self-certified expert on everything from military hardware to home improvement to the endangered species list. Somehow he twisted his newfound knowledge in a way to support his moronic thesis. Sweeney was also renowned in the neighborhood as a counterfeiter of one-dollar bills, which local gin mills had been accepting for two decades in a nod to a certain devious industriousness.

"Last time you paid taxes?"

"Whatever. That's beside the point."

"No, Larry, that is the point. You don't pay taxes, have not paid taxes since I know you, which is close to fifty years, so shut up about it."

"I'm a war veteran."

"You never left Fort Dix."

"Someone had to man the home fires."

Last Stand Larry took his drink and brought it to his lips. When the door opened he turned instinctively toward it, curious to see who was coming in. Mike hoped it was one of Sweeney's drinking companions, someone else he could vent to. A look of confusion crossed Sweeney's face, and Mike turned to see an Italian-looking man coming toward him smiling. The man wore tinted glasses and an expensive-looking coat over a fancy suit. He was certainly not a regular and was too stylish to be a liquor salesman. Mike looked to his right down the bar, trying to figure who the man was smiling at, then he heard "Dolan!" and turned on his stool, pulled by the sound of his name. He watched as the man, no longer smiling, raised a pistol. Mike felt all the air around him go tight, all sound ceased. He froze, unable to move, concentrating on the man's trigger finger. He watched the finger curl backward and saw the crescent of black metal move back and meet the trigger guard. He braced for noise and the strike of hot lead, the muzzle flash, a waft of cordite. Instead, there was a bright beam of red light, a laser, and only the sound of the man cackling. The man turned and moved quickly out the door.

There was silence in the bar. Silence and an awful stench. Mike looked down and realized it was Sweeney who was befouling the sleepy afternoon air of the bar. The bartender came over and, holding his nose with one hand, gently nudged Sweeney. "Come on now, Larry, hit the can. Fix yourself. It's okay."

Sweeney nodded numbly and shuffled off to the bathroom. The other patrons had turned back to their drinks. They did not wish to shame Sweeney. They sat avoiding all eye contact, not quite sure what to make of the episode. Mike Dolan turned back to the bartender and ordered a whiskey. His hands were shaking so hard he could not lift the glass. He placed them under his ass on the stool.

The bartender said, "The fuck was that all about?"

Mike cleared his throat. He could not stop shaking. The fear was alive in him. He thought he was going to be killed. "A message." His voice was high, girlish.

Seamus was watching the door as if he was expecting the man to return. He placed an old .38 service revolver on the cooler at his thighs. "Next time that scumbag comes in the door, he's getting a little lead poisoning for his effort."

Mike knew the man was not coming back. The message was delivered, and he was sure that's all the man had been there for. By the look of Seamus's weapon, it had not been fired or maintained in some years. Finally calmed, Mike spun off his stool and went to the bathroom to check on Last Stand. He had cleaned himself and was standing over the sink, running water over his hands. "Goddamn, he got the jump on me."

"Yeah, Larry, he got the jump on all of us. Sorry."

"Right, Mike."

Back at the bar, Mike noticed that he had peed himself a bit. Thankfully, he was wearing dark pants. After what seemed a safe time, he walked home, panic dogging his steps. He had not felt it since Nam, that jolt of fear that comes from looking eternity in the eye. Over there he had developed a shell that he pulled himself into, had defined the parameters of death. Understood that it was to a great extent out of his hands, that all you could do was keep your shit tight, be aware. After that it was all luck and fate, cruel or kind. Black or red, heads or tails. When it came at you over there it was heat and noise and blood pounding. It bordered on a twisted euphoria. This was different. It was personal and calculated. But even in the bad old days with the local, when he was the target of threats and beatings, he did not imagine being killed. Now he was not sure.

He climbed the stairs to Isham Park, his senses on alert, spying rooftops, glancing warily about. Menace seemed to hang in the air. Even with all the changes he had never felt threatened in his neighborhood, until now. There was a sense of safety, a familiarity. He looked down on Seaman Avenue and remembered the old football games at Baker Field when Columbia used to play Army and the cadets would parade with their marching bands and old donkeys, shouldered arms, a pageant, thousands of neighborhood people lining the streets, festive. Inwood was always a harbor for them, cut off from the rest of the city by water on three sides, a long climb up Broadway to the south. Was it such a happy place? Or was he becoming a sentimental old fool, revising history, clinging to a past that never existed? It was a different place now. A place so many of his neighbors had fled, while he refused to go.

He left the park considering his options. Keefe was proving nothing was sacred. Was it really worth it? He did not want to die. He believed that they would kill him. It was a sign that he was closing the gap, that they were worried, that the secret ballot was of great concern to his opponent. He imagined Keefe and the fake gunman having a laugh over the incident. Ha ha. You should have seen the look on the guy's face, and the old guy shitting his pants. Ha ha.

He walked into the lobby of his building and was confronted by Mrs. McMartin. "You okay, Michael?"

"Fine, Annie, why?" He wondered if they had been here. They would not have escaped her vigilance.

"You look like you seen a ghost, Michael," Mrs. McMartin said.

Mike managed a smile but thought, I did. My own.

St. Patrick's Day broke clear and cold with a sun intent on burning the last of winter air from the city. Jimmy Dolan slept soundly. He was in the throes of a vaguely sexual dream, grappling with an unidentifiable partner, when he felt a tapping on his head. He opened his eyes to see Liam hitting him with the stick of a small Irish tricolor. Liam sat in a chair pulled close to the bed with his feet up and a can of Bud in one hand. "Up an' at 'em, laddie, it's our big day."

"Go way."

"Good to have you back in the 'hood, bro. It's just like old times."

Jimmy pulled the pillow over his head and willed Liam to be gone, for this to be just one of those dreams when you think you're awake but you're really still under. He wanted to retreat back to the fleshy

133

embrace of la-la land. After a moment he peeked over a pillow and Liam was still there, incarnate, a grin on his face. "Come on, bro, the day's a-wasting."

Jimmy groaned and tossed the covers aside. "All right, you sick bastard. Let me get ready."

Liam sat with Mr. Dolan at the kitchen table while Jimmy showered and dressed. Mike was dressed for work—jeans, flannel shirt, work boots. Liam knew as well as anyone that he had no work to go to.

"How's it having Jimmy back home, Mr. D? Hope you got a curfew for him."

"I was thinking midnight, but that might be a little permissive, don't you think?"

"Yeah, maybe in the old days that was okay, but the neighborhood ain't what it used to be. I'd say ten p.m. Do you know where your children are, and all that jazz. I'd keep a short leash on him."

Mike folded his newspaper and smoothed it flat on the kitchen table. He got up and went over to the junk drawer for a pen, then sat and started the crossword, sipping his coffee. "How's your mother?"

"She's good, little sick and all, but pretty good mostly. Took her to Mass this morning." Liam got up and poured himself some more coffee. He alternated sips from the mug with the can of Bud. "I heard about that thing at Johnny Mac's. You need any help over that stuff, Mr. D, I'm available."

Mike dropped his pen and looked at Liam. "I appreciate that, Liam, but no. It's just games the assholes like to play, is all. You say anything to Jimmy?"

"Ain't seen him since 'fore it happened."

"Do me a favor. I haven't had the chance to talk to him yet. Keep it between you and me?"

Liam rolled his eyes. "Mr. D, you forget where it happened? My mother knew about it before I got home from work yesterday. Place is soap opera central. I'm surprised Jimmy ain't heard."

"I just don't want it being blown out of proportion. You guys go and have fun downtown. I'll talk to Jimmy about it later."

Liam shrugged and finished his beer. "No big deal. To me, I mean." He crushed the can in his hand.

Jimmy came in and poured himself a cup of coffee. His hair was wet and combed back behind his ears. He pulled a chair from the table and sat. He bent and pulled on his boots, lacing them and tying them quickly. "This is gotta be the first St. Paddy's in five, six years I'm not in a suit making the rounds of all those political breakfasts." He scooted his chair in and took a sip of coffee. "It's a relief. I used to wish I could just bolt and have fun."

"You file for unemployment?"

"Not yet, Dad, tomorrow." Jimmy buttoned his shirt and took a doughnut from the box in the middle of the table.

"You want to get there early, else you'll be there all day."

Liam also took a doughnut. "Hey, Jimmy, things are picking up with the local, they'll be putting new guys to work next week. You want to do some real work, I'll hook you up."

Jimmy wiped the powdered sugar from his lips with the back of his hand. "I'm a goddamn educated man." He laughed.

"You're a freaking hobo, is what you are."

"Concrete's not a bad racket," Mike said.

Jimmy stood and took his and Liam's cups to the sink, rinsed, and set them on the drainboard. He had done nothing but lay about since his firing, enjoying the short break. Now it was time to get serious. But first, St. Paddy's Day. He dried his hands with a paper towel, which he crumpled and tossed in an arc over his head into the trash can. "Bingo. Hey, Dad, you want to come with us?"

Mike looked up over his reading glasses. "Don't think I could keep up with youse."

"You guys want some eggs?" Jimmy took a heavy skillet down from a cabinet above the sink and placed it on the stove while turning on a burner. He took a stick of butter from the refrigerator and hacked off a chunk of it and dropped it in the pan, where it melted into greasy bubbles. Jimmy cracked open four eggs and ferried them into the heat. When the eggs were ready he made himself and Liam egg sandwiches. Liam squirted about a pint of ketchup on his.

"Maybe we'll catch you on the rebound at Johnny Mac's."

"Possible. Drink responsibly, boys."

"Mr. D, look who you're talking to here."

"That's what I'm afraid of."

Jimmy and Liam put on their jackets and, eating egg and bread, headed out to meet the day.

Tara was picked up at 7 a.m. in a black unmarked car and whisked toward Gracie Mansion. The driver, one of the Mayor's detail, wore a buzz cut, a too expensive suit, and a regulation blank face. He said little. His head looked as if it were jammed down into the collar of his shirt and he gripped the steering wheel like he wanted to sever it from the column. His ear was tilted ever so slightly to the prattle emanating from the police radio. He wore a subtle cologne that was not unpleasant. As they passed through the gate of the mansion he said, "I saw your thing on the news. Nice piece of work."

Tara thanked him and left the car, stepping into the crisp morning air. Nice piece of work. He was not the first cop to describe the shooting that way. Work. Two dead boys. Nice work. But that was part of her chosen profession, right? She buttoned her police dress jacket and straightened out the front of it with her hand. She felt a nervous flutter in her stomach. Gracie Mansion. She had never been here before. She took in the nineteenth-century construction of the place, its wood siding and gabled entranceway. The tree-lined grounds. It was almost as if she had stepped out of Manhattan altogether.

She was intercepted at the door by a decked-out three-star chief she recognized from special details. He stood ramrod straight and tight-lipped, a martial presence, a man who burned through calisthenics every sunrise of his life. The handshake was crushing. He seemed to be appraising her, not in the sexual way she had grown used to on the job, but as a field marshal inspecting one of his fighting men. "Good to see you, O'Neil. You are a credit to the uniform. The Mayor is waiting for you." He very nearly snapped his heels together.

Tara followed his starched back into the mansion. She felt a welling of anxiety. She hated being put on the spot in any way and figured this was going to be an occasion where the focus would be on her like a laser. They passed through the vestibule and up some steps, skirting the main function room. They came upon a half dozen bagpipers gathering themselves for a procession, donning elaborate hats, sliding knives with long blades into calf sheaths, pumping air into the bladders of their instruments. Odd bleats escaped. The room was dense with their presence. They were all large men, fearsome in their thick mustaches, descendants of warrior clans, of humans who met in fields to holler and bash skulls as the sun rose. Tara found them sexy in their kilts and muscles.

In the next room the chief waved for her to stop. She could see into the dining area where the VIPs were gathering. They all seemed in good cheer, sipping from cups of hot tea or coffee, greeting each other, priming for the day. She recognized the odd politician: a hyperactive borough president, a lithe congresswoman from Queens known for her diatribes against the gun lobby. She spotted celebrities: a television anchor who, even in person, seemed cut from plastic, too perfectly turned out to be real, an up-and-coming actor from Long Island who was the toast of the theater season, an aging starlet who spent more time whining about injustice than acting. Other faces she recognized, but could not place, like lost acquaintances happened upon. The room thrummed with import, with the buzz of We are it, we are at the center of things in this city, on this day. Someone dropped a coffee cup. The crash brought a stillness on the room, a hiccup of quietude, and then laughter and the knowing chatter went on.

The chief tapped her on the shoulder and she turned and followed like a good soldier. They came to a door, in front of which another of the Mayor's detail stood. The sharp suit. The blank face. She wondered if they were requisites for the job. He nodded and stepped aside. They entered and came upon the Mayor. He was huddled at a long wooden table with an aide who was pointing his finger down a sheet of paper. The aide seemed to be defending himself feebly. The Mayor's steep forehead was knotted with annoyance. The chief cleared his throat and the Mayor looked up. He glared, but as he looked at Tara his face softened and then was lit by an awkward smile. He rose and took her hand in both of his. His grip was cold and dry, and his head bounced up and down as if he had just been awarded a prize. She vaguely remembered him at her bedside, but had been a bit behind the narcotics at the time.

"Officer. Great to see you again. I can't tell you how much the city respects what you have done for us, for everything. How important people like you are, how without you we'd be, we'd be lost. Without the blue line. I can't imagine being in that situation. Shooting, gunfire. Wow. I just can't imagine."

The Mayor had a sheen to him, an earnestness. He seemed to be playing out a hellfire scenario in his mind. He often showed up at tragedies sporting Police Department hats or jackets. He craved respect from the emergency services. She sensed that he wished he'd been in the firefight, that he saw it like most desk jockeys, as a way to prove his manhood. How stupid. How little they realized it was mostly dumb luck. He still held on to her hand with both of his, drawing her closer. She felt like he wanted to embrace her. She leaned back slightly.

"Are you well? Are you better? Fit for duty?"

"Getting there, sir." She caught the chief over the Mayor's shoulder, casting her a cold but imploring look. "Ah, much better, thank you." She still had trouble mastering the ass kissing required in the presence of superiors. It was the thing she hated most about the job.

"Great. I am so happy you can be with us today. Will you sit with me?"

"Ah. Sure, sir." She had feared this.

The Mayor was one for pomp. They strode in the wake of the Emerald Society band: the wail of the pipes, the steadfast, ominous drumming, the rigid gait of the pipers, elbows high, biceps straining against their navy woolen jackets, thick fingers working the reeds, cheeks swollen from the effort. It was deafening. The assembled stood and gawked like children, applauding, oohs and ahhs. Tara grinned with embarrassment. She was mortified when the Mayor took her hand as they approached the dais.

She was placed to the right of the Mayor, which separated him from the chief. She felt the boss's stiff, officious presence by her side and realized she had knocked him out of the chosen spot. Round tables crowded the room. The feeding was buffet style and a steady stream of well-wishers passed to greet the Mayor, who sat like a sultan receiving homage. He introduced her to the politicos and moneymakers like she was a daughter who had just made the honor roll. She played the wounded valiant to the best of her ability. She had never been a fan of this mayor. She found his bullying behavior offensive, and he had repeatedly screwed cops over money. She soon began to feel like a trophy, an election year prop. She noticed his hands, soft and pale, almost lifeless. A smudge of butter shone on his cuff.

She downed an orange juice and smiled weakly. The crowd was mostly male and hearty. There was a collective strut to them, the kind you saw when too many frat boys or wise guys or cops got together. They seemed to feed off each other. They projected a confidence that said we, and only we, belong. They shook the Mayor's hand with a knowledge that they were the lucky ones who were all somehow in on a great secret. She noticed Frankie Keefe, the man Jimmy had knocked down. He was engaged in vigorous handshaking and back-slapping and seemed to be in great spirits. She thought he was handsome in an edgy way.

After the assembled had wolfed down an Irish breakfast complete with buttered scones and blood pudding, the Mayor rose to the podium. He brushed a crumb from his cheek while he waited. Tara was sweating from the heat and crush of the room. She noticed the Mayor's cops spread out, holding up the wall. Occasionally, they spoke into their sleeves or adjusted their earpieces. The Mayor was introduced with great fanfare by a man with a perfect head of white hair who presided over a financial concern that employed thousands downtown. His face was as red as a sailor's sky, and his blush deepened as he spoke. He had the manner of a church deacon, supercilious. He was moneyed in the peculiar way of the Irish. They never carried it off the way other groups did, as if they were always expecting someone to come along and snatch it all back.

"And now, ladies and gentlemen, it gives me great pleasure to introduce to you the best thing to happen to the Irish in this city for decades. The great and honorable Mayor of New York."

A roar of approval. The Mayor stepped to the microphone and placed his hands on the lectern. He told a tasteful joke about a leprechaun lost on the IRT, then droned on about the contributions of the Irish to New York. Tara scanned the room. The assembled sat enthralled by this man. He strove to remake the city into the place of their warm and hazy nostalgia. A mythical place when old ladies could sit out at night and everyone was so nice to each other, the place of their lost and distant youth. She wondered how many of those present actually lived within the city limits.

As the Mayor went on, she looked about and felt more and more out of place, as if she had wandered into the wrong banquet hall. She wanted to fart or belch, to rattle them somehow. They were so goddamn smug in their belonging.

She tuned back in. "Now, my critics, none of whom are here, I hope. My critics like to bash the police officers of this city. They like to describe a force out of control, a force rife with brutality. They seize on every incident and politicize it. They criminalize every action taken by the police officers of this city. Officers who are here to protect you and me, our children, from the predators among us. The criminals, the thugs. Every police misstep is magnified, every action is questioned, is turned into something sinister. But let me ask you this. How come when officers of this city's police force rise above themselves, when they act with courage and decency and valor, when they put themselves in the line of fire to protect society, to stop wanton violence, to save innocent civilians, where are those critics?"

"In jail!" someone barked from the back of the room. Laughter. Rough, scattered applause. A hoo-rah.

The Mayor held up his hand. "For all I know, they may be. Because they sure are nowhere to be seen. But let me just say how fortunate we are to have the very kind of officers that would do such a thing, risk their lives for us, which they do every damn day. And let me just say how lucky we are in this very room to have one such example of that heroism here with us today. One of New York City's very finest, a great example of what I'm referring to, and Irish to boot. Officer Tara O'Neil." The Mayor turned and looked down at her, offering his pale hand. She took it and rose, waved, her face flushed. There was applause, then they were on their feet, some actually hooting and

140

whooping. She winced from the pain in her side but managed to smile for the benefit of her new admirers.

The Mayor was waving off the applause. "But wait. Hold on now. I made a mistake. How stupid of me. Did I say Officer O'Neil? Is that what I said?" The Mayor played with the crowd. "My mistake. I meant Detective O'Neil."

Tara was shocked. She turned to the Mayor, who was grinning like an ass. She knew cops in shoot-outs were often promoted, but she did not expect it here, now. The Mayor motioned to the chief, who produced a gleaming gold shield and pinned it on her with a flourish. The three of them turned and the cameras let rip. Shit, Tara thought. Politics ain't so bad after all.

The bagpipers marched into the room, announcing the end of formal proceedings. Tara was looking about for an escape route when the Mayor turned to her and said, "Detective. I was hoping you'd march with me." He leaned in close, scrutinizing her with his dark eyes that were too close together. She was about to beg off politely when Chief Knucklehead said, "She'd be honored to march with you, Mr. Mayor."

"Excellent."

Tara smiled. She had no options and she knew it. "My honor, Your Honor."

The chief looked as if someone had just pissed on one of his citations. The Mayor placed his hand on her shoulder, a fatherly gesture. "I just want you to know how proud this city is of you."

She had planned to have lunch in Inwood with her father, go to Good Shepherd and light some candles. Flee the pandemonium. Now she was the official St. Patrick's Day mick sidekick of the Mayor of New York. She worried that her chest might ache mightily as they went up the green strip on the avenue. She knew she would be ribbed by her colleagues for consorting so closely with the man they all considered the enemy by now. She asked to use a phone.

"There's pay phones downstairs."

"Nonsense." The Mayor waved off the chief and motioned to one of his security detail. He took Tara in through the doors to use a private line. She sat at a table that looked to be as old as the city. It was of dark wood and inlaid with a floral design of a lighter color. She looked at the paintings on the wall. The place had the tight, dead air of a museum. She caught a glimpse of the river through one of the windows, silver under the dazzling March sun. Her father picked up on the fifth ring. She explained her predicament.

"Good for you, honey," her father said. "I'll watch for you on the TV."

Tara hung up the phone and realized she had heard genuine pride in her father's voice. She smiled and turned to rejoin the Mayor. The room had emptied, and the Mayor stood speaking heatedly to a man whose back was turned to her. Already, a crew was breaking down the tables and removing the buffet. She watched the man turn and leave in a distinct huff. She was surprised to see who it was. Jimmy's Teamster, Frankie Keefe.

Punchy put in brief appearances at the key political breakfasts—Gracie Mansion, the Roosevelt Hotel for the Speaker of the City Council, and of course McManus's Midtown Democrats on the West Side, then hoofed it toward his place on Second Avenue through the thinning crush of morning rush hour. It was a day he had never toiled on, and was the most sacred on his calendar. While making the rounds people had commented endlessly on his eye patch, so much that he was beginning to like it. He wished he had thought to produce a green one for the occasion, or maybe one emblazoned with a shamrock. He felt it lent his fleshy face a hint of danger, aroused the swashbuckler in him. Of course, he worried that someone would learn the story behind it, that he had been pounced upon and humiliated by a band of dysfunctional ghetto youths.

At Lexington he turned south, moving along with parade marchers heading for their staging areas. He came astride two blond young men and a pudgy woman wearing lavender tee shirts that said IRISH and QUEER. He muttered, "Fruitcakes," under his breath, but apparently he was overheard. The woman craned her neck up at him and spat,

"Look at you, Captain Ahab and Moby Dick had a son." Punchy found himself in the middle of a chuckle storm. He swallowed a retort and crossed the avenue.

His life of late seemed to be a string of humiliations, some great, many small, suffered at the hands of people around him, strangers. Just yesterday he had gotten into a shouting match with a Sikh taxi driver over the best route to take downtown. The argument ended when he leapt from the cab. Unfortunately, the cab was moving at the time. He landed on his knees and tore gaping holes in both trouser legs. But today was a whole new day.

He entered into the cool gloom of his establishment and took a seat at the bar while the day unfolded around him. He nursed several Bloody Marys while the staff whisked about stocking the bar, setting up the free buffet, the best corned beef in town, large trays of shepherd's pie. Upstairs you needed an invite; it was a VIP section of sorts. This white mayor had emboldened the exiles to return in growing numbers. The cops would arrest a truckload of gays, and it was on with the proceedings. The papers would be sure to track down and photograph the few drunk and out-of-control teenagers, Irish Catholics being one of the few groups left that the press had no trouble disparaging. The parade had taken on a corporate tinge in the last few years. Before long it might be the Anheuser-Busch or the AT&T St. Patrick's Day Parade.

Punchy's place had been a must stop for at least a decade. Sandwiched between the political breakfasts and the tuxedoed formality of the Friendly Sons dinner, it was fun time for all, an Irish Festival. Over the years he had never had any trouble, and reveled in the diverse crowd he attracted. Cops and firefighters, college kids, Wall Street hotshots, drank right alongside pick-and-shovel men, tourists, well-known actors, doormen from the swank buildings, the odd novelist, racket guys—all were welcome and all came. It was one of the busiest spots on Second Avenue.

Assured that things were going well, he went to his private bathroom and washed his hands and face. He inspected his brow. It was stubbly, but was finally growing back. He opened a bottle of diet pills he had glommed from one of his waitresses. She took two twice a day, he gobbled six. At 9:30 he opened his doors and regained his stool, a glass of whiskey in hand, a nice amphetamine buzz kicking in. He refused to let his mounting difficulties darken the hour. It was a fine day, indeed.

Jimmy and Liam emerged from the subway at Columbus Circle with pint cans of beer in their hands. The sky was high and clear, more May than March. Jimmy was not thinking about being out of work; he wanted to run amuck, to feel the throb of drums and bagpipes in his chest, to cut loose. He'd not been out and about in months and was jittery with the prospect. He caught a cloying whiff of nuts roasting in a vendor's cart. A dark-skinned man stood at the top of the stairs smiling and trying to sell green carnations and "Fuck Me I'm Irish" buttons for a buck apiece.

Hordes of teenagers on the lam from high schools across the tri-state region emerged with them, carrying six-packs in brown-paper bags that were promptly snatched by the police. Many wore hip-hop fashions that looked ludicrous on them: baseball hats askew, enormous pants that could clothe any three of them at a time, brand-name jackets that must have set their parents back the price of a top-line oven. Some of them looked eleven or twelve, although Jimmy figured they were older than that. When they passed, they spoke the slurry slang of convicts they learned from watching MTV. God, he thought, their parents must be appalled.

Liam shook his head. "It's a whigger parade. Look at them all wanting to be black. Not just black like Bill Cosby or Martin Luther King or Michael Jordan—but stupid, poor, locked up, and black. Fucking idiots. Follow me. I need to make a stop."

Jimmy waited in the shadow of the new building as Liam made his way through the construction site. The place was jumping and humming. A mason tender, short and gnarled with a broad lined face, pushed a wheelbarrow filled with sand past him, whistling a familiar tune Jimmy could not name. A stout Jamaican woman, her hard hat on backward, bulled a section of scaffolding into place along the wall, while three skinny and tattooed Polish laborers argued and smoked with vigor. The air smelled like every site he had ever been on: a mix of wet cement, damp earth, diesel fumes, dust, sweat. He felt the urge to work. Men shouted to be heard over the rip of table saws, the clank of machinery, and the constant backbeat of hammer blows. He stepped back as a truck laden with block nudged its way by him. He noticed a Keefe bumper sticker on the door.

Liam approached, carrying a pay envelope in his hand. He spoke to a man who wore rubber boots, canvas pants, and a flannel shirt. His face was thick and leathery from years of outdoor work, but his body looked twenty years younger. He bounded along. "This is Jimmy, he's gonna come to work with us. Jimmy, this be Thumper, the foreman of the month, a man among mongrels."

Jimmy shook Thumper's hand. He looked up as Liam pointed out a man in a white hard hat coming toward them with purpose, fists swinging at his sides. "Look at this asshole. His old man owns the company, else he'd be working in a diner, cleaning tables, mopping the floors. They wouldn't even let this prick sell soda."

The super came to a halt before them, thrust his arm out and bent his elbow back, bringing his wrist to eye level. His Tag Heuer glinted in the sun. He wore a fleece jacket over an oxford shirt. He bared a set of perfect teeth and his eyes twitched when he said, "Bank hours, Brady?"

Liam looked down at him and laughed. "I don't work on Paddy's Day. Plain and simple. I was Jewish, you wouldn't ask me to work on Passover. I was Muslim you wouldn't ask me about Ramadan. Am I right or what? I'm just here for my money."

Thumper laughed as the super spun and scurried. "Thataboy, Liam. Show that fucking runt."

"Half a runt. Musta forgot his Prozac today. See this prick busting my balls about taking the day? Tell him, I'll file a lawsuit for anti-Irish discrimination." Liam waved at the retreating boss. "More importantly, Jimmy's got a book. We put guys on next week, do me a favor. Put him on."

"No problem. If he's half the man you wish you were, he'll do fine."

"You're a prince, Thumper."

Walking away from the site, Liam said, "Best foreman I ever had. Guy cares about one thing and one thing only, getting the job done. He don't play any bullshit games. And no one's going to give you any shit about Keefe. My business agent hates that guy. He don't have any say over the concrete laborers. Besides, you don't want to work as a Teamster, you'll get fat."

Jimmy laughed, realizing he was probably going back to work. It could be worse. He could stay unemployed. He actually looked forward to some time busting ass, getting muscled up again.

"Come on, let's head to Spillane's so I can cash this check."

They shoved into the place and made their way to the bar.

"Liam, Jimmy. Tricks?" the harried bartender asked.

They shrugged as Liam signed his check and slid it across the bar.

"Same old Paddy, different day."

The bartender gave them two beers. "First round's on me." He took Liam's check and put it on top of the cash register. He moved quickly down the bar, shimmied past his partner, stopped, and leaned over to take another drink order.

"Place is mobbed."

Jimmy squared himself at the bar and thought about what he'd be doing if he had not lost his job. He'd probably be in St. Patrick's Cathedral for Mass. He'd sit with the Mayor in the front row. He had to admit he had liked being at the center of things. He took in the crowd at the bar. There were guys he had worked with and a few from the old neighborhood. It was as if he had entered his own little time warp. A decade step backward. He did not hold these people in less regard. He was comfortable here. But he had moved on. He had taken all the civil service tests, had gotten his union book, and then set his sights upward.

Liam was talking to a guy he recognized but could not place. He had the hard face of a cop or a con, wary eyes that stayed blank when the rest of his face broke into a smile. Jimmy looked down to see Liam, his back to the bar, pull a pistol from his belt and pass it to the guy, who slid it into his jacket. Jimmy glanced quickly about to see if anyone had noticed the transaction. Nobody seemed distracted from their drinking and good cheer. The place was so crowded most people had their arms bent upward at the elbow and their drinks pressed to their cheeks.

Liam's customer patted him on the back, then shouldered his way toward the door.

"I wish you wouldn't pull that shit when I'm with you."

Liam pulled back with a look of mock hurt. "Don't worry about it. I'd never let you get jammed up over me."

Jimmy shook his head. "You work steady. I don't see why you want to risk getting locked up."

"Easy money, Jimbone. Easy money. Besides, I know my clientele. Not to mention the Fourth Amendment protection."

"Fourth Amendment? What are you babbling about?"

"Just doing my thing, Jimmy. We ain't all college boys."

"College got shit to do with it." Jimmy was bumped from behind. A crew of cops, dress uniforms in disarray, were crowding around them. "I don't want to see you locked up. I hate going upstate. Hate the mountains."

"I'll do my very best to stay out of the Catskills, or wherever the new joints are going up."

Jimmy turned so he was facing Liam, pushed by the crowd almost to the point where their faces were touching. He smelled the beer on his friend's breath. "Your mother."

Liam laughed. "Bringing out the secret weapon so soon? Point made. Point taken. New subject."

The bartender came back with a wad of bills and counted out twenties on the bar, then picked them up and tapped the stack on the wood like a dealer with a deck of cards. "Good luck."

Liam took his pay and left a ten on the bar. "Let's get out of here. Place is like a submarine, packed with guys, not a chick in the whole place. Circle jerk. Here." He handed Jimmy some bills. "Just take it. I know things are tight. Fix me up when you can."

Jimmy looked at the money. A Black 47 song cranked from the jukebox and people started bouncing up and down and bellowing along with Larry Kirwan. Firefighters and cops started trading professional insults. "White man's welfare!" squawked a patrolman from the

33rd Precinct at a smoke-eater, whose riposte was a wave of a small tricolor and "Zookeeper!" Charged, boozy laughter. Jimmy took the cash and thanked Liam. Man, he thought, you just never know when things are going to go bad on you.

Out and about they went. The city had the feel of a carnival. They careened around midtown, ducking in and out of bars along the avenues, making a mad, sodden swirl. The city was in full holiday swing. Jimmy made an effort to pace his drinking, knowing it was going to be a long day. Liam did not seemed worried by the prospect.

On their way to the firefighters' party at the armory they stopped and took in the parade. There were no floats, no cars, no political statements. There were contingents representing all thirty-two counties in Ireland, high school marching bands, pipers from as far away as Japan, a wizened witness to the Easter Uprising, alumni associations of Jesuit colleges, soldiers, cops, a nun on crutches, sanitation workers, union men and women, vote seekers, fraternal orders, and patriots, veterans of wars, priests, teachers, a fat man in a green cowboy hat. Though the crowd was five deep, Liam spotted a cop he used to work construction with who let them stand in front of the barricade. Jimmy loved the pipe bands. They played the background music of his life, dirges, songs for the forsaken, rousing jigs.

Most spectators came for the parade but some had stumbled upon it. Jimmy stood next to a woman who wondered aloud in a Southern twang, "What y'all celebrating? It's just like Mardi Gras?" Wide-eyed kids from the suburbs perched on the shoulders of parents who had been born in the city and now came back for work or spectacles. Old, churchgoing ladies from the far reaches of the boroughs, from Rockaway and Woodlawn and Bay Ridge, made their rare visit to Manhattan, stylish in white hair, wrapped in sweaters bought on hard-earned, parish-sponsored pilgrimages to the shrines of the Old Country.

Jimmy heard the Mayor before he saw him. Scattered boos drowned out by lusty cheers. A buzz through the crowd, rising to a roar. Suburbanites howled for him. He showed the world that the city was a shithole before he came on the scene, he validated their abandonment, their white flight. He vanquished the grubby panhandlers, the bums, the squeegee men, the dangerous darkies, put the welfare cheats in their place. "We love you, Mayor!" screamed a sixtyish woman next to him wearing a Massapequa High School jacket. Jimmy stood and watched his former boss approach, waving, smiling, smiling, waving, basking in a glow he would never receive from a more urban throng.

Jimmy felt exposed. He wanted to duck back into the crowd, to hide. A woman in a suit, tall, dark blond hair, a striking figure, walked along with the Mayor. Jesus Christ. It was Tara. Now he really did not want to be seen. Mrs. Massapequa screamed again, a schoolgirl rooting for a home team win. Jimmy did not want the Mayor looking his way. He leaned over and said, "Shush up, lady."

The woman wheeled on him and came up on her toes, a thick homemaker finger in his face. "Fuck off, buster," she growled in toxic Brooklynese. "You don't own this parade."

Liam was yelling, "Hey, Tara! Hey, O'Neil!" At the same moment the Mayor and Tara swiveled to focus on them. Tara waved and smiled, blew them a kiss. The Mayor stared at Jimmy, his smile leaving his face. His Honor shook his head as if he was deeply disappointed and turned to bless the other side of the avenue with his awkward smile.

Liam was saying something. "Hey, Jimmy, Tara take your job or what? Looks like that to me, boy."

Jimmy did not respond. Instead, he stood riveted to the spot and watched his previous life, accompanied by the swirl and bleat of pageantry, pass him by.

The sun fell over Queens, lighting the outer borough sky with a flare of blood orange. Magic waited for darkness to settle. He was watching *Jeopardy!* with his wife. She was answering one question after another, every time right, and he was batting maybe 150, only scoring when they were about entertainment, singers and movies. She was wearing her robe, and by her side was a stack of books, crappy novels, two feet high, and a taller pile of magazines, all kinds. She was a reader, his Ruthie. There was a time when he was really going patzo over things, when he was seeing the government in every design, in the shape of the clouds, and he thought they might somehow be sending in listening devices in the magazines, but he had that ex-FBI guy who worked for Keefe come in and check everything, do the sweep, and he said it was all okay, so he let her send away for them again. It made her happy to sit all day and half the night and read, as if she were being taken to some other place. Which, on some level, he understood. It was no picnic living on lockdown with the government watching your every move.

When it was good and dark he went to the bedroom and dressed in one of those suits the young guys liked, looking like he was going for a jog, sweatpants and sweatshirt, with FIT across the chest. He wondered what the hell that stood for. He put on some black sneakers that Ruthie had picked up at the mall and pulled a Mets cap down over his eyes. He peeked out through the blinds and saw the Fed car sitting across the street, could make out the tip of a cigarette, probably some civil service fuck not smart enough to get a real job. His driver pulled up and this was his cue. He hurried down the stairs and kissed Ruthie goodbye.

Instead of going out and getting in the car he went out the back door and scurried across the yard to the fence. It was a redwood job that came up to his chest. He needed to haul himself over the thing and tried to remember when was the last time he jumped over a fence. Maybe sometime right after World War II. His gym outfit was not helping him. He grabbed the lip of the fence and felt the grain of the wood. He tried to hoist himself up. He got his feet about six inches off the grass and his elbows up on top of the fence. His arms started to quiver and his feet scraped for a grip. He was suspended for maybe ten seconds, his ascent halted by the stonelike weight of his own body. His arms gave out and he slid back down, foiled by the millions of calories he consumed. He leaned against the fence; his breath started coming short and fast. He went over to the shed and took out a stepladder, then put it against the fence and climbed. He got up on top of the fence, his belly folded, one side of him in his airspace, the other half in his neighbor's. With great effort he rolled off and gravity took over. He fell to his neighbor's earth with a great thud. He lay dazed for a minute, trying to figure out if anything was smashed. He rolled over and got on his hands and knees, then pulled himself upright. A sharp pain shot up his leg. He could not picture Carlo Gambino or any of the other old-school guys resorting to this shit. If there was a heaven they were snickering down at him.

He crab-walked through his neighbor's yard, head hung low, arms swinging from side to side, a slight crouch, legs akimbo. He imagined that, to the casual observer, he looked like a two-bit pervert out trying to snatch a pair of panties off a clothesline or sneak a peek at a young babe in the shower. He affected a jogger's type of shuffle, moving slower than a walk, a nice old fat man trying to get in shape. There was the car. The night was crisp, and his breath came in white puffs. A van rolled toward him, and he tucked his chin. He reached the car and opened the door. The keys, as arranged, were in the glove box. He started the engine and immediately dropped it into drive, pulled away from the curb, and headed for the intersection. He braked smoothly and looked both ways before proceeding.

He took a circuitous route to the LIE, winding his way through a stretch of little look-alike towns. The only things to distinguish them were the names on the local police cars. Every few miles he pulled over to the shoulder and waited half a minute before heading on. After a time he was confident that he was not being tailed.

He made his way along the Cross Bronx Expressway and noticed that all the old abandoned buildings had been rehabbed. This was news to him. He pulled onto the George Washington Bridge. Traffic was light and the view of Manhattan to the south was spectacular. There was a time not that far in the past when they owned that town. In his younger days they controlled much of the commerce. They were street kids who told mayors, developers, judges, and juries what they could and could not do. There was nothing they could not attain. Now he felt marginalized, a bloated emperor of late Rome surveying the massing hordes at the city gates. His father was always going on about the greatness of the Roman Empire when they were kids, drilling it into their heads. Have pride in your heritage. He never talked much about Mussolini joining up with Hitler.

Magic was being harassed on all fronts; usurpers were probing his defenses. He lived like a recluse, avoided the spotlight, the authorities. He tried not to commit the fatal mistakes of others who liked to strut around in public throwing off fuck-yous to the world. Look where they ended up. He was Old World and reveled in it. For over a decade now he had been living underground, dressing like a fucking bum off the Bowery, affecting a profile so low he was down with the sewer rats. But now his body was going to hell on him. He took a decent crap maybe once a week, in a good week. The heart was shot. He had exactly eight real teeth left in his head. Still, he was not going to fade away. It was time to stir things up, roil the waters, live a life worth remembering. He would go out with a fucking bang.

He rolled his window down and let the chill night air blow his still-thick hair straight up and away from his head. He turned on the radio and caught a Frankie Valli tune. He held his hands on the wheel at ten and two o'clock, kept the needle on the speed limit, precise. To the passing motorist he was a citizen, a taxpayer, a by-the-numbers asshole. Crossing into Jersey he felt release, leaving New York behind for the first time in over two years—no, three. The music triggered remembrance of his youth in Brooklyn. A simpler time, when it was us versus them. Summer nights in the city, sneaking into Ebbets Field, day trips to Coney Island, gang wars. Ruthie, young and curvaceous in her swimsuit. He had sixteen-inch biceps and a belief that he was bulletproof.

He found the strip mall that Bobby had suggested for the meet. There was the liquor store tucked into the corner. He was a half hour early. He waited in the parking lot forty yards from the store with a clear view of the front door and the entrance and exits of the parking lot. There was a row of a dozen or more stores—a pharmacy, a stationery, a bakery, a luncheonette, a photo-developing place—all dark. A pizza place and a Chinese joint were open. The mall was anchored by an A&P, in front of which a half dozen kids were hanging about drinking from bottles wrapped in brown-paper bags. They all wore those giant-sized pants. He thought about the kid back by his shop who was now missing a tongue. Bobby had said he was surprised that the thing came out in pieces when he got the pliers on it, and not all at once. A woman with three kids in tow came out of the pizza place carrying two pie boxes. She put them on the hood of a car and loaded the kids into the vehicle. She turned and her gaze found Magic. He nodded as if he recognized her.

He popped a nitroglycerine pill and considered his doctor's warning. The old Jew was pushing an operation on him, a quadruple bypass. Fat chance. He figured if he was lucky he had a year before the indictments came down. He'd certainly be held without bail, so much for the fucking Constitution. They'd take their time, maybe a year, putting him on trial, which could last months. Then with the way things went these days, even on reduced charges, he was off for a long bit, at least a decade. He was sixty-seven years old. He used to wonder what he would do if he ever got the news his brother Gino had. Cancer—six months to a year. His brother went and got religion, went around apologizing to people for things they were not even pissed off about, things nobody remembered but Gino. He had to take him aside, his own dying brother, and tell him there were certain things you better keep your mouth shut about. You might be dying, but lots of people still left living are worried about the lack of a statute of limitations for certain crimes. Poor Gino, he never had the balls for this life. He was too much like their mother. Guy went out like a real mope, head hanging low, a family embarrassment. Twenty years gone already.

He watched the Lincoln pull up, and the Russki get out. He looked like those weight lifter guys from the old Olympics, all heft and muscle, the side-to-side shuffle when he walked. Kind of guy that ripped phone books in half at parties to liven things up. The Commie, Ivan, that was his name, liked to do his killing up close, bare-handed if possible. Said he enjoyed watching the light leave a guy's eyes. Sick prick. Ivan looked around checking for cars with people in them. He looked up at the roof like he thought there might be a sniper sitting up there with a bead on his forehead. He made his way through the parked cars to the liquor store. According to Bobby, there was a bar in back. Some strange Jersey thing, putting a bar on the inside of a liquor shop.

Magic got out and followed the Russian into the bar. Through the door there was a small liquor store with bottles stacked high on shelves. In the rear there was an entranceway and then a little bar, no windows. The Russki was back in the corner, a glass of vodka in his thick hand. His back was to the wall, and his hooded eyes seemed to see everything. Magic took the seat next to him and nodded hello. The barman came over and he ordered a glass of beer.

There were about fifteen other people in the bar, half of them old drunks lined up in a row, nursing drinks and bullshitting about God knows what, their fucking hemorrhoids, Magic thought. There was a gaggle of younger guys and two girls huddled by the jukebox, playing darts. The guys wore football jerseys and most had on baseball hats. If any of them were agents, they were as deep-cover as you can get, Magic thought. At the far end of the bar, two lunks sat with drinks before them. Ivan's muscle. They stared down at the wood in front of them.

"So, how are you, Mr. Magic Man?"

"Not so bad, Ivan."

"I read in the newspaper you are on the run, no? You are the last one they do not catch."

Magic sipped his beer and held his tongue. This bit of news seemed to please the Russian. You never knew if these guys were busting your balls or not. He knew this monkey sitting next to him was the future of crime in New York. They would never attain the same place that his people had but they had enough stone killers out of the shitholes of Russia to muscle in on whatever they wanted. There were even rumors these guys had nuclear bombs you could fit in a shopping bag. Magic shook his head. The whole thing was sad, really. The Feds liked to beat their chests and crow over the demise of the Cosa Nostra, but the fact of the matter was, the idiots were just opening the door for legions of depraved cocksuckers like this Ivan, who did not go by any rules. These pricks would start killing cops, agents, judges, lawyers, reporters, and schoolkids. And the Commies were not the worst of them. For years, the Italians had been preventing the mongrel hordes from running amuck, were doing more policing than all the fucking cop agencies combined. They had a sense of decorum, an awareness that violence should be a last resort. Now, to prove a point, he was going to let them in.

"You want some work done?" The big Russian signaled for another round of drinks.

"It's a big job. It'll get a lot of attention. You'll need your best people."

"All my people are the best."

"So you say."

"Of course. This is the truth. We don't have any of your rats. We have no fear of your justice system. In Russia, we have real prisons. Here you have . . . what do you call them? Country clubs."

"Right." Magic did not drive out here to swap braggadocio with this guy. Down the bar one of the younger guys was dancing to some rock-and-roll crap out of the jukebox. He had a hat on sideways, like the Little Black Sambo kids by the social club. His shirt said "Lifestyles of the Drunk and Stupid" in big block letters, and he was obviously pie-eyed. He slugged from his beer and was staring at Magic. Magic shook his head and averted his eyes.

"There's a guy. He needs to go. We need it done out in the open. Broad daylight. We want people to think long and hard about what it means."

"This good. No problem. You see, in America the people are weak, too many years of good times. Nobody knows to suffer. By suffering you become strong. You think Soviet Union is finished. But here, same thing will happen."

Blah, blah, Magic thought. He was willing to let the Russian be cocky. It was always easier to take someone down when they were flush with success. He looked up and the young guy was coming down the bar toward them, a dopey booze grin on his face. A catastrophe waiting to happen.

"Well, fellas, what do we have here? A couple of blockheads. You guys got two of the biggest heads I think I've ever seen. Anyone ever tell you that?" He belched softly and swayed. His eyes were plum red and heavy from a weekend's intake of booze.

Magic could feel the Russian tensing next to him. Magic did not drive out here to get in a bar fight with a bunch of suburban punks. He affected a laugh.

"Where you guys from? My friends call me Merv. You look like a couple of mooks."

Ivan said, "Hey, my friend, are you a pussy?"

The drunk swerved a bit and looked over his shoulder as if for backup. "Me, a pussy? No, you fat foreign fucko."

Magic cursed softly as the Russian exploded up off his barstool and grabbed the drunk by the throat and lifted him a full two feet off the ground and slammed him off the wall like he was a bag of leftovers. The whole bar seemed to shake from the impact. The kid crumpled at Ivan's feet. He peeled off a crisp hundred and dropped it on top of him. "Have a drink on me, my American friend." Nobody in the bar moved or spoke. He waved at the bartender. "Please, drinks for everyone."

Magic waited for the Russian to sit back down.

"Now, Mr. Magic, we can do our business."

"Right." Magic watched as two of the drunk's friends came over and helped him back to a barstool in the corner. "It's a union problem. We got a guy who is making a lot of trouble for us. You take care of it, the regular price, then I'll cut you in on a piece of the action. It will be good for you."

Magic turned to see Ivan brighten. He knew the Russian was drooling at the possibilities. "Good, Mr. Magic. We make you very happy. We become partners."

Magic stood and shook Ivan's hand. Right, he thought. How fucking bad things have gotten. The Russians in the business. Tommy Magic in New Jersey.

On his way home Magic stopped in midtown and left his car off in a municipal parking garage. He walked down Sixth Avenue, by himself, anonymous, no hulking bodyguard. Unhurried, no surveillance. He could be a tourist, he could be anything but what he was. He stopped in a deli and had a pastrami sandwich, washing it down with a sweet root beer. He strolled over to Rockefeller Center. He remembered, Christ, many, many years ago, coming here with his parents and his three brothers. To see the tree. His father had worked some years before as a stonemason on the job. And although the Rockefellers were popular for building the Center during the Depression, his father had another take on them altogether. Blood money. His father had a bit of the anarchist in him. He was an antigovernment guy from way back. Christmastime and the old man would be going on about Bloody Ludlow and the coal miners killed by Rockefeller's goons, and how nothing would make this money clean. Tommy Magic laughed at that. He had a grudging respect for the Rockefellers and the Kennedys and all the others who went legit and got away with it.

He leaned against the wall, his breath short again. He fumbled in his pocket for another pill, put it beneath his tongue. His blood was thick with explosives, little eruptions keeping his heart moving. If he had any regrets, it was not having children. But he knew this to be a bullshit sentiment of a man at the end of a life. He watched groups of tourists move along with kids craning their necks in awe up at the towers. He worried about getting back over the fence. Fuck it. He'd walk right down the sidewalk and wave at them on his way up to his door.

The ringing was insistent and fully inhabited his dream. Mike woke and reached for the phone. "Yeah."

"Mikey, it's your lucky day."

"This?"

"It's Lou Condo. Listena me. I'm sending you out on a job. I need a guy on Fourteenth Street. You want it?"

Mike was alert now. Condo was the rare business agent that did not blindly follow Keefe. "Driving?" he asked.

"No. I want you down there as a shop steward."

Mike took a breath. "Louie, you sure?"

"You think I get up at five a.m. to screw around?"

"Keefe's not gonna be happy."

"You telling me something I don't know already? Listen, I'm retiring, end of the year. He wants to make my life miserable over this, I'll put in my papers tomorrow. You deserve the shot. Besides, how bad is he going to look? He takes you off the job when one of his business agents put you there. It's a win, win."

Mike hung up and dressed quickly. His unemployment was running out in two weeks. It had been six months since his last Teamster paycheck. He took the A train to Fourteenth Street and decided to walk crosstown to the site. He moved along in the urban dawn, the city muted under a lightening sky. A sanitation truck passed him, then a bus with only a driver and two passengers, one seated toward the back, staring out into the morning gloom, the other behind the driver talking into his ear. He stopped at a deli and bought a jumbo cup of black coffee. An old Korean woman looked at him with reddened eyes and pushed dull coins across the counter.

Walking east on Fourteenth Street across the fat part of the island, he could see to the end, where the street met the East River and beyond where the Con Ed stacks punched the sky. He walked with purpose, his breath steaming the cold air, his boots slapping on the lonely concrete, his shoulders and hips loosening with the distance covered. He was going to work. The idea of it thrilled him. He loved to work.

He turned the corner and came upon the job, dark and skeletal in the dawn. A few early birds from upstate sat in cars under the scaffolding. They propped tabloids open on their steering wheels and smoked casually, the tips of their cigarettes fiery in the gray interiors. He found the watch shanty and pushed his way in. The guard, sitting in a blue office chair, had one good eye, which was shut, and a scarred hole which was looking at Mike. It took a second for Mike to realize the man was sleeping. A copy of *Jugs* magazine was splayed open on his chest and a faded green tattoo of indistinct design ran under the collar of his jacket. Mike nudged him with his foot. The man grunted, wiped a bit of tobacco juice from his chin, and said. "Hah?"

Mike introduced himself and the man replied, "Said you'd be coming." He led Mike to the Teamster trailer. He swung a thick bundle of keys up from his hip and worried through them. "This'll do her." He opened the door, and Mike followed him in.

"Said the other fella got a heart attack. Seemed like a nice fella."

Mike waited for the man to go, then set about starting the day. Shop steward was a job he'd been awarded rarely. It was a plum assignment doled out judiciously by Keefe to his prize followers. The responsibility was basic. Record every delivery to the site and turn away any drivers who were not Teamsters. Mike preferred driving to the administrative nature of the steward's job, which was to enforce the contract, something that, under Keefe's tenure, was done erratically. Often it was a license to rob mightily. Every bit of material coming on the site had to be delivered by a Teamster driver and unloaded. This created a natural bottleneck that the steward controlled. It provided many opportunities for shakedowns and kickbacks, all of which made their way up the wise-guy food chain to Keefe, and then, Mike knew, on to Tommy Magic.

He found the coffeepot half filled with murky swill, dumped it out-side the trailer door, and rinsed it thoroughly. He gathered the old newspapers into a stack and took them out to the Dumpster. He turned on the electric heater and warmed his hands. He spread out the papers he read every day. The *Post* and the *News*, then the *Times* and the *Journal*. He noted that the only paper with any coverage of a major ma-chinists strike out West was the *Journal*. So much for the liberal media.

He was almost done when the first truck of the day docked along-side the trailer. He heard the door open and the Teamster leap to the ground, slamming it behind him. He stacked the papers in a neat pile and finished his third cup of coffee. He cracked his knuckles and looked up as the door opened. He was happy to see Ron Parsell.

"You?" The driver stood and smiled.

"Hey, Ron."

"What'd you do, sell your soul to the devil?"

"Not yet. Coffee?"

"Shit, yeah."

"Got the call this morning. Nobody was more surprised than me. Who was on before me?"

"Johnny Longo. Took a heart attack driving home on Monday. Rear-ended an ambulance, of all things. They grabbed him, tossed him in, and off they go. I guess if you're gonna take one while driving, it's pretty convenient to do it that way. Say he would've died elsewise. Turns out good for you, I guess."

"What do they say? One's man's sorrow."

"Yeah, but what kind of crap's this clown trying to pull by sending you out here?" Parsell took off his gloves and dropped them on the table. He took the cup from Mike and poured himself a measure of milk and plunked in four cubes of sugar.

Mike shrugged. He watched Parsell stir his coffee with his finger, oblivious to the heat. "I need the money. I figure I just keep doing my job, his motives will present themselves. I don't think our president is a very complicated guy."

"That prick. You better watch your p's and q's. What I see in the papers, his brother-in-law don't have much left except this local. I doubt they want to lose it to an up-and-up guy like you."

"Yeah, I got to believe that's the case. What's the word about the election?"

Mike sat on the desk as a few trucks rumbled up outside, their air brakes engaging with a snap and a hiss. He noticed two men in suits milling about with rolled-up plans under their arms and white hard hats on their heads.

"Good coffee." Parsell drained his cup. "Guys that give a shit? They seemed excited by the idea of a secret ballot. I think you got a better chance than anyone is giving you. Not too many of the fellas are going around saying, Hey, Dolan's my guy, 'cause they still worry about what the little sack of shit can do to them. But behind the scenes, I think you got better than a long shot. I was a betting man, which I ain't, since the wife threatened to leave me, 'sides the occasional pony, I'd say you're a medium shot and closing."

Parsell turned for the door as someone rapped on it. "Time to earn my money."

Mike opened the door and stood on the top step, watching the line of trucks curl around the corner. Tradesmen dressed in denim and canvas work clothes filed onto the job. They tugged on hard hats and bantered, buckled tool belts. Mike felt good, but wary. He was not sure what to make of the assignment. Condo had always been a good man. Still, he was not so sure Keefe would take kindly to the situation. He'd do his job and keep his eyes open.

A t One Police Plaza she retrieved her weapon. The sergeant on duty slid it across the desk in a plastic bag. She picked it up and removed it from the wrapping, placed it in its holster, and then into her gym bag. "Use it in good health," he said. His eyes were dark with fatigue.

Tara nodded and made her way out to the courtyard, passing

through the shadow of the bleak Orwellian structure where everyone seemed beyond uptight. It would be a sentence working any unit that made its headquarters here. She crossed the plaza, bypassing groups of people taking cigarette breaks on the benches. Old municipal buildings rose around her, monuments to the bold corruption of looser times. She loved the ornateness, the heft and permanence of these buildings. They might have been sinkholes of graft, but they were built to last. She stopped at a vendor for a knish and a Diet Coke. The man was bundled against a cold only he could feel. The day was overcast but had turned balmy, a Gulf Stream wind soothing the city. The man, an aged refugee from South Asian holy wars, stared into her eyes.

"You are most beautiful," he said with an earnestness devoid of lechery.

"Why, thank you," she said as she moved past him. She certainly did not feel beautiful these days. She'd been experiencing a low-level depression since the shooting, a creeping malaise. She lacked her usual confidence, found herself jumping at noises, sudden movement. The department psychiatrist assured her it was a typical reaction, a post-traumatic stress. She made an effort to downplay its effect so as not to jeopardize her position. She, like most cops, had little trust of the department's apparatus for helping its employees. Nobody wanted those little red flags in their files.

Enjoying her knish, she climbed into her Chevy Blazer and battled through downtown streets clogged with transport. She squeezed past a garment truck stuffed with sweatshop booty, a van unloading buckets of plump silver and orange carp, a dirty Mack straight job from JERRY'S BROOKLYN CHEESES. She pulled her side mirror in. Desiccated pigs hung in some windows, greasy duck carcasses in others. She caught a briny whiff of pickle juice. After Houston Street, things got easier.

In her apartment she took out her weapon, a Glock nine millimeter, and placed it on the kitchen table. She stared at it, black, metal and plastic, sleek and deadly efficient in design. German engineering at its purest. She opened the closet and took out her gun-cleaning kit, placing it next to the pistol. From the stack of old newspapers she took a *Post* and spread it on the table. She slid the kit to the left and unholstered the weapon. She placed it flat on the table and opened the cleaning kit. She picked up her gun and felt it in her hand. She squeezed the grip, wrapped her finger around the trigger, and pointed the gun at her refrigerator. She cleared the rack and pressed the button, dropping the clip into her left palm. She pointed again and dry-fired three times. Click, click, click. She put it down and took a deep breath, holding it for a three count, then releasing it. Telling herself, You wanted the job.

The wall clock ticked over her head, voices—a faint chatter from a neighbor's television, a child yelling beneath her window. She disassembled the gun. She took a rod and erased all trace of the projectiles from it. She snapped it together and reholstered it. She hung the holstered firearm on her chair and put the kit away. She gathered up the newspaper and saw, as she balled it up, the faces of the dead perps staring at her, adolescent, alive. She felt a coldness in the base of her spine and swallowed. She tossed the paper into the can and dropped the lid on top.

She fought an urge to call Jimmy and thank him for coming by the hospital. What was she thinking? What good would that do? She needed to concentrate on herself and not allow herself to slip backward. Loneliness could be perilous. She filled the tub with steaming water and bath oil, then undressed. She sank gingerly into the hot, wet embrace of the tub, letting all the tension ease out of her body.

She would turn thirty in two months. What the hell was she going to do with the rest of her life? She used to scoff at women who obsessed over that milestone as if it were some tolling of doom. Thirty, she realized, was still young. Maybe because she was alone, maybe because she was feeling a sense that she was languishing, that she was not focused on large enough goals, she was being beset by a creeping anxiety about the event.

She remembered thinking as a girl how everything was going to be so linear and ordinary in her life, a belief based on examples of older cousins, sisters, neighbors. Life in Inwood was arrested in some ways. There was still a great sense of traditional beliefs and rituals; you grew up, you got married, you had kids, you stayed married, you had grandchildren. Even if all that was really falling down around them as the neighborhood changed. People told themselves they were not like the rest of the world.

She had thought all along she would be married with kids by now.

Even when she had moved away and gone to college and adopted a marginally feminist outlook on things, the notion of tradition still appealed to her. She wanted the starry-eyed marriage proposal, the church wedding, the honeymoon. She wanted to be carried over the threshold, even if she did not want to wind up a housewife with no career of her own, no life outside the husband and kids. She wanted it both ways. Even in terms of men, she wanted a blue-collar boy who was a white-collar man. Someone from her tribe who understood the strengths and the limitations of that tribe. Someone from the neighborhood who wanted more than a civil service pension and an engraved barstool down at Johnny Mac's. Somebody who was interested in the larger world. She'd always wanted it both ways. Her mother used to get a big kick out of all the plans she had, the notions of life that were not always endorsed in the neighborhood.

Her mother had come to her in her feverish hospital dreams. She was there with her smile and her kindness and her amusement. She remembered moments as a girl when it was just the two of them. They lay in bed and read until they fell asleep together. They used to take turns brushing each other's long hair. A wallop of loss hit her, a feeling close to despair. It was times like these that her mother was the only person she could talk to, glean understanding from. She began to sob quietly, tears mixing with the steam on her face.

After a while, she calmed. She stood, the cool air tingling on her skin, and dried herself with a towel. Again, she considered calling Jimmy. She wondered if she was capable of forgiveness. She wondered if there was any turning back, or if she would just be resentful and expect him to disappear again. She wondered if she just wanted to punish him.

She was going back to work. That much she knew.

Jimmy typed up his résumé thinking, What a load of horseshit. It was something he had never done before. He had gone from construction to political jobs, where you were hired on what you could do and who you were sponsored by. In that insular world, one job led to the next, and as long as you were ambitious and diligent, you prospered. Until you knocked someone on his ass. He printed out the résumé and read it. It was as good as it was going to get. He read it again and realized he had used his downtown address. Shit. He changed it to his Inwood address.

He took out his union cards, which were a little smaller than playing cards. His Teamster card was adorned with the two horse heads and wagon wheel, references to the days when a teamster was someone who made deliveries with a team of horses. His Laborers card displayed crossed American and Canadian flags. Laborers International Union of North America. The two cards had helped him pay his way through two years of Manhattan Community College, his BA degree and master's from Fordham, which he earned at night, sitting at those desks dirty and tired from humping all day. After graduating, he had kept paying his union dues, almost without thinking about it. He wondered if he was hedging his bets all along, keeping fallback options open. One bit of advice from his father was don't burn your bridges. He was glad he had kept up his dues. You never know in life. There was no way Keefe would let him work with the Teamsters. But the Laborers were another story. His father was right, it was a decent racket. There were worse fates. He placed his résumés in a manila envelope and shut off the computer. It was three o'clock. He fought the temptation to head to Johnny Mac's. He did not want to get in the habit of drinking away his days in the bar.

He took Quill's leash off the back of the door, and the dog came scurrying across the floor, digging its nails into the linoleum in a futile attempt to stop at Jimmy's feet. The dog careened off the cabinets, rolled on its side, where it lay looking up at him.

In the park he let the dog run free and walked along, enjoying the day. He looked about the park. All the other people in it were retirees, old ladies, or bums. Not fuckups who screwed themselves out of a job. He could not help but feel guilty about being unemployed. After a time, he coaxed Quill back into his collar and retraced his steps home.

His father stood bouncing a handball off the hardwood floor of the living room. He was dressed for exercise. "You want to go?"

Jimmy shrugged. "Why not. How was work?"

"What do they say? Too good to be true."

"What's the story with that? You go from the dole to one of the best spots in the local. It's at least a little suspicious."

"Never kick a gift horse in the mouth. Lou Condo arranged it. He's a good man. But I'm staying on my toes. With Keefe nothing comes for free. And hey, at least someone in the house is working."

Jimmy had no response to that. His father snatched up the handball.

"I seen you brought your things back."

"Yeah," he managed. Being on the brink of thirty and moving back home was something he had never envisioned. Not once. "All right if I stay a while? Till I get things sorted out a bit? Won't be long."

His father laughed. "Why not. It's nice to have someone back home. I'm turning into a lonely old man. Besides, you can do all the chores."

"Yeah, no problem." Jimmy stared at the floor.

His father placed his hand on Jimmy's shoulder and squeezed. "Come on, don't worry about it. It's temporary. Let's hit the court."

"Thanks, Dad."

"Least I could do, James Patrick." Mike rubbed his head. "Now grab the trash, will you?" His father had quite a guffaw over that one.

As they neared the court, Mike said, "First time I ever came to Inwood was to watch my father play right here. Him and a bunch of old TWU guys. Coming from St. Jerome's, this was like the promised land. Elevator buildings, this park. It seemed like a different planet altogether. We thought if you lived here, you were rich. When we moved up here, we figured we had made it."

Jimmy watched his father windmill his arms and start deep-breathing exercises in order to limber up. He then did a series of toe touches. He looked like a drill sergeant in an old war movie. He wore gray sweats and black Pro-Keds, a torn fingerless glove on his right hand. He was so old-school, Jimmy wanted to laugh. Jimmy bounced the ball several times, then began tossing it softly above his head, a bit higher each time.

"You look like a gym teacher from, like, 1948."

"What those set you back?" His father was pointing to his sneakers.

"About a C note." Jimmy shaved a bit of the ticket price off his New Balance cross trainers.

"They must've seen you coming." He pointed to his own. "Eighteen bucks. You think yours make you run any faster?"

"Let's go, Grandpa."

The blue sphere ricocheted hard off the concrete wall, slicing in defiance of physical laws. Jimmy, carrying the wear of ten thousand days fewer than his father, was hard put to compete. His father was all deft strokes, quick feet, and mastery over angles. Jimmy's breath was coming hard as he scurried about trying to get to the ball. He'd hold his own for a short, hard volley, and then his father would lean as if to hit one way and Jimmy would bite, committing, losing his balance, and his father would shift his feet and cut the ball hard in the other direction. Jimmy chased the ball, diving despite the hard surface, and landed on his chest. He got up and tried to breathe through his nose.

"You gonna be okay?"

"I'm fine. Let's go." His father was hardly breaking a sweat, pissing Jimmy off. His plan was to wear the old man down, but this was not going to happen if he could not make him move.

After the third loss his father said, "We done here?"

"No."

Two more games, same result. Jimmy put his hands on his knees and leaned over, gulping for air. He watched as fat drops of his sweat slid down his nose and splattered on the court surface, making darkening circles like wet paint. His breath hurt his lungs. His father stood beside him whistling softly and sending the ball off the wall, whack, whack, whack, easy motions, hard rhythm.

Jimmy straightened. "You taking your Metamucil?"

"It's all a matter of finesse. You're too young to understand that, all full of piss and vinegar."

"Shit. I'm gonna be thirty."

His father stared at him as if he was remembering something. "My baby's going to be thirty. Now that can make a guy feel old."

Jimmy intercepted the ball. "Come on. You're doing fine for your age. Let's get a beer."

Cronin drove the Cadillac while Keefe prattled away. They were headed for one of three gyms his boss belonged to. This one, within a few miles of Keefe's home, was the one he frequented most often. Cronin approached a light that had turned yellow and was about to gun it through when he spotted a patrol car on the far corner. He braked for the light.

"Should've run it. Condo sent that prick Dolan out on a job."

"Why's that?"

"Johnny Longo took a heart attack, so he put Dolan out there. I first heard, I wanted to straighten them both out. But I figure it's best to keep your enemies guessing. Fuck with his head and all. Come on, the hell with this light."

"Cop over there." He indicated the squad car.

"Fuck him. I play golf with his boss. Guy wants to be a hero, he'll be sorry."

"Next time I'll run it, makes you happy."

"Everybody's a Boy Scout. So what was I saying? Oh, yeah. So Dolan is down there doing exactly what I figured he'd be doing, playing J. Edgar and the Lone Ranger all rolled up in one. I figure I'll just let him run the show, play it straight like we knew he would. So nobody can say I'm such a bad guy, right? I sanction this prick going out as a working Teamster foreman even though he's running against me."

"What about Magic?"

"Magic. Fuck Magic. I'm starting to look around and I wonder who has he got to back him up on anything? Things are different nowadays."

"He's still the man."

"Yeah, well, we'll see about that. Besides, it's just a few weeks and then it's goodbye asshole Dolan. I figure it's worth what we lose on the skim, a few weeks."

Keefe reached into his gym bag and took out a wrist grip and started squeezing it. "I can't wait to see the fat prick's face, I tell him that." A car had pulled in front of them and was driving along slowly. "Come on, pass this asshole." Keefe's face reddened.

Cronin stayed behind the car as much to annoy Keefe as anything. He did not care to be ordered around.

"Come on, pass him."

Cronin waited till a car was coming in the other direction, jerked the wheel, and headed straight for it at great speed. At the last second he swerved out of its way back into the right lane and said, "You want to drive?"

Keefe cleared his throat. "Ninety minutes, then we go see that guy downtown."

Cronin pulled into the parking lot of the gym. "Right, Frankie." He watched his so-called boss go through the health club doors, then turned out of the lot and quickly backtracked to the man's house. He parked the black Cadillac curbside and made his way to the door with racing heart. It was a twice-a-week ritual that had started a year before, these clandestine visits to see Marie. Keefe was a two-timing rat of the worst sort, and often he was forced into facilitating his liaisons with various secretaries at the union hall, waitresses, and other tramps attracted by Keefe's edgy good looks and money. He'd even endured the guy's grunting and snorting back-seat encounters while he drove around town.

What had started as a simple grudge fuck had turned into something he had not felt in a long time. It was something along the lines of love, or what he figured it to be. He found himself thinking of her more and more. He genuinely looked forward to their encounters. It was a foolhardy and dangerous game, one the man would certainly finish with violence. Keefe believed in the sanctity of his wife's pussy, no matter how much he ignored it. Any violation of that would be repaid in blood. And while Keefe did not scare him, Magic gave him pause. Greaseballs had rules about their women.

But nothing seemed to matter anymore except being with her. She waited at the door, her black hair piled on her head, a touch more makeup than he liked, her sundress snug over aerobically honed hips. She had her left arm stretched up and held the doorway with her manicured fingers, her doctored chest on display, bringing to mind the come-hither bar girls of his war years. Her tan skin looked smoked in the dazzle of midday. He had hardly made it inside when she was on him, pulling at his clothes. "Jesus, Pete. What the hell took you so long? I can't stand to wait anymore."

Their hungry lovemaking was, for her, a means of revenge, but he knew it was also a kind of connection Keefe was incapable of providing her. Keefe admitted as much to him, referring to his marriage as a business arrangement. Something that gave him Tommy Magic's sanction and protection.

"Hey, hey. Easy, Marie. Here, I brought you something."

He took out the necklace he had picked up for her that morning. It was gold with small diamonds surrounding an emerald. It was by far the most lavish gift he had ever bought. She opened it and put it on.

"Oh, my God, Pete. It's gorgeous. I never seen anything like it." She fingered it, turned it so it sparkled in the hallway light. "Of course, I can't let the weasel see it. I'll wear it whenever we're together."

"Yeah, it looks nice on you."

"Jesus, Pete. It must have cost a fortune."

He pulled her to him. "You're worth it. I missed you."

"Tell me about it. I can't stand looking at him anymore. I feel like every minute I'm not with you is a waste of time."

"Yeah, I know, I know. Same way." They kissed. Then she went down on her knees and pulled him free of his pants. There, just inside the door of the man's house, she savored him until he was beyond grateful.

They never made it off the floor. In her arms, his clothes half on and off, they dozed. When he came to, he held her warm, sleeping body to his own. He found her more attractive each time they met. For fifty, she was in damn good shape. An aging Annette Funicello. Beach blanket bingo, all right. She had spunk, dressed to the nines, liked to laugh. Did her aerobics five days a week, ate right, didn't smoke. Worked it. He liked that. Plus there was a hunger in her, a desire to right the neglect and abuse she suffered at the hands of her husband and she poured that into their lovemaking. She could bop with the best of them. He felt his beeper buzzing by his ankle.

"Shit. I got to go." He untangled from her warm embrace.

"I wish you could stay. I wish we were the ones together. Not me and the moron."

He stood by the door and bent to kiss the top of her head. "Yeah, babe, me too."

He bounded to his car, thinking that it was starting to sound too good to him. He had better back off.

"Where were you?" Keefe rolled his head on his shoulders and massaged his face with his fingertips.

"Stopped for a bite, hit a load of traffic." Cronin could feel himself blush. For Christ sake.

"I don't like being left standing around like that, my prick in my hand."

"Sorry, Frankie."

"You keep it up, you'll have to work out with me. Speaking of working out, you should see this personal trainer I'm gonna start using. The tits on her, holy Jesus. I'd give my left nut to wrap them around my schlong."

Cronin grunted in response. He was beginning to be offended by Keefe's foul descriptions of women.

"What's that smell?"

"Smell?"

"Yeah, smells like Marie's crappy perfume."

Cronin stopped at a red light. "I don't smell nothing." He attempted an air of unconcern. He knew he had one thing going for him. Keefe was beyond the ability to conceive that his wife might be cuckolding him. He was far too narcissistic, far too impressed with himself to believe for a moment that his long-suffering wife might attempt to seek fulfillment outside of her lousy marriage. He probably believed the occasional fuck he tossed her was more than enough.

Keefe nodded. "I know that smell. That toilet water costs me a yard and a half for an ounce. A measly fucking ounce. A shot glass full. Jesus, broads."

Cronin tensed, tried to play it cool. "That's steep. What's gold going for? Three-fifty an ounce, right?"

"Broads." Keefe waved his hand across the front of the car, like he was wiping all thoughts of women away with a flick of his wrist. "So you think it's the wrong idea, letting that prick Mike Dolan work on a job?"

"You think it's right, it's gotta be okay." Cronin let out a breath. "But shop steward? Dolan gonna mess with the extracurriculars?"

Keefe was looking out his window. "Yeah. We got a few things. Plus the numbers and the loan sharking. That stays. Magic wants to bust my balls. I can play that game too. I'm sick and tired of the way that old prick treats me. Like I'm his nigger servant. Enough already. I make more money for him than anybody. Ever. He's gotta learn to appreciate that."

Cronin thought this was a very bad idea on Keefe's part. He also thought it was potentially harmful to him. He was seen as being Keefe's closest associate these days. If Magic decided to react badly to Keefe's lack of discipline, the old gangster might straighten Keefe out by attacking him. He figured it was time to start being more alert, keep his guard up. He also wondered how long he should stay in this thing. He was in deeper than he needed to be. He brought his wrist to his face and smelled Marie on him, could summon the heat of her body, her movement, almost hear her when she came. He should back off on that too. He just wasn't sure he could.

Jimmy pulled on a suit in his boyhood bedroom. He straightened his tie and smoothed his hair. He walked to the A train feeling out of place in his business dress. Punchy had told him to come down and talk about pension funds. Punchy was a senior vice president, a muckety-muck, charged with bringing in union money. Jimmy might fit in nicely, he had said over his whiskey on St. Paddy's Day. Jimmy figured, Why not?

Punchy's office was on Fifty-seventh Street. Jimmy entered the lobby and told the man at the security desk he was there to see Mr. Dolan. He took in the opulence of the place. It was hushed, past lunchtime, with suited folks moving in and out, talking quietly to each other. They all seemed to have a grave and important air. They were

171

responsible for large sums of money, he imagined. Directed to the thirty-first floor, Jimmy signed the ledger and took the visitor's pass.

The elevator door opened on a woman receptionist. Behind her was a glass wall that looked out over the park, stretching northward.

"I'm here to see Pun . . . Pius Dolan."

"Punchy?"

"Yes."

"Have a seat. He'll be right out."

The couch was black leather. Jimmy could get used to this. Plush offices, expense account, corporate travel, secretaries. Money. More money. A life he aspired to. After a while Punchy emerged, his suit looking rumpled, bags under his eyes.

"Jimmy. You meet Esmeralda? You're both from Inwood."

"Oh, really, whereabouts?"

"Sherman Avenue."

"I live on Seaman."

"Small world, small world, indeed. Come on, Jimmy, follow me."

Jimmy followed Punchy through a warren of cubicles until they emerged in a hallway lined with offices. Most doors were closed, but as they passed the occasional open one, Jimmy caught a glimpse of the view northward. They arrived at Punchy's office and on their way in passed a secretary reading a fashion magazine. Jimmy was sure Punchy could sign him up right there and then. He'd fill out a few forms and get busy. He knew plenty of labor guys, men with whom he could arrange meetings, induce them to conduct business with the firm. Commissions would flow into his account, he'd buy a large apartment in the city, a house in Greenwich, dine at the finest of restaurants. He started counting the money he was going to make.

"You know anything about finance?"

"I was an economics major."

Punchy stared down at a folded copy of the *Daily News*. "These New York Knickerbockers have been killing me. You know anything about ERISA? Pension funds?"

"A little. I can learn fast."

"Nets four and a half over Philly. What do you think?"

Jimmy shrugged. "What do I know?"

Punchy pulled a couple books off the shelf. "Here, bone up. I get you an interview with these guys it don't hurt to be able to throw a few of the terms around. Now, in reality, they won't be hiring you for your wizardry with numbers. Numbers crunchers are a dime a dozen. They need people who can relate to their client base, which is union guys. Guys that will like the fact that you come out of the rank and file."

"What does the job entail?" Jimmy winced at the earnestness in his own voice.

"A lot of shmoozing. Lot of travel. You go to conferences, take guys to dinner, sponsor events. It's not as easy as it sounds. You get a lot of guys been doing business with the same firms for years. Not easy to get involved. Plus with the government all over everything, guys are wary. We offer a good product, but it might take you a year or two to bring in your first piece of business. In the meantime you make an okay salary but you're not going to get rich off of it. Sometimes you'll catch a break early, guy might take a shine to you or you might get a guy coming in like on an election, he's new, wants to set up his own relationships. You get a few accounts, you can make out nicely. There's about a trillion dollars of union money out there, between the public and the Taft-Hartley, and it all has to be handled by somebody. Seattle over Portland? Gotta be a lock, right?"

"You guys are looking to hire someone?"

Punchy hesitated. The truth of the matter was, his biggest account was Keefe's local. It was almost a billion dollars of Frankie Keefe's money that made him so popular in the firm. If Keefe heard he was sponsoring Mike Dolan's kid for a job, they might find pieces of him in all five boroughs. Christ, he really needed to stop making barroom promises, especially to his relatives.

"To be honest, they're just in the thinking-about-it stage. We're waiting to see what the quarterly earnings are. But I think things look pretty good. I'll tell you what, though. Let me get a pile of résumés off you, I'll send them around. I'd hate to see you work for the competition, but I'd hate even more to see you waiting around and then it ends up we don't hire anyone. Can't have that, can we?" Punchy stood and extended his hand to Jimmy. "I got to run to a meeting with the big bosses. But thanks for coming by. How's the old man?"

Jimmy rose, pretending not to know he was being given the brush-off. He still held out hope. Punchy was his father's brother, after all. That counted for something. Even if they rarely got along.

He pulled out an envelope with a dozen copies of his résumé and handed it to Punchy.

"What's this?"

"Résumés."

"Oh, right, of course. Good man." Punchy placed his hand on the small of Jimmy's back and steered him out the door of his office. "Find your way out okay?" He glanced at his watch. "I'm going this way. Running a little late." He smiled his best.

"Yeah, Punchy. I'll be okay." Jimmy left, lugging books. Why was he counting on Punchy? On the way to the subway he bought a copy of the *Times* and right there on page one above the fold was the Mayor being led into a two-million-dollar RNC fund-raiser at the Waldorf by Greg Rubin. He felt cut off from the life of the city, exiled within its walls, disconnected. He'd gone from the white-hot center of things to the margins. Ostracized.

He began to feel down, but fought it off. At Columbus Circle he passed three haggard men arguing over a garbage bag full of empty soda cans. Things could be a lot worse. He grabbed the A train and rode toward the Inwood he had spent his life getting away from. As the train smashed through the subterranean dark, he knew he was about a week away from having to beg money from his father. That would not do at all, was totally unacceptable. He also knew he was going back to work with the concrete Laborers. He detrained at the last stop. A trio of teens in Rangers jerseys held footraces on the platform. He doffed his jacket and loosened his tie as he ascended to the glare of 207th Street. Shit, there was a time when he enjoyed concrete work. He just thought he had done it for the last time.

Why do they call Sergeant Lopez 'Hippy'? He's bald," Tara asked.

"That would be short for Hipólito."

"Got it." Tara and Angela sat in a black van and watched for drug activity in a bodega. Routine buy-and-bust. She had asked for the assignment to Manhattan North Narcotics and was immediately granted it. Gee, it was neat being a hero.

"He's a good egg. Got problems with the wife. She's on the job too. Likes to picket outside our station house when she's off duty."

"Picket?"

"Yeah, you believe it? She stands out front with what do they call those, sandwich boards? It lists a whole bunch of complaints against him."

"Complaints? Like what?"

"You know, he hits her, drinks too much, cheats on her, stays out all night. And my favorite, 'can't get it up.' "

"It says that?"

"Yeah. Ain't love grand. It's like she's an employee on strike or something. Crazy, crazy stuff."

"He hits her?"

"I can't see it. Hippy's a sweet guy. Ask me, she's an EDP. Certifiable. What about you? Last time you were talking drunk about your ex. What's his name, Mr. Made Good? Sounded like you were gonna crawl back to him. You didn't make that mistake, did you?"

"No. Not yet at least." Tara hated the way she got nostalgic when drunk.

"Come on, what you told me he put you through, fuck that. He'll think he's all that and a bag a chips, you crawl back in his direction. He wants you back, make the dickhead beg."

"It's not always so easy. But I don't think you have to worry about me and him getting back together." Tara figured that, even if she wanted to be with Jimmy, their history was simply too overwhelming, the darkness was still with her, the scar of betrayal.

"I don't take no guy's shit. I learned that a long time ago."

A silver-gray late-model Lexus with Jersey plates rolled to a stop on the corner. The driver, wearing a black Oakland Raiders cap backward, jumped out, shot sharp looks in all directions, then ducked into the bodega. The passenger slid over to take the wheel.

"Here we go. White boys, Jersey plates. Look suspicious?"

"Nah. Last whites moved out of here when Nixon was President."

Tara was having trouble focusing. She shifted in her seat and squeezed her fists repeatedly. She was anxious about the first job, itching for some action. She was still not sure how she might react and wanted to get it over with. She watched as the Lexus turned the corner, the new driver looking around, his eyes moving quickly. His head rocked to "Smack My Bitch Up" by The Prodigy, which pounded from oversized speakers like an assault on civilization itself. He spotted them, but his eye kept roving. Tara knew this was because he had seen two females. It was almost its own kind of undercover, working with another woman.

The car stopped on the corner, but was forced to move forward when a truck went to pass it. Tara saw the Oakland Raider come out of the bodega and move with determination for the car.

"Let's go."

Angela hit the gas and cut straight across Broadway.

The roof lookout came over the radio. "Let 'em get outta sight."

They rolled slowly after the Oakland Raider, who had no idea about how bad his day was about to turn. Just as he reached for the car door, Angela jumped out with her badge around her neck, her hand on her holster. Tara took a breath and followed. Back in action.

"Police! Stop!"

"What the fuck, man?" As Angela closed the distance between them, the Oakland Raider put his hand to his mouth.

Tara reached in through the open window of the Lexus and snatched the keys from the ignition. Angela grabbed the buyer by the hair and started slapping his face. "Spit it out!" She jammed her forearm into his neck and he gagged, spitting the two-inch-square manila envelopes onto the hood of the car. Angela cuffed him behind the back and spun him around. Tara was dragging the driver from behind the wheel, speaking to him softly, "Keep your hands in front of you, sweetie," as she pulled him by the ear. She tossed him, cuffed him, and leaned him against the car. "There you go." His eyes were filling with tears. Tara almost felt bad for him.

"Well, lookie here, pardner, a controlled substance." Angela held up the contraband and smelled it. "Yeech. Angel dust? The drug choice of champions. How very fucking seventies." She reached into the Oakland Raider's pocket and extracted his wallet. "What's your name?"

"Wally, man."

"Well, Wally, can I call you Walter?"

People passed by on their way home from work, took in the scene, and seemed to approve, white suburban kids getting some comeuppance. A street-corner jester stopped, staggered to his left, staggered to his right, a muscatel two-step. He savored a little wine through a straw and cackled, "Yo, momi! Check out the Cagney and Lacey."

The Oakland Raider laughed and Angela kneed him in the thigh. "Pay attention. This is important." She read from his license. "River Vale? I used to go out with a guy from there. Man, he was a little momma's boy. You look like a momma's boy. You a momma's boy?"

Angela passed her the license. Tara also checked the registration and insurance forms. Wally drove a brand-new Lexus, registered to his father. He wore urban hip-hop gear, probably purchased in a mall in Paramus with his mother's credit card. His Oakland Raiders cap was on backward and pulled to just above his brow. Wally from Jersey was eighteen. Too bad for him, because that meant his mommy could not save him from going through the system, which meant forty to sixty hours of standing in a shit- and piss-reeking holding tank with a few dozen skels and getting a little moldy bologna on soggy white bread for the effort. A character-building exercise.

"You a gangsta, Walter?"

"She-eet."

"I mean, I'm looking at those fine threads and this car. I mean, you must be the phattest, baddest homey in River Vale, New Jersey. You got a street name? Come on, you can share it with us."

"I ain't saying nuttin."

"Code of silence, hah, badass?"

"She-eet. Can't believe I was busted by a girl an' shit."

Tara slapped him across the face, like a nun might slap a sixth grader.

"Hey, you can't do that!"

"You're right." She slapped him with her left hand.

"Ahh, shit."

"Think this might be your lucky day. I mean, you can't be a gang-banger without a little jail time to your credit."

"She's right, Wally. You'll be the toast of River Vale."

"Daddy's gonna lose the car, you know. Think he'll be happy about that?"

Now the driver's eyes were filling with tears.

Tara mussed his hair. "Don't worry, Walter. Someday you'll look back on this and it will all seem funny."

As they loaded the pubescent dustheads into the van, Tara knew it was a bullshit collar. But still, it was a relief to be back on the street.

Jimmy trudged onto the site dreading the coming toil. His father stood talking to two other Teamsters and held a cup of coffee in his hand. He nodded at Jimmy, just a slight recognition, and continued his conversation. Jimmy yelled, "Hey, Pops!" and smiled as the men turned to regard him.

He followed Liam to the trailer and filled out his employment forms. Produced his driver's license and social security card on request. The company man looked at him for a minute, then stared down at his license. "You look familiar somehow. You ever work for us before?"

Jimmy shrugged. "Not that I can remember."

The man looked at the license once more. "That's weird." He went over and photocopied the documents before handing them over to Jimmy. "All right. Payday's Tuesday. Knock yourself out."

On the fourteenth floor, Liam introduced him to the crew. "This is my pal, Jimmy. Best concrete man in the city." There were two Jamaicans Jimmy vaguely recognized from his days in the local, three Irishmen, one of whom had a large knot in the middle of his forehead, and a squat, homely Italian from Brooklyn named Leo, whose tee shirt read: "I was born beautiful instead of rich." The men nodded in his direction. The sky above them was dark and bore the threat of a storm. The foreman, Thumper, came over and looked to the sky as if searching for the clue to a riddle. He shook his head. "Don't look good, boys."

Jimmy followed his gaze and felt a yearning for rain. He was not sure he was up to this. It had been almost three years since he last held a concrete shovel. He rubbed his soft hands and anticipated the blood blisters. On the other hand, he felt an exhilaration. He missed working with his back, missed the exchange, the ball breaking, the heat in his muscles, the strain, the sense of something done, built, poured, so many yards a day.

The men milled about as Thumper walked over to talk with the super. Jimmy looked across Union Square to the north side of the park and the row of buildings that lined it. He imagined the men putting those up more than a century ago. He heard the burp of a siren and looked down to see the Mayor's motorcade snake through the early morning traffic. He pulled back as if embarrassed to be seen, and realized how ridiculous that was. He told himself this was only temporary, a pit stop on the way back to where he wanted to be. A means to pay bills.

"What are you doing tonight, Jimbo?"

Jimmy turned to look at Liam. Behind him the Irishman with the knot on his head was digging his thick finger into his nose as if he were trying to mine gold. Jimmy turned to face away. "Jesus Christ."

Liam turned around and laughed. "Yeah, that's just Cyclops the Muck Savage. See that knot on his head? He fell three stories and landed right on his face. All that happened to him was that lump. I was ten feet from him when he fell, job up on the East Side. He was back to work two days later. I don't think he qualifies as human. My ma was telling about this show she seen where they think Neanderthals was fucking early humans? Cyclops is the result."

"It's permanent?"

"Yeah, the poor fuck. But I tell you what, wait till you see that hump work. Only guy I ever seen can shovel concrete with two arms, one shovel in each hand. Like he's spooning oatmeal."

Jimmy looked back at him. Cyclops was still digging around, but now he was smiling right at him. Jimmy shuddered. Liam laughed. "Ah, it means he likes you. Man, you been in the land of the cupcakes too long." The clouds broke apart and a silver blast of sunlight fell over the site. The wind stirred and the clouds began to move off as if cued by a stage director.

Thumper came over. "All right, let's get set up. It's show time."

They laid out the concrete pipe and hooked the hose to it. Jimmy was sent to get shovels out of the gang box. He passed them to the Laborers as they waited for the flow of concrete. Liam was on the hose. He hefted it, holding it to his side, as the concrete, liquid and silver gray, began to spill out at their feet. Jimmy bent over and started spreading, thinking, Goddamnit, life is funny. The gravel, sand, cement, and water designed to last centuries. He liked to think about archaeologists of some distant future stumbling across his work and contemplating its origin. He was going to make the best of it, enjoy working with his hands again.

By lunchtime Jimmy wanted to weep. He was ready to drop to his knees in the cold and beg out of the job. If it wasn't for Liam, and his father downstairs, he would. His hands were raw from the friction of flesh against wood. Each shovelful felt twice as heavy as the last. He tried to keep the pain off his face. His breath came short. He did not remember the work being so strenuous. Liam moved the concrete hose back and forth as if it were no heavier than a garden hose. He whistled some tune Jimmy could not recognize.

"What's a matter, Jimbo, not used to the old bump and grind?"

"I'm ready for a sandwich."

"Yeah, well, eat while you're moving, bro. We don't take lunch on this one. All OT. We separate the men from the girls on this job."

"Jesus. No lunch break?"

"We're working six tens on this one, straight through. Don't worry, we get a lull every now and then. You can wolf some shit down. Make you lean and mean."

"Fabulous. This is a union job?"

"Hey, they pay you for it."

"Yeah."

The concrete pump started its rhythmic beat. Liam picked up the hose and the men fell back into the task. Jimmy blew his nose on his shirt, then grabbed his shovel and joined in.

The line of agitator trucks wrapped around the block. Plump metal behemoths waiting to discharge their hot gray gruel. The pump was broken, and the superintendent pranced around, his face red, screaming, his arms flapping like a deranged bird. Each truck held thirteen yards of concrete hardening to uselessness, the only perishable product in the construction business. Up above, on the floors, union men at a good wage waited, shooting the shit, relishing the momentary rest. Rolling their shoulders, keeping loose in the cool air while traffic snarled, horns brayed, drivers shouted at each other.

There was nothing Mike could do about the pump. He ducked back into his trailer to avoid the spectacle of the out-of-control super. At least there had not been an attempt to deliver scab material in over a week. By the third day on the job, he had turned away eleven nonunion delivery trucks. As he expected, his predecessor had quite a racket going on and he knew it was with the full cooperation of Frankie Keefe. He was still perplexed by the fact that Keefe was letting him keep the assignment. He figured Keefe wanted to keep him tied down to a job to prevent him from going around the city to other sites, campaigning. He could not have resisted taking the job. The money was too good.

In the mornings he used to meet Liam on the corner of 207th and Broadway and they rode the train together to Fourteenth Street, where they transferred to the Canarsie line. He felt good having Liam with him, like a kind of bodyguard. The kid could handle himself. And now Jimmy would be with them. They had not worked on the same project in ten years. He liked the idea of spending the time with him, of going to work again, with his son.

Mike watched out the window as a gaggle of Keefe supporters took the delay as an opportunity to hold an impromptu rally for their man. They held signs exhorting Teamsters to vote for Keefe. They approached the trailer hooting and calling out to him, taunting. Mike pulled the blind down and turned on the radio.

Liam popped his head in. "Hey, Mr. D, just checking. You need any help?"

"They're entitled to their fun, Liam."

Liam came into the trailer. "What's with the assholes?"

Mike went over and looked out the window of the trailer. There were now almost a dozen picketers. He noticed among them some of the local's worst element. A collection of ex-cons and leg breakers Keefe sent around to deal with recalcitrant contractors or members. Among them was Kieran Patten, who had just beaten a homicide rap. There were rumors of jury tampering, secretive payoffs. Keefe supposedly had a line on jury members through connections with certain court employees.

"Just breaking my shoes. Par for the course with these guys." Mike tried to affect a nonchalant air but he was growing more concerned. The incident in Johnny Mac's was a sinister warning. The thought that Keefe might actually have him killed was starting to fester. He realized now that taking this job might have been a mistake. It was a perfect trap. Keefe knew exactly where he was each day. This was a six-day-a-week job. His movements would be monitored. A truck loaded with rebar pulled up. It screeched to a halt. Mike looked out again and saw the driver jump out and engage in a round of backslapping and handshaking with the goons. The concrete pump started again, the rhythmic pop and hiss, and the men moved back to their trucks. Somebody threw a bottle at the trailer.

Liam took the arrival as his cue. "I better hit it. Listen, any problems, I'm right here. You let me know. I'll swing down here like Batman and Robin, James Fucking Bond and Bruce Lee all rolled into one. I got your back, Mike. Jimmy woulda come down, but his first day and all, I told him I'd check it out."

"Thanks, Liam, I'll be okay."

Mike was convinced that outside of a couple dozen hard-core bad guys who used the local as their own private racket, most of the men wanted change. They wanted Keefe gone, three decades of Keefe domination backed by the mob gone. But most guys just did not want to rock the boat. People who spoke up were ostracized, blacklisted, or worse. For the first time in his twenty-year crusade, Mike was actually afraid for his life. He finished his coffee and pulled his jacket back on and donned his hard hat. It was time to get back to work.

Later, as the sun was falling behind the site and the air was cooling, Jimmy worked alongside Liam, rinsing down the equipment. He washed the concrete off the shovels and then jabbed them into a pile of sand to remove the residue. Despite the soreness, he felt good to be using his body again, and realized he had missed labor. They locked the tools into a gang box and rode the lift down to the ground floor, where his father was waiting for them.

As Jimmy shuffled up, his father stood smiling. "Tough day, huh, kid?"

"Nah, Pop, I was hoping we would work straight through to midnight."

"You look like something run over by a truck."

"It's genetic."

"Ol' Jimmy was gasping for air by lunch, crying for mercy."

"Well, that's the problem. There was no lunch."

"Shit, eat lunch, it only slows you down. Wanna take a nap, you're done eating."

"I think our Spanish friends have the right idea, that siesta thing."

"Lazy spickeroons."

"Who decided lazy was such a bad thing to be, what I want to know. Probably some uptight asshole, somebody who never had any fun, wants everybody else to be miserable right along with them."

"Work is good for you."

Jimmy felt the weight of the day's work with each step. As they walked off the site, his father put his arm around his shoulder. "Good to have you back, Jimmy. Good to have you back." They walked toward the subway, carrying their hard hats under their arms, as dusk came over the city.

Gregov Duskin, forty-three and put together like a collection of bowling balls, watched the job from a dulled-down Buick LeSabre. The back seat was littered with orange peels and coffee cups, the odd half-eaten donut, a deflated soccer ball. Beside him was his cousin, a whippet-thin man made jumpy from all the ordnance and slaughter he'd seen in Grozny. They had to be brazen, to shed blood spectacularly. Their boss wanted an impact hit. It was Gregov's job to make his boss happy. He was ex red army, a trained assassin, confident in his ruthlessness. In Russia he was the man they called in for high-profile hits: foreign businessmen, government officials, other crime lords. When his bosses decided to invest time and resources in America, he was one of the chosen. As always, he insisted on bringing his cousin. After passing by the job site one last time, they sat in a diner on First Avenue. The waitresses were Polish and kept their distance. Gregov watched his cousin dig a wart out of his hand with a pocketknife. He was absorbed in his work; the blood trickled down his wrist. A woman at the next table looked over, retched, gathered her shopping bags and left in a hurry. Gregov waved his cup for some more coffee, smiling to the best of his ability.

He enjoyed his cheeseburger, savored its greasiness. His cousin wiped the blood up with his napkin and sipped his Coca-Cola. He was not much of an eater, his cousin. He had spent much of his youth in Russian prisons. A ruthless street killer by the time he was thirteen, he was freed to join the war in Chechnya. When he spoke of his time there, his eyes brightened. Gregov wondered if there was anything left of the man's soul. Mayhem seemed his only entertainment.

Gregov thought one of the waitresses, an attractive brunette, recalled a whore he knew in Brooklyn. Maybe he would come back another time and ask her out. He finished the last of his french fries, sopping the ketchup off his plate with them. He sat back and lit a cigarette, smoking it down slowly. He watched his cousin watch the people pass by outside the window. The day was gray, and everyone seemed dour and in a hurry. It reminded him of home. He figured his boss was working with the Italians on this one. Gregov felt a strong disdain for the Italians. He thought they were weak and old, or young and stupid. He estimated maybe ten years before they were pushed aside, permanently. He lit a fresh cigarette off the end of his finished one. He ran the plan over in his head. It was a routine he had used many times, in many places. They would steal two cars and use a third driver, a follow car. Hit, drive two blocks, change cars; the streets would be busy, much traffic. A coin toss would determine the shooter. Thirty minutes later he would be back at his apartment in Brooklyn with his French girlfriend, a student at NYU. Easy American money. He pushed back from the table and his cousin, as always, followed.

Cronin left Marie dozing in the hotel room and hustled through Times Square. He stood on the corner disoriented by the razzle-dazzle, the smooth glow of the place, the touristy swirling. He had lost his virginity just steps from here three floors up in a flophouse hotel for a worn twenty-dollar bill. Almost forty years later and he could still smell the crude sweet perfume and liquor breath of that whore. He came on his second stroke, and the whore had chuckled and patted him on the head in a gesture he recognized now as being strangely maternal. Now he looked at all the sterile blandness around him and felt a yearning for the furtive, seedy midtown of his youth.

He walked to Eighth Avenue and ducked into the subway, where he made his way past the quartet of musical Peruvian Indians who seemed to be stationed there round the clock. The leader played a flute while some fresh blond Connecticut girls looked on. On the uptown A, he put the headphones of a Walkman on. Dion crackled with Bronx street-corner energy. As he sped along the underground rail, he considered Mike Dolan. He recognized the man as a true believer and a do-gooder, qualities he both pitied and envied. It was time to sit down with the man, have a little heart-to-heart, see if he might talk some sense into him. They were, after all, contemporaries and men from more or less the same place. He did not want to see the guy get hurt, or worse.

Cronin got off at the last stop and walked to Seaman Avenue, where he sat on the hood of a parked and battered '72 Nova. He waited, listening on his headset to a breaking news story about a cop shooting. He imagined the sorrow that would follow in its wake. He watched as young mothers pushed strollers along, far outnumbered by the ancient holdovers of a dying city, the retired bus drivers and cops and motormen and firemen and elevator operators. He watched them shuffle along. Most were solitary figures slipping toward death on their civil service pensions. He knew these were the diehards, the ones who would not leave on their own volition. He admired their resilience. The sun cast a light and it might be 1957 or 1937 or 1977, a timeless snapshot, but then a car rolled by blasting some rap music that rattled windows, a quartet of homeboys slung low and sipping from bottles draped in brown paper, tattooed arms tapping the side of the car to the hyperthyroid beat. The pedestrians, young and old, glanced quickly in annoyance. Here was the present, intruding rudely on their daydreams.

Cronin watched as Dolan came toward him up the street. He slipped off his headphones and put the Walkman in his pocket. Here was a guy, if he lived long enough, would certainly be one of these white-haired shufflers. He already moved with the weight of solitude. His shoulders were just beginning to stoop toward the sidewalk. His hair showed a lacing of silver in the afternoon light. He carried a cup of coffee in one hand and held several folded newspapers pressed between his arm and his side. He tossed the coffee cup in a trash can.

Cronin waited till he was a couple doors down and then walked to cut off his entrance. Dolan pulled up and took his hands out of his pockets. Cronin held up his hands as if to say, Take it easy. Dolan looked around quickly to assess the threat level.

"Hey, Mike, let's take a stroll. We need to talk."

Dolan stood for a minute. He stared with a level of disdain that made Cronin feel uncomfortable. Cronin felt a kinship with the man that he was unable to articulate. "Come on. Just a stroll and chat. I ain't here to give you any grief."

Dolan shrugged. Cronin figured the man realized that he was not about to deal out any violence here on a sunlit afternoon with so many witnesses. They walked up toward Baker Field, where Columbia track-and-fielders were being put through a limbering routine by a potbellied coach.

"You know, Mike, I grew up in the Heights. Incarnation." He let that out there, a Catholic parish up the hill. The two neighborhoods

186

were just blocks apart. Most people considered them the same thing. "We used to come down for all the games here. Kind of funny us rooting for Columbia and all when those people didn't want to have anything to do with us."

"I suppose so."

"I remember one night, shit, sometime in the sixties right before, no, right after I got back from Nam. We got in a fight with this pack of hippie assholes who were trying to break up the game. Protesting about a war none of them would ever have to worry about going to."

"I was there."

"No kidding. You were there that night?"

"No. I was in Nam."

"No shit." Cronin, of course, knew this. The man had been at the Ia Drang valley in November of '65. Eight hundred U.S. soldiers were overrun by twelve thousand North Vietnamese Army regulars, sustaining a casualty rate of over eighty percent. It was considered one of the most horrific American experiences of the war. A firefight that raged for almost fifty hours. Things went so poorly that the GIs called in arc-light bombing strikes on their own positions. At night the Vietnamese wandered around giggling as they castrated the wounded. It was when Cronin learned this that he realized Dolan might be impossible to deal with. How do you scare a man that's seen that kind of hell? The man would not rattle easily and this is what worried Cronin. They walked silently down Indian Road to Inwood Hill Park. They walked to the edge of the water and looked out over the Henry Hudson Bridge, which spanned the Spuyten Duyvil, where the Hudson and Harlem rivers met. Cronin knew it was Dutch for Spitting Devil.

"You know this boss of mine. The guy ain't the most reasonable guy around. I wanted to come talk to you before things get too crazy. I'm here on my own accord. I mean, Mike, you seem like a decent, stand-up kind of guy. I think we came up the same way. I think the smart thing here would be maybe to kind of lay low, you know what I mean, not rock the boat so much that everyone ends up in the drink."

Dolan just stared out at the Bronx. A boat crew from Columbia slid into the water and pulled its way to the middle of the river. Cronin felt his efforts, as he had suspected, were going to be futile. He picked up a rock and rubbed the grit off it. He skipped it across the surface of the water. It bounced a half dozen times before disappearing. He felt a strain in the back of his arm. Christ, getting old was no fun.

Dolan pointed to the bridge. "When we were kids we used to jump off of that and swim. I was the only kid that jumped off the car bridge. Well, me and a kid named Chickie Donohue. It was just one of those things. I made up my mind and I went and did it. My best friend at the time begged me not to do it, was practically in tears. The other guys were yelling jump, jump, jump, but no one believed I would do it." He stared up as the cars slowed for the toll, looking as if he was tracing the arc of his plummet decades ago. "Well, I jumped."

"Mike, no one is accusing you of being the kind of guy that won't go all the way. Listen, you are in a good spot here for getting something for yourself. Work is booming, couple jobs coming up, long-term, ones you can retire on. You know you're not going to win. Keefe has the local sewed up, Mike, you know that. Why not just take something for yourself? We'll leave you in that spot, you can run the show, do things your way. Soon as it's over, we send you to the next one. It's the smart way to go." Cronin felt a powerful need to confess to him, to bare his true identity. He had to try to keep the man alive. He knew his bosses had no great incentive to do so.

Dolan pointed to the tree line. "You know, there were Indians living in these woods, in caves up there, right until the 1920s. That's three hundred years after their ancestors sold them out. For how much worth of beads? We had skyscrapers, airplanes, luxury liners, telephones, assembly lines."

Jesus Christ, the guy's a dreamer. The most dangerous kind of man. "Way I see it, them selling out was a hell of a lot better than getting burned out." Cronin could not keep the disdain out of his voice.

They stood in silence. A young couple came out of the woods and sat on a park bench a hundred yards off. The girl straddled the boy and they started dry humping right there. Cronin turned and looked Dolan in the face. "This thing is a lot bigger than you against Keefe. Lots of people are not happy about your fucking crusade, Dolan. There are a lot of heavy people, way above and beyond Keefe, that are rooting against you. You keep it up, you're gonna end up on *Unsolved Mysteries.*"

Dolan returned his look and nodded. He paused for a minute, then said, "You know something, Cronin, you might be right about us coming up the same way. I don't know. But what I do know is you sure as hell ain't the same as me now. Tell Keefe he can kiss my Irish ass."

Cronin watched as Dolan walked away. He breathed heavily through his nose. Out on the river the coxswain started barking instructions. A police helicopter rattled overhead and turned to follow the wide expanse of the North River back downtown. On the park bench, oblivious to all else, the young lovers went at it with a spastic rhythm. Cronin walked down to the river and watched the mad current swirl and grind. Dolan survived the Spitting Devil and the NVA, but he might have a harder time with a psycho Teamster, not to mention the mob and the government. He turned and caught a glimpse of Dolan retreating toward Seaman Avenue. He figured he was watching a dead man walking.

For two weeks, Jimmy rode the train downtown with his father and Liam. After the first few days his body settled into the new rhythm, the strain became bearable, and he slept like the dead. He accepted the needling over his new status. He looked at it as a reprieve, a way station, and was determined to make the best of it. After work they headed toward the Old Town Tavern on Eighteenth Street. As they walked along, Jimmy felt the strength of his body, the muscles thickening from the work. It was something he had missed in the white-collar world. There he felt a strange type of inadequacy. He had always earned money with his back, as had everyone in his family going back to the beginning of time. When he had finished school and made the change to the professional world, he felt as if he was cheating somehow, that if you were not sweating you were not working. Now, back in the blue-collar world, he felt the satisfaction that comes from exerting yourself for money.

They pushed their way into the tavern. He had not heard from Punchy and decided to call him. The receptionist, his neighbor from Inwood, acted as if she did not know who he was. He reclaimed his stool. Liam was twirling a quarter on the bar.

"Who you calling?"

"A guy about a job."

"You got a job."

"Yeah, well, a guy about a new job."

"You're just dying to get back in a monkey suit, ain't you?"

Jimmy waved the bartender down. He was Richie O'Rourke, a guy from Kingsbridge in the Bronx, who worked days at the bar. "Hey, Jimmy, how's your father?"

"Good, Richie, good. He's waiting on some trucks."

"He still running against that skel Keefe?"

"Last I heard."

"Your father was always a stubborn bastard."

A man claimed the barstool next to Jimmy, took out a cell phone, and began jabbering away. He waved to Richie. Richie ignored him, then started his ritual, quizzing Liam and Jimmy. He was a master of sports trivia.

"Today's easy. How many World Series did Yogi Berra play in?"

Liam said, "Come on, Richie. That's bush league. Fourteen."

"Jesus, how'd you get past ten? Take your shoes off?"

The man on the cell phone was waving frantically to Richie, trying to place a drink order with some type of sign language. Richie looked at him and shook his head.

"You believe this prick? So, Liam, you still live uptown?"

Liam nodded his head as he chewed on a drink straw. The man was now slapping his hand on the bar and waving with his head.

Richie said, "Hey, hang up the goddamn phone and order like a human, you want a drink. I don't understand monkey signals."

The man placed the phone down and said, "I would like a Beefeater martini with three olives."

"Yeah, I'll be right with you. How's your mom holding up, Liam?"

"She's good, thinking about running for office as of this morning. Put an end to immigration."

"She's an immigrant, from the other side, right?"

"According to her, it's different."

"Ahem."

Richie shot the man a withering look and said, "Hang on, fellas." He mixed the requested cocktail. He placed the martini in front of the phone man and delicately dropped three olives into it. Richie bowed and made a sweeping wave with his hand as if to say, There you go, my man. Sweat on the glass glistened, light sliced through the drink and glowed. It looked like a setup for a liquor ad. The bar was quiet before the rush-hour crush. The man nodded and stretched his hand out toward the drink. Richie snatched it, downed it in one long gulp, then slapped the empty glass on the bar. The man jumped back startled and Richie said, "You know something? When I was drinking whiskey out of a jam and jelly jar with Rootie Kazootie on the label, your mother was sucking my dick. Now, you want another drink?"

The man blanched and looked around for support. "I was only looking for a drink. I mean, I, well, I. You are the rudest bartender I have ever met."

Liam started howling.

"That right? You see that door?" Richie pointed. The man looked. "Now, you see that window?" Richie pointed, and the man nodded. "In three seconds you're leaving through one of them. The choice is yours." The man backed away from the bar and headed for the door. Richie watched him go, saying, "Jesus. People really have no manners today."

They nursed a few beers, and when darkness had settled, they moved toward the job site. As they walked past the fashionable eateries on Union Square, Liam was saying, "I was on the subway the other day, the A train, and this guy gets on at West Fourth Street and he's wearing that fucking perfume the hippie chicks wear. What's that shit called? Something oil?"

"Patchouli oil."

"Yeah, that's the shit, patchouli oil. Crap makes me want to puke. He's pushed up almost against me, and to make matters worse, you know what drives me crazy? Guy's wearing earrings, you know, one in each ear, like a girl. I seen this family the other day, guy walking down the street with his wife and two kids. First off, they're wearing Chicago Bulls jerseys, Michael Jordan shirts in New York, which I have a problem with right then and there. I mean, not that I give a flying shit about basketball, car jackers in shorts, but the two boys, maybe ten, twelve years old, they're both wearing earrings. I mean, what kind of parent lets that kind of shit happen? Earrings on boys. They're gonna grow all confused about all kinds of shit that's pretty straightforward. So where was I?"

"West Fourth Street," Jimmy said.

"Yeah, West Fourth Street. So this cupcake with his hippie chick perfume and his earrings, is trying like practically to rub up against me and shit."

"Practically?"

"Yeah, more or less. I start to think, Jesus, this shit is so heavy in the air. I figure I'm so close to this guy those patchouli molecules are jumping all over me like fleas as I'm riding along. I'm on my way to meet this chick, first date and all that, I'm gonna show up stinking like half a fag. Now, you think, just move away from the guy, right, but the subway is packed. And besides, I ain't the guy polluting the air. So now I'm getting a little pissed off."

"Oh, boy."

"What?"

"Nothing, go ahead."

"So we stop at Fourteenth Street and a few people get off, giving me a little more room. I turn and whack him, just kind of nail him with an elbow in the solar plexus. Nothing that's gonna cause any damage, just a nudge, like, Get the fuck outta here, you stinky queer bastid. The guy's like, ooomph, and falls right out the door just as it closes. I laughed my balls off."

"You're out of your mind."

"Nah. It was a goof. Whoomph." Liam made a jabbing motion with his elbow.

Jimmy shook his head. Liam had an interesting way of dealing with irritants. But the truth was, Liam simply acted the way most people wanted to but were afraid of the consequences. "You still on probation for that thing downtown?"

"Yeah, that. Another six months. Plus they make me go to these anger management classes. What horseshit. I tell the judge, I didn't knock the guy out because I was angry. I was angry, I probably would have killed him. I was just annoyed. You know, I was beefing because this waiter puts the beers down in front of me and says—get a load of this—fourteen bucks for two Buds! Fourteen! So I says, I ain't never paid fourteen dollars for two Buds. This fuck with a Texas twang says, This is Manhattan, everything is expensive. He's talking to me like *I'm* some kind of out-of-town hick, some apple knocker. So I get up and I say, Listen, you prick—and, Jimmy, you know how I feel about this— I say, Listen, this is my island. I was born and raised on this fucking is-land, so it's my island, not yours, asshole. My island. Now, this big doofus, guy in a black shirt and pants, little gizmo in his ear, like he's protecting the President, all muscled up, comes over and he's getting in my face. You know, Is there some problem here? So I look up, guy's gotta be six-six, six-eight. I say, Who the fuck are you? He says, I'm the doorman. I go, Oh yeah? Bang!" Liam demonstrated a nasty uppercut. "He goes boom, right on his face. I say, Now you're the door-*mat*, motherfucker."

"You were just annoyed."

"Yeah. If I was angry, it was at the pussy waiter. Thing is, I hit him, it would've been like hitting somebody's grandmother. So I was glad the other guy jumped in. Let me feel good about hitting somebody."

"Thank God for small favors."

"You got that right, bro."

They stopped at an intersection where a construction site was fenced in, the steel frame of a new building rising above it. "Come on." Underneath the shadows of cranes, they worked methodically, covering all the Keefe campaign bumper stickers with Dolan ones. When they finished, they hit several more sites, then went up to the East Side, where they plastered all the approaches to a concrete plant with Dolan stickers.

They stopped for a nightcap at Johnny Mac's. Jimmy sipped his beer and listened to some singer he could not identify wail about love being like oxygen. This put him deeper into a funk that had been creeping up on him for days. He'd watched as Liam hit on women to

193

unusually poor effect but was unable to join in on the banter. He had not stopped thinking about Tara since that day in the hospital. He tried to sort through it and figure what had changed. He wondered if his current status as loser was responsible. Maybe he needed someone to soothe him, someone to unburden himself to. He hoped it was not something so selfish, something that would vanish once his situation tilted toward the better.

Liam returned from the jukebox and took his stool. "You know, you are the prince of darkness tonight, man. I wanted doom and gloom, I could've stayed home with my mother. Here, I played your theme song for you."

"I had a job, I had a girl . . ." Springsteen moaned a lament of pissed-away opportunity.

"Fuck off. What happened to that cute chick from the Island?"

"The Jewish girl?"

"Yeah," Jimmy said.

"Her grandfather was a garrote and ice-pick man for Murder Incorporated. Let's just say the nut didn't fall far from the tree."

Jimmy stared at the fresh Bud before him. It was a work night, and any more beers would be pain in the morning. He looked around the familiar bar. A quartet of stragglers were spaced along the wood, fastened to their stools by gravity, men he had watched grow old as he grew up, guys with no particular place to go. Liam tapped his thigh to the beat of the song. Fuck it. He wanted to be drunk. The hangover would take his mind off Tara. He sucked down the icy brew. Right back where he'd started from.

Cronin lay in the weak dawn light and waited for the wail of his alarm clock. Sanitation trucks grumbled below his windows. He always beat the alarm awake in the mornings, was always up, anticipating its shriek. He had had trouble sleeping lately and last night was harder than usual. He awoke several times with a tightness in his chest. He felt he was right to be afraid. He knew, somehow, that the man was haunting the margins of his subconscious, lurking, exacting payment for his untimely and violent death. He played the night over in his mind. One reporter had called it an execution, and though he was cleared by a grand jury, he knew that the word was exactly right. He had put his gun in the face of a man and taken it from there. He had gotten away with murder, they said. He thought, On one level, yes. But on many others, he had not gotten away with anything.

He listened to the chatter of the workers and the clanking of bottles hoisted for recycling. He lit a cigarette and smoked it halfway down. He was trying to quit and was down from two packs a day to one-half pack. The alarm went off and he hit it and stubbed out the butt. He stood and made his way to the front room, where he had installed weights. He lay on the bench and knocked off three quick sets of chest presses.

He thought of Marie, of her breathless and reckless phone calls, with Keefe right in the next room, and wondered if the day would present an opportunity to see her. It had been over a week. Keefe was increasingly erratic with his schedule. Dolan's candidacy was driving him to distraction.

As he dressed, he realized that he was losing the line, the boundaries were blurring to a point he knew was dangerous. Yet part of him was beyond caring. He knew that his true employer was unconcerned about the niceties of legalities, was only concerned with making cases, building a portfolio that would one day lead to a directorship. He zipped up the jacket of his clownish warm-up suit, his costume for the part, and stood briefly before the mirror. The light had brightened and was streaming in from the east, illuminating him. He realized he needed a vacation badly. Needed to go somewhere far away and be his true self. As he shut the door behind him, he wondered who exactly that might be.

Cronin drove up from the city sipping contemplatively from a cup of coffee. The reverse commute was smooth. He hurtled past near-gridlock trying to go in the opposite direction. He felt optimistic about the day. Figured he'd be able to get a couple of hours with Marie. An image of her splayed beneath him on Keefe's expensive carpet came to mind. He gripped the wheel and smiled, stirred by her hunger for him. He marveled at her ability to exhilarate him to breathe life into his daily routine. What a wacky world, he thought.

Keefe was standing in his cathedral-ceilinged living room sipping a glass of orange juice. His face was twitching. "You want to hear a good one?"

"Yeah, Frank, what is it?"

"Sol Rosen? This prick, treacherous Jew? This fucking Judas? Word on the street is he's going with Dolan."

Cronin considered the weight of that defection. Rosen was a tough and wily retired Teamster who was still revered by many members of his old local. He also controlled the retiree voting bloc, which was substantial. Keefe's local allowed retirees to vote in elections.

"Are you sure?"

"Sure as I need to be."

Marie came into the living room as Keefe was pulling on his suit coat. They locked eyes and Cronin felt the urge to coldcock Keefe and have at her right there. His face flushed and a heat spread through his body. Jesus, this is crazy. Marie was dressed in a red terry-cloth robe and her face was soft from sleep. She smiled and flashed her tits behind her husband's back.

"Hey, Pete."

"Marie." He worried that his voice would crack, would reveal his true feelings for her.

"Her fat brother hears this, I'm going to get a shit storm of grief."

"Don't talk about Tommy like that."

Keefe looked around like he was trying to place the source of a sound. "I ask you? Oh, yeah, that reminds me, you two are going on a date."

Cronin stiffened. "What?"

"You gotta do me a favor, Pete. Marie wants to go to some god-damn doo-wop show out on Long Island. You mind driving her and her pals out there for me?"

"No, Frank, shouldn't be a problem. I don't mind doing a little wop every now and again."

Marie laughed out loud.

Keefe stared at her. "Doo-wop. Aptly named," he said as he walked toward the front door.

Marie came up and said over Cronin's shoulder, "Have a good day, honey." She goosed him so hard he yelped.

"What's that?"

Cronin shrugged. "Not a thing, Frankie. Not a thing."

As they drove down the block, Keefe chuckled. "Funny guy, that Rosen. Funny, funny guy." He then just sat and stared out the window, speechless and dark-hearted.

As they pulled onto the highway, this placidity worried Cronin far more than the hysterics.

Punchy prepared the envelope for Frankie Keefe's bagman, Pete Cronin. He filled it with thirty-five crisp one-hundred-dollar bills, thinking, Jesus Christ, Mother of Mercy, how did I ever get wrapped up with these no-good greedy rat bastards. The thirty-five went out every two weeks. Just part of kickbacks that allowed Keefe and Tommy Magic to prosper from Punchy's management of the Teamster pension funds. Of course, Punchy had to admit, these also afforded him a healthy living, one which he promptly pissed away gambling like a mad drunken sailor.

He took a stack of hundreds and slipped them into his pocket. It was Tuesday, so he had to make the rounds and pay up. He had taken another beating over the weekend. He watched as Cronin, that big ugly son of a bitch, lumbered into the restaurant and sat at mid-bar. He couldn't come down to the end where I sat, Punchy thought. Guy is a hard-on like the weasel he works for. Pulling this crap just as a little show of power, who's bowing to whom. Irish guys acting like guinea assholes. Punchy sighed and walked down the bar.

He sat next to Cronin and waved the bartender over. "Joe, get me a little whiskey and a drink for Mr. Cronin here."

Joe placed a glass and poured Punchy's Jameson. Cronin watched this silently and when Joe looked up said, "Same."

Punchy lifted his glass, said, "Slainte," and Cronin did likewise. Punchy waited to see what the man had to say. He had never accepted a drink before.

"I hear you had a bad weekend," Cronin said.

"Jesus Christ. Can't I get a bit of privacy to blow my money in peace?"

"Dolan, I don't give a shit what you do with your money. Some of my best friends are degenerate gamblers. Don't make them bad guys. Unless maybe it takes money out of someone else's pocket or food off their kids' table, that kind of situation. So no, I don't care."

"Mighty white of you. I didn't figure you as a guy with friends."

"What about this brother of yours?"

Punchy sighed. "I tried, I tried. Let me tell you about my long-lost brother. The guy is a dreamer, he's got ideals. He might as well be a Buddhist from fucking Tibet as much as I understand the guy. Gimme a break. I can't control him at all. Never could. Like I told your boss, we're barely related. You might as well ask me to petition the Cardinal to sanction gay marriages. I mean, he's my brother. So I guess I love him. But to tell you the truth, I don't like him much at all. And he returns the favor in spades."

Cronin finished his whiskey. He stood and put his hand out. Punchy handed the envelope to him. "Listen. The guy is in trouble. Not fucking-around trouble. He's in about as much trouble as a guy can get into in this world. Between you and me and the barstool here, try to talk some sense into him before it's too late. You understand me?"

Punchy nodded and thought, Why me, why the hell me? "I'll give it a shot."

Then Cronin shocked him when he said, "Thanks." And turned and walked out into the afternoon.

Punchy nursed a few more whiskeys, then decided it was time to head across town to Quinn's Bar and settle his weekly gambling debt. He flagged a cab and settled back, silently counting his losses in his head. He thought of his older brother Mike and how, for a time in his life, he had more than liked him. He had worshiped him. His brother, several years older, was a natural leader in the neighborhood who was looked up to by all the kids of Punchy's age for his charisma and derring-do. He remembered wanting not just to emulate him but to be him. It was the type of brotherly love that transcended all other considerations. I will kill or die for you. Christ, he had even followed his lead into the madness of Southeast Asia.

The cab swerved to avoid an oncoming bus that had strayed into the wrong lane. Punchy, pushed up against the door, tried to place when his relationship with Mike had soured. He could point out no cataclysmic event, no major betrayal or disappointment even. No squabble over money or a woman. No sidings with or against other siblings. He guessed it was just an accumulation of slights that eventually reached a critical mass. The fuck-you-too stage of irrevocable estrangement. It probably began at that pivotal moment when a younger brother ceases to idolize and begins to try to best. The cab lurched to a stop on Eighth Avenue in the shadow of the fourth and ugliest of the Madison Square Gardens.

Punchy pushed his way into the smoky and poorly lit, faded gin mill. He passed a line of kamikaze boozers perched over low-grade hooch. Each sat ignoring the others, their eyes locked on some indistinct distance. Men with lost pasts and no futures—a clientele tolerated to mask the real activity of the place. A television at each end of the bar provided background gurgle and tremulous light. Punchy made for the rear, where, seated over the racing form and a Johnnie Black, was his bookie.

The man, a chunky Sicilian with outsized ears, looked up at Punchy's approach and made the sign of the cross, rolling his small dark eyes to the tin ceiling. He wore wire-rimmed glasses and reeked of something chemical, something Punchy could not name. A neon beer sign bathed him in cathouse red. He said, "Thank you, God. Here is the man putting my babies through college."

Punchy dropped the envelope on the table and said, "Don't gloat. It's beneath you."

The bookie hefted the envelope, peered toward the front of the establishment, and dropped it down between his legs, where it landed, Punchy knew, in a shopping bag with other envelopes. "Fourteen grand. And still you keep calling me."

Punchy sighed. "Even the losers get lucky sometime."

"You really think that?"

"I don't have a choice."

The bookie seemed to think deeply on this. He pulled a pencil from behind his ear and scratched some hieroglyphics on the back of a Labatt's coaster. "I got a visit today from some gentlemen looking for you."

Punchy did not like the sound of that one bit. "And?"

"They were interested in your wagering."

"Anyone you know?"

A phone rang. The man stood and answered one of the six pay phones lining the wall behind his table. His side of the conversation consisted of a series of "ah-ha"s, "yeah"s, and "right"s. Before he sat, two more of the phones rang and he repeated his side of the dialogue nearly word for word. Back at the table, more hieroglyphics.

"Let's just say I am known to them and vice versa. We are competitors of a sort. Men engaged in endeavors on opposite sides of the legal fence."

"You tell them?" Punchy felt a tremor of paranoia. His palms began to perspire. He rubbed them on his pants.

The bookie tapped his pencil on the table. "This and that, some things."

"Come on, Vince, everybody wants to break my shoes. I have never come close to putting you in a bad spot."

"This is true. I told them you are an impeccable gentleman gambler. A throwback of sorts. Someone with the old-fashioned values. Hard work, diligence, promptness in payments. Placing a wager is no crime in our state. I am, however, a bit concerned about this intrusion today. Taking said wagers, as you know, is a felony. And these men take their paychecks from DC, so they don't like to negotiate."

Punchy nodded as a bead of sweat raced down between his ass cheeks. He aspired to nonchalance. "Five dimes on the Knicks. Screw it."

"I need to maintain a certain image, a perception. Please tell me, Dolan—you know, for old times' sake—that this is not going to be a regular occurrence. I want you to assure to me that these fucking guys, with the funny accents and crew cuts, won't be part of my daily schedule because of you."

"Vince, we go way back. Relax, I'll square this away."

"Good. Because in this business, unlike many others, no business is better, much better, than bad business."

Punchy left the cryptlike air of the bar and scurried several blocks south on the avenue. He tried to fathom the reasons for today's events. First Cronin's message about Mike, then this ominous tale from Vince. While there were a half dozen bookies around town he gambled with, Vince was his main one, the one he tried to stay current with, the one who knew him best. He stopped on the corner of Twenty-ninth Street and waited for the light. The streets were surprisingly empty. He stood beside a dirty water dog vendor. Despite his fears, he could not resist the temptation. He ordered one, which he ate before the light could change. It was quite savory. He paused, then decided he was still hungry and bought two more with mustard and sauerkraut.

He felt dark forces marshaling against him. Feds checking on him with Vince. Was he to be arrested? Forced to inform on his partners? Both? These possibilities poisoned his world with dread. And his brother. He owed him at least a phone call. Cronin seemed to be trying to tell him something was about to happen. Something horrible. Why was Cronin bothering to warn him about Mike? He walked over to a pay phone and dialed his brother's number. When the machine picked up, he left his older brother a message of some urgency, then decided to head home and lie low. He needed to sort things out, to get ahead of events, to maintain some control over his fate.

Mike registered the last of the concrete trucks and turned his right wrist up to check his watch. Six-fifteen. They would be finished by seven, another twelve-hour day of nonstop work. He was loving all the overtime. The driver of the truck wore a black hooded sweatshirt with the sleeves cut off over a flannel shirt that was stiff with flecks of dried concrete. He put together his chute, hooking the metal conveyance together, and pulled the lever, letting the concrete flow into the waiting bucket. He leaned against the chute to steady it and took a pack of Pall Malls from the fold of his watch cap. He knocked one out, put it to his lips, and lit it. Mike walked over to him and nodded.

The Teamster blew a plume of gray smoke out his nostrils and said, "Hey, Mike, just want you to know, I'm with you all the way. Lot of the guys are the same way too. They might not want to come out and say it, but they're sick of that prick. Good riddance."

"I appreciate that, Gerry."

"No problem. You want a smoke?"

"Not one of my vices."

"Lucky you. Three packs a day and climbing. I'll be driving this thing around in an iron lung, time I'm fifty."

"Look on the bright side, that's only what, three or four an hour."

"You must be a politician."

The Teamster scraped the last of the concrete off the chute into the bucket. He stroked his thick brown mustache and hosed down the equipment. The rigger hooked the bucket to the crane cable and stood back while the operator lifted the bucket up and away over Broadway, and arced it up over the gathering gloom of a spring twilight, faster than usual, a bit of recklessness at the end of a long day. Gerry wiped a smudge off the truck's fender. He moved the rag lovingly like a teenager tending his first car.

"You know what bothers me the most about that guy? He ain't worked a day in his life that I can see, he walks around in them suits—they gotta go for a grand a pop—hair all pretty, like he's some twat of a movie star, and he comes around the job with all that 'hey, my union brother' crap. I say horseshit. I gotta be honest. I'm no tough guy, just a guy trying to make a living, feed my family is all, but I want to smack this guy like it's nobody's business. Every time I see him I walk the other way, 'cause if I don't, I'm afraid I'm gonna end up jammed up. And that, Mikey, I don't need." He flicked his cigarette to the ground and stepped on it.

Gerry jumped in his truck, called out, "Good luck, brother," yanked on his air horn twice, and stabbed the agitator into the downtown flow of New York traffic.

Mike tilted his head back to watch the bucket rise high above the street against a darkening sky and disappear over the twenty-story lip of the building. The bucket held the last of the eight hundred yards of concrete, the most they had poured in one day. He expected the boys to be pretty ragged from the day's endeavor. Eight hundred yards was a lot of humping.

He went back to the trailer and finished his paperwork. It was all done on computer, the log of trucks and materials that came on the site. Carrying steel and wiring and plank and pipe and marble, bathroom fixtures and concrete, drywall, loads of block, brick, various conduits. Word was out. No scab deliveries on this site. Keefe's underhanded business had shifted to other sites. This afforded Mike a sense of satisfaction, but also worry. He was now taking money out of some very dangerous pockets.

He shut off his computer. He wiped down the desk and locked the drawers. He picked up the picture of his wife and felt a wallop of longing. He wiped the dust off the picture and put it back down. Nothing had been the same for him since that day. At least he was not going home to an empty house. Having Jimmy back, however temporary, was a nice break from being alone. He had never considered bringing another woman into the house. Pushed by friends, he had gone on a couple dates a few years back that he felt, though he knew it was not rational, had soiled his wife's memory. They were also excruciatingly awkward. He knew he would never love anyone else, so why bother? Till death do us part was only half of the deal as far as he was concerned. He shut and locked the windows. Turned out the lights. Some days he recalled her so vividly that it was as if she was still alive. Her gestures would come to him, the way her face changed when a smile broke over it, how her body felt in the late hours of the night, the rhythm of her sleep. She would grind her teeth, mumble to herself, as if all her turmoil was reserved for the night. During the day she was always calm and in control and possessed of an even temper he marveled at. He thought of how she could defuse the tension in the house with her laughter and sense of humor. She made it hard to leave the bed and go to work. He fought off a stab of self-pity.

He put on his jacket and felt unsettled, as if she was close by, in the trailer with him. He preferred this to those days when she would recede, and feel dim, lost to him. He pulled the door shut and checked the lock. He buttoned his jacket. The air had turned chill over the course of the shift. He walked down the three steps of the trailer and waited for the cage to work its way down the side of the building, bringing the concrete crew. He turned to see Liam coming toward him from the inside of the building. The kid never waited for the cage, he took the stairs from the platform no matter how high up they were. He wished he had half that kid's energy. He stepped away from the trailer. Traffic was crawling past, rush-hour horns honked. He looked forward to getting home.

The Russians were parked on Thirteenth Street. Gregov took a pistol and laid it on his lap. He pulled a glove onto his right hand and then carefully wiped all prints off. He checked to make sure the gun was loaded, chambered a round, and flipped the safety to off. He slid the pistol into the jacket pocket of his windbreaker and watched as the target came out of his trailer and stood with his back to Broadway. Gregov took three sharp breaths and nodded to his cousin, who said only, "Is good." He stepped out of the car.

The light turned and the car went west. Gregov crossed the street and, as he moved alongside a UPS truck, pulled the ski mask down over his face. He gripped the pistol and moved toward the target. The blood rose in his temples, he felt his breath quicken, the acid taste of controlled fear on his tongue. He passed shoppers, tourists, a woman with green dreadlocks. He focused on the Teamster. He was light, fast, hard, accustomed to bloodletting. Stalking, up on the balls of his feet, he was singular in purpose.

Jimmy crowded onto the cage. As the crew rattled down the side of the building, he stared out toward the World Trade Center. His father had been working on that project when he was born. He looked down and saw his father waiting for him outside the Teamster trailer. He thought about the time his father took them down to the observation deck and pointed out with pride the work he had helped on. Jimmy noticed a figure in dark clothes moving along the building behind his father. He took a second to recognize that the man was wearing a ski mask, and, by the time the oddity of this on a decent spring day registered, he saw the man raise his hand as if to point at his father. Jimmy started to scream, to call out his father's name over the racket of the cage. His father seemed to sense something beyond hearing. He looked up and Jimmy saw the man's hand jump and spark. He saw his father's head move and his knees buckle and then he was on the ground and the man in the ski mask was standing over him and shooting lead into his body. Jimmy banged the cage with his fists as the other men started to realize what was happening, and all around him the men yelled, the cage still going down, as if it might make some difference.

L iam bounded down the last deck of stairs and turned to make his way to the street. He spotted Mike Dolan watching the cage on its way down, his face turned up to the face of the building. He saw a man come up behind Mike and raise his arm. He could not hear the shots, but he saw Mike go down. It took Liam a moment to realize what was happening. Then he started running toward Mike, and the man stopped firing, looked quickly side to side, then twisted around, pointing the gun at anyone who might make a move. Liam skidded to a stop and dropped to his knees. The man pointed the gun at him and Liam just held up his hands, as if to say, I'm not going to do anything. Then the shooter turned and started moving away, not running, but walking quickly. Liam stood and pulled the zipper on his gym bag open. He fumbled around the clothes, a half sandwich, a newspaper, and grabbed his pistol. He took off, running in the direction of the shooter, holding the gun by the side of his leg. When he turned the corner he saw the man getting into the back seat of a dark blue sedan. Liam yelled, "Hey," and the man turned, raised his arm, and fired once.

Liam flinched as the bullet snapped and cracked the air above his head. He raised the pistol and paused. The driver, thin-faced and deathly pale, turned to look at him. The car was pulling away, but he thought the hell with it, and squeezed off three quick shots, shattering the back window of the sedan. The car accelerated and moved out of sight. Liam stood, holding the gun, the adrenaline thick in his blood. He looked at the gun in his hand and then at the people in the street, some ducking, some sprinting, others stuck, jaws agape, frozen and fearful in the moment.

He shoved the gun in his waistband, turned, and ran back for Jimmy.

When the cage landed, Jimmy pushed men aside and sprinted to his father's prone body. Mike lay twisted like a kid in a midair leap. His eyes stared straight up without light in them. A pool of blood was widening around him. Jimmy dropped to his knees and lifted up his father's head. He felt the softness of the shattered skull, and when he pulled his hand away there were bits of brain and thick, viscous blood on it. He rocked back and forth beyond all caring, the shock coming over him like paralysis. Hard hats stood and shook their heads in disbelief, trying not to stare.

Keefe flipped his secretary over and took her doggie style. He watched himself in the mirror as his stomach and chest muscles rippled. His triceps were looking good too. All that set work at the gym was certainly paying off. He made a note to get more creatine. He worked into a steady and vigorous rhythm, slapping his pelvis off her tight ass, enjoyed the sound of flesh against flesh, the little yelping noise she made when she was working up a good head of steam. Sweat started to trickle down his chest, he leaned back slightly so the light caught him differently, a slick sheen defining him even more. Lorene grabbed the sheets and moved back to meet him. He picked up his pace. It was like another workout, his third of the day, decent cardio. He felt a swelling, a ripple starting to roil through him up from his toes, and he pressed his hands against her ass, flexing his chest and arms, his lats. He thought he might like to videotape this. Then, with a shudder and a grunt, he was done.

He rolled off to the side and lay on his back. Lorene stayed face down. He listened to her breathing, rapid and hoarse. "Oh, God," she muttered, and he took this to be high compliment. He held his fingers to his neck and felt his pulse come down to normal in less than a minute. Amazing. He slapped her on the ass. "That was fantastic, sweetie pie. Terr-if-ic."

She was silent for a minute, her breathing coming down slowly. "Frankie, I want to get some business cards made up. You said I was getting a promotion."

He chuckled. "That's great. What are they gonna say? Lorene—fuck buddy of Frankie Keefe?"

"Very funny." A note of hurt crept into her voice.

"I'm just teasing, honey, you oughta know that."

"I want to have a kid."

He yawned. Yeah, right. "That's nice to hear."

"Frankie, I'm thirty-two."

He thought about that. She could barely keep up already. She had a nice figure but was lazy and would eventually go to seed. It might be time to put her on waivers, bring someone up from the farm system, fresh blood. But, nah, he was actually fond of her. She never complained to his face about anything and she still had some decent miles on her. He pulled the soiled, juice-laden prophylactic off his wilted cock and flipped it on the floor. She'd get it later.

"Listen, we'll talk more about that another time. I gotta get the divorce first, all right?" he cooed. Like he might ever walk away from Magic's sister. "I'm thinking of heading down to the islands for a week soon. Whaddya say? We'll head to the Caymans, charter a sailboat. Watch the sunsets. Drink champagne, eat fish they catch right off of the boat. It'll be beautiful, baby, just the two of us. Real class."

"I get seasick."

"Nah, you'll love it. We'll hire a masseuse, a top-notch chef, the whole nine."

"What if I puke?"

"They got pills for that crap."

"Maybe that would be nice." She rolled on her back. Her tits stood straight, like traffic cones.

"Maybe? What are you, crazy? Jesus, I spoil you too much." He held his arms above his head and stole glimpses at his biceps.

"Keep dreaming, Frankie. I'm spoil-proof."

"I got to get going."

"Running home to the warthog?"

Keefe looked down at her. Her unruly hair fell all about the pillow, her lips curled in a pout. He wished he had time for another go. "Nah. She's out to some doo-wop show. I got a business meeting. I need a shower."

Keefe walked into the shower, turned it on hot, and quickly scrubbed himself. He used an excessive amount of soap and worked it to a thick lather, spending extra time on his genitals. He hated to wait even a minute before cleaning himself after a shtupping. He did not like the idea of other people's germs festering on his body. Little colonies of filthy microscopic creatures wreaking havoc. He imagined epic battles of the little fuckers cavorting up and down his body like it was some Civil War battlefield.

He toweled and then stood in front of the mirror and blew his hair dry. He opened his gym bag and took out a small jar of hair gel and worked it in meticulously, massaging his scalp, moving it back and forth, and finally slicking the hair down. He rinsed his hands. He replaced the hair gel and took out a jar of Oil of Olay from which he had removed the label. He did not want anyone at the gym to think he was some kind of fag. He squirted the pink stuff into his palm, rubbed his hands together, and worked it over his face, paying close attention to the skin around his eyes. He was fighting a running battle with crow's-feet. He leaned for a closer look. Surgery? Nah, not yet. It was something he might consider. On the QT. He trimmed his nose hairs. Turned side to side to make sure there were no errant hairs popping out of his ears, like some freaking immigrant plumber. He poured talc on his chest. He buffed his nails, put his gold crucifix on.

"Turn on the TV. New York One. I want to hear the traffic."

"Yes, Your Highness," she called from the other room.

Your Highness, some kind of wiseass she was. Keep it up.

He dressed and went into the bathroom. He peed and was shaking his cock when he heard the squawk of a breaking news story. A murder downtown. Who cares, some mook probably deserved to die. No need for a special story. Then he heard the words Teamster and Dolan, and recognition hit him like a three iron between the eyes. He yanked up his zipper and caught the flesh of his penis in the metal teeth. "Yeeow!" Clammy, cold sweat, a wave of nausea. "God, oh God." He forced himself to be calm. He leaned on the sink with one hand and clung to his zipper with the other. His hands trembled. "All right, all right," he hissed. He tried to listen to the story, tried to take his mind off his cock, the pain. He gritted his teeth and yanked down on his zipper. A patch of skin came off. He yelped again and looked down at the rivulet of blood. His penis shriveled to a fraction of its normal size as if it were trying to crawl back into his body away from further assault. He muttered. "Oh mother of God, mamma mia, fucking eggs and bacon, oh shit shit shit, you dumb ass, oww oww oww. Fiddle fucking sticks." He sat on the bowl. "Turn that up," he barked. He patted his abused manhood with a bit of toilet paper, sopped up the blood. He heard a story of a shooter and a dead Mike Dolan. "Turn it all the way up!"

He stood and pulled open the medicine cabinet. He grabbed a bottle of alcohol and poured it on the wound. He screamed again. Grabbed the edge of the sink and stared at his face. It was bleached of all color, chalky and lifeless. Aged. Dead. Like he was laid out in a box in some mick funeral home. O'Connor's or McManus's. He wrapped a wad of tissue around his wound and hoisted his trousers, then staggered into the living room. "Try the other channels. Four, Two, Seven! All of them!" Nothing. Soaps, Jenny Jones, a spunky brunette hawking a douche, Muppets.

But he knew the significance. He knew how it looked. He stood by the end of the bed, his hair spiked up and crazed, his prick bloodied, and his world flipped on its ass. He whispered, "What the hell did I do to deserve this?"

"Oh, Frankie, you don't look so hot."

He shook his head. His cell phone chirped. His beeper started a rhumba across the dresser. This was all bad. He picked up the offending gadgets and slammed them both off the wall. Lorene jumped, pulled the blankets over her head. Frankie Keefe watched her cower. He beat his fist off his chest. "What? You think you got problems?"

Cronin made the stop at his safe-deposit box just before the bank closed. The assistant manager, a meticulous gay man of sixty, led him to the room that held his nest egg, his escape hatch, his copper parachute. Cronin bowed his head slightly, and the bank man receded graciously, a prim nod in return. Cronin flipped the lid and surveyed stacks of hundred-dollar bills. He took an envelope from his pocket and added it to the stack. He thumbed through it, reveled in the touch, fanned the bills, and breathed in the aroma of dirty money. He wanted enough to buy a nice little cantina, somewhere in the islands or overseas, some place it never dropped below fifty degrees Fahrenheit. A golf course nearby. He'd grill up fish for *turistas*, serve it with iced-down beer, tropical drinks. He knew the lay of the land well from his Marine days. After his tour in Nam he'd finished his time in Gitmo Bay, Puerto Rico, and Panama. There were plenty of places in the tropics where they were relaxed about a man's past.

He closed the box, hefted it, and slid it back into its berth. The bank was an old granite-and-marble monument to financial rectitude. It was opened in 1886, and although the ownership had changed twice, it had always been a bank. He'd wager that some of the accounts here had been opened before he was born. This comforted him somehow. He might be safer in an offshore account, but something about the electronic age made him nervous. He needed to be able to heft his loot, to feel that it was real. He passed through the main room, where widows were lined up to sock away more savings for rainy days they'd never see.

A retired cop sat watchful, a huge revolver on his belt. The bank man nodded as Cronin passed under the chandelier. The place was a sedate oasis, sealed off from the outside world—marble, bronze, heavy hard-woods, plush carpet. There weren't many banks like this anymore.

His magic number was 250 large, the number he felt would buy his freedom. He was more than halfway there. He knew it was time to pick it up a bit, get a little reckless. He was putting the squeeze on dangerous turf. Word might get around. He was skimming here and there. His timetable was changed because of Marie. He checked his watch. It was time to pick her up.

He made good time to Westchester, and Marie was down the steps and at him as soon as he stepped from the car. He moved around the front of the Buick and opened the passenger door for her. She wore a leather jacket over a short red dress, strapped heels. Her hair was newly fashioned and he commented favorably on it. She looked, in the setting sun, to be younger than her fifty years. Her face was smooth and her eyes bright with anticipation. She was a knockout. He had purchased a new sport jacket for the evening, splashed on an ex-pensive cologne named after a Norse god that she had said she liked.

This, ironically arranged by Keefe, was their first date of sorts. A night on the town. Most of the time it was furtive coupling that always left him depressed, with a kind of hangover from the excitement. He fought the urge to embrace her right there, lest a neighbor might spy them. He held the door for her.

"What a gentleman. Frankie hasn't held a door for me since the honeymoon."

He made his way around the car. When he sat he said, "Let's make a deal. Just for tonight, he doesn't exist, okay? He's not your husband and he's not my boss. We'll have a nice time without him."

She leaned over and rubbed the inside of his thigh. "Deal."

She groped him as they drove. They stopped in a shorefront lobster house and dined on two-pounders fresh from the icy waters of the Labrador Current. He liked the way she tucked into a meal, did not pull that dainty eater crap so many women did. They shared a piece of Key lime pie and washed it all down with a bottle of crisp Chardon-nay and a couple of cognacs.

He took an exit ramp off the LIE and presently came upon the Holiday Inn. The marquee declared it DOO-WOP & FIFTIES NIGHT. Cronin slipped a breath mint into his mouth and took Marie's jacket as they came upon a coat-check girl who was anxious for the show to start so she might get back to the fright paperback splayed on the counter. The lobby swarmed with aging boppers. They tried to carry the extra pounds of middle age with aplomb, but for the most part failed. Flesh strained too tight skirts and bellies tested the limits of sport coat buttons. DAs and bouffants ruled the night.

Cronin placed his hand on the tight top of Marie's ass and steered her to a prime table. He leaned over an Ecuadoran waiter and while slipping him a twenty said, "More where that came from, amigo." He settled down over a scotch on the rocks. Marie sipped Campari and soda.

He felt stupid. Did he look like one of these fools? But the music put him back on the corners of his youth, the summer nights when all was possible and life would stretch forever. And this woman made him feel more alive than he could remember. Marie insisted they dance. He moved self-consciously at first, but she placed her head on his chest and pulled him close until she was his only focus, all else faded to background. There was just the music and the two of them. After a series of turns on the dance floor, they repaired to a table. She scooted her chair around till it was next to his. She draped her arms over his shoulders. Cronin, as was his habit, surveyed the room.

"I want to leave, Pete."

"Now?" He looked around, surprised.

"No. I want to leave Frankie. I want the two of us to go far away. Anywhere you want, just the two of us. I can't spend any more of my life in that house."

"Yeah, baby, me too." He leaned over and buried his face in Marie's hair and let himself relax for the first time in months. He wanted to run away with her, to have a partner for his adventure.

It was on the way home that Cronin heard about Dolan. He had dropped off Marie and was heading south in a trance, excited. They had coupled with incredible heat in the car, right in Keefe's driveway, like kids high on the promise of escape. Near Yonkers he turned on

1010 WINS to hear the traffic report and was crossing into the upper reaches of the Bronx when the announcer related Dolan's killing. Teamster Shot Union Square No Suspects. Nothing between the lines. Cronin wondered what it might announce. What the hell could have happened? Did Keefe do it? He could not believe that he would defy Magic on such an audacious scale. The guy talked a big game but rarely had he taken any action that was not ordained by his brother-in-law.

Traffic on the FDR brought him to a standstill. He had an impulse to turn the car around and pick her up now, grab his kitty, and head south pronto. But no, it was too soon. An hour later he pulled into the parking garage on Nineteenth Street. He drove to his spot and saw that someone was parked there. Damnit. He had complained to the attendant a couple of days before. This was the third time in two weeks the same car, a sparkling new Lexus, was in his place. He parked next to it in someone else's spot. He was tempted to punch out a window or pop a tire on the offending vehicle. He heard footsteps, a couple passed. The man wore a dark, tailored topcoat, the woman was blond, furred, and drunk to the point of collapse. He half carried her head on his shoulder, half supported her with an arm around the waist. Cronin waited for them to pass, wondering how they had driven in such condition.

He took one of his Teamster business cards out of his wallet. He wrote on the back: "Please Do Not Park in My Space Again. Thank You." He lifted the wiper blade and placed the card on the windshield. Next time he was not going to be so polite.

The doorman looked up from his book, a heavy tome of codes and zoning variances, and nodded the dull stare of the somnambulant. A Slavic immigrant, he was studying for a real estate license and often expressed his capitalistic Yankee fantasies to Cronin. "First five million by thirty" was his credo. Cronin never asked, but he guessed by the shadows around the kid's eyes that his deadline was fast approaching. He wished him all success. Some of his own ancestors had arrived on these shores with the same delusions and hungers.

He stopped and checked his mail. There was a letter from his mother, her pinched scrawl instantly recognizable. The return address was a new retirement home in Florida. Eileen Cronin, down with the millions of other snowbirds, was not content to play Parcheesi and knit scarves for her grandchildren up North. She was not an idle one. Last winter he had received a picture of her tooling up the Intracoastal on a Jet Ski. As of late she had become an avid weight lifter. Her farm-girl genetics were serving her well as she approached eighty. He believed that she would outlive all her children. He planned to visit her on the way out of the country, make some type of amends.

Waiting for the elevator, he checked his pager. Eleven beeps from Keefe and five from Roth. Christ. He tossed it in his gym bag.

Except for the various welcoming doormats, it might be a hotel. On his floor, the hallway carpeting was dull green. He entered his apartment, dropped his bag on the kitchen table, and made his way to the living room. His answering machine light was blinking like a maddened stop signal. He picked up the remote control and clicked to Channel One. He crouched before his aquarium and studied his collection of tropical fish.

He poured a scotch and took a deep breath. The news turned to the shooting. Dolan's killing could only mean bad things, but so far there was nothing but confusion and suspicion. Or so the man holding the mike said. The fade-out shot was of the kid, the one who smacked Keefe, kneeling over his dead father with bloody hands and a look stuck somewhere between shock and rage. It was not a pleasant image.

Cronin found himself making the sign of the cross, something he had not done in a very long time. He had genuinely liked Dolan and imagined the kid would be vengeful. He finished his drink and poured another. He paced the room wondering what went down and why, thinking through the possibilities, an old habit from his law enforcement days. Could Keefe have sanctioned it? Was Tommy Magic just cleaning house? Improving his odds? Could Roth or someone in the government have okayed it or at least let it go down? He knew nothing was beyond the range of possibility. People would be shocked, they knew how these things played out on the street. Mike Dolan had placed himself in an untenable spot. The fool had been warned.

Cronin fed his fish. He wondered if it was possible that somebody else was trying to make a statement. He watched as the fish, luminous, cut their way through the tank, gobbling food. The big fish chased the little ones away and fed. He picked up the phone. He had two bosses to call and a world of shit to deal with. Fucking Mike Dolan. The guy should have known better.

Jimmy tried to sleep, but kept coming back to his father's ruined head. His father had turned to him and smiled, then turned back toward Liam. In the next second his head was obliterated by the bullet. Every time he started to go under, the image of his father's death flickered across his brain. Around dawn he jerked alert, his body tense, clammy with bad sweat, poised to shove his father from harm's way. But his father was gone. All that was left was the cold empty silence of his room. He lay on his back unblinking and stared at the ceiling. He realized sleep was not a possibility and took a hot scalding shower. It was too early to call anyone, to make preparations. He made a pot of coffee and sat, utterly alone.

After a time, he wandered into his father's room and sat on the bed. He listened as the sanitation crews started their morning rounds, could hear muffled sounds of alarms calling people from slumber in other apartments. Someone met the day with a wet, gravelly hacking that persisted. He lay back on the bed and pulled a pillow over his face. He caught his father's scent, sparking a rush of memory and sickening knowledge. Quill rubbed against his leg and he picked the dog up and put him on his lap. The dog whined low and constant, sensing the loss.

He got up and put Quill on the floor. He clenched his fists and stood saying no, no, no, trying to believe this was some crazy dream that he was going to wake from. He sat back down and buried his face in his hands, pressing his fingers into his skull with force. His father's clock radio went off, and he jumped at the sound. He stared, confused by the racket, until he realized that his father must have reset it after he woke the day before. The announcer was describing the shooting, and Jimmy ripped the radio from the nightstand and smashed it on the wall.

He moved into the kitchen and tried to calm himself. But he thought of Keefe, and his mourning was transformed into a rage as pure and strong as any feeling he had ever known. He was going to make that piece of shit pay. If he had to march into the man's house and hack him to death in front of his wife and kids, he would get his revenge. His father had put the *Daily News* cover of Jimmy knocking Keefe down on the refrigerator. Now Jimmy beat a vicious tattoo on the picture, wishing Keefe was there with him. He picked up the microwave and slammed it off the door. He punched and kicked and let out a scream. Finally he lay spent on the cool linoleum floor with the knowledge that nothing in his life was ever going to be the same again.

Tommy Magic was up and in his garden before the sun warmed it. He had not slept as well in months, maybe years, a deep narcotic slumber of vivid and harrowing dreams. The Commies had delivered. He had watched the news, then drunk a cup of warm milk and pulled the covers over his head. He had risen with the sun and taken a hearty crap that seemed to set his equilibrium in order. Even his heart felt as if it were purring along; he was yet to pop a single nitro, a record these days. He spread manure and fish emulsion onto the black soil. The stink of it was invigorating. He worked the rows for what seemed the hundredth time. Today he would spread some seed, spring vegetables, snap peas, some herbs.

He listened as car doors up and down the street opened and shut, cars fired up for the drive to work. It was promising to be a helluva day. He had forgotten how good killing made him feel. The sense of power—like fuck you, I am God. He'd give a pickle barrel full of fazools to be inside that prick Keefe's head this morning. Magic chuckled. The mope was probably going crazy trying to figure out what was going on, the bullet coming like a bolt of lightning up his ass. It ought to set the smug little prick straight for a while. He planned to string him along, rant and rave about it. Mess with the asshole's head, make him believe the Magic man thought he was responsible for an unsanctioned hit.

He stood up, wiped his hands along the front of his trousers, and considered the Russians. Maybe he would not bother to pay them. Maybe he would kill them. Maybe he would march right into their little clubhouse and blast them straight to a Commie version of hell. He figured the best way to straighten out the government was to build up his business and hand it over to a group that might not be so willing to take the load of crap the G wanted to hand them. He pushed his wheelbarrow over to the shed and felt a rattle in his heart. He sat at a picnic table and fumbled for a pill. He remembered the days when they might work things out with the agents, do favors for each other. But things had changed with all the Goody Two-Shoes taking over. Lawyers and bean counters who knew nothing of the street. There were more than a few times in the past when the bastards came to them for their dirty work. Like that civil rights thing down in Mississippi, when those Jew kids were buried along with that blackie. He was the man that the FBI unleashed on the fat sloppy Ku Klux animal who would not tell the government where the bodies were buried. He took a hammer to him till the next thing you know the guy's singing like a sweetheart through his busted teeth. The guy had lasted a few hours, he'd give him that. The pricks in the skinny ties had promised to pay a hundred large and only paid twenty-five. The twisted things they did together down in Cuba. All those poor working stiffs with busted heads or worse trying to get decent pay. Well, now it was his turn. He'd get one last shot in at those motherless fucks. He smelled the coffee his wife was making and headed back inside.

When Punchy heard about his brother's death he decided it was time to take a break from his little health kick. He went directly to the bar with every intention of drinking enough whiskey to float a water buffalo in. He sat on the corner stool and dialed in bets that were insane even by his degenerate standards. He was beginning to believe that his safety might not be assured. The killing was appalling, brazen beyond anything he had seen in his long association with bad guys. There had been others, quiet little rubouts with lots of questions and scant news coverage. But nothing so open. The media was on fire with the story. He spread the papers before him, flipped the TV channels continuously, pausing whenever there was a mention. He wondered if it was Keefe. He did not think the man had it in him. For all his pseudo guinea swagger the man was not a killer, as far as he could tell. Those men lurking behind him were another matter altogether. But why so audacious? And why now with the government all over the place? It was better than risking defeat in the election, he guessed, but still.

"Francis." He pointed to his glass. "The holy trinity."

The day bartender regarded him with some alarm. He came over and poured a triple shot of Jameson. "Do not stray," Punchy told him. "I mean business today, son, business."

Punchy watched as the lunch crew came in and took their stations. He did not speak to any of them. He usually engaged them in light banter, a little repartee. But not today. His world was grim, sinister even. He had been contacted the day before by agents of a certain federal law enforcement agency looking to bring down Tommy Magic. They had hinted at various levels of immunity in exchange for testimony. Tried to have him identify with their side, we and you, us, together. It is not too late, they told him. He might even keep a property or two, some cash. The bastards approached him here, at the bar. In plain sight. Two guys in suits and muscles, righteous zeal. He picked up the phone, still warm from his last round of wagering. "Let me get fifty dimes on my brothers from Seventh Avenue."

"Hold on." The smacking of the phone on a table. "Say again."

"You got it right, fifty grand."

"I should be alarmed?"

"Fifty. Vince, you want me to shop around?"

"Fifty. You got it."

Punchy did not stop at that. He placed a call to his financial adviser. When she answered he simply announced, "I need cash."

A pause. Why did everyone always have to wait before they felt they could respond to him? "Hello. I pay you. You give me what I need."

"Punchy, you are not very liquid. I, ah, I mean we can cash in some T bills, maybe move some funds, but we really need to get together and reevaluate your position."

"My position? I am about a mile out of hell, lady, and closing fast. Cash, cash, cash. Get me cash or you are . . . well, just do me a favor, will you, Jennifer." Punchy made two more bets. One on the Denver Nuggets and another on a soccer game in England prompted by a tip from his Irish bar back. He settled in, letting the whiskey work its numbing magic on his dancing nerves. For the first time, he was afraid for his physical safety. My God, if they could whack Mike like that, right on a Manhattan street corner? In broad daylight? He tried to console himself that he was a valuable asset, an earner, as the goombahs were so fond of calling themselves. Still, he was merely a figurehead, a beard, a dupe, a spokesperson, a front, a facade, more easily replaceable than a monkey on an organ grinder. The mob merely needed to threaten one of his business partners. They all knew what was going on. They would protest at first, beg off, try to maintain a distance, the appearance of propriety. But all it would take is an ape like Cronin showing up at some function and accosting them in the men's room, on the way to a car, anywhere. These were not rugged men, schooled in the hard ways of the street. Not a bit. A slap across the face was about all it would take. He envisioned them blubbery and acquiescent. The Feds might have a worse effect. These men lived in fear of things like a dank cellblock and a gang of darkies coming for tribute. They were smart. He came to the terrible conclusion that he was expendable. He waved the bartender over.

"Another, and keep them coming."

Punchy sipped deeply. Whiskey, whiskey, my dear friend. What if word of the little federal flirtation was making the rounds? Assassins might be lurking already, might be bearing down on him, sizing him up, drawing a bead. He had laughed it off, but the bastards knew exactly what they were doing. The day of his brother's murder they decide to lean on him. They were exposing his flank, preying on his fear. Planting a poisonous seed that could quickly lead to his death. Jesus, he did not want to die. Not yet, not violently. He picked up the phone and called Sean Holyfield, a Bronx bookie he employed only when he was in the direst of straits. "Gimme five grand on the Bulls." He placed the phone down. "Hey, Francis, C note says the next one through the door is a broad."

The bartender looked up toward the street, then back at Punchy. He shook his head with a look of sadness, but took a hundred-dollar bill out of his pocket and slapped it on the bar. "Right you are, boss."

Punchy matched it. He sipped from his drink and waited. The door opened and someone came toward them backlit by the harsh light of noon. He saw long hair and laughed, then reached for the bills. Francis clamped his hand. "Hold yourself there, boss man." Punchy turned back to see the beard. "Jesus Christ."

"Nah, not Jesus at all. Merely one of the apostles, I'd say."

"Yeah. Just my luck."

"Or lack thereof."

Punchy considered this. And then he realized, fully, that his brother Mike was gone. My God. Dead. Killed, and probably by people he was close to. Cronin had warned him. What was that all about? He sat on his stool, a fat and lazy middle-aged man who he knew would be incomprehensible to the street kid he had once been. He had a sudden flash memory of Mike rescuing him from a gang of hoodlums who had jumped him on his way to a CYO basketball game. Mike had come in swinging, his face set and deadly calm, a fierceness to him that sent the punks scurrying for safety. It had been a chilly Inwood Saturday many, many years ago. Punchy could hear the crack of blows his brother landed, could taste the salty blood as it snaked from his nose into his mouth. He stood at the end of the bar and looked around, shaken. He took a steadying breath. Mike had never let him down. And now this. A bloody, violent end. Punchy felt a flood of tears come on. He beat them back, snatched his whiskey, and retreated to the sanctuary of his office.

Tara finished her tour and begged off drinks with the crew. She had tried Jimmy a dozen times through the night but got only a busy signal. She was going to go home for some sleep but instead drove toward Inwood. The sun was cresting on her right, a fat and bright globe devoid of real heat. She doubled-parked in front of Jimmy's building and took the stairs. The hallway smelled of Pine-Sol. These buildings that were once so grand now served as either a type of elder hostel or overworked tenements. She stood on the worn bristle welcome mat that had always been there. She knocked, and when there was no response, found the door unlocked, opened it, and came upon the wreckage. She touched her gun, called out, "Jimmy?"

She turned into the kitchen and saw him sitting beneath a shattered window. His hands were buried in his face; a line of blood snaked down his arm from his fist and pooled between his legs. The dog was by his side whimpering, its tail worrying the floor.

She sat next to him and draped an arm around his shoulders. She wiped some of the blood away. Nobody deserves this, she thought. Jimmy was still, tense, pulled tight within himself.

When he spoke it seemed to come from some lost place. "Fuck. Tara. It's all my fault."

"It's not your fault, Jimmy." She held him closer and wished she could somehow ease his pain. He stayed knotted as if he was unable to yield to her embrace.

"No, Tara, it's my fault and I have to make that scumbag pay. It's up to me."

"Jimmy, this is no more your fault than my mother getting cancer was mine."

"That was a disease."

"I still blamed myself for a long time, that I couldn't save her."

"I know that. I was with you. But nobody shot her like a fucking dog on the street."

She knew there was no convincing response to this, so she sat without speaking for a long time until finally he said, "Thank you, Tara. Thanks for coming, being here. But I have to deal with this."

Yes, but I hope you do it the smart way, she thought. Sometime later, they moved to his bed, where together they fell off into a troubled and erratic sleep.

s this some kind of fucking joke? You fucking disappearing on me? I can't have this kind of crap, Cronin." Keefe was twisting his head from side to side and stabbing his finger at the windshield as he yelled. "I'm up to my eyeballs in crocodiles and you are off gallivanting at some fucking doo-wop show with my own wife no less and you somehow manage to misplace your beeper on the one occasion that it actually was an emergency. I am left with a dead, make that assassinated—that's the word used in every paper I got, assassinated—opponent. His head blowed off on a job that, as far as the general public is concerned, I sent him to. Now, how does this look to a casual observer? Do I come up smelling like a pile of fresh dog shit on this incident? I ask you. Tell me. How the fuck does this look? I just might be, what do they call them, a prime suspect, a likely candidate. It's bullshit." He swiveled in his seat and glared at Cronin. "And why was I forced to call you thirty-seven times?"

"Frankie, we been through that already." Cronin was hoping the man would get hold of himself. His ranting was wearing thin, and the day had just begun.

"Well, ain't that nice. We been through it already, like that makes everything okay."

"Christ, look at this." As they turned onto the block of the union hall, they came upon a half dozen news trucks and a swarm of photographers.

"Ahhh, fuck me. Should we keep going?"

Cronin thought for a minute. "You're gonna have to face them sooner or later. Might as well get it over with."

"What the hell do I say?"

"Frankie, tell the truth. You don't know what happened, right?"

"Got a point."

"So go with that. And don't forget to express some sorrow. You know, make believe you feel bad, the guy getting killed."

Keefe shook his head. He was starting to ratchet down a bit.

Cronin decided now was as good a time as any. "You got any ideas on this thing?"

"Ideas? You think I know? I mean, what the fuck. I come out looking worse than bad here. My top suspects? I want to say my brother-in-law, but I can't be sure. The guy, the fat miserable fuck, he's never pulled anything like this before. Even for him, this would be insane. You know the guy hates attention." Keefe waved at the press. "If he did it, what was he thinking? I can't say I'm mourning for the Dolan asshole, but still."

"Anybody else?"

"What, Son of fucking Sam?"

Cronin wanted to raise the possibility of government complicity, but he knew he had to be careful. "Maybe some Young Turk, thinks it's a way to move up?"

"What, and keep it to himself? Which might be par for the course these days with the imbeciles I see. I don't know. I got a bad feeling is all. Things ain't so cut and dried like they used to be. I got a bad feeling."

Yeah. Me too, Cronin thought, me too.

As they pulled in, the press scrambled after them, cameras hoisted, mikes aimed like accusing fingers, all heat and crush, all give us what we want, now. Cronin parked and watched as Keefe smoothed down his hair and straightened his tie. He took a deep breath and said, "All right, let's give these assholes something to do."

As soon as he stepped out questions flew through the air like shrapnel, staccato bursts, an unintelligible cacophony. Keefe held up his hands like a messiah, imploring for order in the crowd.

"We are deeply saddened by this tragedy. Mike Dolan was a good Teamster and a worthy opponent. We will do our best to assist law enforcement in their efforts. I am personally putting up a fifty-thousand-dollar reward to bring the killers to justice. Now I have to get to work on behalf of my membership. Thank you."

Cronin watched and took his cue, moving between Keefe and the reporters, using his bulk to lead the way, lifting the odd elbow. The press retreated under his weight, shouting provocations.

"Why'd you kill him?"

"You afraid he was gonna win?"

"Where's Tommy Magic?"

"Are you a member of the Ferucci crime family?"

Cronin picked up the pace. He imagined Keefe behind him biting his tongue so hard the blood must be trickling down his throat. He felt Keefe's hand on his back. They moved across the lot with the press as in a rugby scrum. Someone barked, "Is this because his kid knocked you on your ass at the mansion?"

Cronin felt a yank on his shirt. Keefe had wheeled, was snarling into the cameras, his eyes pinwheeling with rage. "Who said that? Who fucking said that? Daly, that you? Where are you?"

The crowd parted to reveal a reporter, wearing a rumpled tan trench coat, pen poised over a notepad. "It's a logical question, Frankie."

Keefe lurched forward and Cronin held him by the belt. "Logical? And who the fuck are you to call me Frankie, you twerp." Cronin spun him around and marched him toward the front door.

When they pulled into the office, the staff were all standing at the windows. They turned toward the door. Keefe stood, his breath coming hard and fast, his face muddied with rage.

"What the fuck are you people gawking at!? What? Hah? What? You think I'm a fucking killer? Hah? I'll kill each and every one of you, you think I'm a fucking killer."

At his kitchen table Jimmy took his father's worn but hard-polished boots from the morgue bag. Each was spotted with several drops that looked like redwood paint, but weren't. He looked briefly through the clothes and tossed them in a garbage bag. Quill slouched over and started snorting beside the bag as if he were trying to conjure up his master's presence from the scent of him. Jimmy took out his father's wallet and emptied it. There was his union card, a health-care card, an ATM card, two Mass cards, one for his mother and one, he realized, for his Uncle Ray, and several photographs.

There was one of his mother and his father, just home from Vietnam. They were in the Catskills in their bathing suits holding each other, a river in the background, the trees lush from summer. Dad still bore an angry scar across his shoulder and down his chest from where he had taken shrapnel from NVA mortar fire. He was muscled and tanned, a bright tattoo with his new bride's name on his biceps. Mom wore a conservative two-piece suit and her hair was long and bright from the sun. They were so alive then. Another battered picture was of Jimmy and his siblings at Christmas when he was maybe six or seven. They were lined up in front of a Christmas tree surrounded by a pile of gifts that looked as if it might be enough for the whole neighborhood. The last was of his grandparents back on the farm in Ireland. Somber and tough, looking like they had no illusions about life. Three pictures, three generations. He turned the picture over. "Kilnaleck 1925" was scrawled across it in faded ink. Within a year they would be in New York. His grandfather would find work on the IRT, eighty-four hours a week for thirty dollars; his grandmother would raise six kids in a cold-water walk-up, scrounging to make ends meet. What a leap. From a stubborn little farm in the middle of nowhere to a stinking tenement in the South Bronx.

Jimmy considered their hardship. He wondered if he had the fortitude to do what they had done. He had been raised with the stories, heard of the struggles, the toughness. Immigrant America. He figured it was part of what drove him to succeed. He had wanted to validate their sacrifice and their gamble.

He looked at his mother's funeral card, which had a picture of Jesus the Good Shepherd on it, carrying a lamb over his shoulder. He read the prayer. He sat and stared. He looked down at his father's boots. He picked them up and turned them in his hands, looking at the bloodstains, the concrete dust and site dirt in the creases. He flipped them up and looked at the soles, worn and smooth where they had borne most of his weight. His father would be about ready to have them resoled. He'd bring them down to the old Italian shoemaker whose shop had not changed in the last quarter century. Jimmy took the boots and walked to the door, where Quill was still nosing around the bag of clothes. He bent and stroked the dog's neck and nudged him aside gently. He opened the door and placed his father's boots outside, next to the welcome mat.

Cronin sat at the bar and watched Keefe canoodle with Lorene. It was the first time the lunatic had calmed down since the Dolan hit. Cronin enjoyed his beer.

"That's some wild shit went down in Union Square," the bartender said.

"I'd say so." Cronin looked at his watch. Ten minutes he'd call Marie. He turned his back to the room, positioning himself so he could monitor his boss in the mirror behind the bar. The guy was half convinced they were going to come for him. He had been ducking Tommy Magic, which Cronin figured was really stupid. Yet Keefe seemed to have forgotten his troubles the minute they picked up his squeeze. Cronin ate a grilled shrimp appetizer, washed it down with a cold beer. He licked the garlicky oil from his fingers and watched as a crew of Wall Street types started clipping the ends off plump Cuban cigars.

Their cigars lit, they ordered several bottles of Cristal champagne to toast a deal. They roared with good cheer and fat success. Cronin envied them. They seemed oblivious to all but their own good fortune. He dealt in half-truths, lies, and violence, and operated on the cold margins of a system that these revelers knew little about. He'd made a career of keeping the bad things under control.

Cronin heard a commotion and turned toward the door. A man, decidedly old for this crowd, was arguing with the bouncer, who stood with his sinewy arms folded across his chest. The older man started stabbing his finger up to the face of the doorman. Cronin noticed, with alarm, that the gray-haired guy was Tommy Magic. He stopped drinking, put his beer down on the bar, and moved quickly to the maître d', who was watching the scene with detached superiority. Cronin pulled him by the elbow and informed him whom his underling was harassing. The man jerked his head back and yelped, "Andre!"

The bouncer shut up in mid-sentence and stepped back to let Tommy Magic pass. The mobster muttered, "Scumbag," and came to where Cronin stood.

"Buy me a drink."

Cronin watched him stare at Keefe, who was so wrapped up in Lorene that he did not even realize who had entered the place. The Wall Streeters, who had watched the scene at the door, moved away, smiles dying on their faces. He might be gray-haired, but Magic still projected enough menace to chill their celebration. This is not a man to be trifled with.

"Gimme a cigar." Magic pointed at a bespectacled broker with glazed eyes. The financier handed a plump stogie over and offered to cut it for him. Magic waved him off and bit the end, spit it on the floor.

"You're welcome, Pops." He held himself erect and smiled sloppily.

"Pops? Oh, yeah, that was your mother I fucked. I coulda sworn it was just ineee ass, though. So how the hell you popped out is anybody's guess." He turned his back as the broker folded into his clique.

"What kinda booze they got here?"

"Whatever you want, Tommy."

"Scotch." Magic looked over at his brother-in-law. "Will you look at this asshole? I can't believe I'm related to him. A cock relation, mind you, not blood. Let's see what kind of bullshit this asshole's gonna try and sell me."

They moved with drinks to the table. Keefe turned to see them approach. He did a double take and then jumped like a man caught masturbating by his sister. "Tommy! Jeez, what a surprise." He was reaching out to shake his hand, grinning stupidly. Magic ignored him and sat down.

"You whack this guy, I tell you not to?"

"Tommy, I . . ." Keefe stood, still stunned by the arrival.

"Don't you Tommy me, you two-bit mick son of a bitch. If you didn't whack him, who did? Tell me this, bright guy. Where's my Marie?"

"Ah, she's . . . home." Keefe sat.

Lorene stood. "Maybe I should go, Frankie."

"You sit right there," Tommy said to her without taking his eyes off of Keefe. "Who's this?"

"This is my secretary."

"Yeah. And I'm that black Reverend Jesse Johnson."

"Tommy, I really. Listena me, this thing. The guy, wow, I mean, when I heard." Keefe's face took on a sheen. A woman at the next table cackled, a hyena outburst. "Shock, this happens, and as much as I know, it might as well've been, I don't know, lightning. A bolt. Kapow. Zap. Gone."

"I'll give you zap. Shuddup. You think you're something special. You're nobody. This guy is dead."

"Tommy, I got no idea over that."

"I better not find out you kilt him. I'll rip your ears offa your head."

"Tommy. Tommy."

Cronin knew Keefe was seething over being treated like that in front of Lorene.

Magic finally turned to look at her. "Hey, sweetheart, go powder your nose."

"Powder my nose?"

Keefe snarled. "Take a walk."

"Oh."

When she was gone, Tommy leaned in, three teenagers huddling over a skin mag. "So he's gone."

"Yeah, Tommy, you got it."

Magic held up his hand. "Hey, Frankie, this is bad? He's outta the way. Relax. Let's celebrate here. You got a clear path, be happy. Long as nobody catches wise, we're in the money."

"But . . ."

"But my ass. Somebody did us a favor. Let's get some more drinks over here. They come to see you?"

"Yeah. The fucking Feds, the city, the state. I'm waiting for Interpol and Scotland Yard."

"You got the alibi?"

"Yeah. I'm good."

Cronin knew Keefe's alibi was that he had been in a condo banging Lorene. Three doormen and Lorene had corroborated that, as he had himself. Tommy would not like that too much, he guessed. He watched Tommy Magic sit with a fat, strange grin on his face that said nothing and everything about the Dolan hit. Keefe was not about to press it, and Cronin thought, Neither am I. They drank, and Magic was expansive, laughing, exhibiting a natural good cheer that Cronin had never witnessed. He watched Keefe and was more impressed. The man had to be the best bullshit artist in the history of the planet. Two guys just sitting and carrying on over their drinks in a fashionable Manhattan nightspot. Lying to each other's faces like there was no to-morrow. Mike Dolan may as well have never existed. The spilling of his blood was to these guys a way to deal with an irritant, a possible impediment to their cash flow. Cronin finished his drink and chewed on an ice cube, thinking it might not be so easy. There was still the son.

Tara reluctantly left Jimmy and headed for work. She dressed in the locker room and waited for the shift to assemble. She picked up a newspaper and looked at the follow-up coverage of Mr. Dolan's murder. It was splashy and sensational, hinting at dark motives and shady dealings. Jimmy's father was portrayed for the most part as a high-minded reformer. Except in the *Post*, which couldn't seem to help itself. They said, "Murky Teamster Business Ends in Rubout." Even the victim was tarnished because he was a union man.

"LT says you know the guy?" Hippy was looking over her shoulder.

"My boyfriend's father."

"No shit. Sorry to hear that. Looks like heavy OC to me."

"That's what we figure." She realized she had referred to Jimmy as her boyfriend. Present tense. It sounded odd. But she felt she needed to be there for him, that, despite what happened between them at the end, there were bonds that would never be broken. She remembered how he supported her when her mother died, how no one else could console her. She worried he might do something really stupid, like answer violence with more bloodshed. It seemed like their relationship was directed by death; it pushed them together or pulled them apart.

She partnered up with Angela and they moved away from the precinct in the roundup van. Angela drove with the seat pulled all the way forward so she could reach the pedals.

"You think there's any way they catch the shooter?"

"I hate to say it, but I doubt it."

"That's tough. You know, when they killed my dad, all I wanted to know was who did it. I didn't really expect justice because of who my dad was. I mean, I looked at it like an occupational hazard, to tell you the truth. I mean, it was like he was a construction worker who got whacked on the head by a brick or fell off a building. But I would go to family things, funerals, weddings, and the way those people work I had to guess it was somebody he knew. It just made me crazy to know that the scumbag who killed my dad was probably right there in the room with me, maybe one of them kissing me on the cheek, slipping me a little cash for tuition. That's the hardest part. Not knowing."

Tara opened a bottle of water and listened. She had spent many hours alone with Angela, knew about her dad being a mafioso who was killed, but she had never talked about it and Tara had never felt it was the kind of thing to ask about. Angela turned onto Broadway. They stopped at a red light. A car pulled up next to them, slung low with tricked-out wheels and custom lights strung along its chassis.

"I'm worried about Jimmy."

"You think he's gonna go after the guys?"

"I don't know. Well, maybe I do. Jimmy's, well, Jimmy's a nice guy. You know, he was never like some of the maniacs we grew up with. He'd charm his way out of a jam before he'd fight. But I've never seen him like this. I mean, well, you gotta know what it feels like."

"I used to dream. You know, I had these recurring dreams. I wouldn't call them nightmares, because I loved the dream. I used to look forward to it. I was just this girl, fifteen. There was nothing I could do. I mean, I was helpless. But at night, for months and months, no, a few years, really, I would have these dreams, not every night but a lot of nights. I would come up on the assholes when they were killing my father. They shot him in the cemetery, at my mother's grave. He used to go there every Tuesday, the day she died, like a ritual. He never missed it. So they knew he was gonna be there. But in the dream I come up on them and I have something in my hand; usually it was an ax, sometimes a bat or a pipe. I just start swinging and swinging and screaming and there's blood everywhere and I just keeping whacking the assholes. And when I kill them all, I grab my father and I say, 'Daddy, I'm so sorry, I'm sorry it took so long.' And he smiles and says, 'I knew you would come.' That's it, every time. 'I knew you would come.'"

A car stopped in front of them and two guys came over to the driver's side window, laughing and carrying on. Someone behind the van started leaning on the horn. The guys in the street just went on yukking it up.

"Look at this." Angela put the cherry top on the dash and hit the siren once. The guys pulled back and the car moved down the block. "I still have that dream once in a while."

"Jesus."

"So, I can understand him wanting to get revenge."

"I'm really worried about him."

"Well, I hate to say it, but you should be. I know how he feels. You guys getting back together, you think?"

"No. Yeah. I don't know. Maybe. Shit, who knows. There's something about him. I can't explain it. We connect on so many levels. It feels right. I mean, the more I think about it, the more I realize what broke us up is that we are both so thickheaded. We don't like to back up."

"Thick micks."

"And then some."

"You got to give a little to get a little."

"I just can't think of anybody that I felt I could be honest with, open. I could tell him anything. And he'd actually listen."

"That's a first. Most guys."

"Don't I know it."

"Well, baby, go with it. He fucks you over again, you got a gun, shoot his balls off."

Tara laughed. "Now there's an idea."

Cronin waited on a Riverside Park bench and watched New Jersey. It had been one of those pleasant days in spring that bring people out to enjoy the sun. Despite the encroaching darkness there were many cyclists, joggers, and Rollerbladers still working their way along the promenade. He watched as a middle-aged man made his way toward him on skates. He looked to be at least a little out of control. As he passed, his face was twisted with concern, his arms flapping, like an ostrich trying to achieve liftoff. His beer belly hung over his sweatpants like a wet sandbag. Some people, Cronin thought, need to look in the mirror before leaving home.

His peace was interrupted by Roth sitting down next to him.

"So?"

Cronin knew exactly what was on the man's mind. "If he killed Dolan, he's a far better actor than I'll ever be."

Roth smoothed his pant leg, bent over, and picked a blade of grass from a crack in the macadam. "There's going to be a certain amount of collateral damage; other agencies will be involved. The NYPD will want to solve such a high-profile case. It's not generating the kind of press this mayor enjoys. It creates a perception of lawlessness."

Roth's attitude was bothering Cronin. Here, a decent guy, a taxpayer, gets splattered all over Union Square and Roth expresses not a hint of regret, no concern that this is not the way things should be. He realized Dolan was nothing but a nuisance to the man, that his ideas were repulsive even. Roth enjoyed manipulation, inducing paranoia, gamesmanship, intrigue. When Cronin signed on as a contract player he had been motivated by several things. The idea of going after corrupt union leaders was one; the opportunity to get back in the game another. Cash, of course, and some kind of redemption also figured into the equation. He had pissed away a promising career for reasons he still was not clear on. But he was tiring of doing Roth's dirty work. Rules had always been bent, the Constitution worked over and around. Roth seemed guided by a sole principle: don't get caught.

Roth's real goal, besides furthering his career, was to cripple the unions, set people up, hit them with RICO suits, drain resources, take over on the pretense of cleaning things up. The federal decade-long control of the Teamsters union had gotten rid of a gangster element, but it had also weakened the union and bankrupted it in a way no wise guys ever could. Cronin knew ex-colleagues who had retired and were being paid three hundred dollars an hour to do background checks from chaises longues in Florida, all paid from membership dues. And while hundreds of Teamsters were drummed out of the union, maybe five had been indicted for anything. Cronin suspected larger forces were at play. He had heard rumors about Roth taking payoffs, but he doubted this. Money seemed the least of the man's motivations. But you never knew.

"If not Keefe, who?"

"He went to his brother-in-law and was shot down. At least that's what he says. He's been beefing about it nonstop ever since. But I doubt he was serious about making a move. He just needed to look like he was capable of it. You got any ideas?"

"Nothing that makes sense."

Cronin considered the chilling thought that Roth might have arranged it himself. Keefe was his prize pet, his moneymaker. The man had connected the dots for them on so many cases that he was more valuable than any passel of agents or any brilliant prosecutors. Roth would not want to lose him. It was not your garden variety Cosa Nostra rubout, two in the head while you were parking your car. This was a brazen, professional hit done in public to make a point. Anytime, anyplace. No matter who authorized the hit, it was a contract job. Just how valuable was Keefe? Cronin was not privy to his meetings with Roth, and operated on a need-to-know basis. But who knew? Why not reel Keefe in, offer him some type of immunity, the witness protection program?

"What about Magic?"

"There has been some unusual activity in that area."

"I'll say. He almost gave our boy a coronary the other night."

"We've tracked him. He's been out more in the last few weeks than he has in the previous three years."

"What the hell is he up to?"

"We don't know. We can only wonder at the complexities of the Mediterranean psyche."

An awkward silence fell over them. The sky turned a brilliant red. The sun dazzled from beyond the horizon.

"Some of your extracurricular activities are drawing more notice than we're comfortable with. People end up dead for pulling such stunts."

Cronin chose not to respond. What was there to say? He needed to watch himself. It wasn't just Keefe, or Magic; there were turf wars between agencies. He might be set up for any number of things by some G branch he didn't know existed. He remembered what happened to Jim Phillips, an asset who did the same type of work. They cut him loose, turned on him, and labeled him a burnout. Last he heard, Phillips was living out in Brooklyn, tending bar in a local saloon, gobbling Prozac, and ranting about liberal conspiracies. Cronin expected to be long gone before he ended up compromised or dead.

"I don't begrudge someone in your position picking up some pocket change in your spare time. But it has to be low-profile. I don't have to spell out the kind of difficulty any attention drawn to that will cause." He let that sink in, then said, "Let's walk." Roth stood and pulled his trench coat closed. Cronin walked along with him, an uneasy feeling in his stomach. Something in Roth's carriage, the lilt of his voice. The Dolan hit, things were shifting, his world was being impacted, he needed to stay ahead of the curve, outpace any changes. Contain things. Keep his plan intact.

"On the other hand, your little adventure in adultery needs to come to a quick end. I don't think it is wise. If you wish to covet another man's wife, it should not be an asset's. Things get too murky. We might wind up losing you both. If we know, eventually he'll know."

Cronin expected it sooner or later. Roth was one to keep tabs, not to let surprise be an option.

"It's not a problem."

"You are wrong. Whether it's a dalliance, a way to screw the boss, if you will, or some misguided attempt to find love in middle age, it is dangerous, and you know it. End it, before Keefe does."

Cronin considered a response. He'd been raised to follow orders, the Church, the Marines, the NYPD, the Bureau, it was all about charging the hill when told to do so. His training was at war with a desire he had never known before. Part of him screamed to tell Roth to fuck off. But here was a man who, if he knew desire of the flesh, managed to ward it off, never to let it show. He seemed a man incapable of indulgence. Up on the avenue, the screech of tires was followed by loud cursing in Spanish. Cronin knew what he needed more than anything was time.

"Yeah, I guess you're right."

Roth studied him for a moment.

"All right. Good. We don't want to lose you. Now, what about the son?"

Cronin inhaled. He should have figured Roth would be way out ahead of things.

"Dolan's?"

"James Patrick Dolan. Jimmy to his friends. Should we be worried about Hibernian notions of vengeance and bloodletting?"

"He's a college kid." Cronin braced for what was next.

"We need him neutralized."

"Neutralized." He wondered if Roth was reading too many spy novels.

"I want him to be a nonfactor in the election."

Jesus. Not bad enough the father was killed; now they want to visit some hell on the kid. "I'll keep an eye on him."

"I know you will. And remember how important it is to keep your priorities in line."

They parted and, as Cronin walked on, he found himself thinking of his own dead father. That cold and tormented man. He wondered if he had lived and things had been different, could they ever have sat down as men and talked. From what he knew about the Dolans they had had a relationship he envied. A closeness. He wondered what, if any, sacrifice he would make if someone he cared that much for was murdered. That made it easy to guess what the kid might do.

Cronin flagged a cab and considered his next move.

The tables and counters of the Dolan apartment were piled high with dishes of cakes, cookies, cheeses, and meats. There were casseroles and bottles of whiskey and wine, soda, bowls of cracked ice. A mourning bounty. Mrs. McGovern came up from 1B and appointed herself organizer and de facto family member. She shooed him and his brothers, his sister, away from chores. Liam's mother, encased in black from head to foot, sat with the rosary, muttering, "It's a shame. He was a nice man, a wonderful man." And then she went back to her beads. For once, even she seemed at a loss for words.

Jimmy paced the kitchen floor and looked at the clock. His aunts moved about affecting good cheer, mouthing Irishisms, a wall against unseemly displays of lament. No old country keening in the New World. He too had resolved to put up a good front. He bussed the powdered cheeks aging aunts offered up, shook the hands of thick-necked uncles. The sad occasion had brought them back from suburban exile, back to the neighborhood of their youth. His Uncle Timmy swirled a beer mug filled with whiskey and ice and muttered about the decline of Inwood. He was dressed in his Sunday best, a vertigo-inducing outfit of checks and stripes and paisleys, punctuated by black wing tips and white socks. Jimmy figured he was about an hour away from picking a fight with his wife, who, in defense, would berate him to the point of muteness.

"I can't believe it. I wanted to get a drink at the Looney. It's a Spanish restaurant now."

"A Mexican cantina," his Aunt Tina specified.

"Same difference, ain't it?"

"What's worse, you can't even buy a Mass card at the bars anymore."

Jimmy felt as if he were drugged, and the mix of emotions were canceling each other out. He had to hold up, maintain a facade, yet he thought it strange that no one spoke about the fact that his father had been murdered. He might as well have taken a heart attack. It occurred to him that there might be some level of shame relating to his means of departure from this earth, a blame-the-victim sentiment not uncommon with the Irish. Jimmy grabbed a glass of ginger ale, dropped in some ice cubes. His Aunt Mary cornered him by the refrigerator. Her perfume was sweet and cloying. Jimmy wanted to get away.

"He was a great guy, your father, Jimmy, my favorite brother-in-law. We're going to miss him very, very much. Are you going to be all right, honey?" Jimmy assured her, indeed, all would be well.

The mourners turned to reminisce. Jimmy listened as stories were offered up as proof of his father's vitality, that he was once quick and not dead.

"Remember the time he knocked the shit out of Jimmy Harkrider?"

All heads turned to the source of the crudity. His Uncle Timmy looked down in embarrassment. The apartment was beginning to feel crowded. Jimmy moved out of the kitchen. In the living room several aunts and cousins watched the Rosie O'Donnell show with his sister. Liam stood by the window, somehow comical in his suit. It was too loose in the waist, too tight in the shoulders. His shoes could use some spit and polish.

Although Jimmy was the youngest, he was looked to as the leader for the day. He was the closest to his father. He moved into his room and shut the door, looking for a minute's respite. The bed was piled high with coats, and the air was thick with the commingling of perfumes and colognes. At the church, he was to offer up a reading from scripture. He was nervous. He picked up the Bible and read it to himself, slowing his pace, articulating it in his head. He wished he had enough composure to come up with his own words, but he knew he would be unable to.

He wished Tara was there. She should be coming off her tour soon. He felt a powerful need for her company, that she was the only one who truly knew how he felt. They had shared this before, had helped each other bury their mothers. As an adult, he had never cried in front of anyone else, and knew he never could. Theirs was a bond thickened by blood, by tragedy.

Liam came into the room.

"Jimmy, what's up?"

"Hey, Liam, where's your mom?"

"She's banging out the novenas. Headed down to the church already. You gonna make it?"

"Yeah. I don't have a choice, do I?"

"Not a fucking one, bro."

Punchy waddled out to his waiting limo. He'd barely slept. He tried to tally his losses of the past couple days, somewhere around a quarter of a million dollars. That was just the bets he remembered. There were times he wagered while on a raging bender that he did not ever remember, fucking bookies don't give a shit, as long as he pays. Till someone showed up with a marker. He did not want to go to the service, felt some complicity, felt he should have done more. Mike was his brother, no matter what he told Keefe or his gorilla. Somehow he had blood on his hands. He was considering running, fleeing, becoming a fugitive from dark forces he felt marshaling against him. "I am but hunted," he whispered as he ducked into the sleek black vehicle. He was in a position to topple many unsavory characters, was the keeper of many unholy secrets. This made him a ripe target. Someone whose life will be deemed a nuisance, a danger, a possible stool pigeon of great help to the authorities. A prize canary, a super rat.

The things he could say. He could send quite a ripple through a few circles of hell. He cracked the seal on the pint of whiskey and sipped as the limo whispered away from Trump Tower. He was dressed in his best dark suit, best that still fit him at least. The losses were numbing, but not a personal worst for him, far from that. "Stop here. Get me a pocket rocket, Jameson." The driver, a man he had employed for years, a former dockworker, gave him the look. "I'm grieving, damnit. Run along."

He couldn't make it up the aisle unnoticed. He dropped his bottle and it skittered loudly across the polished, sanctified floor of the church and disappeared under a pew, the racket like an accusation. He staggered sideways, a seaman on a storm-tossed deck of his own making, and followed the whiskey to the floor, a loud bellow emanating from deep within him. The black sheep's triumphant moment, the ultimate fuckup, making a horse's ass of himself at his murdered brother's funeral Mass. He heard gasps, a murmur, whispers. The priest stared stonily, mortified. They serenaded him, those lost friends and relatives, with a chorus of disapproval. No, no, he thought. You don't understand. I am hunted. There is blood on my hands. Suddenly, men in cheap suits and syrupy cologne were about him, stout lads, Teamsters, he assumed. They hoisted him like they might a dead workhorse from the middle of a country lane. Murmuring murderously in his ears, and despite his protestations that he was Mike Dolan's kid brother, they escorted him brusquely out through the hush of the vestibule and into the harsh reality of Broadway. As the doors closed behind him, he looked up from the vantage of his backside on the sidewalk and heard with heightened clarity. "Fucking useless drunk asshole." Yeah.

The Irish-American Teamsters had sent a phalanx of bagpipers. Jimmy, following his father's casket, came out of the church and was stunned by the scene. As far up Broadway as he could see, there must have been a hundred trucks idling, their motors growling. Concrete trucks, flatbeds, other locals. As the limos pulled from the curb, Jimmy looked back and saw the trucks fall into line behind him. A salute to his dead father.

Later, at the Knights of Columbus hall, Punchy, slightly recovered from his fall, hovered over him, hot whiskey breath in his face. He did not look well. "Jimmy, we need to talk," he slurred. His eyes were badly bloodshot, beady from the booze. "They came to me, Jimmy. They came to me. Your father. I . . . they came, they wanted things."

Jimmy looked past his uncle at the thick gathering. He sighed and turned up to look at Punchy. He tried to make sense of what he was saying. "Who? Who's they?"

"I'm hunted, Jimmy, I'm next. The fucking Corsicans."

"Come on, Punchy, give him a break. It's his father's funeral, for Christ sake." One of his other uncles pulled Punchy away. Jimmy watched as Punchy was escorted out the door for the second time that day. He would have to talk to him and try to figure out what he knew. For the moment he was pissed off at him for showing up blasted.

Jimmy sat at the bar maintaining a hearty good cheer despite the occasion. It was expected that he be strong. His nephew, a Yankee hat on backward, his suit jacket off on the floor somewhere, ran up to the bar and ordered another cherry Coke. Jimmy envied his childish oblivion to the seriousness of the gathering. He felt a sudden wave of fatigue and wanted to be far from this place. He felt overwhelmed by the ritual. He watched Liam's mother worry her rosary beads while she made idle chatter. His Aunt Alice, the oldest, indestructible at eighty-seven, drank beer from the can and puffed on a Pall Mall. She was voicing her objection to doctors to anyone who listened. She had not seen one since her last child was born in 1951.

Jimmy watched and felt the strength of connection. He saw Tara laughing with one of his aunts. He was grateful for her presence and support. When everyone was gone, back to their lives, she would still be there, he hoped. He watched his elder relatives who were living bridges to another time. They were the last of the Americans who had lived through the Depression and the wars and remembered a time before television. They often remarked how at the time they did not know they were poor. Everybody was in the same boat. They looked out for each other and appreciated what they had. They came of age in a time and place where your word was your bond and shame was still possible.

They were still churchgoers for the most part. He envied the strength of their faith, faith that seemed beyond his generation. Maybe we need to suffer more. He laughed. He knew their reliance on the spiritual helped to ward off the obscenity of the physical, of bodies failing, bones turning to dust, organs bloated and weak, skin sagging, senses dulled, functions beyond control. Ritual and tradition defined their world for them.

He wondered if his father would have lived a different life if he had had another chance. If he had known it would lead to a barrage of bullets on a city street. He wondered if any of the assembled would. They had all bought into the belief that everything always got better in America. Your kids would do better than you, if you just did the right thing, lived the right life. Sure, we'll build your buildings and police your streets and clean your houses and drive your trains and buses. We'll even fight your wars, honorable or dirty, just as long as you give us a shot at supping at the big table. I pledge allegiance. Justice for all. In God We Trust. Jimmy swirled his drink and looked over the room. He realized not one of the men here had ever left the country without a rifle in his hands.

He felt grateful for the family and the love and the solidity of it. You can take everything away but this you cannot fuck with. Blood is thicker than all. He felt the restlessness leave. He basked in the love and respect his father had earned over his life. Now Tara was by his side. She wore a plain black dress, a small gold crucifix around her neck, her hair pulled back in a bun. Funeral dress. They'd been to too many of them. She knew him better than anyone in this life. She touched his arm and kissed the side of his face. She smelled of flowery soap.

"Hanging in there?"

He simply nodded and put his arm around her waist, felt the heat of her. He watched a group of Teamsters approach. They were a thick-necked and solemn bunch. He recognized most of them. Over the years they had often come by the apartment to futilely conspire with his father against the Keefes. One he knew to be Lou Condo said, "Jimmy, we think you should run."

"Me? Run?" Jimmy thought he was kidding. Taking up his father's cause was not something he had considered. But he saw in their faces a sincerity. "Thanks, guys, but no, I couldn't."

"Jimmy, your dues are paid up, you're still a member in good standing. According to the bylaws, you're good to go."

"You want to get at this prick, there's no better way," Condo said.

Jimmy did not know what to say. It was one avenue to vengeance. "I'll think about it." This did not seem to satisfy them. They looked down at their feet. Jimmy stood. He felt Tara nudge him from behind, a sign. He trusted her instincts. "I'm serious, I'll think it over. It's just, I had no idea."

"Good, Jimmy, good. It's the right thing to do. You got experience on the job, that big-money education, the connections downtown. And the right name. Think about it. Nobody else is gonna run. That means everything your father stood for was buried with him today." Condo put a hand on Jimmy's shoulder. "We'll help you any way we can."

Each of them shook his hand before putting on their jackets and heading for the door. Jimmy watched them go and wondered just what made them think he had a chance if he did decide to run. Tara held his hand.

"What do you make of that?" Jimmy asked.

"It beats risking a homicide rap. You know your father would approve."

"I don't know. I just don't know." He turned his attention back to the gathering wondering if they were right.

When all were gone he sat at home alone and had a drink. It had been a long day. Tara was dropping off two of his aunts out in New Jersey. He walked the empty rooms of the apartment listening to echoes of forgotten times. He wondered if he should give the place up, or if he should keep it forever, a shrine to what was, all the life that was lived within these walls. After a time he lay down, knowing sleep was still far beyond him. He allowed himself, for the first time in days, to contemplate the future, to imagine a plan of action, a response to his father's killing. Later, as darkness came over the neighborhood, he sat in his father's old chair and thought about running. His dad would have loved the idea. And even if he ran and lost, it would be an action his father would have appreciated. There was a time when he thought he would get involved in union politics and that would be his life. But somehow he had gotten on another track. He sometimes wrestled with the idea that he had somehow sold out, but pushed it aside. Part of him just wanted to make money to prove that he could, that he could compete in that world. He was not immune to the idea that wealth meant success, however dubiously it was won. He was a product of his generation. Quill came over and he rubbed the dog's head. He wondered about running. He did not feel secure about his Teamster credentials. He had not worked full-time in years and he had always looked at it more as a way to pay for school than anything else. Besides, he was only twenty-nine. Why would anyone take him seriously? He did like the idea of going after Keefe and beating him legitimately, of getting right in his face and making him pay for his father's murder. Kill one Dolan? Here's another, asshole. He only wished he had a fraction of his father's tenacity. But, then again, maybe he did. His father never had so powerful a motivation. He closed his eyes, the fatigue nailing him in place, and waited for Tara to come back into his life.

The morning after the funeral, Liam returned to the job site. The shooting had not stopped work for a minute and he noticed two more floors had gone up. The place crawled with workers; machines started up for the day. Thumper put on his hard hat and gave him a grim wave as he entered the cage. A crane boom rose from the ground, slowly unfolding as it pointed toward the Manhattan sky. This was the signal to get busy. Liam stood outside the Teamster trailer. The pavement still bore the stain from Mr. Dolan's blood. He thought for a moment he might cover it with paint. But then he changed his mind. He made the sign of the cross and took three wooden horses and placed them around the blood to form a triangle barrier. He ignored the stares of the other men. He took a can of spray paint and wrote on the sidewalk: "Mike Dolan Teamster. RIP." As he finished, he saw the superintendent come out of his trailer toward him, his face all worked up ugly, ready for a tizzy. Liam was in no mood for this prick today.

"What the hell is this?"

Liam hated the way the guy stood, with his hands on his hips and his chest puffed out, like he was some kind of badass. Liam stood right in front of him and looked him in the eyes.

"You do not fuck with the dead. Or you might become one of them. You follow?"

Liam had not liked the guy from day one. He figured the guy had been a fan of John Wayne movies when he was young, the way he strutted around barking orders and making wisecracks at people's expense. Now he watched the guy's face as he went from big shit Mr. Honcho to all confusion, till his brain registered what was up. He opened his mouth to say something, then shut it just as quickly. Liam liked that. You get in someone's face, they usually show their true colors.

Liam went to the deck and helped the crew set up for the pour. He figured Jimmy would be out for a few days. He was not going to let him mope around feeling sorry for himself, and he sure as hell was not going to let that Keefe off easy. Jimmy had mentioned that some of the guys wanted him to run, and Liam thought that was a great idea. If it was his call, he would put two rounds behind the asshole mobster's ear and stuff him in a drum headed for Jamaica Bay, but he and Jimmy were different. He eased into the rhythm of the work.

At lunch he sat with his legs dangling over the side, sixteen stories up. Down below, he saw Keefe's Cadillac make its way through Broadway traffic and park beside the Teamster trailer.

The nerve of this scumbag. Liam could not believe the man was coming by the job so soon. We'll see about that. He took a twelve-inch concrete block and sat it on the edge of the floor. He watched the asshole and the gorilla emerge from their car. He put his finger in his mouth and then stuck it in the air as if to gauge wind direction and speed. He spit on his palms and rubbed them together. He picked up the block and gave it a little toss over the orange safety barrier. He looked down as it flipped end over end.

K eefe was ranting and raving. "You see what's happening here? I am being fucked with. I got six kinds of cops with their noses up my ass, I got smartass reporters trying to make a career out of me, and I got half my members convinced I killed the guy. Then my brother-in-law, that asshole, he must be losing his mind. He's been locked up with that lunatic wife of his for so long it's wearing off on him. He's become demented. They're gonna fit the bastard for a padded room. What was that shit in the restaurant the other day? Here's a guy that don't leave his house but once every three years, and he finds me in a joint like that? What was that supposed to mean, 'long as nobody catches wise'? About what?"

"You talk to him yet?" Cronin asked.

"No. You don't exactly talk to a guy like that. You try and communicate somehow to him, but you don't talk to him. I'd be better off sending up fucking smoke signals. Now, who the hell else wanted Mike Dolan dead? What, am I supposed to believe he gets whacked like that by a jealous husband? This fat fuck Magic, he just decides he's gonna have a little fun and, wham, I'm in the middle of a fucking murder investigation. Then, on top of everything else, he tells me to start cutting these fucking Russians in. I was speechless."

Cronin knew Keefe was scared to push Magic on anything. He was becoming like one of those animals that stick their heads in the dirt when things get dicey. For all his bluster, the man was a little short on balls. But this business with the Russians was bizarre. What it all meant was impossible to tell. Cronin guessed Magic saw the future and decided the Russians were it, that maybe he had them whack Mike Dolan and the business he was throwing them was payback. A contract was a contract, but why he was doing them favors was hard to figure. While the Russian mob was a growing concern, they still treaded carefully around Italian strongholds.

Cronin turned the car off Fourteenth Street and considered Roth's warning about Marie. A skateboarder came shooting into traffic, headed right for him, and swerved at the last second. As the mutt shot past his door, Cronin fought the urge to open it and splatter the little prick. He pulled alongside the Teamster trailer and parked. He had tried to discourage Keefe from making the rounds. The man felt it was smart to get out and start rallying the troops, to take on an air of concern about Dolan's death, to assure the men he had nothing to do with it. Cronin thought this was stupid. A week or two lying low while proclaiming he was pressing the authorities to solve the matter was the way he would play it. Let some doubt settle in. Right now even his biggest supporters were sure he had killed the man.

Keefe flipped down the vanity mirror and ran a hand through his hair. He bared his teeth, then reached into his inside jacket pocket and took out a small case, from which he produced a gold toothpick in the shape of a cavalry sword. He picked a small piece of breakfast meat from his teeth and replaced the pick. "I gotta get the guys behind me on this. Come on."

He followed Keefe out of the car. He looked around, then up, where he saw legs dangling many stories above the ground. Opposite the Teamster trailer was a row of makeshift benches where a gang of workers sat and ate lunch. Few showed any signs of recognition. They chewed on sandwiches and watched the two guys in suits with a studied disinterest. Cronin looked at the memorial to Dolan, was surprised the bloodstain was so vivid.

A Teamster tied down a load on a flatbed as Keefe approached. Cronin watched as Keefe turned on his smile and extended his hand. The Teamster, whom he vaguely recognized, kept working a come-along. Cronin trailed a few feet behind Keefe and heard him say, "Hey, brother, how are you?"

The Teamster kept securing his load and stared at Keefe. "Brother? I been in the local eighteen years. You know my name?"

Keefe, his hand suspended in the cold void between them, kept smiling. Cronin watched his face twitch with the effort of remembering. He opened his mouth to speak and there was a loud crash behind them. Cronin ducked his head as bits of glass peppered him. Keefe dove to the ground as if he were under mortar attack. The Teamster flinched and kept working. The men eating lunch whistled and hooted. Cronin turned to see the cinder block somebody had dropped onto the car. Its impact had crushed the roof in the middle and busted out all the windows.

Keefe stood, his suit marred by sand and powdered cement and oil. His face was scraped, and a trickle of blood fell down off his chin. His hair was standing straight up, untamed and free. He looked as if he had just been sucker-punched. Cronin turned away so as not to laugh in his face.

He looked back at Keefe, who was brushing his suit front, his face red as he started screaming at the Teamster. "You see this shit? I'm the victim here, I'm the victim. Me! I'm the victim!" The Teamster secured his last tie-down and jumped in his truck and roared off, leaving Keefe babbling in a cloud of dust. Cronin walked over and pulled him toward the trailer.

"Come on, Frankie. Let's get out of here."

Keefe turned to him. "You see this shit?"

Jimmy jogged to the top of Inwood Hill Park. It was ten past six and he stood among trees that were starting to go from buds to leaf. He had barely slept in days, had not left the apartment since the funeral, until now. He was plagued by restlessness, by a gnawing sense that he needed to avenge his father, to make Keefe somehow pay for his father's death. The light was pink and soft, warm. He looked out across the river to the Bronx. The buildings along the ridge in University Heights looked pristine in the morning light. He remembered visiting relatives when he was a kid, going to Mass at Tolentine. A neighborhood that seemed to go from middle class to a scarred ghetto in about a year after NYU pulled out. A neighborhood that served as an omen for the people of Inwood, just across the river. People seemed to dig in harder and move toward escape all at once.

He sat on a boulder near the remains of the park house. When they were kids, he and Liam and Bobby Belson had stolen some dynamite from a construction site. They had rigged it along the base of the house, a granite-and-concrete testament to the largesse of city contracts from the Depression era. They wanted to blast the steel door off it so they might use the place for a clubhouse, but they badly miscalculated the amount of explosives. The explosion laid the house to waste. They had staggered back to the neighborhood with singed eyebrows and ears that rang for days.

He felt that only he could avenge his father. His brothers and sister all had kids, families. He was single, with no children; and most important, he felt responsible for his father's death. Was the beef at Gracie Mansion the last straw? It was a distinct possibility. He watched as a pack of wild dogs, matted and mangy, galloped along the tree line, stopped to smell the air, and then dove back into the underbrush.

He considered his father's struggle against Keefe. His father had died for what he believed in. He thought of the way the men had shown up at the funeral, the procession, the words of encouragement. He had never considered a struggle that was not primarily for his own benefit.

He turned and started jogging, a slow, loping gait, easing himself back into it. He knew he needed to stay busy, to channel his anger into something. He was not ready to go back to work, did not think he would be able to handle bumping into Keefe without trying to beat him to death. Liam had offered to use violence to settle the score and, though Jimmy did not doubt his friend's willingness or ability, he turned that down, pronto. There was no need to operate on Keefe's level. Not yet anyway. He wanted to be smart, to think this out, to figure the best way to take him down.

He thought about the offer from Lou Condo and the others at his father's funeral. He wondered if he had what it took to make a run against Keefe. If they killed his father, what would stop them from killing him? He was not sure he had the kind of balls his father had. The courage to look death in the eye for a cause. It could be that he'd be running solely to avenge his father and that this would not be fair to the members. On the other hand, on his most selfish day he was more committed to helping them than Frankie Keefe could be in a thousand years. He knew a lot of the men, had put in enough time so that he would not feel like an opportunist or a carpetbagger, and believed his education and his time in politics were further qualifications.

He wove his way through the woods along the path. He came to stone steps laid here decades ago and started running up them. He made it to the top and stopped, jogged down, and raced back up. He was planning to see Tara for lunch. He would run the options by her, see what she thought. He needed her and he appreciated her support. He knew that if their roles were reversed he might not be so generous. He realized how incredibly lucky he was that she still wanted to be in his life. His father had been a huge fan of hers, and Jimmy thought it interesting that his death was the thing that was driving them back together. He wondered if he was ready to go after Keefe. And he wondered how fair it would be to get involved with Tara now, in case anything happened to him. Maybe it would be better if he kept a little distance between them. He ran down through the woods and hit the field at a full sprint, racing toward his building. One thing he knew for sure. He wanted Frankie Keefe to regret the day he ever messed with the Dolans.

K eefe watched the building from across Broadway. He glanced at his watch, then made his way to the corner. Traffic was thick as he waited for the light. He recognized a pair of the Mayor's aides walking toward him, back from some lunch maybe. They strutted along in sharply cut suits and an air of authority. Keefe turned his head and let them pass without being noticed. He waited again for the light, then walked across Broadway and ducked into the building. It was only the second time he had been to this office. His contacts were usually out and about, random spots designed for secrecy.

He pulled a protein bar from his pocket, tore it open, and started chewing. A dozen years of dirt and damaging scoops. This is how he's treated? He'd been feeding Roth rival Teamsters and mob guys, making his career, and the guy can't return his call? He had been trying to get hold of him for three days, and the Fed fuck had not called back. Keefe was furious. Furious and half scared to death. He wondered if the Fed had any prior knowledge that Dolan was going to get hit. It would not surprise him in the least.

On the sixth floor a woman in her mid-fifties sat at a desk and flipped through a magazine. Her hair was the color of a warship; her glasses were pointed and maybe three decades out of style. She looked bored, but her eyes were bright and took him in as if judging him on some higher level. Keefe stood before her, refusing to even announce his presence. He knew that she knew who he was and what he wanted. Finally, she closed her magazine and raised her eyebrows.

Without speaking, she lifted her right arm and pointed down the hall-way. To his back she said, "Last door."

Most were closed, but he passed one where a group of men were huddled, as if in deep conference. At the end of the hall he came to an open door. There, Roth, a man he had been doing dangerous busi-ness with for the last dozen years, looked up from his desk, where he was engaged in a phone conversation, and waved him in. He went back to the phone and spoke in a murmur. He laughed, looked over at Keefe, and laughed again.

Keefe felt the heat rise in him, tasted bile. He pulled at his neck, loosened his tie. He fought the urge to pick up his chair and throw it through the window. Let the guy know he was not here to listen to him laugh. Roth did it again, this time tossing his head back so it came from somewhere deep in his gut. A regular guffaw. Ha ha ha. Keefe wondered if it was a joke at his expense. The shit was coming down around him, and this prick was giggling like a schoolgirl. He stood up. He paced back and forth and glared at Roth. He opened the door and slammed it so hard the windows rattled. He coughed. Roth quietly hung up the phone. He stared and did not say anything, his mouth curled up at the corners. Finally he said, "Frank. Good to see you. Bit of a surprise, though."

"Yeah. Great. You think I got time for this?" Keefe slapped the desk. "Hah? I got shit up to my ears and you make me wait until you're done making ha ha on the phone?"

"I was talking to my wife. We're taking a vacation next week, with the kids."

"Vacation."

"Yeah. I feel the need to unwind."

"Unwind." He heard the pitch in his voice, like a woman's. Un-wind. He was wound so tight he was about to take off like a fucking space shuttle. This guy was headed to some resort to take in the sun-shine.

"You needed to see me. Has something come up?"

"Something? Has something come up? Let me ask you something. You're the law here, right? The detective, the snoop, the spook, the fucking guy with all the intelligence? I got people fucking with me, killing people so's I get blamed for it. I'm being stalked and harassed, raked over the coals by half-wit cops, I got people dropping concrete blocks on me, and you ask me has something come up?"

"Nothing that can't be handled."

"Great. You going to handle my brother-in-law? What about all the other shit I been through? What the fuck are you doing for me? You tell me, with all the agents you got, you ain't heard nothing of what I'm going through? Are you kidding me?"

"Frank, please, relax. Those are matters of local jurisdiction."

"Local what?"

"There really is not much we can do."

"Not much."

"We've looked into the Dolan matter and we are certain you were not involved. We notified the right people about this. Of course, if you were, that would be in violation of our agreement. We cannot condone any criminal behavior on your part."

"Don't give me that legal blah blah bullshit, you prick. You trying to play me like some jerk-off? You're up to your fucking neck in this thing. Don't forget that I know that."

Roth stiffened. "Maybe you should get out of town for a while, Frank. Let things iron themselves out. You look a little peaked. Unless there is something else, I've got a meeting to attend. And, I was you, I would not come here again."

"Yeah. How am I going to get out of town? They're talking about Dolan's kid running against me. You know what happens to all of us if I lose? Who's gonna be your guy then? This kid? If he's half the fucking Goody Two-Shoes saint his old man was, forget about it. This comes out, we all get hurt. You think long and hard about how much we need each other, pally."

Phones rang up and down the hall. Out on the street a car alarm wailed. Roth heard the distant rumble of thunder. He watched Keefe scurry alone across Broadway. Maybe it was time to pull the plug on the guy. Or put a stop to whoever was pushing him. Keefe had been a valuable asset for a long time. But he was becoming too hot. And he had the audacity to march in here and make threats. Keefe did have certain knowledge, but that did not worry Roth. There was no proof.

And this Jimmy Dolan—what were his chances? Could he be made to cooperate? He'd been around city politics for a couple of years. He knows the game. Maybe it was time to create a situation where Dolan needed him. It would mean canceling his vacation plans with Christen. But what the hell, he needed to focus on this Teamster mess and figure out what outcome was most beneficial to him.

Tara sat with Lieutenant Lincoln Mitchell at the bar of Marty O'Brien's. Mitchell was running her squad and had been her instructor at the academy. She knew that he had worked for several years on construction rackets, infiltrating minority coalitions that were really fronts for organized crime families more interested in shaking down contractors and unions than in finding jobs for the disadvantaged. Mitchell had agreed to have a rare drink with his subordinate. Tara wanted to find out as much as she could about Frankie Keefe. She'd always liked Mitchell. She felt his being black and her a woman in a predominantly white male organization gave them a bond.

Mitchell twirled his glass of Courvoisier and said, "The big dog gets off the porch, you best look out. I'll tell you what I know, and this is all off the record, so far off that it never happened. I spent time in OCCB and we were working with the Manhattan DA doing some labor racketeering cases. Just let me say this, that your man—Frankie Slick, we called him—no matter how dirty he came up, he was labeled a hands-off. Now, this is not so unusual as you might think. Sometimes it's a little pissing match between agencies or jurisdictions. This business is all about numbers and pictures. Numbers of drugs stopped or millions of dollars confiscated, pounds, tons, ounces— money, money, money. Then the pictures is all about who gets to pose for them nice newspapers and the six o'clock news. All smiling, we are the ones making America safe and sound for all you taxpayers. PR is what this is all about, making somebody look good so all the mommies and daddies out there who are forking over lots of their hard-

252

earned money in taxes feel like they're getting a bang for their buck."

Mitchell held his drink to the light as if inspecting it for flaws, sipped, and continued. "Now, your man, well, he's got to have an eight-hundred-pound gorilla for a rabbi somewhere, 'cause the man stinks like a rotten fish and everybody knows it, but nobody moves on him. And if they do, they get straightened out right quick, and in terms that are loud and clear."

Tara sipped her drink and contemplated what she'd heard. She watched as three women with showy hairdos and tight dresses came into the bar and joined a table of similarly coiffed and clothed women along the wall. As if cued, "Dancing Queen" by Abba spilled loudly from the jukebox.

"So it looks like he's working for somebody."

"Well, Detective, if it walks like a rat and talks like a rat, chances are it's awful fond of cheese."

"So no matter how dirty he gets, they let him stay in place." Tara was not surprised. She'd been a cop long enough.

"Must be feeding them something real tasty. It's all a matter of the lesser of evils—least it used to be. Our government has made nice with a whole line of scumbags to get what it wants. That's just how it goes. Truth is, that's how it has to go. We want to get the bad guys locked up. This guy is probably in a position to make more than a few careers for some Federales. I know an agent who doesn't like your man either. Way he was talking, it ain't the FBI that's running him, but you never know once you get involved with all that spook business. They got the FBI spying on the CIA, who's spying on the DEA, all of whom are spying on each other, and the shit gets so out of control they all end up not knowing what's going on. Regular Keystone Kops. And the citizen, the taxpayer, well. I've heard of operations where you got three different agencies out on the street all on different radio frequencies tripping over each other."

Lincoln Mitchell seemed to be in a reflective mood. Now he said it again. "I'd be careful you wanna start looking into our Teamster. He must have some real interesting friends. You do not want to get that big dog off the porch."

Tara ordered another round. Hippy was pleading with a waitress to have children with him. She decided this would be her last drink. She wanted to be up early, go for a run, and stop by school to talk to one of her professors. But she wanted to help Jimmy, find out what made Keefe so prosecution-proof.

She peeled the label from her beer bottle and stuck it on the bar, smoothing it out. "Do you think anything else might happen?"

"Like what, Detective?"

"I'm a little worried about Jimmy."

"From what I know? Like we discussed, Frankie Slick has a guardian angel on his side. But on the street it's general knowledge that he's run by his brother-in-law, Tommy Magic. Now, the It-lo-Americans have been hounded so bad they're on the verge of extinction in the lying and thieving business. But I always figured you push them so far they're gonna show their true colors. You got to give them the fact that they did play by certain rules. Mostly. No women, no cops, no citizens. Most of the people who caught lead poisoning were crossing lines they knew all about. Now, maybe we see the desperate animal side of things. I was you, I'd tell your boyfriend to keep his wits about him. They hit his father on the street like that for a reason. Frankie Slick makes a lot of money for people who are very, very stingy. You don't want to be seen as somebody messing with their cash flow."

"So you're saying he has people on both sides that need him to stay right where he is?"

"Excellent, Detective. Frankie Slick is a rare bird who has elevated himself beyond the usual good guy vs. bad guy scenario. He has made himself *necessary*."

Tara knew Jimmy well enough to know he had plenty of his father in him. He was not going to walk away. The Model Citizens came on the jukebox singing about some shlep in over his head forced to take desperate measures. If only life was as neat as a song. She watched Hippy kissing one of the big-haired women. "You mind if I call you, time to time, bounce things off you?"

"I'll do what I can, Detective. Just be careful. There are people who can turn your relationship with your boyfriend into something that can hurt your career."

"Gotcha. Say, it ever bother you doing that undercover work, with the coalitions?"

He looked at her as if it was a stupid question. "That was a long time ago. But no, it did not. They were bad guys who did bad things. And bad guys are bad guys no matter how much time their ancestors did or did not spend in the sunshine."

He finished his drink. "I am gone. One more and I'll be here all night, which will lead to my wife giving me a whole lot of shit I do not need." He nodded toward Hippy. "Keep an eye on the sergeant." He put on his coat and, as he was about to walk away, said, "Remember, you and your boyfriend do not want that big dog off the porch."

Tara sipped the beer feeling a little drunk. Mitchell had been around the construction rackets, he knew what he was talking about. It was unsettling. Hippy had repaired to a table with his new paramour, and Angela came and sat by her side. "You brownnosing the loo?"

Tara laughed. "Yeah, why the hell not?"

"What's the matter, girl? You don't look so hot."

Tara checked herself out in the mirror behind the bar. She looked beyond tired. "Ah, this thing with Jimmy's father. I don't know how it's going to play out with Jimmy. I'm worried."

"Well, baby, I know better than most, and you have every right to be worried. Those are bad, bad people."

"I'm sorry."

Angela waved her off. "Hey, that was a long time ago. I've come to terms with it, made my peace. Where's he at now?"

"Jimmy?"

"Yeah, Jimmy, your one true love. So called."

Tara glanced at the wall clock. It was later than she thought. She wondered how Jimmy was doing. She worried about him being alone. She finished her beer and realized what she really wanted was to be with him, and to be there for him. What the hell was she doing here getting drunk when he was uptown by himself? She tipped the bartender and said her goodbyes. She pushed out the door into the stillness of 3 a.m. on a Manhattan Monday, and drove north with a recklessness. She rang Jimmy's bell. His voice came over the intercom as if he had been waiting for her. "Come on up. Just in time for last call."

He sat at the kitchen table leafing through photo albums. Tara thought he looked ill. His face was gaunt, dark crescents forming under his eyes. She pushed a chair next to his with her foot and sat close.

"You're fucked up," he said in a manner that was not accusatory.

She shook her head no. "I'm okay, Jimmy. Just a girl out and about. Offer me a drink?"

"Good thing you're a cop. You don't lie good enough to be a bad guy." He took two beers from the refrigerator and popped them open. "You like a glass, madam?"

"Aluminum's fine with me. I look forward to Alzheimer's. Least I won't know I'm old and broken-down, wearing diapers. What are you doing up so late looking at pictures?"

"Late?" Jimmy sipped his beer and made a face. "Nasty. My father was not much of a drinker, now I know why. This shit will kill you." He took a photo out of an envelope and tossed it on the table. It was his father, in a tee shirt wearing a Teamster hat. Jimmy, about three years old, was perched on his shoulders. A group of men, thick-armed with tough faces, stood around him with picket signs. The city was in the background. "My first strike. Here, look at this, that's the Teamster convention in Miami."

Tara didn't know what to say. It worried her that he was up alone at this hour, dragging himself through the past, consorting with his dead father.

"All he knew was the union, you know. He just wanted to get rid of the assholes. Fucking Keefe. I want to kill him, Tara, I want to walk up to him right on the street and blow his fucking brains out."

"Don't be stupid, Jimmy."

"Stupid? What the hell is stupid? You want my definition? To me, stupid is letting that piece of shit walk around with that fake smile of his, while my father is rotting in the cemetery. I got nothing to lose, Tara, not a thing. If it costs me ten, fifteen years of my life, every second is worth it."

"Jimmy, you do that, it goes premeditated. That's first degree. They got the death penalty these days."

"So what. Don't be such a cop, Tara. Your colleagues tell me they got nothing to go on. I don't need hard evidence. The whole world knows he did it. What can they do to me? It won't be any worse than walking around knowing I caused this shit to happen. If I hadn't slapped the asshole, my father would be sitting right here with me instead of you. If I hadn't slapped the guy, my father would get to retire, spend his days with his grandchildren. My father would be alive. Tara, you got no idea what this is doing to me. I got to do something. I ain't afraid of doing time." He reached down and took another picture. "This was when we won the Gaelic football title. He was trying to get my nephew involved, took him up to Gaelic Park."

Tara nodded her head. "This is not just about you. You got family. Friends. People who care about you."

"Don't tell me, Tara, what this is about, who it's about. You have no idea what it is like to be sitting where I am on this one, Tara. I know you've been through a lot of shit. Trust me, it ain't like this. You're a cop, a detective. Tell me what the NYPD is gonna do about it. All they know is that Keefe was nowhere near it. He ain't stupid. Even that mook Cronin has an alibi."

"I been looking into some things, you know, on the QT."

"Yeah, Sherlock. Gee whiz."

Tara fought off a flash of anger, turned away for a moment, so as not to respond with any heat. She figured he had a right to be upset. "Jimmy, I'm not the enemy here." She paused till he nodded. "You're right. There is not much to go on. A professional, maybe even from out of town, high end. But what I hear is some people believe your guy might be in bed with the government."

"Yeah, and they all got together and killed JF fucking K."

"I'm not saying they helped him. But if he's ratting, maybe someone is not too eager to take him down, if he can't be tied directly to it. Or maybe someone is setting him up."

Jimmy waved her off. "I don't give a shit. I'm gonna kill him."

She sat in silence. "Yeah, well, I hope you change your mind." After a minute she leaned over, put her arm around his neck. "Because if anything happens to you it's going to kill me, Jimmy. 'Cause I love you, Jimmy. No matter what happened, I've always loved you."

Jimmy's face softened. The anger slipped away, and he pulled her to him. "Shit, Tara, I'm sorry. I know you want to help. I'm sorry about . . . I'm sorry about everything. I just want to get the guy. I'm not going to kill anyone. I just sit here alone at night, and it seems like the easy way out, the cleanest, easiest thing in the world is to walk up to him and shoot him dead. And that pisses me off even more because I know I'm turning into him, or them, or whoever killed my father. And I know that would hurt my father more than anything I could ever do. I just feel sometimes like it's the only choice."

"Jimmy, we make our own choices in this world. You can play this any way you like, but you're smarter than they are. My call? You should run against him. Take those Teamsters' advice. That would hurt the guy more than anything else, and you won't get jammed up over it."

She pulled him up and they lay together in his bed. They were still and quiet in the warmth of each other, mourning the loss and hurt and regret, but together.

In the hard white light of morning they made love for the first time in years. Afterward, they lay wordless in a tight embrace, as Tara began to feel that maybe it was time to look to the future, to let the past die. After a time, she felt Jimmy fall into a deep sleep. She dressed and left for work.

When he awoke, Jimmy lay wrapped in the sheets and considered Tara. The bed held her warmth and scent and he wished she was still there. He pulled himself into the new day, showered, and ate breakfast. He noticed some calls had come in while he was in the shower. The first message was from Tara: "You're still the big man on campus—can't wait to get back there. Love and kisses." Jimmy laughed, anticipating her return, excited by the prospect of their renewed relationship. The second message played. He heard someone say, "Hey, asshole," followed by the unmistakable sound of a chain saw roaring to life. The caller revved it several times, then shut it off. Jimmy heard a cackle and then a click. He sat down on his couch, his good mood gone, a sense of dread settling over him.

After a while, his fear subsided and he felt a cold heat, a desire to strike back, to start moving on his enemies. His father's killers. They wanted to scare him off. Well, fuck them.

He called Liam. It was time to pay a visit to his Uncle Punchy. Upset by the call, he told Liam to come armed. They drove down to Trump Tower. It was their good fortune that one of the doormen was a buddy from grammar school. "That asshole Punchy? I'll let you right in."

In the elevator Liam was rambling on. "I mean, riddle me this, Batman: this guy Trump, you think he'd get a single piece of ass, he wasn't a trillionaire? Every day I read the paper, I see this twerp with a different model, actress, movie star. Don't these women have any self-respect? I mean, if you go out with someone because they got money, that makes you a ho'. Am I right? I done it myself, I'll admit it freely. I mean, the guy is ugly. Look at him. That hair, the way he walks, like spastic. This guy could not keep his lunch money, he didn't have a half dozen bodyguards with him. Goes around bragging about being a self-made man. His old man give him a million dollars to start out with. That don't count? Self-made is when you come from nothing and then you get something."

They were met at Punchy's door by a maintenance man with a key.

"The one thing I give him, though, is he does not give the workers a bad time on his sites. I worked on a few myself. That, I'll give the guy."

As they entered the apartment, Jimmy called out, "Hey, Punchy, where are you?" They came upon him sleeping on his couch, wrapped in a monogrammed silk robe. The manor lord in repose.

Liam stood slack-jawed at the view. "Look at this fucking place, and he's related to you?"

Punchy pulled his eye patch down and groaned. He did not seem perturbed by the intrusion. "Water, water. I was dreaming. I am in the Gobi Desert. Nomads on camels passing me by laughing, ha ha, die of thirst, you American scum. Instead of water, they poured dollar bills on me." Punchy sat up. "I can't even catch a break in my dreams these days."

"Too bad. That's what happens when you show up shit-faced at your brother's funeral. Now, what did you mean when you said they came to you. Who's they?" Jimmy asked.

Punchy shook his head. "Listen, I don't know anything, except they wanted me to talk to your father, tell him to back off."

"They?"

"Come on, kid, you need a map? I'll give you one." He stood and pulled a robe around himself. He moved to the kitchen and made a cocktail of vodka and tomato juice, spooned in a hefty dollop of horse-radish, and gulped it down. "Wow. I need to lay off this. I get you kids a drink?" He wiped his mouth with the back of his arm. He steadied himself on the counter. "Jimmy, I don't know. I mean, these people, they are not nice. They can do things to a person, they can make you suffer, they can make you disappear. This man's brother-in-law, they don't call him Tommy Magic because he likes to pull rabbits out of his hat or do card tricks at cocktail parties. These guys are killers. They do not live by any moral code. They don't have qualms about shedding blood, playing judge, jury, and executioner. I could never figure that out about some people. They go to church, we share the same God, the same saints, give or take." Punchy mixed another drink and moved back to the couch.

"Jimmy, your father knew all of this. I mean, I hate to say it, but people tried to talk to him. To show him the light. I was one of them. I begged him, for Christ sake. I'm sorry, but he was around a long time, your father, rest his soul. We were brothers, we were blood. I . . . maybe we went our different ways, but I was fond of him. He was a good guy. The last of the Mohicans in his own regard, but hardheaded as they come. He was always like that, even when we were kids."

"I want you to help me nail him."

"Him? Who's him?"

"Keefe."

"If only life was so simple."

"What does that mean?"

"When I first started in business I worked for an old-timer from the

260

Heights. A guy from Lithuania who was supposed to have made his first bundle with Arnold Rothstein."

"Who?"

"Who? The guy who supposedly fixed the World Series. That's who. In 1919. Anyway, he had a favorite saying. Anything came up, it was follow the money, follow the cash. If you think this begins and ends with your Teamster you are sadly deluded."

"I don't care about anyone else. It had to come from or through Keefe, end of story. You're going to help me."

"Hah, Jimmy, Jimmy, please, don't. I mean, what do you want to do that to me for? These people will kill me before I can hurt them."

"Punchy, what do you think I will do to you?"

"Jimmy, please. You are not in the league these guys are. You're a kid, for crying out loud, a babe in the woods. You can't compete in the menace department. Please, don't make more of a mess out of this. They'll kill us all. You can bank on that."

"Maybe. But there's a difference between me and them. They care about one thing, money. I care about doing the right thing, Punchy. They killed your brother. Does all this shit in your life"—Jimmy indicated the grandeur of Punchy's apartment with a sweep of his hand—"mean more to you than your own flesh and blood?"

"Mother of God. I am but a football. Please, stop with the Irish guilt. You want me to be honest about that? There were these three brothers, the Doyles. Tough guys. Thought they could buck the system, go up against Keefe, Tommy Magic. When it was over, they were all dead, decapitated, mind you, along with a cousin and two childhood pals. The family had to bury headless bodies. All that death just to prove a point. These people, no, these animals, Jimmy, you do not want to fuck with."

"You're not gonna help me because you think they'll kill you? You know why you are going to help me, Punchy? Because you want to do the right thing. Either way, you are fucked. So what do you do? Do you reach down and find the little bit of a soul you have left and help me get the guy who killed your own brother? Or do you help them because you have become such a low-life piece of shit? Look in the mirror, Punchy. They can't stop me. You know why they can't stop me?

261

You want to know the one reason they can't? Because I ain't afraid of dying. I'll be in touch."

"See ya, fat man." Liam said as he followed Jimmy out the door.

Punchy watched them go. He pulled himself up and made another drink. Not afraid of dying, he thought. How quaint. Right about now, dying appeared to be the least of his worries. He dialed in a bet on the Knickerbockers, lit a cigar, and sat naked overlooking the city. It was a clear day and helicopters hammered by at eye level over the river. He wondered if they could see him in all his glory.

He considered doing the right thing. Dialing up the Feds, ratting on Keefe. He had enough on his skimming commissions from the pension funds, and various kickbacks, to nail him for a pound anyway. He might cut his losses, enroll in the witness protection program, get a new identity, a home in a quiet suburb outside a Sun Belt city. He had a vision of himself retrieving the morning paper off his front stoop. No, out there they call them porches. Maybe water the lawn, drop about fifty pounds, romance a honey-haired divorcée of solid midwestern stock. A schoolteacher perhaps, or a librarian, or nurse. Someone with a good heart and narrow horizons. He'd father a child, attend local functions, sponsor a Little League team. His past would lead to thrilled speculation at the local mid-level country club. He could hustle the rubes at golf, wager over the Internet.

What was he thinking? He was being harassed on three fronts. He considered fleeing. He still had enough stashed away to live right if he could curb the gambling. Maybe he could move to some island, or a country without extradition treaties with the U.S., somewhere he could purchase protection from the Corsicans on the cheap. His own private army of Third World underachievers, heavily armed, lightly educated, and grateful for his largesse.

He got up and rummaged through a desk drawer for the Fed's number. Maybe he should sit down, see what they had in mind. Maybe he could get Uncle Sam to finance his expat future. He found the business card, stained, with simply a contact name and a number. It bore no official letterhead of a government agency, no embossed seal. He rubbed the card in his fingers and picked up the phone. He hung up.

He would tidy up first. What's the hurry? He gathered the newspapers and magazines from the coffee table. As he was throwing them out, he noticed the racing form. He saw a few picks that looked interesting. He dropped the card back in his desk and called his bookie.

He needed to think things over some more, see what was up, how things might lie. He'd then test the waters, here and there first. He was going to take care of numero uno. He thought about his nephew. The kid was dangerous, a loose cannon. He had no idea what he was getting into. Something he would not have expected. He felt some guilt over Mike's death, felt it was a terrible event. But Jesus, the man had been warned. He was not an innocent, not just the victim of some random act of violence, some indiscriminate cross fire. Mike had known better than anyone what he was up against, who he was upsetting. He was a proselytizer and, like many before him, was martyred for his cause. At least it was swift. A bullet to the brain.

He wondered about Jimmy. He would not take odds on the kid's survival. He was a worse dreamer than the old man if he thought he could win a battle against Francis Michael Keefe and his Italian sponsorship. What the hell was wrong with people? Why not cut a deal and live happily ever after? He had not mentioned it to the kid, but he suspected this thing went beyond even Tommy Magic and the mob. How the hell else was Keefe still in place with the government running the International? And just what the hell was behind Cronin's warnings?

He dumped his drink in the sink and washed down a couple of diet pills with carrot juice. He turned on the TV and watched an exercise program. Three tight-waisted, well-busted women in blue spandex with some kind of tropical paradise in the background put themselves through an aerobic routine. They shouted instruction and encouragement and wore microphones that wrapped around their heads like those of reservationists in some dreary back office. A type of jungle music pulsed.

Punchy stood and made a halfhearted attempt to follow them, arms one way, legs another. His breath was soon ragged and short, his face flushed. He sat down and watched the remainder of the show, but did not try to get up again.

The buzzer rang. It was the building manager bitching about his tardy maintenance fee. "Ah, shit," he muttered. "A fourth front."

Tommy Magic sat in the back room of a beauty parlor in Brighton Beach, fat and happy, shooting the shit with Ivan, his new pal, to whom he offered his sage counsel. "I can't stress this enough. Stay offa the fucking phone. Any fucking phone. I ain't picked one up in twenty-five years. I think in my head that every one of them is covered in shit. You don't put your hand in shit, do you? That and mumble, mumble like a fucking retard, like you got rocks in your head. They got equipment, this day and age, that can hear you through a fucking wall of concrete, like they're sitting in the room with you, these sneaky fucking government hard-ons."

Ivan smiled, then looked up and waved to one of his comrades, who was holding up the wall. The mook wore a bandage over his left ear, which had been shot off his head as he was leaving the Dolan hit. Magic watched as the guy, unusually skinny for one of these Commies, who all looked like they might have played football, if they had football over in Commieville, walked out the door. Magic stared at his face and saw the eyes. Dog eyes, like a fucking pit bull's, dull, stupid, mean eyes, maybe like a shark's. Eyes of a guy that kills, then goes home to play patty-cake with his kid. My kind of guy, Magic thought.

Ivan was trying to find a soccer game on his satellite television. He held three different clickers at a time and jabbed them at his wide-screen TV like a man emptying a pistol. He babbled in Russian. The room smelled like a boiled cabbage. Magic took in all the stereo and electronic crap piled around. Place looked like a control tower. The black marble table they sat at still had a price tag on it. A red velour couch was piled high with leather jackets, all right off some truck somewhere, he guessed. It made him miss the old days.

"I come up as a hijacker."

Ivan stared at him and continued to work his remotes. The skinny guy came back in with a plate of sandwiches, which he placed on their table. Tommy picked one of them up and regarded it. It looked like half of somebody's ass between two slices of soggy cardboard. Fuck it, when in Moscow. He chomped.

Ivan put the remotes down on the table gently. He stood and crossed the room, where he punched the TV screen so hard it exploded into glass confetti. He sat back down and smiled, picked up one of the sandwiches, blood trickling off his knuckles. "You like?"

"Sure, what is it?"

Ivan just laughed and attacked his food.

Tommy Magic liked these guys. He was really looking forward to killing some more people. It actually made him happy to kill. He just wasn't sure if it was going to be the Dolan kid or that weasel of a brother-in-law of his. Maybe he'd flip a coin. It was fun not giving a fuck.

Jimmy passed through the glass doors into a marble lobby that suggested long-held wealth and quiet living. Broadway vanished behind him. A man in a brown uniform with sharp gold trimmings sat at a desk, and another, similarly attired, stood at parade rest by a bank of elevators. Jimmy approached the desk and said, "I'm here for Breslin. The name's Dolan. Jimmy Dolan." The man put aside a paperback he was reading and looked Jimmy up and down, taking in his dirty work clothes. The man's nose twitched ever so slightly, and Jimmy followed his eyes to footprints he had left on the running carpet. He wondered if snobbery was contagious, a consequence of hanging around the rich. Jimmy looked back and shrugged. "Hey, I work for a living. Sometimes that puts you near dirt."

The man picked up a phone, dialed, and said, "Jimmy Dolan." He listened, then nodded.

"Thirty-fifth floor."

"What apartment?"

The man picked up his book and looked at Jimmy as if he was tired of him. "You'll see the man." He waved toward his partner and flipped his book up. Jimmy clocked the title. *Nine Secrets of Successful People.*

The elevator pulled him skyward with a quiet rush. His ears popped from the change of altitude and he worked his mouth open and closed. The doors slid open on a long hallway, at the end of which was a single door. He walked across plush carpeting and rapped lightly on the door.

"Come in."

Jimmy turned the knob and entered the apartment. Up three stairs, at a long table, sat a man beating a vicious two-finger tattoo on the keyboard of a sparkling new computer. He was hunched over, dressed in a white button-down shirt and flannel slacks, his salt-and-pepper hair spiked out at mad angles.

Jimmy took in the spacious grandeur of the place. The view was southerly and jaw-dropping. He never thought the writing business could afford such luxury. He stood uncertain as Breslin continued to pummel the keys. Finally, Breslin stopped and said, "Come on, get up here." Jimmy climbed the stairs and shook his hand.

"Sorry about your father. He was a good guy, the best. You want something to drink?"

Jimmy declined and they sat at the table.

"So what can I do for you?"

"I'm thinking of running against Keefe, taking my father's place. I was wondering what you think about that. You know, what my chances might be."

Breslin raised his bushy eyebrows. "You really like to pick the easy fights. I guess the nut don't fall far from the tree. How you going to run against that? The guy's got a ton of money and more people that like him in there so they can keep robbing the joint blind. Plus I don't need to point out what happened to your father. These people are the worst, killers."

"I know it won't be easy. But a lot of the guys want me to run."

"You don't think maybe you should lie low for a while?"

"It's something I need to do."

"Well, I can't argue against that. You just better watch yourself."

"I want to go after him in as many ways as possible." Jimmy hoped one of those ways was in the mainstream press.

"So?" Breslin offered nothing.

"I was hoping you might write something about him. If you think it's a good idea. There's been a lot of rumors he's being propped up by the Feds. I mean, you know, with all the takeovers of Teamster locals, what's amazing is that this guy, who everyone figures is as crooked as they come, is still in there. He must be doing somebody a lot of favors."

"He's a bum, like his old man. The two of them don't have a legitimate bone in their bodies—thieves. I seen your guy once at a picket line. He's nothing unless he's surrounded by his apes. Who's your source?"

"A detective I know." Jimmy had little solid to go with. Tara had agreed to talk to Breslin, but what did she really know? He wondered how much bluffing they would need in order to get the story done.

"My guess is they won't be going on the record."

"No, but they'll talk to you. It's just an opinion piece, right? Kind of why is he still here?"

"Kid, I don't need no freakin' blueprint. You don't see me coming around telling you how to pour your concrete."

"I get you."

Breslin stood and walked down a long hallway corridor. He came back momentarily, sipping a cup of coffee. "You're a nice young kid, you sure you want to get mixed up in all this? Why dontcha take one of those Wall Street jobs, make yourself a fortune? Screw 'em. Leave the dirty business alone. It'll only cost you. Your integrity, your sanity, maybe your freaking life."

"I have to do this for my father. And for me," Jimmy said quietly.

Breslin studied him for a minute. "I'm not going to tell you what to do about that. I mean, we all had a father one time or another. Mine walked out when I was nine. Didn't stick around long enough to put me in your position. I'll see what I can do. I'll make a few of my own calls. Now let me get back to work here. I'm on deadline. I'll call." He waved Jimmy away. "I'll call, leave me your number. I'll call."

Jimmy passed through the doors onto Broadway and felt good, like he was finally starting to take some action, was doing something instead of just thinking about it.

267

You got to be kidding me," Jimmy said to his Uncle Punchy.

"Joke?" Punchy shook his large head. "Joke? No, Jimmy, this is not something I'm kidding about. You want the job, it's yours. You start at eighty grand plus expenses. You bring in business, you get points. It's a nice deal, Jimmy."

Jimmy swallowed his disappointment. He had asked Punchy to do the right thing and help him avenge his brother's death, to get rid of Frankie Keefe in the process, and his uncle comes back with what was essentially a bribe, an attempt to buy him out of the race to unseat Keefe. Jimmy decided to mess with him about it. "Eighty? Tell him I want two hundred."

Punchy looked perplexed. "Him? Who the hell is him?"

"Your friend Keefe."

"Ah, Jesus, come on, Jimmy. This ain't nothing like that. This is a legitimate offer, a nice job. You'll be in a good spot. Come on. Take the money. It's a nice life. A month ago you came to me for the thing."

Jimmy stared at him. "A month ago? A month ago was last lifetime, Punchy. A month ago was a different fucking solar system. Tell your friends they can stick the money up their thieving asses. Now get the fuck out of my father's house."

Eighty grand. Nice money, Jimmy thought. Almost twice what he had ever made in a year, not to mention big upshot potential. It was something he would have jumped at before his father's murder, was the life he aspired to. But now, there was no way he could take it. Money suddenly did not mean that much to him. He had something more important to achieve.

Punchy rode the elevator down and hurried out of the neighborhood. The place held too many bad memories for him, what he had run from for so long. Too many ghosts. He wondered what to do now. He wondered if he should have mentioned to Jimmy that the offer was not from Frankie Keefe at all. That it was from the government guy who was presently breathing down his neck. From the man who, with his threats and pressure, was making his life a living hell. Punchy decided it was time to go underground for a while. To stay on the sidelines while things sorted themselves out.

R oth looked over the various reports from his field agents and their informants. There was a surprising amount of activity involving what looked like cooperation between established Italian mob elements and upstart Russian gangs. According to Cronin, Tommy Magic was encouraging this. He had a communication from the local FBI office detailing Russian attempts to infiltrate labor unions, following the old Cosa Nostra pattern, as a way of gaining a foothold in legitimate business. He found this troublesome. It could only lead to the type of jurisdictional squabbles he had spent years avoiding. With a presidential election coming up, his mandate might be revoked. He decided he needed to stay on top of these developments. He realized Frankie Keefe would be of little use to him with the Russians.

Besides information, Keefe had been supplying him with a monthly package that would see him into a nice retirement. Roth stood up and looked into an envelope. It was thick with bills sent by Keefe. He picked up another envelope and took out a series of pictures that captured Cronin and Keefe's wife in various lewd embraces. He dropped the pictures on his desk and took a phone call from Punchy Dolan. He listened as the man described his nephew's rejection of the job offer.

He stood and looked out over Broadway. Maybe it was time to change horses. Keefe's threats were annoying. He started considering variables. If Dolan won, if Magic killed him. Roth figured he needed to act and not react, that he needed to dictate the situation. The FBI had stayed out of his way for a long time only because he fed them enough information from Keefe that helped them build their own cases. But many Bureau agents resented his exclusive access to Keefe.

He wondered if maybe it was time to put some more pressure on young Dolan.

'm going to run."

They walked through the park in the late-day sunshine hand in hand like new lovers, their shoulders touching, moving easily, the friction of the past faded.

"Where?" Tara knew what he meant and was not surprised but wanted to keep things light, kid a bit. He was serious so much of the time since his father was killed.

"After you, so I can hit you on the head."

That's better, she thought. "You think so? I'll kick your ass, cuff you, and strip-search you."

"The woman of my dreams. What do you think?"

"You scared?"

They came upon a bench. She sat and watched as Jimmy stood on the back of it balancing on one leg, curling his other foot behind him like a gymnast. "Of course I'm scared. I'm scared shitless. But every time I start to think about how scared I am, I begin to realize how pissed off I am. Sometimes I think about walking away, you know? I think that it will get easier, that I'm going to accept it, and deal with it. I went down to the church. I talked to Father Keith. But I don't really believe in that anymore. If there is a God that let that happen to my father, then what good is He? All this turn-the-other-cheek shit is for suckers." He leaped off and landed on the footpath. He sat and put his arm around Tara and pulled her head to his shoulder. "I'm going to meet with some of the old-timers in the union, see if I can get the kind of support I need to win."

Part of her wanted to dissuade him, because she knew it was going to change him forever. It might ruin any chance they had of a life together. She knew that if he went after Keefe, legally or otherwise, it would consume him. There was no way to roll in the mud with someone like that and not come away tainted. At least he seemed to have moved beyond the idea of murder. She looked at him. There was a tightness to him, his face, his carriage, as if somehow he was being sucked inside the vortex of his own self. She knew he would never be the same again. She wondered if she wanted this Jimmy. Maybe she needed the carefree fuckup somehow.

"So you're gonna run?"

"I figure I have two choices. I beat him the right way or I beat him the wrong way. All I know is, I can't live in my own skin if I let him get away with this shit. My father knew what might happen, and he never walked away."

Tara put her hand on his shoulder, felt the knot of tension, and thought, You are not your father. He was from a different time altogether. "Good. Jimmy, anything you want to do, I want to be there. Just promise me you won't do anything stupid. 'Less I say it's okay."

"I might look stupid, but it's just a disguise."

"Let's go do something, have some fun. You need to relax."

"Fun?"

"Yeah, Jimmy, fun. Hello, you remember what that's like? We can go up to my aunt's house in the Poconos, get away from all this shit."

"Okay." He sounded noncommittal. "I guess a couple days away won't hurt, for the weekend."

A man ran along playfully, chasing two young boys over the grass. They came together in a scrum and fell to the ground wrestling, the boys yelping with joy. A park ranger rolled past in a three-wheeled vehicle. Tara watched as a teenager, dressed entirely in black, emerged from the tree line. He spotted the ranger, froze, then slithered back into the woods.

"Jimmy, nobody says you have to give up your life to do this thing."

"Yeah. But nobody has to live my life either. I've already been threatened and bribed. It just makes me more determined to fight the assholes."

"What about the job they offered you?"

"Hey, it's the easy way out. I just couldn't live with myself."

"Good." She was proud of him for that. She stood and took his hand and they walked back toward his apartment in the gathering dusk.

L iam, did you see in the papers about the flesh-eating bacteria?"
Liam blew air through his lips. "Nah, Ma."

"It's a terrible thing. A simple cut, any type of scratch, and the next thing you know it can be eating you away like it's a pack of hungry wolves and you're a wounded doe that they've separated from her family and pounced on. It'll chew away till there's nothing left of you. What a terrible way to go. Terrible."

His mother related this information with such concern you would think her best friend had just been attacked by the bacteria. Liam sat next to her on the couch and tied his boots. He sipped a beer. His mother wore a tattered housecoat and drank a cup of tea. Her hair was in curlers and she sported her usual full face of makeup, which lent her the look of a clown. Liam stared at her bare feet, veiny and pale. God, he wished she'd put something on them. He hated her feet.

"I really wish you didn't drink so much, Liam. It's hell on the liver and various of the other organs. Now, your father was a man never touched a drop, looked on it as poison. And right he was." She sipped again from her cup, the rim of which was smudged with her lipstick. Something else that gave him the creeps. "We'd go to the county dances and everyone would be sloshed, Mrs. Murray prime among them, the lush. Not that I sit in judgment now; it's just some things are too obvious to ignore. Your father would sip his Coca-Cola. Above it all, he was."

Liam, when he was younger, had made attempts to find out the fate of his father. He carried around a picture in his wallet and, when making the rounds, he would ask old-time bartenders if they remembered him. Occasionally, they did. Most were at odds with his mother's memory about his aversion to booze. Apparently, his father was a nasty drunk, quick with his fists and often in trouble. Once, Liam accosted a man who resembled his father. The man was startled when Liam questioned him and produced a half dozen pieces of identification to demonstrate that he was not Liam's father. It was obvious that the further his father receded into the past, the more his mother idealized him.

She stood and placed her cup on a coaster she'd brought back from her honeymoon in Niagara Falls. When she came back from the bathroom, she said, "Here, Liam. I saw on the news, this is the stuff, if you get it on early enough it prevents that flesh-eating bacteria from sinking its teeth into you. With your job, cuts are all too common. I've a case of the stuff just for you."

Liam took the tube of Neosporin. "Great, Mom. I'll keep it handy." Even though she was his mother, every now and then, he wanted to crack her one.

He bussed her cheek and put on his jacket. He paused in the hall to zip up and looked at the picture that hung there. It was his parents on their honeymoon, his mother slightly swollen with him. She had been quite a looker in her youth with her waist-length black hair and showgirl figure. She looked like an old-timey movie star. He knew if he ever met up with his father, he was going to throw the man a good beating, no matter how old and busted down he might be.

In front of his building, Ralphie, the neighbor's kid, was bouncing a Spaldeen off the wall, throwing with one hand and then catching with the other, switching back and forth. Liam had taught him that as a way to build ambidexterity.

"Hey, Ralphie, you ready?" He produced two Rangers tickets from his pocket and waved them in the air between them. "Next Friday."

"I want to see the Knicks."

"That's enough of that kind of talk. Who sucks?"

Ralphie looked up the block, then turned back, a sly grin coming across his face. "Islanders suck."

"There you go. How's your mom?"

He shrugged. "Working."

"You take good care of her."

Liam headed to Johnny Mac's. The owner, drooling in the corner, was worrying over his racing form. He looked up and gave him his stare. "Errrrr. Behave yourself, Brady, or you're outta here for good this time."

"You some kind of fucking pirate? Errrr? Shiver me fucking timbers, Johnny Mac. I could get the scurvy in here."

"Keep an eye on him, Seamus. First sign of trouble, out he goes."

The bartender offered his boss a mock salute and said to Liam, "Mr. Brady, the usual?"

"Yup. Jimmy been round?"

"Not as of yet, Liam."

Liam took a roll of singles from his pocket and programmed AC/DC's *Back in Black*, the entire album twice. He sat and worked his way through two beers as if they were the last in the city, savoring each sip. He looked up and caught Johnny Mac glowering at him as the music, full of menace, pounded through the bar. Last Stand Larry sat cringing a few stools down. He seemed more forlorn than usual.

"Hey, Larry, where's your bike?" Liam asked.

Larry turned to him and stared, as if trying to gauge whether he was being ridiculed.

"The enemy captured it."

"Your flag too?"

"Sent me a ransom note."

"Yeah? Get outta here."

"In Spanish. They're calling themselves the Committee for a White Boy-Free Neighborhood, best as I can tell. Seeing as how I speak only the native tongue."

Liam fought down a laugh. Larry was one of those people everybody loved to fuck with. "What do they want?"

"They want me to move to Westchester or the Island. They'll settle for Jersey. It's war, Brady. War." Larry turned back to his cheap whiskey.

Liam ordered another beer and looked down the bar to Johnny Mac, sitting like king shit. "Hey, Johnny Mac, how we supposed to have fun with you hanging around like a cloud of doom all day?"

"I'd leave, but there's six Domos having lunch on my car."

Liam looked past him to the street. A half dozen teenagers were eating pizza, using Johnny Mac's car as a picnic table.

"You gotta be the oldest thirty-five-year-old on the planet." Liam reached into his pocket and pulled out his key chain. On it was a key to Johnny Mac's car. One afternoon, while the proprietor snoozed quietly on the bar, he had taken the liberty of making a duplicate. Not a bad thing to have. He patted his money and pushed the empty toward Seamus. "I'll be right back. Keep his attention."

He went to the corner, chased the kids away, unlocked Johnny Mac's car, jumped in, started it, and turned it around, so it was parked facing the wrong way and in a bus stop. He sauntered back into the bar and watched out the window. He sat whistling along to the songs. A tow truck appeared within two beers. He watched as the driver got out. He was a burly black man in a tight tee shirt wearing a weight-lifting belt. Liam wondered if he was going to pick up the car by himself. He watched him hook it, work the lift. As soon as the front was off the ground, Liam said. "Hey, Johnny Mac, you drive a Ford Explorer, right?"

Johnny Mac looked up out of one eye.

"They're towing one out there. Looks a lot like yours."

Johnny Mac dashed out the door and ran screaming into the middle of Broadway, waving his arms, and was nearly flattened by a gypsy cab. The tow truck driver, who had the Explorer secured, looked up at him, smiled, shrugged, jumped in the truck, and gunned it up Broadway, dragging Johnny Mac's pride and joy to the impoundment lot. Johnny Mac staggered after it a few yards, then bent over and placed his hands on his knees and tried to catch his breath. Liam watched him make his way back to the bar, his face twitching from the ordeal.

Liam ordered another beer and shared a laugh with Seamus and the other patrons. Johnny Mac came in the door, and before he could launch into his tirade Liam said, "You oughta watch where you park your car, Johnny. I mean, what with this mayor and his quality-of-life thing."

"Sons a bitches." Johnny grabbed his coat and rushed out to retrieve his car.

A beer and a shot later, Liam watched Jimmy come through the door. Man, he had changed since his dad got clipped. The way he carried himself, his face, he seemed older by a decade, serious in a way he never remembered. Jimmy came down the bar toward Liam, acknowledging somber hellos from a line of regulars.

Jimmy sat next to Liam. "My brother."

"Liam."

After a few drinks, Liam said, "I seen Keefe in the paper again, giving money to some children's charity. Blind and retarded kids."

"Yeah. Me too. A regular St. Francis."

"How does he get such a free ride?"

"He's sucking somebody's dick."

"Jimmy, I known you my whole life. I don't want to tell you what to do here, but the guy killed your father and I see the way you been since. You got to do something. Else it's gonna eat you up."

"I'm running."

"No shit?"

"I ain't taking this lying down. I have a few things going. But I need you to help me out." He told Liam about the two other chainsaw phone calls he had received and asked him not to tell Tara.

"Those fucking pussies."

"Yeah, well, I'm taking it seriously. I want you to watch my back."

"Done deal, brother. Done fucking deal."

Jimmy ordered a beer and said, "And, oh, yeah, one more thing."

Liam held up his hands. "What's mine is yours, brother."

"I need a gun."

"That's my Jimmy."

Cronin, caught in the commercial glare of an enclosed and sprawling shopping mall, moved along with the weekend hordes. It struck him that he had never been in one of these places before and was stunned by the crush and neon glow. He moved along, with longing in his heart. A rendezvous with Marie was in the offing, but he wanted to lose any possible tails. He went into stores randomly, checking out the crap for sale, then came out and switched directions. He meandered for half an hour, then sat and ate a piece of greasy fried chicken while looking down on the concourse. The whole scene made him glad he never had kids.

He made his way out into the sunlit parking lot, walked along the outside of the mall, then ducked into another entrance. His excitement was such that he could barely concentrate on scanning the crowd. He flashed a counterfeit badge in a Gap store, startling the clerk, and cut through and out the back door. He used the employee entrance of the hotel and took the stairs to the fourth floor. He waited at the top flight, and when no one followed, he took out a plastic room key and entered room 404.

Marie was on the edge of the bed with the TV remote in her hand looking as comfortable as if she were in her own bedroom. She was dressed in one of his shirts and nothing else. A talk show was on and, as he moved to her side, two outrageously fat young women started clawing each other's faces with a fury that was unsettling. Marie said, "Look at those animals," and clicked off the set. She smiled and stood and they came together. The room smelled mildly of mildew and previous couplings. He tore at her with a fire and desperation fueled now by something he did not want to recognize.

They finished and lay in a tangle, drenched in sweat, their breath ragged. "Jesus, Petey. What was that all about?"

He rolled on his back. He did not know what to say. He wanted to tell her the truth about the nature of his work, but realized the need for caution. She was, after all, Magic's sister. He squeezed the arm she draped across him. "Nothing. I just missed you. It's been . . ."

"Too long."

"Yeah." He felt a sadness descend. He lay here, the one time in his life when he felt a desire to get close, and who was it with? A woman married to his nominal boss, on whom he was spying for some branch of the government whose motives he was not sure of, a woman who also happened to be the sister of one of the most feared killers in the land. He wanted to laugh.

He had always run from comfort, from safety. Now when he thought he'd found what he wanted, was it really what he wanted, or was it just some sick bullshit way of fucking up his life and that of everyone around him? He knew one thing. He wanted out. And he knew another. He was taking Marie with him. It occurred to him he might have to kill Keefe and maybe even Magic to do this. He wondered if he was capable. He had killed in war and in and out of the line of duty. He recalled that night and the one angry bullet he'd fired while drunk into the face of a suspect they simply could not nail legally. The man had taunted them, hiding behind his cleverness. He had decided in the blind heat of booze to make him pay for his sins, had played God and executioner. It had cost him his career, but not his freedom.

She stroked his chest, twirled his hair around her fingers. "I don't know what's going on. My whole life it's been a requirement that I did not know what was going on. But I know this, Pete. I'm happy for the first time in my life."

He picked up his cigarettes, then put them down, realizing the smoke would bother her. He turned on his side to look at her face. The eyes were so full of something that he had never seen, not even in the beginning with the wife he had thought he loved. "You know, Marie, we could get in a lot of hot water over this. The guy might not care about you either way, but he's not about to let us ride off into the sunset. Think about it. He'd kill me, he knew. This is not a guy you can waltz into divorce court."

"I don't care. I can't take it anymore with the creep. We can run. My brother won't let him hurt me, Pete. I'll talk to him."

Cronin squeezed her shoulder. "No, no, no. Don't talk to anyone. Let me figure it out."

"My brother will understand. He's always been good to me." She stroked his face, her fingers lingering.

It worried him that she believed this to be true. He stood and waved her off. "No. Your brother won't understand. I'm sure he's fond of you and whatnot. But, Marie, you know this as well as anybody. The man is of a world, of a time and place where certain things are not acceptable. He might be a lot of things, but there are rules, Marie. You know what happened, couple of years ago, that guy in Queens?"

She sat up on the bed and wrapped her hands around her knees, looking as though she might cry. Hard sunlight striped across her from the window blinds. The air in the room was thick with the humidity of their coupling. She shrugged. "Lots of things happen to guys in Queens."

The muffled groans of other lovers reached them through the cheap walls. "Not what happened to this one." He pulled on his trousers. As he was buckling his belt, he said, "He was sneaking around with a mob guy's wife. Having the time of his life."

"That what this is to you?"

He held up a hand. "Stop it. You know better. Long story short, they found him on the side of the BQE with his"—Cronin pointed down the front of himself—"apparatus in his mouth."

"Come on, Pete, Frankie's Irish."

"You may know that, and I may know that. Problem is, he don't seem to know that." Buttoning his coat, he bent to kiss the top of her head. He lingered, inhaling her scent. It seemed to calm him. "We go, babe, it's a two-person tango. Me and you." He stood. "Nobody's going to want to help us on this one. Nobody. So please, no matter what you think about Tommy, let me figure this one out, okay?"

She looked up at him and, without speaking, nodded. He hugged her once more and knew it was time to get busy. The next few days would mean everything to them.

It was the kind of work that made her crazy. Her knowledge of computers made her a logical choice, but it was nothing more than drone work, data entry that any primate could handle. It made her wish she had kept her computer expertise to herself. She sat in a cubicle with a Diet Coke and a computer in front of her. There were two dozen identical cubicles in the room. It reminded her of modules in college.

The room was in the bowels of One Police Plaza and was part of the new electronic era of law enforcement. The Mayor was a freak for numbers, stats, hard measures of his crime-fighting prowess. Look, see, it's right here in black and white. Tara knew what anyone with a half-assed statistics background knew, that numerical analysis was a lot softer science than people wanted you to believe.

She moved quickly through the names. She thought it was a decent idea. Building a data base of buyers and sellers, in an attempt to track the narcotics trade as it moved from block to block and precinct to precinct. It was part of a federally funded joint task force with the DEA. She sat and sipped her Diet Coke. She took the names and typed them in. The task force then ran background checks—names, addresses, employment records, medical histories, credit checks, surveillance reports. They were even pressing for DNA sampling. She wondered about this. That it might be overkill for some poor mope from Connecticut busted buying a ten-dollar bag of pot. A little too much Big Brother.

She decided, on a whim, to type in the name of Thomas Vamonte, aka Tommy Magic. She had the second of four levels of clearance. His name came up with listings of his associates, a short bio, and areas of influence. It seemed he was the target of a task force investigation into racketeering in the construction field. She typed in Francis Keefe, but the computer asked for a password for higher clearance. She typed in a few silly attempts. Nothing happened, so she turned off the computer and left.

L iam lay prone on the lush lawn of the house across from Frankie Keefe's. He was dressed in a dark sweat suit and running shoes, elbows propped in sniper position, and his patience was on the wane. He wanted the asshole to be home for the show. The place was as quiet as a country lane after a blizzard. Occasionally, a luxury car would glide past him, splaying light across the lawn. The grass was damp and smelled rich, like a little bit of summer. It might be cozy, sleeping out here on a warm night. The faint warble of a TV reached him from a distance. He imagined a well-scrubbed family catching the last dose of boob tube before beddy-bye. This was prime home invasion territory. He imagined lots of jewels and thick stashes of cash. Things ever went bad in construction, he might have to come back this way.

Finally, the Cadillac pulled up, and he watched Keefe get out of the car. The Teamster boss waved his driver off, and when the car pulled back, Liam saw an older, dark-haired woman in the upstairs window, waving to the bodyguard. Liam figured Keefe's wife was getting a little side action.

He set his watch and waited fifteen minutes, long enough for the guy to get into bed, not long enough for him to fall asleep. His weapon was a single-shot twenty-two, a starter rifle for kids all over America. He placed the tube from a roll of wrapping paper over the barrel of the rifle, a primitive but effective silencer, and slapped home a twenty-shot clip. Then he sighted on the big house and started firing methodically, working the windows first, staying away from the one he figured to be the bedroom, hitting high on the second floor to be safe. He squeezed off shots, nailed the porch light, the rear tires of both vehicles in the driveway, a bird feeder. He imagined Keefe diving around his floor, screaming, trying to dial for help.

When the gun was empty, he tossed it into the hedgerow where he had stashed it just after nightfall, and started working his way back through the posh yards of the Westchester well-to-do. Every yard he traversed contained an in-ground pool and most had tennis courts. He hugged shrub lines and fences, moving through the night with a steady trickle of adrenaline keeping him on high alert. He fought an urge to rummage for plunder in toolsheds. He leapt easily over fences. Nothing could stop him. The wail of sirens pierced the night.

He pulled his baseball hat down over his eyes and jogged the last six blocks to the train station, where he sat in the bushes till he heard the air-horn signal. A northbound train eased to a stop and spilled its cargo of late-night commuters, the go-getters who forsook family to chase the big bucks. They seemed all to be in uniform—dressed in trench coats and carrying briefcases. Mixed among them were a few boisterous drunks back from an evening of good cheer in the big town. He watched this parade and thought it would be fun to pop a few rounds off, nothing serious, just flesh wounds to lend their lives some dimension.

He melted in with the commuters heading for the cars. He'd boosted a Ford Taurus for the operation and made his way to it through a lot ridiculously full of sport utility vehicles. There were even several humvees, not unlike what they'd used in the Gulf War. He found this comical. He had not even seen a single pothole in this neck of the woods. Just roads paved smooth. What a flock of assholes. He pulled out of the lot like any of the other late-night commuters coming home from the city. Jimmy might not have the stomach for the dirty work, but Liam did not mind at all. He actually enjoyed it, got a kick out of it. It was all shits and giggles to him. He'd just keep Jimmy out of the loop. Need to know, Jimbo. Need to know. I got your back, all right. What you don't know can't hurt you. He hit the Taconic and popped in a Guns N' Roses tape. He thought about Keefe and laughed out loud, a cackle, a joyous exclamation. Welcome to the jungle, motherfucker.

Frankie Keefe looked at the bullet holes in his triple-pane windows and felt the anger roll up from the balls of his feet, up through his legs and gonads and stomach, felt it climb into his chest and then explode in his brain with the white-hot flash of a phosphorus grenade. Somebody was going to die for this.

He forced himself to calm down. He placed three phone calls. One to the local cops, one to Cronin, and one to a man who would soon be whispering into Tommy Magic's ear.

Jimmy listened to Detective Sergeant McCabe. "It's got all the earmarks of a high-profile mob rubout, but the only suspect with a motive, this scumbag Keefe, was under federal surveillance at the time. And, of course, nowhere near the scene of the crime. We found the car, and the gun, which was foreign and clean. There was some blood in the car, and a piece of someone's ear, so if we grab a suspect we can at least put him in the car. Listen, Jimmy, your father was a good guy, we all know that. We want to nail these humps as bad as you do. Anything breaks, you'll be the first person I call." Jimmy thanked him and hung up, knowing that they would be moving on to fresher bloodletting. Life in the big town.

The next morning he woke with the sun and dressed for work. He made coffee. He walked the dog. He paced back and forth in the living room considering the election. Quill, still missing his master, followed his every step, whimpering quietly as he moved his arthritic joints along the parquet floor. Jimmy squatted and stroked his head. "Yep, it's me and you, Quill."

If he was going to make a decent run at Keefe, he would need a lot of help. He was not about to sit around and wait for some miraculous break in the case. He needed to assuage his heartbreak and rage and guilt. He went to his bedroom and looked through the papers on his dresser. He found the cocktail napkin from the funeral and looked at the name and number. The Teamster who had urged him to run, Lou Condo, had written his cell phone and beeper numbers on it. Jimmy put it in his pocket. He filled the dog's water bowl and stepped into the hallway. He took his boots and sat on the top step, laced them up, and descended into the dawn street.

He walked down to 207th and turned left, passing Mr. Oates walking his dog. "Morning, Jimmy." Jimmy returned his greeting and thought it amazing that when he bumped into people from the neighborhood he had not seen in several years, they greeted him as if he had never left.

On the corner, a man was trying to start his thirty-year-old car. The hood was up and he had one foot on the gas pedal and the other on the street. "Please. Please. You don't want me to lose my job," he pleaded with the car. He turned over his engine and the starter engaged, but the motor merely coughed and sputtered like a tired coal miner. The man leapt from the car and kicked it viciously. "You stupid bitch."

Jimmy caught up with Liam standing on the corner, a hard hat under his arm, eating a bacon-and-egg sandwich. Liam tossed a rolled-up newspaper at Jimmy and said, "Page three, bubby, nice piece of work."

Jimmy forgot it was Tuesday. He ripped open the paper and read the bold headline: TEAMSTER BOSS PLAYING BOTH SIDES? He walked along almost giddy. Breslin's article went further than he had hoped. Someone in the Labor Racketeering section of the Manhattan DA's office, as well as an unnamed detective he knew to be Tara, described a turf battle over Keefe. There was even an unnamed FBI agent expressing his frustration at Keefe's ability to duck prosecution. It was perfect, a public announcement of Keefe's duplicity. It suggested not only that he was a suspect in Mike's killing but also that he might be an informant. Jimmy knew that at that very moment Teamsters all over the city were reading the story, giving them another reason not to vote for the man. He hoped Tommy Magic was enjoying the column.

"This ought to shake the prick up."

"Oh, I think he's shaken already."

Jimmy ignored the remark.

"Homey, don't you know me? Shall we?" Liam gestured grandly. "This way to the A train." Jimmy followed him down the stairs. He fished a token out of his pocket while Liam jumped the turnstile. "Fuck the MTA, I always say."

They sat in the front car. Liam started throwing his hammer up in the air and catching it as it spun. First one somersault, then he worked two, and as the train pulled away, he was flipping it for three tight circles.

They left the train and walked over to the building site. Men came to the site from all directions, some in cars, others on buses, most from the half dozen subways that stopped at Union Square. A minivan pulled up, and five Jamaican carpenters got out, followed by a cloud of reefer smoke. Liam nodded. "Fucking coconut wagon. Good guys, though. Put in a day's work for a day's pay." Jimmy watched as they fitted their hard hats on top of piles of dreadlocks.

Jimmy, feeling some weird good fortune, called out to the site bookmaker, who was writing down bets in a small notebook. "Hey, half a sawbuck on 408." The bookie looked up at Jimmy and winked. 408, his father's birthday. He passed the shrine Liam had erected. He could have been assigned to any job in the city, but he chose to come back here, to the scene of the crime. He made his way to the cage and squeezed on with some of his crew and a dozen other assorted tradesmen. As the cage rumbled its way up the side of the building, they were afforded a spider man's perspective of the city. Somebody had doused himself with a sickly aftershave.

"Man, who the fuck stinks like a French hoo-er?"

"It's me. Why? You want to fuck me?"

"Your old lady let you outta the house stinking like that?"

"No. But yours did."

They left the cage and Jimmy followed Liam to the gang box, where they placed their coats and Jimmy put on a hard hat. He bent slowly at the knees, then did some slow squats and a few trunk twists, trying to limber up for the work. He bent from the waist and scraped his knuckles across the tops of his boots.

Liam watched him with a wry grin. "You look like some old fuck limbering up on a cruise ship before shuffleboard."

Jimmy carried on. "I'm not going to pull a muscle to impress you."

"Well, you better be loose, it's gonna be a long-ass day. Old numb-nuts wants to set the record. Thinks he's building the Empire State or some shit."

"Yeah. I like the OT, though."

"Changed your tune. Few weeks ago you were crying over half a day."

"Yeah, well, lots of things have changed in a few weeks." He pulled on his rubber boots.

Liam motioned with his head. "Look at the freak of nature."

Jimmy turned to see Cyclops pulling on his size-sixteen work boots. Despite the morning chill, the man wore only a tee shirt and dungarees. His arms were muscled like a Thoroughbred's thighs and richly tattooed. He picked up a McDonald's bag and pulled out half a dozen Egg McMuffins and set them on the plank next to him. His tee shirt read FUCK THE WORLD. He proceeded to devour the breakfast sandwiches as if they were cookies, one after another, pausing only to wash mouthfuls down from a half-gallon carton of milk.

Most of the crew had gathered to witness the feeding frenzy.

"Jesus, how long's he been in captivity?"

"Shhh. You can't disturb them when they're eating."

"Somebody should call the Discovery Channel."

"All right, you Marys in the woods, let's pour some concrete," Thumper barked in his best drill instructor cadence.

They were pouring the twenty-third floor; Jimmy stood and took in

285

the view of the city laid at his feet. He loved working up high. He inched forward so his toes were past the edge of the building and looked straight down at people scurrying to work, insignificant specks, at the cars and buses and trucks streaming along Broadway. The wind picked up and he rocked back on his heels, then leaned forward again, felt a dizzy rush. He would have made a hell of an ironworker.

Liam yelled, "Hey, either jump or get to work."

Jimmy turned as a concrete bucket came up over the lip of the building. A hard wind started to gust across the site, picking up papers and cups and swirling them about. Far out over New Jersey, the sky was darkening, and Jimmy felt electricity in the air. He picked up his shovel, and as the concrete started to flow, he dug in hard. He lost himself in the work, his muscles straining. Soon, sweat ran down his back and chest and his breath came short and hard. The crew worked together in a steady rhythm, efficient, almost mechanized, men with a fanatical devotion to the work ethic, men who defined themselves by their ability to bust ass for dollars. They spread the stuff about them. Thumper stood to the side and smoked a cigarette, staring off into the distance. Jimmy knew he appreciated having a crew that needed little supervision.

He moved along wondering whether he was capable of filling his father's shoes. He was not blessed with his father's idealism, and he hoped he wanted the job for the right reasons, to do the right thing for the members, not just to punish Keefe. He would figure that out later. Getting rid of him would be a service to the honest guys in the local. He moved aside as an empty bucket was lifted away. He wondered what would happen if he lost. He knew one thing; he was not going to let Keefe get away with it.

Later, after long hard hours and eight hundred yards of concrete, Jimmy descended to the street with the rest of the men. Waiting for him was Paddy Cullen, the new Teamster shop steward. Cullen sported a black crew cut and was dressed in dungarees and a blue polo shirt that showed off his thick biceps. Cullen handed Jimmy a photograph of his parents and his father's lunch pail.

"Hey, Jimmy, sorry about your dad. That's all he left here. I thought you should have them."

"Thanks, Paddy."

As he started away, Cullen said, "I hope to hell you beat that weasel. Good luck."

Jimmy turned back. "I'm going to give it my best shot. You can bet your bottom dollar on that."

The bar was lit by buzzing fluorescent lights that lent the patrons a sickly pallor. Just inside the door to the right, a steam table contained metal trays of thickly marbled meats and vegetables stewed to the point of colorlessness. The air was dead and so heavy with smoke that it seemed a different medium altogether. Jimmy stood still for a minute and let his senses adjust to the change from the crisp sunshine and windswept air of the avenue. His eye wandered down the long, dark wood bar. Most stools were occupied by blue-collar guys coming off shift. They sipped from mugs of cold beer and had piles of cash in front of them. They seemed intent on their drinking.

He did not see Condo and was about to make for the back to check the tables, when he heard his name called. He looked to his left and saw the Teamster at the corner of the bar with a *Daily News* spread before him. He held a glass of whiskey in his right hand, and there was a ballpoint pen behind his ear. Even in the piss-poor light of the bar, Condo looked good for a man of his age. His smooth complexion put him a dozen years younger than he was. He had the features of a fading actor who, because of his presence and intelligence, wins better roles as he ages. His eyes were large and liquid brown and his shoulders were thick with hard-earned muscle. He had a type of calm about him that Jimmy found reassuring.

Two businessmen in suits sat next to Condo. Jimmy shook his hand. Condo spoke to the men. "Hey, you, get up and let a working man sit down." He said it with a smile, but there was no mistaking the seriousness behind his request. The men looked to be high-level financial types not accustomed to being ordered around. They gave Jimmy and his concrete-dirtied clothes a once-over, then looked at

Condo and, still uncertain, to the bartender, who nodded. "Come down here, gentlemen, I've seats for you."

Jimmy took one of the vacated stools. A piebald cat wandered along the bar top, rubbing its head against the taps. Halfway down the line, a man lowered his face to the wood as if it were his pillow, knocking over a glass of beer. The bartender, a ruddy Irishman with a humorless face and a shock of white hair, righted the glass, pulled a towel off his shoulder, and mopped the beer off the bar. He placed the glass on top of the man's money, and let him be.

"Guy's taking his nap," Condo said. "Nice to see you. I was hoping you'd call."

"Thanks."

"You a drinker?"

"I'll take a beer. Bud."

"Your father, he wasn't much for the booze. You don't overdo it, do you?"

"Not these days."

Condo studied him. "Yeah, I guess you got other things on your mind nowadays. Which is good if you're going to do this thing. You better be prepared to give up everything else."

Jimmy decided to say as little as possible. He recalled a piece of advice Chickie Donohue had drilled into him. "Shut up and listen, kid, you might learn something." Besides, he was running, no matter what Condo had to say.

"So you think you can do this?"

"Yeah. I think it's the right thing to do."

"You realize they're gonna come after you."

"They?"

"Yeah, they. The families, the guys on the job that are happy the way things are, the government. Maybe the press. And let's not forget numb-nuts himself."

"Right."

"You hungry?" Before Jimmy could answer, Condo said, "Of course, you worked all day, you must be." He called to the man behind the steam counter. "Hey, Pepe, get us two pastramis, rye, mustard, a pile of pickles, you refugee."

"Ah, funguuul." The cook flipped his hand out from underneath his chin.

"See that? I taught him that," he said to Jimmy, then called out, "Keep it up and I'll drop a dime, call immigration." Condo turned back to Jimmy. "Your father was a good, decent guy. He had brass balls, but he didn't always use his smarts. Don't get me wrong, but he knew he was up against the jackals. Sometimes backing up ain't such a bad idea. What do you know about your opponent?"

"Less than you, obviously."

"Yeah. You spend much time talking to your father about this?"

"Not really, tell the truth. He kept most of it to himself."

Condo nodded. He sipped his whiskey and regarded Jimmy as if he was making an assessment. "Probably didn't want you all caught up in it. Your father would be like that." Condo put his glass down and said, "Keefe is the nephew of a guy who ran the local for years."

"Billy Keefe."

"Right, whose brother, the current asshole's father, was a bad guy, name of Frankie too. He was a real Irish rum-dum with an attitude. Kind of guy was nasty when he drank, but this one was almost the same way without a drop in him. I think there was something wrong with his head, maybe he was dropped on it five or six times when he was born. His brother Billy, he was the smart one. Not a bad guy, far as things go. Now, he did business with all sorts of rotten apples, but this is the forties, fifties, sixties, even the seventies. You see, now things are known, but in them days you had Hoover denying the families existed, Kennedy cutting his deals, everybody was crooked. Just some people lied about it better than others. Billy Keefe was no angel. But he was his own man. He did deals here and there, but the funny guys came around, he never let them take the thing over.

"Now, his moron brother Frankie was the one. He got slapped around in a bar one night in Brooklyn. So, instead of taking his beating like a man—like so you got your ass kicked—he runs home and gets a gun. He waits outside the bar and the guy comes out. Bang-bang, he puts two bullets in the guy's face. Dead." Condo waved at the bartender. "Benny, fresh us up here.

"So he goes to the can, seven years, I remember, eight maybe. All the rumors are going around, he's some Mafia hit man. Over the fact he couldn't defend himself. Still, his brother Billy wants to take care of him, since it's his brother and all. He puts the guy in all the right spots. But he is a fricking zero, he's robbing everybody blind. And worse than all that, he's buddies with a crew of cannibals from Brooklyn he met in the joint. They use him to get in the door. Soon as that happens, of course, they start trying to take things over from his brother. Like they can't help themselves. Most guys fold then and there. Hey, it usually means they got some brains.

"Billy Keefe goes to visit a job, and he catches one of the cannibals trying to take over the little book they got going—you know, nickel-and-dime stuff. The numbers, a little sports, maybe a loan or two—strictly in-house and small-time. Now, this is a made guy and all the world knows it. But Billy Keefe, he was one big tough Irish SOB. He smacks the jamoke to the pavement. I mean, he beats him like I ain't never seen anybody get beat, worse than a stepson who peed the bed. The guy's bleeding, trying to crawl away, and Keefe walks along beside him, kicking him in the ribs. The mope finally goes out, and Billy Keefe, he yanks off the guy's pinkie ring. You know, like an insult-to-injury kind of thing, and tosses it into the foundation they're pouring. A meat wagon had to come and scrape the slob offa the sidewalk."

Pepe came over and placed the plates in front of them with a flourish, as if he was serving dignitaries at the Four Seasons. "Yours I do not spit into," he said to Jimmy with a crooked smile that revealed a mouth holding only a few teeth.

"Let me see your hands. You're touching my food." Condo made a show of inspecting Pepe's nails for cleanliness. "Not bad. Now get outta here, you cockroach farmer." Condo slipped him a bill for a tip. Jimmy noticed it was a twenty.

Condo tucked into his sandwich for a few mouthfuls, then continued. "Where was I? Oh, yeah. Two days later they found his brother nailed to the floor of a job site. The old eye-for-an-eye, a little worse. Now, I don't know if Billy Keefe was left alone because they couldn't get to him, or they were scared of him, or they figured killing his brother was enough, or maybe the guy he stomped is on somebody's shit list, or what. There's always a lot of maybes and ifs when you're

dealing with those people. Now, you got Billy Keefe, he's feeling remorse over what happened, so he starts grooming the nephew,
Frankie, our current problem, to work with him. Coupla years go by,
and it's obvious to everybody this little prick is about as useful as tits
on a bull. He's no Billy Keefe. Now, during this time a few of us who
was always having problems with the way things were run, your father
and me included, tried to run candidates, one of which was your father.

"So Frankie's running around making noise like he's set to be the
next business agent. Billy Keefe makes it clear this ain't gonna happen
as long as he's alive to prevent it. Then one day out of the blue sky,
Billy gets popped for whacking a trucking company exec, and next
thing he's tied up in this RICO trial and, ba-da-boom, he goes away.
Gone." Condo waved his arm and pointed out through the window as
if indicating a particular place. "He dies up there. And, of course, in
his absence, who gets in but this ham sandwich with a fancy haircut
and a suntan."

Jimmy watched as a gaggle of postal workers from the General Post
Office made their way in for an after-work libation. They slapped
federal-issue paychecks on the bar and ordered drinks. "Why'd he kill
the guy?"

"Who?"

"The trucking guy. Billy Keefe."

Condo shrugged. "One of those things. But it always struck me as
wrong. Billy Keefe was a tough guy, but he was no killer. You never
know what gets into a guy, you never know."

Jimmy sipped his beer. This litany of mayhem was giving him
pause. Condo continued.

"So this pissant takes over, and right away he's doing business with
all kinds of slobs and degenerates his uncle would never let in the
door. As bad as he was, he got us decent contracts and only robbed for
himself. Now, remember, any other profession the top guy takes, it's
called a salary, maybe a finder's fee. With a union, it's extortion or
some other crime. His nephew, this guy Frankie Keefe, he's making
parasites rich, bloodsuckers. Then he marries that slob's sister and for-
getaboutit. They got it all sewed up."

Condo tossed the last bit of his sandwich down on his plate and shoved it away from him. "Just thinking about the prick ruins my appetite." He pulled out a small bottle of Tums, laid a half dozen out in his palm, and popped them into his mouth. He washed them down with his Johnnie Black.

Jimmy drank the rest of his beer, felt himself getting in deeper and deeper: This is where I fathom myself. "Why do you want to help me?"

Condo paused and put his hand on his belly as if he was waiting for the concoction to transform him. "That's a good question. I came up the old way. Me and your father didn't always get along. Sometimes we was together on things, other times we were at odds and ends. He was from Manhattan, I was from the Bronx. He was Irish, I'm Italian. In them days, both those things meant something, like we were different tribes. But we all had our problems with the Keefes.

"In the bad old days, a guy wanted to go against the system, he risked a beating or worse. One night, a guy, I'll never forget, name of Bobby Oreo, like the cookie, he was bitching and moaning about I don't know, job assignments? Whatever. Point is, he pissed off the powers that be. Three gorillas jumped him on the way to his car. I come upon this, I say screw it, some things you just can't let happen. I jump in, and of course, I take the beating too. They give me this." Condo turned his head and bent to show Jimmy a vicious scar that ran along his hairline from his forehead to the bottom of his ear. "And these." He popped out a set of false teeth, turned them in his hand, and put them back in. "I come close to dying that night. Till someone jumped in to stop it. That guy was your father. Without him, I ain't been here for the last twenty years. A new lease on life he gave me."

Jimmy took this in. He had never figured his father for a brawler.

"You think I got a shot with this thing?"

"Let me tell you something. This thing with your father, it's got a lot of people that was going along to get along, it's got them to talking and wanting to do something for a change. Lot of guys weren't crazy about your father, because he stirred up a lot of crap. But outside of his collection of goons, not too many guys give a rat's ass about Keefe. Most guys worry about this new, so-called secret ballot. Like how secret is it really going to be? If the thing is legitimate, you get a lot of guys who might be nervous, but they'll vote for you. I think, you run, you got a chance. I just need to know if you are willing to do what's gotta be done."

Jimmy felt a chill in the close air of the bar. He wondered what that meant. "Yeah," he said, just to fill the space between them. Condo twirled the ice in his rocks glass. "I want to make the fucking guy sorry he was ever born. I go to bed at night thinking about it, I wake up thinking about it, and in between I dream about it. He killed my father and he's a thief who screws ninety-five percent of the guys he's supposed to be representing. He's got to go."

Condo pursed his lips. "That's well and good. That's the spirit, but you seen what happened to your father. This ain't a kiddie ride. There's a lot of people counting on Frankie Keefe for a lot of things. You need to know how bad you want this." His tone hardened. "This ain't a joke, kid. You win this election, let me tell you something, you'll be sitting on eight, nine hundred million dollars of benefit funds and you're gonna have a ten-billion-dollar-a-year industry by the balls. One yank and you can make or break a lot of heavy people. Good guys, bad guys—et cetera. All a sudden, you are going to have a lot of new friends and a lot of new enemies." Condo looked him in the eye. "You go in for a penny, you better be in for a pound."

Jimmy nodded his head. He would not be running half-assed.

Condo waved a hand at the bartender and indicated their drinks. "Let's have one for the road."

Jimmy decided to ask the obvious. "How come no one, the Feds, city, state, ever took him down?"

Condo shrugged. "Sixty-four-thousand-dollar question. One I never figured. Especially now with the government running things. Somebody's in love with the guy. He's gotta be somebody's sweetheart. Although he took a hit in the paper." He stopped to look Jimmy over like he was waiting for an admission of complicity in the Breslin story.

Jimmy thought there was no reason to tip his hand on that. "I seen it."

"As far as you're concerned, that shouldn't matter. Worry about the votes. Fifty percent plus one and you win. Simple math."

"How come Keefe hasn't come after you?"

Condo paused, twirled his drink again, as if he was considering Jimmy's need-to-know status. "I have an uncle. Downtown. One of the last of the guys from way back. Way, way back. He's old and he's getting feeble, but he still scares a lot of people. Long as he's around, this punk don't have the stones to come after me. I just have to hope my uncle lives longer than this tomato can stays head of the union. And besides, I don't give much of a rat's ass anyways. I've lived a good life. Nobody can subtract that, this stage of the game."

Benny the bartender brought their drinks. Condo downed his quickly, stood, and put his coat on. "Here's a list. Call each of these guys. I talked to them already. Most of them are ready to help, a few others are willing to talk. And, hey, keep your eyes open. You seen how they got your father. Anytime, anyplace. That was done for a spe- cific reason. These guys are running out of options. They're gonna want to hold on to whatever they got left. Always remember: *Nothing's on the level*. You might think something or somebody is, but nothing's on the level. You keep that in mind, you might be all right."

Jimmy stood on Eighth Avenue and watched Lou Condo disap- pear into the night crowd. He put his hands in his pocket and felt the list Condo had given him. A yellow scramble of taxis hurtled past him toward Penn Station. He walked up the avenue to the A train, a bounce in his step, feeling victory was possible.

Cronin pulled up to Keefe's house and saw the car, a black Crown Vic, with the two bodyguards parked out front. With the shooting up of his house, Keefe's paranoia had grown to the point that he had added around-the-clock protection to ease his mind. Both the bodyguards were sleeping. The one on the driver's side was lean- ing against the window, his mouth open as if he was dead. His breath fogging the window proved this was not the case. He had a thick head of black hair and a nose that had been banged around. Cronin chuck- led. The other bodyguard was leaning over, his head resting on the driver's shoulder like a lover's. Crack squad here. He rapped his ring on the window and they both jumped as if lit on fire. "Morning, ladies." He moved past the car and up the drive to the house.

He rang the bell and Keefe answered, knotting his tie. Keefe looked outside and tossed his head back toward the vestibule. "In," was all he said. Cronin followed him and saw Marie sitting on the couch with an array of suitcases at her feet. He looked to her but she did not meet his eyes.

Keefe was pulling on his jacket. "You see the fucking newspaper this morning?"

Cronin nodded. The column was a follow-up article by Breslin and had provided quite a shock over his pancakes. The piece contended that someone with proof about Keefe taking kickbacks from contractors was about to come forward.

"I need this? As if things ain't going bad enough, I got some prick with a pen spreading lies about me like that."

Cronin realized what a virtuoso liar Keefe was. If he did not know better, he would believe Keefe's indignation was legitimate.

"What's with the luggage? You going somewhere?"

"Me? Fuck no. I'm going to stand and fight. I'm sending Marie to the country house for a few days. I can't have her around with bullets flying through my fucking windows and papers making me out to be some rat. Like living at the O.K. Corral." He turned to his wife. "All's I need is you getting shot, your brother will be over here trying to unscrew my head and shit down my windpipe. My life will be even more miserable than it is today."

"I don't want to go to the country. I'm not particularly fond of spiders and mosquitoes. Not to mention the shitty shopping." She sounded like a schoolgirl who was being grounded. When Keefe turned away she made a yucky face.

Cronin realized she was using child psychology on her husband. She was eager to be away, a little adventure.

"Tell those two galoots to get up here and load the luggage so she can be on her way."

Not quite. Cronin said, "Frankie, I come up on those two. They were sleeping."

"You shitting me?"

"Regular slumber party. I'd give them a load of grief, I were you. Anybody could have come up on you." He watched Keefe consider this. He knew the man was scared, as much as he tried to cover it up.

"Goddamnit. All right, you take her."

"Frankie, you shouldn't be by yourself." Cronin faked concern.

"I'll have one of the apes drive me before I shit-can them. Long as they're awake they can't be too bad. Come on, Marie, give me a kiss goodbye."

Cronin turned away while they embraced, feeling a ridiculous stab of jealousy.

"Oh, I forgot," Marie said. "Tommy called. He wants to see you tonight, he said."

"You forgot?" Keefe turned a shocked shade of pale. "How the fuck you forget that with what you seen in the paper? Oh, for the love of God, Marie. Tommy called, himself? On the phone? Your brother used the fucking phone? And you forgot?"

"Frankie, I'm sorry. I was distracted about everything. I ain't used to getting shot at."

Keefe regained some of his tan. "Bring her up there and turn back around as fast as you can. I want you to come to the meet with me."

Cronin knew the man was straining to keep it together in front of his wife. He was not looking forward to the meet himself. If it was not in a public place, he wondered if they were going to come out of it alive. He considered it might be time to run. Cut his losses and get out while he still could.

Cronin dumped her bags in the trunk and took the wheel. On the thruway he said, "Let me ask you something."

"Yeah."

"Your brother, on the phone. How did he sound?"

"Sound?"

"Yeah, did he sound mad, different than when he usually calls?"

"He don't usually call. He's not one for the phones. He'll have his wife call. But I'd say he sounded like always. You know, in person, a lot of grunts, a lot of fuck this and fuck that. That's my brother. I don't think he likes Frankie much. Speaking of which, you should have seen him over that story this morning. He was screaming like a madman. I had to fight not to laugh in his face, the jerk. But I'll tell you, it's all nonsense. Frankie's a lot of things, but no way is he a stool pigeon."

Cronin thought, We never really know people, do we?

She leaned on his shoulder and turned the radio up a click. "Love this tune. I've been thinking, Pete, I want to do this now. I want to just go away. Screw that asshole."

Cronin was convinced the time to move was at hand and was glad he would not have to do any convincing. He knew that he was playing his hand beyond any sensible level. He was still short of cash. He knew Marie might come up with some, but nothing he could count on. That prick Keefe made her practically beg for money. She had to go to him for cash, like a kid looking for an allowance. He let her have the credit cards, but he would shut those down the instant he knew they were gone. Besides, Cronin was not about to leave that kind of a trail for the man to follow.

Cronin tallied the few pickups he might still make. He had seven of the regular contractor stops, which meant another seventy, eighty large. It was not enough. He needed a big grab. He had a pretty good idea when that was going to be. The timing was good. He wondered about the meet Magic wanted. If he knew, or even believed, Keefe was really a rat, things might go badly for them. He tried to calculate what the marriage to his sister might mean for a killer like Magic. God only knew. Probably nothing.

As they made their way up Route 17, the traffic was fast and light. He thought Marie might never go back to that house again, if he could put things together. He fought the urge to confess the real nature of his involvement with Frankie. There would be plenty of time for that later.

They stopped for some burgers at a rest stop. Back on the road, she asked about his timetable. "I'm putting it together. Things go right, I'm thinking a few days, a week on the outside."

"I can't believe we're really going to do it."

The thrill in her voice roused him. Christ, the two of them. They were like a couple of kids out in a big car on the open highway, music blaring and nothing but promise ahead. He stomped on the gas and blew the carburetor wide open. She placed her hand on his knee and gave a reassuring squeeze. Damn. He might just pull this off.

Tara rolled out of Jimmy's bed and for a moment watched him sleep, the tightness gone. He looked vulnerable somehow. She dressed without showering and drove down to work. She parked around the corner and threw her police parking plaque on her dashboard. She was surprised to see Lincoln Mitchell waving to her from his own car. She walked over to him, and he pushed open the passenger door for her. "Detective, come take a little ride." She slipped into the car and Mitchell pulled away. "I got an interesting call last night about your boyfriend."

"Jimmy?"

"Jimmy Dolan. Seems to be making a lot of people nervous." Mitchell parked alongside the Native American Museum. Across the street, a funeral motorcade was arriving at a church. Two black limos followed the hearse to the curb. A woman, thick-legged and dressed in black, was led sobbing from the lead car. She carried a floppy hat in one hand and a Bible in the other. Lincoln Mitchell waved a dark brown hand at the unfolding ritual. "We all gotta go. Sometime."

"What kind of people is he making nervous.?"

"Good question. What I know is this." The radio played softly, an old R&B classic. Tara, feeling the sudden need for air, cracked her window. Mitchell continued. "We talked about the Big Dog. It appears he is stirring. Frankie Slick's friends are worried about losing him. I guess what it is, is that your Jimmy is now seen as a serious contender, and that makes people unhappy."

Tara knew this could only be bad. "What does this have to do with me?"

Mitchell exhaled. "The way these people work, they look to exploit a weakness. They look for links. They know a lot of people, most people, might not want to do something for themselves, but they'll act differently if someone they care about is in trouble. They like to present choices."

The low-grade fear she'd been feeling kicked up a notch.

"Two things. They know you were in the computer. Unauthorized, and looking into OC suspects. They can easily make it look like you were passing on information."

Tara sank down in the seat and cursed to herself. Jesus, how could she have been so stupid? This wasn't a game.

"And your shooting, they have not officially closed it. You can be called into question on that. This department, if they want, can hang you out to dry, and in public. A leak in the press. Questions. Scenarios floated. They can ruin your life, Tara."

Tara felt her fear being replaced by heat. She sat up. "Why the hell me?"

"Jimmy Dolan. They want you to get him to drop out. You don't, they're going after you. Your shooting, the fact you were in the computer. They can do what they want. This is not like a real job. This is an organization, baby, that eats its own. They want you, they got you. End of story."

"But what stake do they have? I thought you said it's a federal thing, this Keefe."

"It is. But apparently somebody is doing somebody a favor. Or maybe somebody owes somebody. I don't know. What I do know is they came to me because they know I know you. Which means they already been looking closely at you. I know what you're feeling. But, Detective, think on this real hard. I've seen what they can do. I've seen good tough cops end up eating their guns. 'Cause when they turn on you, you're going to be the loneliest person in the world."

"My lucky day."

Mitchell drove back around the block in front of the task force building. "They mentioned time. A week."

Tara got out of the car. She thanked Mitchell.

"Look," he said through the window. "I'm not sure at all what this means, who is who. I'm just letting you know what I heard. Are they bluffing? I wouldn't bet my ass on it. You need to sit down with your Teamster boyfriend, figure out what it is you two want in life. You want your career, he's got to take a walk on this election."

"I can't believe this shit."

Mitchell drummed his fingers on the steering wheel. His face was lined with concern. "If it's any consolation, this job ain't what it used to be."

Tara nodded and walked toward the building, looking around. She felt hunted and watched, vulnerable. She passed through the door of the HQ wondering what her love for Jimmy Dolan might cost her.

On the ride down to the East Side, Keefe was quieter than Cronin ever remembered. He gnawed on his lip and stared out the window, like a man on his way to a sentencing. Which, Cronin realized, he might very well be. When they crossed Fourteenth Street, Keefe said, "I hope this guy doesn't believe the shit they put in the papers. I mean, it can only be bad for us."

Cronin winced at the choice of pronouns. He had Roth on speed dial on his cell phone. If he hit the button, they were supposed to come and come heavy. He had no interest in becoming fertilizer in Magic's garden. "Maybe we should turn around."

"And go where? The fat fuck would find us, no matter where we go. He calls, I gotta go in. No ifs, ands, or nothings."

Cronin thought Keefe overestimated his brother-in-law's reach, but who knew. They found a meter spot on Avenue A and parked. Ordinarily, he would drop Keefe off and wait. But not this time. Keefe insisted he come in.

"Look at that pile of shit." Keefe motioned to a half dozen teenagers done up in punk-rock fashions. They sported various spiked and cropped hairdos and were prodigiously pierced and tattooed. "They filming a fucking horror movie?"

As they passed, the one who appeared to be the ringleader said, "Can you give us a dollar for drugs?" His diction and accent placed his upbringing a long way from that street corner. Keefe stopped short.

"A dollar? How about I rip your fucking ears offa your head instead."

"Dude, that's harsh."

Cronin watched Keefe stiffen and thought for a moment he might smack the kid. The punk stood his ground and even seemed to be contemplating his own assault.

"Harsh. You don't know the meaning of harsh."

Keefe pulled open his jacket to reveal the butt of a pistol. The punk looked down at it and began to back up slowly, saying, "That's not even real, dude."

They walked in lockstep to First Avenue. Cronin's senses were on full alert. The light was clear and sharp. He noticed that the joints in the brick wall of a school they passed had just been repointed. He whiffed the greasy smell from a falafel stand, heard guttural chatter coming from a window. He moved along loose-limbed on adrenal buzz.

"This has got to be a good sign, right? Him calling us down here."

Cronin knew Keefe was looking for affirmation, reassurance. He did not answer him.

"If he was going to take us out, he wouldn't invite us down, the middle of the day, right?"

The pronoun grated on him. Us. No, Frankie, it's you. "Wouldn't be smart."

"Smart. He's too fucking cunning for that. I should figure out a way to whack him. That would solve all my problems. I'd have to figure out a way, do it, pull it off so nobody knows who done it. But hey, that's doable. Don't you think?"

Cronin just looked at him.

"It ain't like the old days. I mean, things are so half-assed screwed up, who's left to step in, the guy goes? We could run it ourselves."

Cronin wondered if Keefe was losing his mind, if the pressures were finally getting to him. Whacking Magic was an idea that could only occur to an unsound mind.

As they walked down the three steps to Magic's pastry shop, Cronin surveyed the block for anything that might be the cavalry. Nothing stuck out. Traffic crawled up the avenue, drivers leaning on horns to no effect, a deranged symphony. He considered the possibility that Roth was letting him go in naked. As they pushed the door open, he had to admit that it would not surprise him.

Inside, they were hit by warm, sweet air, heavy with the cloying aroma of fresh-baked pastries and black coffee. Mary, the cashier, sat stone-faced behind the counter. She pulled on a cigarette and gave them a cold once-over. A plump young woman stood with a white box in one hand selecting a variety of desserts and dropping them into the container. She followed the prompting of an old widow in black who pointed a bony finger through the glass.

Keefe said hello to Mary, and moved for the back. Two men, one large with the insolent gape of a third-grade bully, the other wiry and sharp-eyed, watched them approach. Both wore track suits. One black, one blue. Gold chains sparkled around their necks. Skinny nodded so slightly Cronin was not sure his head had even moved. Human guard dogs.

Cronin fingered the cell phone in his pocket and felt a sense of relief at the presence of the women. He followed Keefe through the shop and into a back room that was really no more than an overstuffed supply closet. Five-gallon buckets of lard and sacks of flour were stacked all around; great tins held oily coffee beans. The floor was dusted white and a calendar bearing the Sacred Heart of Jesus hung from a nail. It was eleven years old.

In the middle of the room was a card table with a few folding chairs and a seated Tommy Magic. He was dressed in the fashion of a color-blind retiree with his green-and-brown-checked golf slacks and baby-blue sport shirt. A bare bulb hung from a cord and lit the space with enough wattage to show the years on Magic's face to poor effect. His eyes were underscored by half-moons so dark that they might have been the result of blunt-force trauma and not just hard living. He sat and looked up at them glumly. In front of him was a cup of espresso, and to Cronin's surprise, a small tape recorder of the type a journalist might use.

Magic put his fists on the table and pushed himself up, sliding the chair behind him so it scraped on the concrete floor. "Frankie," he said, and then nodded at Cronin. "How's things?" He then put his fingers to his lips and pressed a button on the tape recorder. After a second Keefe's voice emanated in answer and a conversation of no import issued from the device. Small talk between the men that Cronin

302

realized had been taped some time before as a ruse. They all stared at the recorder for a moment. Magic smiled. His plump lips separated into a kind of lupine grimace. It was a facial gesture so rare on the mobster that it looked unreal. He jerked his head toward the back door.

Cronin put his hands back in his pocket and watched Keefe slide his hand into his jacket near his pistol. He hoped the man was not that stupid. If death was waiting for them behind that door, men with silenced pistols, those listening would have no idea what was happening. The recorder was a primitive, but cunning deception. They moved toward the door. Cronin noticed Keefe's lips pulled back in a kind of leer he affected when he was nervous.

The door was metal and dented and had probably hung there since the building went up a century ago. Cronin wondered if anyone had gone through it and not come back alive. He knew there would be a small yard boxed in on all sides by other buildings with many windows overlooking the yard. Witnesses. On the tape behind him Magic was saying, "These agents, motherless fucks." Just a little gratuitous dig at his pursuers. They had all bunched up in the tight space before the door. Magic pulled it open and held it for them. Keefe pointed to it as if to say "Through there?" and Magic waved his arm quickly three times. It looked like a moronic pantomime. Keefe moved for the door looking at Cronin. His eyes were saying, You better be right. They followed Magic into the backyard.

There was a canvas tarp draped over their heads, propped up by poles and tied to a wire that ran from the building, which blocked the view of anyone above. It had begun to rain and the damp reek of the canvas triggered an army memory for Cronin. The rain drummed on the jury-rigged overhang. The air was tight and humid, a mix of smells: Magic's animal musk, garlic frying in a nearby kitchen, and the cold rot of monsoons from his past. He half expected a whiff of cordite or the stench of death.

Magic spat through his teeth. "That fat fuck finance guy, your good friend with the bar on the East Side. I hear things, like he's been talking to people he shouldn't be talking to. I seen in the paper about you. Forget it. I figure they're out to divide us. You gonna have a problem replacing that fuck? He suddenly can't do your business?"

Keefe's relief was palpable. Cronin swore he heard him sigh. "A dime a dozen that guy, Tommy. Not to worry."

"Not to worry. All I do is worry. This kid, your election, he a problem?"

"No. I mean, I doubt it. He never spent much time on a truck, guys don't like that, and he's just a kid."

Magic turned his fat misshapen head to gawk at his brother-in-law. His eyebrows raised with a creak. His pupils shrank. "How much time was it you spent on a truck, Frankie? Exactly?"

Keefe said nothing.

"Just remember, you ain't gonna be my favorite brother-in-law no more, you lose that local."

They followed Magic's fat checkered ass back into the supply room office. The recorder was still on and from it Magic proclaimed, "Who the fuck can root for a team, nothing but dope addicts and rapists? Not to mention they all black as the inside of somebody's ass." Magic hit the stop button and pocketed the recorder. As they passed back into the shop, he called after them, "Take a piece of cake, you want it. Just make sure you pay for it."

On the way uptown Keefe broke into a heavy sweat and rolled his window down.

"See that? No big deal. That fucking Paunchy. I should have figured that the fat bastard was the rat. You can tell just looking at him, he's weak. Soft. Fuck him."

"You never know."

"That thing I said before. About my relative? I'm thinking that's the way to go here."

Cronin just shook his head. Keefe was so full of shit it was unreal. Whack Tommy Magic. Right.

"You want a piece of that? I'll make it worth your while."

Cronin said only, "We'll talk. Not in the car." He punched the gas as the traffic on the FDR loosened up. He needed to get a message to Roth about Punchy. It sounded as if Pius Dolan was not long for this earth. Then he wondered at the source of Magic's misinformation. Who was in a position to know, or care, about Punchy? He swerved to avoid a truck with Ohio plates. At the wheel was a kid with long blond hair and a goatee.

"This moron with commercial plates on the FDR. They should lock the asshole up." Keefe squirted some Binaca in his mouth. "Paunchy Dolan. After all the nice things I done for him."

You're a real sweetheart, Cronin thought. Up on the Cross Bronx Expressway, he wondered again about who might want Punchy out of the picture.

Jimmy spent the week working his way down the list of Teamsters that Condo had given him. The election was turning out to be no different than any political campaign he had worked on. First you identify and solidify your base and then you reach out and try to attract new votes. Build coalitions. Give people a reason to believe. Lie when you have to. He met with the ones he felt certain of first. These were men who did not like Keefe and were mostly concerned with keeping their jobs. They were afraid of Keefe's vengeance, if he won. Most had been around a long time and had survived by keeping their mouths shut. Go along to get along.

Several Keefe stalwarts had not returned his calls. One had pitched into a frothy screaming fit on the phone, threatening to "pound him like a piece of punk meat" if Jimmy ever called him again. He was not sure what that meant. He scheduled a meet with Sol Rosen, whom Condo described as the key to the race. Retired, he was an old ally of Billy Keefe's and controlled a large bloc of votes from Long Island and Queens and most of the retirees who were eligible to vote. These guys had little to fear, since they were not looking for work, but were concerned about crooks handling their pension funds. Rosen had already been moving toward endorsing his father before the shooting. Jimmy figured that was a good sign.

Jimmy sat on the steps of the General Post Office on Eighth Avenue as a daytime basketball game let out at the Garden. The fans from the suburbs flooded the street, making their way to the cheaper parking lots of the West Side. They wore polo shirts and baseball hats, khakis and pressed jeans, in the spring light. Jimmy guessed by their jubilance that the Knicks had won.

In time, the crowd thinned out, and he spotted Condo strolling toward him, accompanied by a beefy man of some years. He took this to be Rosen. He stood and made his way down the granite steps to them. When he reached the bottom, Condo nodded up at him, and without a word, motioned him to come along. Jimmy fell in beside them. Condo and Rosen continued talking in a tone too low for him to hear. Jimmy moved off a bit.

They retrieved Condo's Buick from a parking lot on the corner and drove to Marine Park. Jimmy sat in the back. Rosen had yet to acknowledge his presence. On the Belt Parkway they drove by the graceful steel span of the Verrazano Narrows Bridge. Jimmy realized he had never been on that bridge in his life. He imagined New York to be the only city in the States where that could happen. His whole life in the city and never traversing one if its major landmarks.

Rosen spoke to Condo loud enough for his voice to travel to the back seat. "You know, now I got what, seven grandkids in the college. All those books, all those teachers. This day and age you need that college, but I gotta say, Louie, I wonder if any one of them could hold on to their lunch money, they were on the street. Don't get me wrong. I love that they're there with the teachers and the trees and that nice life. But somebody needs to mix it up, I wonder what college will do for them."

"Nobody mixes it up. They call in the lawyers."

"Imagine. That's what it is, this college. It makes everybody a crybaby, looking for somebody should fight for them."

This went on until Condo pulled up to a marina. They parked the car and came upon a man locking the door of a small shanty. Condo called out to him. The man turned and, seeing who'd addressed him, said, "Mr. Condo, Louie," and embraced him.

"What's going on?"

"We closing, Louie. The cook, he went home. It's late."

"Late? This is New York. We need sandwiches. Call him back."

"Mr. Lou. Of course. I can make you sandwiches." The man turned back and unlocked the door.

Rosen said, "You are unbelievable, kid."

It took Jimmy a minute to realize Rosen was referring to Condo.

They waited while the man sliced open Italian bread and layered on cold cuts and fresh cheese, red peppers, topping them all off with splashes of olive oil and vinegar.

"Don't you skimp on the meat. Make one of them Jewish, for our friend here. Nothing from a pig, poor fuck."

Rosen waved him off. "What do you know?"

They packed the sandwiches along with some beer and wine into a cooler and bought bait. Jimmy sat down at a large picnic table while the marina hand loaded everything onto a boat.

As they motored out past the reaches of Rockaway Beach, Louie spread a cloth on top of a makeshift table. "We got to eat."

"What are we fishing for?" Jimmy asked.

Condo said, "We're fishing for fluke; you're fishing for votes."

Jimmy nodded. As they made their way out into open water, the city was reduced to a smudge on the horizon. They finished their meal and set up poles and baited their lines with clams and mussels. Condo looked at the gray mollusk meat and frowned.

"You don't like shellfish?" Rosen asked.

"I'm with your gang on this one. All they do is hang around the bottom of rocks sucking shit out of the water, God knows where they been. At least with your land animal, I got a pretty good idea where it's been from the day it was born to the day it hits my plate."

Jimmy noticed, after a minute, that fishing was pretty much a pretext. They watched the poles while they sat on chairs. Rosen leaned over. "You look a little young for this position you seek to take."

"Ah, Sol, come on, he's an up-and-coming guy. He ain't no little kid. Think where you was when you were his age."

"How old?"

"Thirty." Jimmy added a couple of months. Admitting to being in his twenties did not feel right in present company.

"Thirty. I was in Sing Sing with a four-hundred-pound Slovak for a cellmate."

"That something along the lines of a Polack?" Condo prodded him.

"Thereabout. He tried to hang himself three times. I got the great white whale swinging in my cell. Nothing would hold his weight long enough so he could choke to death."

"Why'd you go up?" Condo asked.

"We had a strike. The company hired a bunch of goons. We stood our ground."

Jimmy wondered what that meant. He pictured a line of stout Teamsters like Rosen dragging scabs out of trucks and bouncing them along like beach balls. This was before all the battles were fought by the lawyers. He had to admit, he wished he had been there.

"I think I'm old enough, or I would not be running. I want to do the right thing for the members."

"That right? Let me ask you something. You run, you lose. Then what? A lot of guys support you. Two weeks later you're wearing a suit and tie in some office, getting paid. Your supporters are in shit up to their eyeballs. Guys got families, mouths to feed. This other bunch, they kill your father, you think they'll have a problem throwing guys out on the street?"

Jimmy looked out over the expanse of ocean, back toward the city. He thought how these men, and men like his father, had created all of it. He hoped he was not doing something that would cost them in any way.

"I'm not in this for some kind of adventure. Yeah, them killing my father is a big, a huge fucking motivation. But there's more to it than that for me. I know what happens if I lose. I also know I'm sticking my neck out as much or more than anyone, or I wouldn't be running."

Rosen nodded and stared silently at Jimmy for a full minute before saying, "Good. We all want the same thing. But what I need is to be able to tell my people that jobs will be there for them. All this politics is bullshit, you hear me? Bullshit. It's always been about one thing, and that's cash. Green money. Don't you ever forget that, kid. Minute you do, you're finished in this racket. And your father is not the only one paid the price for getting in the way of that. There's been too many, all the way up to Hoffa. Jimmy Hoffa was a great American, who should be on that mountain with those dead Presidents, Mount, Mount . . ."

"Rushmore."

"Right. Mount Rushmore."

Louie stood. "I'm gonna get some more wine over here."

Rosen slapped a meaty hand on Jimmy's shoulder and squeezed it. When he spoke, his tone was lighter. "You're here for one thing, my support. Louie says you're good. Says you're a smart kid. You tell me you're gonna do the right thing. I'm not asking for anything funny, anything underhand. But I have to ask: What the hell do you know about running a union? You ever negotiate a contract? You gonna sit across the table from these contractors, they'll eat your lunch and shit in your hat."

"I'll sit down with the right people. I'll keep you on the negotiating committee. I'll learn from you."

"Good answer. You ain't as stupid as you look. Next scenario. One of this guy's greaseball friends approaches you. Puts a gun to your head. Says it's time to do business. He cocks the gun. What do you do?"

"I watch my back. I don't ever let them in the door."

"Easier said than done."

"Times are changing. Besides, these people killed my father. Do you think I am going to deal with them? They'll have to kill me first."

"They just might. I seen a lot of guys, enthusiastic up-and-comers like yourself, get run over by a steamroller. Never thought it could happen to them."

"I'll take the chance."

"You think you got balls, kid? Lemme tell you about balls. Balls are bullshit. I'd be more concerned with having brains, it'll get you a lot further in this racket, this day and age. Now, speaking of brains, what do you know about Keefe's house being shot up? Somebody throwing a concrete block off the building onto his car? This is not the sign of somebody with brains."

Jimmy wondered what that meant. Damn. Liam? He hoped he kept the recognition off his face. "Not my style. I want to beat him the way it will hurt the most."

Rosen stared hard at him again. He had the coldest blue eyes Jimmy had ever seen. They seemed to chill the air around them.

Jimmy did not want to disappoint him. "Go check the lines. Gimme a minute with Louie."

Jimmy crossed over to the port side of the boat. After a while, he heard Louie call to him.

Rosen extended his hand. "I'll support you. My people will come into line. But I'll be watching you. Don't muck up."

"Listen, I might be younger, but I was raised the same way. You do the right thing, end of story. I'm only looking to hurt one guy. I'm the last guy wants to put someone out of a job."

"Unless his name is Frankie Keefe."

They had a laugh, and Jimmy felt an odd sense of power, like he was making inroads, was on his way to realizing something that was denied his father. Something that his father died trying to achieve. He sat in the rocking boat and enjoyed the slow ride back to the shores of Brooklyn.

Tara could barely make it through work. She had not said a word yet to Jimmy about Mitchell's warning. The one thing that kept her going was her running. She would tear along and see herself as if from on high, above all the stress and worry about her career, about Jimmy, about what the hell she was going to do with her life if her job was done. But now her hamstring was too tight to run, so she decided to go to the gym. She resolved not to let it eat her away, not to let things get to her.

A few older women, dressed in unseemly tights, were lifting small weights. Tara draped her jump rope around her neck and worked on the universal. How did this all come down to her? She thought of calling Mitchell, wanting to know more, but was unsure of what to ask. She moved through her workout as if in a trance.

Jimmy had thrown himself into the campaign, had devoted himself fully. She did not know what to do. Should she tell him and put the choice between his ambition and her career on him? Or should she keep silent and see how it played itself out? She wondered how badly they could hurt her. She knew Mitchell was right when he described how they could ruin a career. She had seen it happen herself. There were lines in the department and once you crossed them you were screwed. You stepped on the wrong toes or transgressed in a certain way, it was over for you. You might hold on to your job but they made it a living hell. They put you as far as possible from your place of residence, assigned you the worst tours, psychopathic partners, heaped humiliations on you. Other cops smelled it and distanced themselves, lest they too be ostracized. She considered Jimmy's reaction and what it might be. Would he drop out to save her job? Would she want him to? How much did being on the cops mean to her?

Whoever was behind the move to dissuade Jimmy knew their business. They like to give you choices, Mitchell had said. Yeah, the worst possible choices. Because no matter which way you chose, you were left with a lifetime of recrimination and regret. The bastards. She jumped rope, fast, skipping to the beat of the music blaring through the gym. She needed to sit down with Jimmy. They needed to consider their options.

Tara walked back to her apartment and rode the elevator knowing that it was time to make a choice.

Cronin selected the restaurant for its location, a forgotten stretch of working-class Queens gone from Italian to Puerto Rican to South American. The restaurant was German, had weathered all the change, and still served up the best veal for miles. He arrived early and sat at a table next to the kitchen door. The place was slow, a few tables of diners who might be teachers or clerks in the nearby city offices. It was hard for him to imagine such jobs.

Cronin watched him come in the door and glance casually around the room scanning the tables, taking a kind of inventory. He had begun to develop serious doubts about where he stood with the man, and the government for that matter. He did not trust Roth to look out for anyone except himself, and he knew way too much about the man's dealings.

"Herr Cronin. Interesting restaurant selection."

"I used to come here with my parents. A long time ago."

Roth looked around and nodded. "Probably hasn't changed since. It induces a certain nostalgia."

"Still the best Wiener schnitzel in town."

"Sounds like a winner."

Cronin motioned the waiter over. The man was long past legal retirement age but still had a strong carriage and bright eyes. He bowed slightly. Cronin ordered two plates of the veal and a bottle of Riesling.

Roth realigned his silverware and said, "So what is going on with Keefe's new opponent?"

"The kid?"

"He's hardly a kid. He'll be thirty soon. Was a time when that was considered the very pinnacle of manhood. No? Alexander the Great had conquered the world by then. Al Capone was already past his peak of power." Roth buttered his bread with a precision that suggested surgical dexterity.

"He seems anxious to avenge his father's killing. Makes sense to me. How about you?"

"I'm not in a position to make sense out of vendettas. I'm trying to protect an asset. We've invested far too much in Mr. Keefe for him to be taken down by outside agitators."

Cronin was stunned at this description. "Outside agitators? It's the guy's kid." He realized he needed to be careful; he did not want to come across as caring too much either way.

"We can't have anyone, regardless of intentions, jeopardizing our operation. We're only months away from wrapping the biggest case against the Cosa Nostra ever. This is a nail in the coffin, a deathblow. If Keefe loses the election it may scuttle the whole thing."

"If you're so close, then what difference does it make?"

By way of answer, Roth simply raised an eyebrow.

"You really think he's going to give you his brother-in-law?"

"We have ways of assuring that, yes."

Cronin considered this. He wondered just how much he didn't know. "So, if this kid gets run over in the process, that's his tough luck?"

Roth finished chewing a piece of veal and placed his fork down. He wiped his lips with his napkin. "No one is looking to hurt him. We just don't want him to win. I'm sure there will be another election down the line. He can take up his crusade again. Tell me about your meeting. I see you survived it."

Cronin wondered if that was a dig at his concern, his plea that Roth provide cover. "Magic wants to kill Punchy Dolan. He thinks he's behind the bad press, that he's the real rat." He did not pass on Keefe's desire to whack Magic.

"He doesn't suspect Keefe?"

"Not that he showed."

"Maybe he's bluffing, trying to lull our man."

Our man. Cronin did not like the sound of that. "Hard to say. He doesn't show a lot, Magic. You'll get a message to Dolan?"

"Of course. Standard operating procedure. Have you gotten the other thing under control?"

Cronin considered what kind of man relished keeping tabs on another man's romantic life. There was the hint of a smile on Roth's face. Cronin thought he might enjoy smacking the asshole. "You don't know?"

"How would I?"

"Gee, Roth, I can't imagine."

"Let's deal with more important matters. Find us something we can use to convince young Dolan his campaign is not a wise one."

"Why don't you offer him something? Try the carrot before the stick?"

"We already have."

That worried Cronin. They were already going around him. That could only signal that he was being pushed aside. It was just a matter of what form that might take. He figured they would find a way to neutralize him.

"How'd he respond to that?"

"Like the little crusader he fancies himself."

Cronin realized Roth could not understand the rawness of Jimmy Dolan's emotion, the fire the kid must feel. Roth was all cold rationality. He figured Roth would find with the Dolan kid that some things are beyond all reason. He wondered if maybe he should visit Punchy Dolan and warn him that he was a target. He did not trust Roth to move quickly on the information. If bad things happened to Punchy in the meantime, Roth might benefit from it. Punchy Dolan was surely in a position to take Keefe down.

"So what do you suggest?"

"I think it might be time for a little rough stuff."

"He's already being squeezed by the wise guys."

"We'll just have to squeeze harder then, won't we? There is some urgency to this, Cronin. Call me by Thursday."

Cronin emerged from the restaurant as a train thundered past on the el. Gypsy cabs trolled for cheap fares. A gaggle of men with faces as dark and hard as mahogany congregated outside the local OTB. They had racing forms tucked under their arms and stunted hopes for a smoother life. He checked his watch and decided he needed to get real busy.

Roth paid the bill in cash and watched Cronin go. He was not pleased. The man was a burnout and likely moving beyond control. Roth considered Punchy Dolan a fool to be used to help him get what he needed. He would get word to him, in time. He was using an agent with a fake gambling problem to funnel misinformation to Tommy Magic, which is what led him to believe that Punchy was a rat. Roth enjoyed the manipulation.

He figured it was almost time to reach out to Jimmy Dolan. The kid must be feeling the pressure. The squeeze was being applied not just on him but on his girlfriend the cop as well. He pushed away his half-empty glass of wine and called for some more water. It was time to test the young man's resolve. As he walked out of the restaurant, a grand idea dawned on him.

C ronin muscled his car through thickening traffic and made for a printshop in Maspeth. He took the ramp off the BQE past a road crew repairing guardrails. He found a parking spot two doors away from the shop. He rapped three times on the window and presently a man hunched forward, bent as if forming a human question mark, emerged from the back, and unlocked the door with a loud snap.

He merely nodded in acknowledgment, and Cronin followed him to the back. The walls were covered with copies of the man's more mundane work: wedding invites, business cards, birth announcements. In the back room several out-of-date printing presses hummed with oiled precision and were attended by a short man with the flat and pronounced features of the Inca warrior. He wore an apron and somehow looked defeated despite the wide smile he showed Cronin and his boss.

"Good fucking kid. Ecuador. The sons of bitches work like dogs. They're happy for the opportunity. Sit down. I'm nearly done."

Cronin sat on a stool and watched as the man spread open a U.S. passport. Despite his bent form, the man's hands were steady as a watchmaker's. He moved a picture of Marie into place and trimmed it down with an X-Acto knife. "Now, they gotta be looking real hard to catch you with these." He turned to a machine and placed the passport lying open. He took out a piece of plastic and fitted it over the page with a picture, using the knife to trim it to size. He pulled the cover of the machine closed in the manner of using a waffle iron. The smell of melting plastic was cloying.

The printer finished and held it up to the light to examine his handiwork. "Here." He tossed it to Cronin, who caught it and looked it over. "Two American, two Irish." He took three more from the drawer and gave them to Cronin.

Cronin looked them over. He was impressed. "Better than ever, Bernie. How's tricks?" He took an envelope out of his jacket pocket. It was thick with used twenties.

"Good and bad. Same as ever. I had a little visit the other day might interest you. Coupla guys, they were asking about a certain ex-colleague of theirs. Federals. Wanted I should notify them if he turned up looking to get some work done. Young guys. Big and stupid, you ask me. And no fucking manners to speak of, this new generation. After all I've done in the service of my country. Like a bum off the street is how they treat me."

"Day was this?"

"What's today?"

"Tuesday."

"Musta been Friday. No, make it Saturday. That's what I get for working on the Sabbath. They really think they can scare a guy my age? What the fuck I got to lose? They gonna cancel my social security? Go ahead. My cousin's a congressman. You want to hear a horrible noise? You should hear him when he raises a stink. One time, we were kids, I punched him in the nose. I can still hear the little prick screaming."

"I don't think they'll bother you, Bernie." Cronin was not sure of this.

"I already lived five good lives. They can rot. They come back, what should I tell them?"

Cronin thought for a minute. He hoped to be long gone by the time it mattered. Roth was just being himself, keeping tabs, maintaining control. He did not fear the government wasting time pursuing him. It was Keefe he worried about. But maybe Roth was so enamored of the asshole he might do it as a favor. It was in the realm of the possible. He had been around long enough to know that much. He wanted to go without a trace.

"Give them a line of shit, Bernie. Send them on a long and false trail. Keep them occupied."

"Yeah. My fucking federal withholding at work."

"The price for democracy."

"My wrinkled ass. I lugged a rifle all over Europe for this?"

Cronin smiled. Despite the shabbiness of the shop and Bernie's attire, he knew the man to be sitting on a small fortune somewhere.

"Take a look." He handed Cronin a twenty-dollar bill.

Cronin held it, smelled it, put it to the light. It was impossible to tell that it was, as he assumed, a fake. "Not bad at all."

"Fucking A-rabs. Don't ask me how, I don't know. Top shelf, though. Give the ragheads that. No wonder we changed our currency. They're looking for two bits on the dollar. You want?"

That was high for fake money, but he had never seen such good counterfeits. Cronin, though tempted, decided to pass. No point in looking for trouble now. "Thanks, Bernie. But I'm a law-abiding kinda guy."

"That's a good one. Whose laws exactly?"

"The law of averages."

"Averages? You'll always end up fucked."

Cronin backtracked to his car, worried about being followed. He dropped a letter to his mother in a mailbox. He planned to drive south, see her, then leave the country via the sailboat of an old friend. When he pulled into his garage he removed the microrecorder he wore in his pocket. He slipped the tape out and dropped it into an envelope. Roth might be in charge, but Cronin was not without a weapon or two of his own. He had made a half dozen tapes over the last few months, each capturing Roth crossing lines that could ruin him. If the man wanted to play rough, Cronin would not go down without a fight. Now he had one more piece of work, and then it was time to move.

Punchy had been staying on the Upper West Side house-sitting for an old flame who was out of town and needed someone to attend to her six cats. Why anyone would want even one was beyond him, but he had little choice. As he left the apartment, he held a hefty bag containing the contents of her several litter boxes at arm's length, and took a halfhearted kick at a calico. The cat did not even bother to move.

He traveled by subway to avoid being seen. He knew few people anymore who used the conveyance. As he rocked along in the IRT, he was shocked by the cleanliness of the graffiti-free car. He realized it had been many years since he had taken the subway, not since the blackout of '77, when he had been trapped in a downtown A train, only to emerge at 125th Street to a scene of rioting he could only describe as orgiastic. There was a madness crackling in the air that night that he had never seen before, not even in war. He had not gotten on a subway since.

317

He had been spinning a web of lies to avoid work and other commitments while hiding from Roth the Fed, Frankie, the wannabe guinea Keefe, and whatever assassins might be lurking. He had been nursing whiskey and had taken at times to hiding in closets when he heard people in the hallway. He was beginning to believe that he would either die on the street, shot like his brother Michael, or be butchered by shank-wielding recidivists in the dank bowels of the federal penal system. During the dark, endless nights he would try to recall a time when he was actually somewhat of a tough guy, a time when he might have risen to the challenges at hand, no matter how perilous. But he had lost his edge a long time ago, the street hardness sucked out of him by soft sheets and larded plates at the poshest of eateries, by high life and fat, good fortune.

Of all his pursuers, Roth was the one who worried him the most. At least with Keefe and his Corsican pirates, he knew precisely where he stood and why. They wanted him dead because he could hurt them. But Roth wanted to use him to some ends he did not make clear. You would think his goal was to take down Keefe and Magic, but he seemed more interested in getting Jimmy out of the election. There was something about Roth that repulsed him, a smugness, as if he knew that he held your fate in his hands, that you were merely a tool, that he enjoyed fucking with you. Punchy knew his life was closing in on him. It had come down to the weighing of several horrors: prison, or testifying against Keefe and Magic, or death. Maybe all three.

Punchy had decided to chance showing himself and visit his restaurant to purloin some cash from the safe. He needed some walking-around money. He slipped into the restaurant and, with a dismissive nod to the shocked wait staff, made for his office. He found the safe empty and slammed it shut. Fuck. He would have to make do with what he might find in the register. As he came up from the basement, he looked up to see Cronin coming through the front door of the restaurant. He ducked back down the stairway. He felt the urge to pass water and froze, his breath ragged, his entire being clenched with terror. Are they here to kill me? Jesus, how bad could one guy's luck run? That the one safe haven he had was in a lady's apartment with six cats. He slipped out through the kitchen and hurried back.

iam, what the fuck are you doing? Shooting up the guy's house? Wrecking his car?"

They were sitting at Jimmy's kitchen table waiting for Lou Condo to show up with Chickie Donohue so they could discuss the election. Jimmy had decided to confront Liam about his extracurricular violence.

"Hey, Jimmy, what?" Liam shrugged.

"You can't do this shit. We do, we're just like them."

Liam shook his head. "So we supposed to sit around like a coupla pussies, let them do what they want?"

"Liam, that kind of shit don't help."

"Yeah, okay. You got no problem, me watching your back. Carrying a piece, putting my freedom on the line, my safety. But I go the extra yard for you, all of a sudden you got a beef with that?"

"Fucking Liam, man. It ain't that. Listen, I appreciate that you're willing to do that work for me. But now's not the time. All right? The time may come. But for now, I got people backing me up, big-time people, they see that shit, they're going to drop me. We can beat this creep fair and square, on the up-and-up. We lose, then we go to plan B. All right?" Liam looked away. "Please, you gotta come into line on this with me. Liam, I need you to play it my way. You don't think I appreciate you putting yourself in the line of fire for me? Come on. I known you my whole life. Let's just give it to the election."

Liam walked to the window and sat on the sill. "Jimmy, I ain't built like you. They did that to me, it'd be all about a blaze of glory. Bang, bang, motherfucking bang, bang. And this all-my-life shit, yeah, you're right. And your father was pretty much the only father I ever had. But you left a while back and this all-my-life shit, you seemed to forget about that."

Jimmy could not believe what Liam was saying. It stung. "What's that supposed to mean? It's some kind of sin I wanted to do something with my life?"

"Face it, Jimmy. You got embarrassed by me, guys like me."

Jimmy flushed with anger but tried to keep it out of his voice. "You're fucking wrong. How can you say that to me? Of all people."

"I ain't saying you are now. But till you got shit-canned by the Mayor, you were leaving us all behind. Inwood, everything."

Jimmy considered this. He shook his head. How to explain to Liam that that is part of the deal. When you move on, you leave some things behind. Liam, though, as crazy as he could be, meant as much to him as anything in the world.

"Let's face it, Jimmy, you were on your way to being one of those dickheads in a suit, thinks he deserves it all. Looks down his nose at the workingman."

"Liam, come on. No matter what the hell I wear to work, that doesn't mean I forgot where I come from."

"So if I want to help you out, maybe some of the shit I can do you ain't got the balls for. Maybe you become one of those people gets too much to lose to make a move. He gets stuck. Thinks being a good citizen is the way to go. Likes to take everyone's shit, 'cause he's scared."

"Liam. I'll give you that. But violence is not the way to deal with this. It's got to be a last resort. This is my beef for now. Okay? Let's just give this a try. Like I said, it don't work out for us, then we move on. I ain't going to let this guy get away with killing my father."

Liam looked to the floor and walked over to the window. "All right, homey. But we lose, it's my turn."

"Fucking A. Fair enough."

"And it's my rules."

Tara leaned against the refrigerator as Jimmy sat at the kitchen table with Chickie and Lou. Liam was in the front room, watching the street from the window, an M-16 propped up next to him. Tara knew Donohue to be a neighborhood guy who had grown up with her father. He had a reputation as quite the operator, and many of his adventures had become Inwood lore. While her father had never once been outside the tristate area, Chickie was legendary for his travels around the globe, including the time, as a merchant seaman, when he hand-delivered a case of beer to a couple of neighborhood guys taking rocket fire outside Danang. The fact that it took a munitions ship, a plane, three helicopters, a half-track, a jeep, and an award-winning load of bullshit to get him and the beer halfway around the world and into a war zone had not dampened his resolve. A number of kids had already come back to Inwood in body bags, and the guys from the saloons along 207th Street wanted the current combatants to know they were not forgotten. Chickie was the natural choice for messenger. He delivered the goods with the aplomb of a pizza boy running a pie across Broadway.

Tara needed to talk to Jimmy, to let him know how they were squeezing her. She watched as Jimmy listened intently to Chickie and scribbled notes on a legal pad. Chickie's delivery was rapid-fire and concise. Lou Condo sipped from a can of seltzer and piped in occasionally, usually to make fun of Chickie.

"Listen, you're on the ballot. Louie and Sol Rosen nominated you. That's all well and good. But let's face it, your father was a long shot—at best. And now you're running, but a lot of guys look at you and they see a college kid, they're not looking at you as a Teamster, and they have to figure the only reason you're running is because of anger."

Jimmy started to protest, but Chickie held up a hand to silence him.

"I'm not interested in what you think. I'm telling you how it *looks*. Now, I think you can play this to your advantage. You need to lull this O'Keefe."

"Keefe."

"Whatever you want to call him. Call him shit-for-brains for all I care. Now you have two of the best, Louie here and Sol Rosen, in your corner and they'll pull some strings. But you want your opponent to take you for granted. Why?"

"Yeah, why?"

Tara guessed that Jimmy was not pleased with this approach. He wanted to dive in swinging, but Tara saw the logic in it. Keefe could easily outmobilize him and outspend him.

"This is a guy, a guy very used to living off the union dime. He don't spend his own money for nothing. He whips out that union credit card for union business. He eats lunch, it's union business. Guys like that get used to living off someone else's money. What do you have saved up?"

"Me?"

"No, your machine-gun buddy in the living room."

"Not much. Nothing actually."

"You see my point? You want this guy to go to sleep. He thinks he's on his way out, he'll start spending on the campaign, he'll have guys getting a new piece of mail every day telling them what a scumbag you are over their morning coffee, how much he's done for them with the contracts. How much more he's gonna do with the new contract. He'll say, What does this college boy know about the affairs of men? It can be all bullshit, it doesn't matter. What I'm trying to tell you is, this is a guy you do not go toe to toe with. You don't have the ammo, kid. You might be *right*, but that and a buck fifty will get you to Canarsie."

"I can't just do nothing."

"I say anything about nothing? Hey, Louie, you hear me say anything about nothing?"

Louie tapped one ear, and then the other, and shrugged. "I don't know nothing about nothing, maestro."

Chickie said, "Kid, listen. This is what you do."

Tara watched as they outlined a game plan designed to build support on the sly and then hit hard the last few days of the campaign, including a heavy presence at the polls. Chickie also presented a way to make sure that the election was monitored by the International and that Jimmy had his own labor lawyers on site in order to impound the ballots if things looked suspicious. He instructed Jimmy to write a letter that would be mailed to the entire membership right before election day.

Jimmy said, "How the hell do I get the mailing list?"

Louie coughed, placed a briefcase on the kitchen table, and opened it with a flourish. He pulled out a thick stack of paper secured by a rubber band. When he dropped it on the table, Tara saw that not only was it the mailing list for the local but it was put on labels.

Condo jerked a thumb at Chickie. "He might be the genius, the big-picture guy, but I'm more nuts and bolts."

"Yeah, you're half right. And I ain't talking about the bolts."

Jimmy picked up the stack and riffled through it. "Jackpot." He now had access to the entire membership in their own living rooms.

"Now write that letter and show it to me and only me. And, kid, don't be showing off your college skills. Keep it simple. The members ain't interested in your pretty prose. Hit your marks and that will be fine. Call me Monday, I want to see it by then. And remember, there is no mercy here, Jimmy. You got him down, it's time for the killer instinct. If you don't have it, get the hell out of this business."

When they all stood to leave, Jimmy walked them to the door. Tara watched as he came back to the kitchen and gathered his notes from the table. He moved with a purpose that he had lacked since the murder. There was a focus to him now, an intensity. She put her hand on his arm. She was unsure how Jimmy would respond when she explained what was happening with her, her job. Mitchell's warnings. She had pondered it for days and still did not know what to do or even how she wanted him to react. Was his campaign more important than her career? Should he sacrifice for her or vice versa? Is this the price of love? Maybe she could just tell Mitchell that she had tried to get him to drop out, but failed.

He stopped and looked up at her, said, "Yeah, babe?"

"I think we need to talk."

Jimmy said, "What's up?" and the phone rang.

She watched him pick it up. His whole demeanor changed. He said, "Yeah, this is him," with a hardness that she was not accustomed to. He spoke tersely into the phone, insistent on something. He hung up and called to Liam.

Then he turned to Tara. "We talk when I get back? This needs to be taken care of."

Tara nodded. She started to speak but stopped.

"Is everything okay?"

"Girls not allowed to play?"

"Tara, that's not the point. You're on the job. You don't want to be mixed up in this right now. Everything okay?"

She paused. That's what you think. "Yeah, Jimmy. Never better."

They got ready to go, and Jimmy hugged her. As she watched him leave, she thought, Well, I guess I made my decision. She got ready for work and wondered how and when they might come for her.

Jimmy did not know whether it was wise to meet Cronin. He considered the possibility that he was being targeted, set up. But he figured if they really wanted him, they would not make an appointment. Besides, he had insisted that Cronin come to Inwood for the meet. To further ensure his safety, he sat on a ridge overlooking the park. Liam was to meet Cronin at the corner of 207th and Broadway and escort him up into the woods. Jimmy had a clear view of the park and the surrounding area. He moved the pistol around to the back of his waistband and watched as Liam led Cronin into the woods, then stopped and searched him. He nodded and followed Cronin.

When they reached him, Cronin was sweating and breathless. "If I knew I was going mountain climbing, I'd've put on some hiking boots."

"Too fucking bad." Jimmy counted Cronin among the chief suspects in his father's death. "What is this about?"

Cronin, still breathing hard, said, "I know how you feel about your old man. I need you to listen to me, hear me out. Put your anger aside for a minute. You do that?"

Jimmy nodded. "I'll listen to anybody has something I should hear."

"Good. Now, I don't know what you know about me, but you probably heard I used to work for the government?"

"Cop before that. Football prospect. Made the Redskins, then your knee started giving you trouble."

"The reason I left the Bureau is a shooting I was involved in went bad."

"Bad?"

"I was in a shitty mood, and I killed a lowlife we couldn't make a case on. Things happen. That's neither here nor there. Truth is, I never fully left the government; officially yes, but my whole thing with Keefe has been to keep an eye on him, verify what he's telling the G. I'm what they call a contract worker. Shit hits the fan, they don't know me. It's more common than you might think."

"So Keefe's been a rat all along?" They stood next to a wall that was built by colonials to offer cover when they fired down on the British. It was the highest ground on Manhattan Island.

"Going on twenty years. One of the most valuable ever. He's brought down more guys than you'll ever know."

"Jesus Christ."

"And I don't think he killed your father."

A middle-aged couple came along the path hand in hand. Jimmy watched them and gripped his pistol. He put nothing past his enemies. The couple smiled nervously as they walked by three men huddled in unknown intent.

Jimmy looked back up at Cronin. "Say that again."

"I said, I don't think he killed your father."

"What? You gotta be kidding me." If not Keefe, who? Plus he wondered at Cronin's motivation. "Whether he did or not, he's the reason it happened. Same difference to me."

"Well, you have to figure that out on your own. Listen, I'm going away. I'm finished. Now, I been trying to find your uncle. He's next. They're gonna whack him. And your name has come up."

Jimmy felt a tremor of fear but swallowed it. "My name?" He was not surprised, but it was unsettling to hear it announced.

"Dolan, you're rocking the boat. The way things go is, they got a nice setup, Keefe and the government. They'll be willing to turn a blind eye, get what they want. It's the best way to get bad guys. Not to mention Keefe and Tommy Magic, who I look at to be the shooter on your father. Not him personally, of course, but his orders."

"I thought the Feds have to let you know if you're going to get hit, if there's a contract on you."

"Officially."

"Officially. That's great."

Cronin said, "Something tells me you'll be a lot less surprised about how things work once you're done with your campaign. 'Cause you're gonna learn that life gets hard when you decide to raise your head up, take a stand. Look at the world. It might be easy to look at people go to work every day for decades to jobs they don't like, pay taxes they don't want to, eat all sorts of shit. Might look lousy, but there's a lot less grief in their lives. I'll tell you that."

"Why'd you want to talk to me?"

Cronin looked back toward Broadway. Below them, Mexicans played soccer across green fields just yards from where the Dutch bought the island four hundred years before. Cronin spit at the stone wall. "The truth? I feel bad about what happened to your father. I liked him. And second, I'm tired. Real tired."

"Why should I believe a word you say?"

"Because I came out of my way to help you out."

"Help?"

"You were offered a job recently."

Jimmy nodded.

"Why don't you take it?"

"I'm not interested."

"It might be time to be smart. This is bigger than you. They'll crush you and everything important to you."

"They'll try."

"Listen, this whole thing started back in the early eighties, Reagan. It was a joint task force, Labor Department, Justice, IRS, even the Postal Service. They were looking to put together RICO cases on union guys. A guy named Roth is what's left of it. He's been handling Keefe for the last twelve years. He's become an entity of his own. Everybody from the Manhattan DA to the FBI hates this guy, but he's still there. This is not a guy overly concerned with dotting *i*'s and crossing *t*'s. His idol is J. Edgar."

"He doesn't have anything on me."

"He doesn't need anything. He'll manufacture it. Or he'll stand back and let other people do what they want. You can't win."

"I'm doing the right thing. End of story."

"Jesus. This ain't about good guys and bad guys, right and wrong, some fucking fairy tale. There is no right and fucking wrong in this life. You ain't that wet behind the ears. You want to be an idealist? Idealists get bought or they get run over. It's about power, it's about money. Take the fucking job, kid, walk away. Live a happy life. You want to do good things? Tithe the church. Work Thanksgiving in a soup kitchen. Help an old lady across Broadway."

"I can't."

"You're not interested in getting old, are you?"

"I have to do it."

"I was afraid you'd say that. In some ways I envy you. But you know what? Mostly, I feel sorry for you." Cronin reached into his pocket, producing an envelope. "Here, for what it's worth. This might help you. Use it wisely." Cronin started back down carefully. "I fall and rip these slacks, I'm sending you the bill."

Jimmy watched as Cronin started down the hill. Something did not add up. "Hey," he called after him. "You said twelve years. Who was running Keefe before Roth?"

Cronin looked up at him and shook his head. "Who else? Your old boss."

"The Mayor?"

"Bingo, bright boy."

Cronin made his way gingerly down the hill. Liam came up and stood next to him. "What do you think? He full of shit?"

"I don't know. I doubt it. I don't know."

"What's that?" Liam indicated the envelope Cronin had handed him.

Jimmy opened it and peered inside. It contained a mini cassette tape. He took it out and held it on his palm. "Well, what the hell do we have here?"

S he walked up to her car, which was blocked in by a dark sedan. Three men in suits emerged and gathered around her, their bodies leaning into her until she could feel the muscle and heat of them. "Detective, come with us please."

"Come where?" Tara yanked herself away from them. Her hand moved toward her gun.

"IAB, O'Neil. Nice and easy now." They produced ID and relieved her of her Glock.

She rode along in silence, the anger growing in her. She knew this would happen. She had not expected it so soon. When they crossed over the Triborough Bridge, she began to worry. She remembered stories about interrogations lasting hours, a warehouse in Queens. "What's this about?"

"Routine stuff."

"I want my delegate."

One of them sported a crew cut the color of new rust. His skin was splotchy and he looked to be wearing a collar that was two sizes too small. He turned his torso to look at her and laughed. "Yeah, right."

They drove down an industrial road lined with squat abandoned structures. There was a silence to the area that seemed impenetrable. They pulled beside one of the buildings and led her inside, passing into a cavernous room empty except for a table and several chairs in the center of the space. Pigeons in the rafters of the fifty-foot ceilings stirred at their arrival, fluttered about, and settled back down. The room was cold and gray, all concrete, chipped in many places where rusted rebar protruded.

They handcuffed her to a chair and then left, their shoes scuffing along the hard floor until she was alone in all that space and silence. She felt a powerful need to urinate, but refused to let this be known. She sat and thought about Jimmy, and whether he would suffer this for her. She calmed herself by flexing and relaxing her muscles, starting with her jaw and working down to her toes then back to the top and down again.

Finally, after what seemed to be many hours, they came into the room. There were three of them, none of them her original abductors. She recognized one, the tall ruddy-faced guy, as an inspector. She wondered what had brought such eminence to this inquisition. "What's your connection to Tommy Magic?"

She considered whether or not to answer.

"Officer, you can try and stonewall us on this. We know you were in the files, we know you are involved with Dolan, from the Teamsters union. We know enough to run you off the force, to ruin your career. And by God, if I find out you have been aiding and abetting a known mafioso, I'll see you to the penitentiary. Now, what were you doing in those files?"

The youngest one, the one with deathly white skin, who had been standing quietly, walked behind her and screamed, "You fucking cunt! You piss on this job, you piece of shit!" Tara jumped. The inspector stood before her and smiled. "You got him all riled up. He hates the Cosa Nostra. Maybe some Italian took his lunch money when he was a pup."

"This is kidnapping. Let me go. I want my delegate."

"You're a bright girl, O'Neil. You must realize you are in no position to want anything. Now, who were you working for?"

"Working? I'm a cop."

"Listen to me, you smartass. You tell us who put you up to snooping in those files or, so help me, you go from here right to Central Booking. I'll not be fucked with by a twat with a badge."

"Twat?"

"Your shooting is still under review. We've been getting some conflicting reports. You know what happens when this job turns its back on a cop? When there is no one to turn to? You can give me a load of crap about the union, but how far out on a limb are they going to go for someone who compromises undercover people? Gets a cop killed maybe? Think about it."

Tara felt things slipping away. She fought an urge to cry, she was not about to give this asshole that satisfaction. She knew his type, the old-timers who could barely stomach the idea of working with women, but wouldn't retire because they'd be stuck at home with wives they liked even less. She knew he'd been on the job since before she was born. They stood and smirked at her, then left. A while later rusthead came in with a bologna sandwich on white. Jail cuisine. She was so hungry she took a bite.

"It don't have to be like this." He bent over. His breath was like sour milk. The start of a five o'clock shadow, dirty pores. "We can work together." He put his hand on her thigh and rubbed it back and forth. "You're a nice-looking piece of ass."

She spit the bologna in his face. He slapped her so hard her ear rang and she saw two of him. He stood up straight, seething, his face turned the color of a brush fire. He looked up to a dark window where someone must be watching them. He wiped his face and stormed out of the room.

Much later, they came back with her ID. As one of them uncuffed her, another threw it on the table in front of her. She saw the red "restricted" stamp splashed across her picture. The rubber gun squad. The inspector was behind her. "You're off the task force. I'll be watching you." They kept her gun and led her out to a waiting sedan. Without another word they drove her to the end of the A train at Lefferts Boulevard. It was 3 a.m. Her jaw was tender, cheek swollen. She thought of calling Jimmy, or her father, or maybe Angela. Instead, she rode the train home. Back in her apartment she dug out her Polaroid, held it before her face, and snapped a picture. Proof, for what it was worth. She waited till the picture dried. She saw an image that repulsed her; she was haggard and aged, her face a white-and-purple swollen horror. She put ice to her face, lay on her bed, and wept as light bled into the eastern sky.

In the lobby, Mrs. McMartin said, "Your cable TV should be fine now, Jimmy." Jimmy waved hello and walked to the elevator. He held his lunchbox under his arm and was wiped out from the day's labor. He needed to make some campaign calls but was looking forward to a hot shower and a meal, seeing Tara. He pushed the up button. When the door opened he got on the elevator and punched 3. As the door started to close, he thought about what Mrs. McMartin had said. He stuck his foot in the door. "What was that? Mrs. McMartin?" The door opened wide.

"The cable guys were here this afternoon. They went up to your place. Foreign fellas. Said they was Russian. Real proud of that. You imagine? Makes you miss the Cold War a bit, don't it?"

Jimmy swallowed. He forced himself to speak evenly. "When?"

330

"A coupla hours ago. They're gone. Is something the matter, Jimmy?"

The elevator rose behind him. He took the stairs three at a time and pushed his way into his apartment, wishing he had carried his gun with him. In the living room he came upon Quill lying on the floor in a pool of dark blood. Jimmy bent down and could see that someone had cut the dog's throat ear to ear, so that tendons and arteries hung in a meaty tangle. Beside the dog's head a note was stuck to the floor with a knife. He picked it up. All it said was: "We'll be in touch." The author had drawn a smiley face on it. Jimmy stood and looked about at the destruction.

He toured the apartment. Nothing seemed to be missing. It was just a violation, a "we can fuck you on your home court." He went back to the hallway and knelt over Quill again. If their aim was to intimidate him, they had succeeded. He stroked the dead dog's head. He considered calling the cops but figured it would not do much good. If they could not solve his father's killing, he had little faith they could solve the dog's. He wondered if Russians were involved in his father's murder. He knew one thing. It was time to lean on his uncle. Enough was enough.

He stood and went to the kitchen. He took the mop bucket, filled it with hot water, and dumped in some Lysol. He grabbed an old blanket from the closet and rolled Quill onto it. He bent and kissed the dog's head, then folded the blanket over him. He dragged him toward the door, then went back and mopped up the mess. When he had finished cleaning, he considered what to do with the dog. He decided to carry him up to the park and bury him in the woods, in the place where he always seemed the happiest. He wondered where Tara might be.

Jeez, these fucking Russians are smarter than they look, Tommy Magic thought to himself. Ivan, the big blockhead mastermind, was sitting there with one of his cronies, the two of them looking like heavies in one of those James Bond pictures. Telling him how easy it

331

was to track cell phones, to pinpoint them down to an exact location. He'd given them a nice slice of the book in Brooklyn, turned it over to them for nothing. He was showing them the ropes in the construction rackets and had given them the drugs, lock, stock, and barrel. He was glad to be out of that shit, dealing with all sorts of fucking degenerate darkies.

There had been a general howling from the crews. Fuck them. He was doing them a favor even if they did not see it that way. He was giving the government another target, something to focus their energy on. He figured what they really needed was a way to get the public to take the Commies seriously, like a Russian Godfather movie. The way he saw it, it was all down a big fucking hill from that point on. Everybody believing that horseshit.

He threw the crews a few bones, to ease the pain of letting the Russians in by cutting back on tribute the crews needed to pay. He had tried to explain it was going to be like the old days when they were in with the Jews. Things were generally better for everyone in those days, but he did not give a rat fuck what anyone thought. They might even be setting him up for a hit. Did he care? No. His single goal in life now was to give the government a nightmare of psychos who did not reason with anyone, who would shoot and fuck and blow up whoever they wanted, even little kids and guys with badges, judges, taxpayers, media guys, whoever. They'll beg for the old days, the old ways, these pricks.

"So you see, simple, even for you Mr. Magician."

Funny guys, these Commie comedians. "Let's get the shitheel. See how simple it is." Magic was out on a hit for the first time in almost twenty years. He was thrilled at the prospect of bloodying someone.

They rolled up Broadway, windows down, a vehicle of destruction. The shooters sat in the back seat. He shared the front with Ivan, who piloted them in search of their prey. He was going to whack that Irish slob Punchy Dolan, who might or might not be a rat. Then he was gonna send his new friends to visit the guy's colleagues in their fancy offices, use the dead guy as an example of what might happen if they did not continue things as they'd always been. Then he was going to see about the college kid who wanted to take the Teamsters away from him. The kid was proving to be stubborn. Magic figured he'd teach him the facts of life.

"Hey, Mr. the Magician. I think we find your friend."

Magic looked at the big ugly Commie. He belched and then popped a nitro under his tongue. "Good. Let's take care of that."

Punchy pulled out his cell phone and flipped it open. He was out for a walk after polishing off a twelve-pack of Bud and a crime novel. He had all of his ex-wives on speed dial and occasionally made drunken calls to them in sodden and melancholy attempts to recapture the past, the brief time when there had been something like real love and peace between them. They took this with varying degrees of reasonableness. He hit the button for wife number two. "I've got to see you. I need you. I'm in the shit."

"Punchy?"

He realized with alarm that he had mistakenly dialed his sister Immaculata. He hung up and stared at his phone as if it had betrayed him. He flipped it shut and decided what he needed was a hot dog. He slouched into the Papaya King on Seventy-second and Broadway. There was a crowd, a haphazard line. A dozen or so frat boys who looked as if they should be rolling kegs of beer across a crisp campus lawn were roughhousing. They wore shorts despite the chill, tee shirts with asinine sayings on them, and baseball hats with the peaks curled down into inverted U's. They brayed and hooted like cavemen crazed on some hallucinogenic root. Punchy was annoyed by their raucous behavior. They seemed to enjoy making fun of the brown folk behind the counter.

Enough of this, he thought. He pushed his way to the front and placed his order. He took his hot dog and grape drink and shouldered his way to the front window, where he ate from the shelf. A dollop of onions spilled out of the bun and landed on his foot. As he bent to clean the mess, the window above him suddenly shattered. He thought he heard a gunshot, then two more, then there came the unmistakable sound of automatic weapons fire. He was back in Quangtri. One of the frat boys started to scream. Punchy wheeled and saw the one screaming, his shirt suddenly bright red, vomit shooting from his mouth. He went down hard. Another kid was lying on the floor, bubbles of bloody saliva coming from his lips. A third stood staring blankly out through the broken window as though he was looking for someone who had called to him. Punchy fell flat to the tiles and heard the screech of rubber, the throaty roar of a getaway car. He shot to his feet and ran.

Out on the street panic hit him with force. He was nauseous. They were out to slaughter him. He glanced about quickly. Everything had come to a halt—pedestrian traffic, cars, the world stuck on its axis. People were gaping, their faces twisted in horror and surprise. He turned left and elbowed his way through the gawkers. He heard shouts, the keening of sirens coalescing on the spot. He moved down Broadway with a speed he had not mustered in three decades, the adrenaline obliterating the years. He ducked into a bar. The patrons were well dressed and sported early tans. They looked up as if he had just staggered into their bedroom mid-coitus. He went for the bathroom and locked the door behind him. He peeked at himself in the mirror. A look of horror glared back at him. His heart pounded in his ears. His hair was wild and unkempt, his eyes dilated with fear, his face speckled with mustard, a bit of onion, a fine spray of blood. Fuck, he thought. They really were going to kill me. He fumbled in his pocket. His phone. His fingers felt like thick, useless sausages. It took all the concentration he could manage just to dial 911. A voice answered, insistent. He stuttered, "I—they—shot—guns, they had guns—bullets. I have blood on me. Blood!"

But, he thought in a flash of clarity, he did not want cops, no. He would have too much to explain. He pressed "end," dropped the phone, bent and picked it up, cracking his head on the underside of the sink. He sat and tried to collect himself. Jimmy. He decided to call his nephew Jimmy.

The kid was calm. "Stay there. Sit at the bar and have a drink."

"I can't."

"You have to."

Punchy agreed and hung up. What else could he do? He stood

and cleaned himself as best he could, splashed cold water on his face, and combed his hair. He went to the bar and tried to get the attention of the bartender, who was down at the end with a buxom brunette. They leaned over the bar and kissed each other deeply. This is what his whole life has led to. Being shot at like an animal on the street and not even able to get a damn drink. He coughed loudly, drummed his hand on the bar. Patrons edged away from him.

"Hey!" he called out.

The bartender looked up at him annoyed and carried on. Enough of this, Punchy thought. He marched down to the end of the bar and broke into the conversation. "I know you're trying to get a piece of ass here, pal, but I need a drink."

The bartender looked up. "Go get yourself a forty from the bodega."

This prompted a chuckle from the brunette.

"Jameson. A triple."

"Let's go, pal, take it outside." The voice was firmer, the smile gone.

Punchy was in no mood for further abuse. He leaned over the bar and spoke in a hiss. "You listen to me, you little pretty boy cunt. There was a shooting up the block. Somebody was killed not two feet away from me. I need a drink and I'm sitting right here till I decide I want to leave. And I am sorry you never got the part in the soap opera, but bartending is a noble calling. Now get me a triple Jameson and leave me the fuck alone. I'll leave when my friend gets here. You got me?"

The bartender started a response, stuttered, and stopped. He looked out the window. He shook his head and moved down the bar to pour Punchy's drink. After a while, Punchy looked up and saw Jimmy's friend, the commando, advancing on him through the crowd. He stood beside him and smiled.

"Rich guy," Liam Brady said.

"A man is only as rich as . . ."

"Yeah. Whatever you say, tubby."

Punchy stood and left a fifty on the bar. Liam grabbed it and took a five out of his pocket, which he put on the bar in its place. "Fuck him."

"Where's my nephew?"

"Home. I'm his go-to guy."

Outside Punchy followed the commando around the corner to a pickup truck.

As he climbed into the cab, Punchy said, "I don't think I've ever been in one of these. Where are you taking me?"

"My buddy Crazy Quinn's boat."

"Crazy?"

"Yeah, Nutsy's brother."

"Gotcha." Punchy hunkered down in his seat. They passed the crime-scene commotion at the Papaya King. It looked like a doomsday scenario. Punchy counted twenty-two vehicles with flashing lights—police, fire, EMT. And the media. The red swirl of the emergency lights was watered down by the newscast halogens. He averted his face and sighed. Jesus, I caused all that?

They sped up the West Side Highway. Punchy felt secure with the commando. He moved with a physical assuredness that he himself once had. He was surprised when they pulled into the Dyckman Street boat basin. He had expected somewhere farther afield. They walked down from the parking lot to the marina. Once they were settled in the hold of the boat Liam said he was going to cook. Punchy watched in horror as Liam took out cans of Chunky soup, a loaf of white bread, and some packaged lunch ham. Luckily he did not have much of an appetite.

"I'm sorry, I don't remember your name."

"Brady. Liam Brady."

"Brady. Any relation to Diamond Jim?"

"I don't have many relatives. Who's he?"

"A hero of mine. Liked to eat and drink and be merry."

"Don't make him a bad guy. Where you from?"

"Inwood, Good Shepherd. Right here."

"Yeah? That I heard. Hard to believe. Where'd you learn to talk like that?"

"I'm educated."

"It ain't helping you too much now, is it?" Liam tucked into his ham sandwich.

Punchy shrugged. "Good point."

After dinner they played cards for nickel ante and Punchy cleaned up.

"Not so bad for a rich asshole."

Liam rigged the alarm system, and took out and assembled an M-16 while Punchy watched. The routine took him back to his army days. This Liam Brady was like many he had met over in Nam. The type of clean-cut killer only America could produce. He'd watch the ones that were there because they enjoyed it, saw themselves as warriors. If they complained at all it was only about their gear. They re-upped happily. Liam handled his weapon in a way that he might call lovingly. He got the feeling the kid was more attached to his weapons than to people.

"You like guns, huh?"

"Like? Respect is more like it. But I don't need them. Someone like you should like them so you can defend yourself."

"I won the Golden Gloves twice, buddy."

"Around World War I?"

"Let me ask you something. You one of these guys who run around looking for black helicopters, think the Jews are running the world?"

"Jews? My godmother is a Jew. Whaddya mean, black helicopters?"

"Just checking."

"You know something, you oughta be a little more grateful. I'm about the only thing standing between you and a shallow grave."

Indeed. This was a sobering thought.

"You sleep here." Brady indicated the hold. "You'll be okay."

"I feel privileged."

"I'm just doing my man Jimmy a favor. You, I could give two shits about."

Punchy lay in the cramped bed, his body barely contained in the space. He was like a fat cat stuffed into a shoe box. There was not even room enough to roll on his side. The boat rocked gently on the river. His mind turned over the evening's events. Panic hovered on the borders of his consciousness, staved off by booze and fatigue, an adrenal backwash. What now? he wondered. His life would never be the same. He would be in hiding for a long time. He realized, with a sadness, that he was utterly alone in the world. All his ambition, his desire to blast out, to get more than they were offering, where had it led? He felt a tugboat drone down river, the vibrations coming through the craft. All his hustling and conniving and dancing and lying and scheming had led him to this dingy boat on the waters of his childhood. He was struck by the thought that he should have listened to his mother and taken the civil service tests, even applied for a job at Con Ed.

He called his sister. In the dark, tight air of the hold, he listened to her say, "Pius? Pius?" No one had called him that in many, many years. Still, he did not know what to say, so he simply hung up. Hearing her voice reminded him of all he had been and all he had run from. His sister in the suburbs was married to a fireman. Four kids, an earnest respectability on a lower rung of the middle class always a paycheck away from disaster, and they thought they were doing great. Maybe they were. He was beginning to think that poverty was highly underrated. Who had said it? He could never remember. We spend our lives searching for security and hate it when we find it. He had hated it long before he ever thought to seek it out. He realized her birthday had passed. God, she was fifty. His baby sister. Fifty goddamn years old. To him, she was forever young, a bright-eyed curious kid. A fearless tomboy. God, how life had smoothed her down, ground her into the careful, anxious woman she now was. We start with such promise. He realized he was crying. Not just his occasional mistiness inspired by an Irish ballad and a gallon of hooch; these tears were real. Grief and fear, exhaustion and self-pity. He tried to remember the last time he had cried like this. It was like trying to remember a verse to a song he might have heard once, but was not sure. Maybe his mother's passing, his father's. Maybe not since he was a boy. He couldn't recall. Gone, unreachable, lost. He wiped the tears and lay silent, aware of Brady's vigilant presence, a thin wall away. After a while sleep finally came over him. He slipped under, wondering how the Knicks had done.

Jimmy rolled on his side and stroked her back under the sheets. "How come you didn't tell me, Tara?"

"I guess I figured you had enough on your mind."

"That right? So you let yourself get jammed up because of me, but you don't bother to say anything. You're losing your job because of me, and I'm not supposed to know about it? I'm not in on the decision? So now, because of me, you're fucked. These useless, cowardly motherfuckers. They don't have the balls to leave you out of it. Tara, you should have told me." He pulled his hand away.

"Would it have made a difference?"

Jimmy sat up. "That supposed to mean?"

The phone rang, and Jimmy snatched it up. It was Liam, assuring him that his uncle was safe. He rolled over and held on to Tara. Lou Condo had said they were going to make him pay a price. He did not think they would make Tara pay too. He wondered that she would sacrifice her career for him. He wished she had not done it, wished she had let him make the choice. But he wondered if he was in too deep to walk away.

"So now what?"

"So now you better win, Jimmy. Because my only hope of keeping the job is your winning. How's Punchy?"

"Good. Liam has him." He needed to figure how best to use Punchy. He had to assume that Keefe ordered the shooting. Maybe now Punchy wouldn't be so reluctant to turn on them. He wished he could talk to Cronin one more time. There were a thousand questions he needed to ask that had not occurred to him at the meeting.

Tara propped herself up on her elbow. "Is he going to do the right thing?"

"I don't know. Depends on how bad he wants to stay alive."

"How can he help you with the election?"

"Tell Keefe to drop out of the race, and we'll keep Punchy from ratting."

"Will Punchy go for that?"

He ran his hand through her hair, rubbed her neck. "That's not my problem. After the election, I don't care what happens to either of them."

"Jimmy, he's still your uncle."

"He sure as hell hasn't done me any favors lately. Besides, the way things are going, I don't think I can lose this election."

"You don't want to be so sure of that."

339

"Everywhere I go, I can feel it. Guys are coming up to me, telling me they're with me. Guys who wouldn't even look me in the eye when I started, would go the other way if they saw me, like I was some kind of disease they wanted to avoid."

"I don't want to be a wet blanket, but just for the sake of argument—you know, devil's advocate kind of thing—who's counting the votes?"

"Come on, Tara. I can't believe the government is going to go that far and fix the election. So they use Keefe as a rat. Let's face it, they've used worse. And I don't blame them."

"All I'm saying is you should go after him on as many levels as you can. He drops out, then nobody can fix the election."

"You should be my campaign manager."

"You could do worse."

"Yeah. Later, I go see my so-called uncle. See how he wants to play it. And, Tara?"

"Yeah?"

"I'm really sorry about the job. I, I didn't think they would pull shit like that. I'm sorry."

"I knew you would be, Jimmy. Let's just get this thing done."

Jimmy reached up and shut off the light. He lay there with Tara warm beside him. After a while he felt her fall off to sleep, her breathing deep and even. He rolled on his side and kissed her lightly on the top of her head. "I'm sorry," he whispered in the darkness. Sorry for a lot of things. He hoped one day they might move to a place where sorrow was not part of their equation.

Keefe sat in his Queens office and made a few bullshit calls he was late returning. He finished, then looked at his pile of mail. On top was a thick manila envelope marked "Personal and Confidential." He looked at the scrawled handwriting, hefted it, threw it back down on his desk. He walked over to the windows and looked out across the East River to the skyline of Manhattan. He had not heard from his brother-in-law since the meeting, and this worried him more than the fact that he was suddenly up to his ass in an election. He still did not think the kid had a snowball's chance in hell of beating him, but still. He thought of going to Roth and somehow discrediting the kid. Finding something on him. He wished the son had been hit instead of the father. Now he was running against a ghost, something he could not strike back against. A freaking martyr.

He picked up the envelope and sliced the end with a letter opener. He expected it to be some form of complaint by a disgruntled member. He was surprised to find photographs. He looked down and realized with a start what they were. They were all of his wife and Cronin, on the street in various embraces. He wondered whether this was just harmless nicey-nice and someone was fucking with him, trying to lead him to believe there was more to it. Then, as he flicked through them, he was getting incensed. Finally, he came to the last one. It was an indoor shot, this one. His wife was on her knees, wearing nothing but a wicked smile. She was positioned before Cronin, his trusted bodyguard, a member of mythic proportion jutting away from his hips. On it someone had written "Ha Ha."

He rose out of his chair as if propelled by a rocket blast. He paced the floor of his office, a red rage rising in him like a conflagration. The intercom buzzed, but he ignored it. He clenched his fists until his manicured nails sliced into his palms. He stalked back over to the desk and picked up the offensive portrait of his wife and Cronin to make sure it was real. "Motherfucker," he sprayed through clenched teeth. He tore the picture to shreds and dropped it on his desk. The mouth of his wife and the head of that . . . that . . . thing. Monstrous. He picked up his chair, spun it like a discus thrower, and heaved it against the wall. A half dozen picture frames fell to the floor. He picked up the rest of the photos, jammed them in his gym bag, and headed out of the office, past his gaping staff. He pulled out of the parking lot and headed for the highway. As he punched the gas pedal to the floor, he thought, Now it's my turn.

Jimmy sat on the boat and watched a hawk soar across the river, cruising the Palisades for prey. Two kids on a Jet Ski roared down the middle of the Hudson. Punchy was a nervous wreck. Though the air was cool, he was sweating profusely. His eyes were swollen, and he fidgeted in his seat. Jimmy tried to reel him in slow, but he was getting pissed off. His uncle's instincts were heavily toward the running part of the fight-or-flight index. Tara and Liam stood behind him.

"Jimmy, I can't let them get another shot at me. I'm not cut out for this horseshit. Maybe your father had the balls for it, but I'm not made that way, kid. The shit hits the fan and I fade quick."

"I thought you were in Nam," Liam said.

Punchy looked over at him. "Yeah, Captain Savage, I was in Nam. I ran a fucking bodega. A colonel needed a case of good whiskey, I was the go-to guy. I drove a powder blue jeep, painted it myself. I tried to stay a long way from the shooting. My fighting ended when I left Inwood. I found a better way."

"Look where that got you."

"Liam." Jimmy held up a hand to silence his friend. "What about this Fed who was looking to turn you? What's the story there?"

"Jimmy, it's not that simple. They got as much on me as they do on anyone. I'm in this up to my eyeballs. This would be a lot easier, I just get in the wind. Now, I appreciate you helping out. But it's just a matter of time before they catch up to me."

"Come on, Punchy. Cut the martyr act."

"Listen, it's not just Keefe and Magic and his guinea bandits. What motives do these Feds have? If what is being said is true, if Keefe is their man, then who needs me? Nobody. You think the government gives a shit that I been helping these people milk union pension funds? Half of the government guys I know would pin a medal on me if they could. The other half will watch the backs of their brothers. Nobody gives a shit about the members of your local. They're the losers here, always were, always will be. You think you'll change that? Good luck. That's gonna be your job, you win. You live long enough to do so."

"Hey, fucko." Liam moved toward Punchy. "Let's just turn this fat fuck over to the guineas."

Jimmy waved Liam off again. "Let me go see this Fed. Feel him out on the QT. If he wants to make a good deal, we'll bring your lawyers in and get it cut before we turn you over. He doesn't do the right thing, you're free to go wherever you want."

Punchy shook his head. His jowls made the left-to-right movement several times more than the rest of his head. "Jimmy, Jimmy, Jimmy. Two things I don't like the sound of. My lawyers. You got any idea who my lawyers are, who they really work for? I don't have a lawyer I'd trust with my life. Number two is: free to go. You imply that I'm some kind of hostage here. A man without free will."

"Your track record sucks when it comes to doing the right thing. We're just here to set you on the straight and narrow."

"Jimmy, come on."

"Punchy, you get a shot at redemption. Consider it a privilege. Now, gimme that Fed's number."

Punchy sighed and rummaged in his wallet for the number. He pulled out the tattered card and gave it to Jimmy, who took it and motioned for Liam to follow him outside.

When they left, Tara sat across from Punchy. She leaned forward and touched his leg, figured it was time to play good cop. "What I don't understand is why you don't do the right thing here, Punchy. Help everybody, including yourself."

He looked up at her with sad eyes, like a stricken walrus. He shook his head. "Can't it be simply that I'm scared? I'm scared to death of those people. They can get me anywhere. Prison, the witness protection program. You don't think there's a hard-up marshal or two out there, needs a little cash to make alimony payments, maybe a degenerate gambler, a drug addict, a guy wants a lifestyle he can't have on a civil servant's pay?"

"I've never heard of anyone getting killed in that program."

Punchy shook his head. "Never heard. Is that supposed to be a meaningful statement? A type of reassurance? Never heard. You probably never heard a lot of things that happen every day. You're a cop, right? You sit there and tell me you haven't come across a few people sworn to uphold the law, protect and serve, that have not taken opportunities as they saw fit? Please."

"This is about your family."

"If I thought I could really help, I would. My brother is dead. I can't change that. I would if I could, but I can't. Do you want to die? Do you?"

"Not at the moment, no."

"So please, cut me a little slack."

Jimmy stood with Liam on the deck of the gently rocking boat. A warm breeze blew upriver.

"You want me to cuff him?"

"Not yet. We need him to help. I don't want the guy seeing us as the enemy."

"Saved his fucking life."

"Yeah, Liam, listen, just keep him happy. I'm going to call this guy. See if he's interested. It should be easy."

"But it ain't. You should let me take care of Keefe my way."

"Liam."

"Jimmy, I'm serious. The guy's a piece of shit. It ain't like killing a human being. We'll be doing the world a favor."

Jimmy looked up to the George Washington Bridge. He had a picture of his grandparents amid the hoopla on the span the day it opened. He wished he could just nod his head and sic Liam on Keefe. Turn away and it would be done. He did not lack confidence in Liam's ability to carry out the hit. He just didn't think he had it in him to kill or order someone killed. He had thought long and hard on it. He wanted vengeance and he wanted it bad. Punchy was the key to that, not violence. He understood his uncle's fear; what he could not understand was his reluctance to take down the people who had

344

killed his brother and were obviously intent on doing the same to him.

"Not yet. Let's see how things go the next few days. Besides, we kill Keefe, who do you think they're going to look to?"

"So?"

"So, I still think there's other ways to get him."

"Fat boy?"

"For one."

"I can't stay here twenty-four/seven."

"Tara's gonna cover for us."

"You want her in the middle of this?"

"Liam. We're not talking about some librarian. She's combat-tested."

"More than you."

"Exactly. Plus this is just babysitting. Now let me go see what this Fed can do for us."

"He tries to leave, what then?"

"Do what you have to. Just try not to hurt him, all right? He's pissing me off, making this difficult."

"Tell me. So much for blood being thicker than water. Fucking rich people. What I always say. They get a little, they stop looking out for anybody but number one. Loyalty don't mean shit to these people. I don't give a fuck where he came from. It's all about where he is now. He don't live like you and me."

"All right. Tara will take over for tonight."

Jimmy left the boat, walked through the park, and flagged a gypsy cab. He wondered what this Fed might have to say, and he wondered what kind of leverage Cronin's tape might give him. There really was not much on it. He had listened to it over and over. The Fed, Roth, urged Cronin to get rough with him, but there was no specific threat, and since nothing had happened, what did he really have? He figured it would embarrass the man at worst. He guessed what he had going for him was there was no way for Roth to know that this was the only tape he possessed. He fidgeted in the back of the car, cracked the window for air. It was time for a little Liar's Poker.

Keefe picked up one of his leg breakers and handed him a pistol. He had him stop at a hardware store. "Go in and buy a roll of duct tape. A big one."

On the ride north, Keefe entertained visions of violence. He'd show the bitch and her boyfriend the price for screwing him behind his back. The oaf at the wheel tried to make small talk, but Keefe cut him off, saying they had a big job to do and it was going to be rough. The man was a convicted killer who had recently completed a manslaughter sentence. He would do nicely.

Keefe watched the countryside roll by. He could not get that picture out of his mind. It was seared into his consciousness. Her smile, the size of the prick on Cronin, which made him as mad as anything. My God, he'd never seen anything like it. His jaw began to ache and he realized he was grinding his teeth, his mouth shut with fury. His heart beat quicker as they neared the house. He prayed silently that she would be there, that they would both be there. So he could end it today. Now.

He'd play it nonchalant at first. Hey, just stopping by. Then all hell would break loose.

As they came upon the house, he noticed there was only one car, which meant Cronin was not there. Shit. That was all right, he thought. He'd just wait the man out, take care of his wife first. "You drive around the back. There's a barn. Park in there and wait till I come for you."

When he walked in the door he flashed a smile as wide and bright as can be. She stood agape, her lips twitching in an effort to speak. She wore a nice short dress he had never seen. It was a sexy cut and showed off her figure. He saw the fear in her eyes. This made him happy for the first time all day.

"Frankie." Barely audible.

"Hey, honey, what's the matter, you expecting someone else?"

"No, I just thought you'd call before you came."

"Oh, yeah. What, I gotta put a call in, let my own fucking wife know I'm coming? Why's that? Hah?" He tried to keep his voice light but it was not working. She started to back up.

"Maybe because you're fucking somebody else? No. You wouldn't do that, would you, honey? Would you? Come on, you can tell me."

He had her backed up to the wall beside the fireplace. Her eyes were wide with fright, and she was starting to tremble. He liked that. "Come on, baby, it's me, your hubby wubby. Till death do us part. That sound familiar to you? You little wacko guinea cunt. Ooops. I am sorry, sweetie. Did I call you a bad name?" He watched her lip twitch. He stroked the side of her face. "You can tell me who you're fucking. I'll forgive you."

"I don't know what you're talking about."

There. She had spoken. A little defiance mixed in with the fear. He liked that too. He punched her in the face with his right fist so hard that she bounced off the wall and crumpled at his feet. He stared down at her. The punch felt great. He could feel something in her face break. Little bones snapping. He rubbed his fist. One down. One to go.

He took out the tape and went to work, wrapping her feet and hands so tight she would need lots of help to get it undone. Help that was never going to come for her. When he was finished, he went out and called for his driver. The big lout actually jogged over to him.

"Bob Drury. I never bothered to ask you. That a Jew name?"

"Fuck no. West Side Irish."

"All right, Westie, you know how to dig a hole?"

"I can do it."

"Great. Make it deep."

"How deep?"

"Six feet'll be perfect."

"How do I know when it's six feet?"

Keefe looked up at the hulking ex-con. "You fucking with me?"

"No. I ain't good with figures."

"How tall are you?"

"Six-two."

"Well, figure it out from there."

"Oh, yeah, that's a good idea."

Jesus Christ. "No kidding. That's great. Start digging."

While his idiot dug, he sat and drank a glass of wine, a good Cabernet, and enjoyed the quiet of the country. He had not been up here in almost two years. What a waste. He watched as his wife came to and started to look around. He watched her eyes, watched as her situation became clear to her. "Welcome back, honey. Where's that boyfriend of yours? He on his way?"

When Drury called that he was finished, Keefe tossed back his glass of wine and picked Marie up off the floor. Black circles were forming under her eyes. He must have broken her nose. He carried her out, whispering, his voice soothing, "Don't this remind you of the honeymoon? Remember I carried you over that threshold in Waikiki? No? I do."

He stood above the hole Drury had dug and peered down. Nice work. Deep and wide. A perfect grave. He kissed her on the head and dropped her in. "Good night, shit bag."

Cronin wondered what kind of luck the gamblers of Manhattan had over the weekend, because his fortune this day was tied directly to theirs. Tuesday was the day all bets were squared, the day bookies had the most cash on hand. It was the day to rob one. If the sporting crowd had hit it big, he was about to make a nice score because Vince would be sitting on a pile to pay off. He perused the sports section. There were quite a few upsets. But how much wagering had been done on the underdogs was another matter. He hoped Vince served a reckless cadre. Then he'd be in the chips.

He was to stop first at his bank and load everything into a designer travel bag he had picked up for the occasion. He looked around his apartment one last time. There was nothing he wanted to take. It struck him as a sad statement for a man in his fifties. That he could pack a day bag and walk out his door without regret for what he left behind. Or maybe, he thought, it made him lucky. He pulled the door shut, thinking it all depended on how you looked at things. And on this day, he decided, things were looking good.

He left instructions for feeding his fish and a set of keys with the local pet store. Told the nice woman he was going on vacation for two weeks. When he did not return, he figured she would take them in and care for them. She was quite the animal lover.

He finished his banking and drove south toward his final stop. The traffic was heavy going down Seventh. He considered calling Marie, but no. She knew he was coming. One of those double-decker tour buses, red, and full of pink people from Europe, cut him off and braked. He swerved to avoid it and sped through a changing light. A cop on a horse shook his head as if Cronin had let him down. He parked two blocks from the bar, aiming his car north. When he entered the place he walked straight to the back without acknowledging the nods from the bartenders. They knew who he was, but that was not a concern of his. No one was likely to go to the cops about the crime he was about to commit. The air smelled of beer gone bad. The smoke was so thick you could part it. He saw Vince talking on the phone. He nodded, and Cronin sat at his table and waited. The man had the phone stuck between his shoulder and cheek and a cigarette in his hand. He wore a white shirt opened two buttons deep so his salt-and-pepper chest hair stuck out and a gold chain was visible. Cronin figured he was one of these old guys gone to seed but unable to recognize it. Like he was still thirty and had some physical appeal.

Vince hung up, and Cronin stood. "How's tricks, Vince?"

"Hey."

"I need a minute with you. The office?" He pointed with his thumb.

"It's gotta be quick. I'm working here."

"Two minutes tops."

When they stepped into the office, Cronin decided he'd oblige the man. He pulled his pistol from his waistband and chambered a round. Vince turned and regarded him with aplomb.

"Are you some kind of fucking nut?"

Cronin said, "More or less. Now, we're both in a hurry, so be nice and hand over your receipts."

"You realize you're a dead man." Vince was smug, unafraid.

"You don't move quick you'll beat me to it."

"You got some pair of stones."

"Yeah, yeah. You two-bit greaseball bookie. You know what's good for you, you'll shut your mouth."

"You're a fucking dead man."

"I'm warning you. Keep it up."

"You know who I work for, asshole. You're pissing off the wrong people."

Jesus, Cronin thought, I got John Wayne here. "You gonna shut the fuck up, or no?"

"What the fuck has gotten into you? You think that Teamster weasel can save you?"

Cronin, his gun trained on Vince, took bundles of cash from an open safe and loaded them into his bag. Vince looked up. The thick lenses lent his face a look of dementia. They were fogging. Sweat was forming on his brow and lip. "Turn around."

"Fuck you."

Cronin shook his head. "You're like a fucking cashier in a Mc-Donald's fighting off a stickup, being a hero for a guy who pays him minimum wage. Not smart. It ain't your money, Vince." He spun the chair around and smacked him over the head with the pistol. The bookie went down, but when he rolled over, he had a pistol in his hand. Shit. Cronin kicked his hand and the pistol discharged, then skittered across the floor, disappearing under a cabinet. The report was deafening in the small office. Cronin stepped back, then turned to look at Vince, who was holding his head and whimpering. The bullet must have hit him in the head. He looked closer. There was a hole in his forehead and a bigger hole out the top, but not much blood. Vince was muttering curses. Cronin took the bag and stepped away from the bloodied bookie. "Had to be a hero." He left through the back door, which led into an alley.

He realized the pistol was still in his hand. He shoved it into his belt and went to reclaim his car.

omething about the guy seemed wrong. He was not what Jimmy had expected. Roth looked more like a college professor than any cop he had ever known. He was tall and skinny and wore a suit that did not fit right. Jimmy half expected him to pull out a pipe and stoke it up while they were talking. He had urged Jimmy to come in immediately, had expressed great interest in what Punchy might have to say about Frankie Keefe and Tommy Magic. But now it all seemed to be backfiring. The other agent, who sat off to the side, just at the edge of his peripheral vision, and took notes, never saying a word, was right out of central casting. Buzz cut and hard angles, ropey neck, spit-polished shoes. He looked as if he enjoyed surreptitious beatings. What struck Jimmy immediately was that they did not seem much concerned with Punchy's plight or with what he might be able to offer them.

Jimmy had barely outlined the situation when Roth confused him more, saying, "Do you think you have a chance of winning your election?"

What had Condo stressed? Nothing is on the level. "I'm not here to discuss that."

Roth looked up at his colleague, and smiled, like they were in on a little secret that Jimmy was too stupid to know about.

"Oh, well, we see it all as part and parcel of the same thing."

"What same thing? Someone is trying to kill my uncle, and he wants to help you find them."

"Your uncle wants help? That's convenient. He gets in a little hot water with his business associates and, *voilà*, he's one of the good guys. A crime fighter." Roth chuckled.

Jimmy was uncertain. What was going on here? "He wants to help."

Roth began twirling a key ring on his index finger. "Maybe he's the one that needs help. You fancy yourself a labor leader. How do you feel about a man who has been robbing the pension funds of the rank and file? Not exactly a Eugene Debs, is he, your uncle?"

"He can give you Frankie Keefe. That's who's behind anything my uncle has done. And Tommy Magic."

Roth looked again to his colleague, and they exchanged smirks. Jimmy was getting pissed off. He stood up and walked to the side so he could see both of them at the same time. He wondered how much Roth was going to smirk when he heard the tape he had in his pocket.

"Well, what the hell does the taxpayer need us for?" Roth said.

"Got me," chimed in the sidekick.

"Let me tell you something, young man. Your uncle had better come to us if he wants to stay alive. We'll make a decision on how important his information is. But if he thinks he can escape prosecution by selling out, he's mistaken. We're not in the business of abetting felons."

It was Jimmy's turn to laugh. "No? What do you call your deal with Keefe?"

"Frankie Keefe? What are you talking about?"

"You know what I'm talking about."

"Don't believe everything you read in the papers."

Jimmy strode over to Roth's desk and placed his fists on top of it, leaning over. "Papers? No, I got better information than that. Your old pal, Cronin, came to see me." He turned to Roth's associate. "Why don't you give me a minute alone with your boss. I think we need to talk." Roth stared at him. Jimmy could see the doubt in his eyes, like a light coming under a door. Roth motioned with his head for the buzz cut to leave the room. When the door shut behind him, Jimmy took the tape out of his pocket and dropped it on the table. "That's one of many. Cronin was a resourceful guy, and I guess you ended up pissing him off. I gotta imagine whoever it is you work for is not gonna be happy with the way you're operating. I don't appreciate the way I'm threatened on this tape. Now we need each other. I can hold on to these or I can give them to my pal Jimmy Breslin. He'd love to stir up a shit storm that lands on you. So do yourself a favor. Think about what you can do for me, and for my uncle."

Roth stared up blankly, his smirk gone. Jimmy moved toward the door. "I'll be in touch."

Jimmy left with his heart beating in his throat. He wondered if

Roth would go for the bluff, and if he did, what it would mean for him and Punchy. He still needed to convince Punchy to cooperate, and he had to decide whether to hold him until the election or let him go. For now, he had to focus on winning. He had to get out the vote and he had to keep anyone else from being killed. Himself included.

Cronin stopped on a country bridge that spanned a dark black lake that was actually a flooded mine shaft, rumored to be many hundreds of feet deep. Marie had pointed it out on their first ride up here, as she had other local landmarks. A number of area kids had supposedly drowned in its cold embrace over the years. He leaned over and let the pistol fall. Ripples moved across the black surface, dissipating quickly. A clean entry. He got back in the car and headed for her, his love. He thought of her now and of escape. He never expected his life would lead to all this.

Keefe loved the look on Cronin's face when he walked in. "Hey, Pete, I got to show you something." He pointed the pistol and motioned him outside. He had Bob Drury, the mutant giant, backing him up with his own piece in case Cronin tried to play the white knight and get all heroic on him.

Cronin walked into the yard, regretfully flashing on the gun he had just dropped into the cold black water. He knew how easy it would have been to kill Keefe right here. If only he had the means. He felt a wave of nausea, a wobble in his knees. He was overcome by his helplessness. Keefe's words seemed to be coming to him from a deep valley, echoing. His lips were dry. He looked to the guy with the gun, recognized him as a leg breaker, then back to Keefe, who was waving at him with the pistol, his face twitching with rage.

"Come on, come on, you fuck. C'mere! You want to fuck my wife?"

Cronin wanted to run, to at least try to escape. But something more powerful pulled him toward the hole. He needed to see Marie, to know if she was dead or still alive. He did not want to escape without her. Maybe this is how they would get to be together. He edged closer to the pit. He looked down at the dirt piled at his feet. He smelled the deep lushness of the spring wood. The sky above was clear and high, full of promise. He would not show fear. Suddenly, he was calm. He wondered if his mother had received the letter he sent, how long she would await his arrival. As he moved toward Keefe, he realized that if he died here, he might never be found. Something in that appealed to him. Those who wondered where he was might think he succeeded. They would imagine him far away, living the high life in balmy climes, thumbing his nose at his detractors, his pursuers. Then he peered over into the hole and saw Marie, bound and terrified, and all hope bled out of him. He saw Keefe's shadow raise the shovel.

The thwack from the shovel made Keefe laugh. It was almost like something out of a cartoon. Boiiing. Only this character ain't gonna bounce back like nothing happened. This is the final episode. Cronin collapsed, tumbling on top of Marie with a thud. "You wanna fuck my wife! You can fuck her in hell, you piece of shit. I made you. You bite the hand that feeds you?"

He heard laughter behind him. "What's so funny?" He raised the gun and shot Drury in the mouth. End of laughter. The ape dropped at his feet. He put the gun down and rolled Drury on top of his wife and her lover. He stood over the hole feeling a surge of power, a vindication. Nobody fucked him over and got away with it.

He kicked dirt on them. "Make a kook-hole outta me? Fuck you!" He started shoveling hard. Shoveling and singing, "Will you love me in December?" He watched them disappear under the dirt. "Have some supper, wormies. On the menu tonight—a lying hooer and a backstabbing scumbag. Oh, and a dopey chauffeur for dessert."

He straightened up and brushed the dirt from his hands. He stomped up and down on the fresh grave, thinking, Holy shit, I've done it, I killed the bitch and the traitor. Drury he did not even consider. He smoothed over the grave and then went into the shed and rummaged around until he found some grass seed, which he sprinkled around the dig site. A few weeks, and nobody would be the wiser. He returned to the house and washed his hands. As he pulled out of the yard, he figured, Why stop here? It was time to get rid of that prick college boy and his slob brother-in-law too. Then, Frankie Keefe thought as he hit the highway, I'll be home free.

Roth listened to the tape over and over again and was irritated by the sound of his own voice. Cronin. He never would have believed he was interested in anything but getting paid. He sat in the kitchen of his apartment and contemplated his next move. Were there more tapes? If the kid won his election, he was still subject to the whims of the government consent decree over the union. Roth had many friends in a position to have Dolan removed from office for any number of allegations, none of which needed to be true. So he still had something there. Of course, this was true only if he won. If the kid lost, he really did not have anything to use against him. But how far out on a limb was Dolan going to go for his uncle? His real motivation was obviously in destroying Keefe. Roth poured another cup of coffee and hit the play button one more time. It looked like it was time to pull the plug on Top Echelon Informant number one.

On his way back to the city, his rage subsiding, Keefe realized his situation. He had just killed his wife, Magic's sister. Now what was he going to do? He knew this meant he would have to make the next move and whack the mafioso. He needed to do it smart, make it look like someone else had done it. He pulled into his circular driveway and shut off the ignition. His house would be empty now.

It was too large to live in by himself. Maybe he would put it on the market. He sat trying to calm himself, to stay in control. He worried about the bodies. Maybe he should go back and move them off the property. Should he report her missing? He opened the bag of money he had found in Cronin's car. It looked to be a few hundred grand. Those creeps had been about to run off.

He picked up a sheet of newspaper that had blown into his hedge. He let himself into his house, jangled his keys, felt his wife's absence. He walked into the living room. He started to pour himself a rare scotch when behind him someone said, "Shitbird."

Keefe jumped a full foot off the floor and spun, his legs heavy, his asshole clenching with fear. "Tommy! Mother of God, you scared the shit outta me."

"That blood on your shirt?"

"No!" He looked down. "I mean, yeah. I, we had some trouble with a member." He laughed. It sounded to his ears like a deranged schoolgirl giggle.

"Where's my sister?"

"She's still up the country, Tommy." Keefe felt a panic coming over him. He fought the crazy urge to blurt out a confession.

"Call her on the phone. I need to ask her something."

"Now? On the phone?"

"You got shit in your ears?"

"Ha ha." He picked up the phone and dialed. Of course there was nothing to worry about. It wasn't like somebody was going to answer.

"Your shoes get muddy? You're fucking up your carpet."

He looked down at his muddy shoes. Real professional killer, he was. He searched Magic's ugly face for signs that he knew anything. It was like looking at a stone gargoyle on a building. Nothing. He considered killing the fat fuck right then and there. He wondered how he'd gotten up from Queens. There was no car out front. "No answer. She's probably out shopping. You know how these women are."

"No, I don't."

"How'd you get up, Tommy? I didn't see your car."

"I got ways."

The next question in his mind was: How the hell did he get in the house? "Any problem with the alarm?"

"Keys."

"Keys?"

"Yeah, keys, you stupid prick. You think I don't got the keys to my own sister's house?"

Keefe affected a look of surprise. He was, in fact, surprised. What other secrets did the two of them keep from him? Magic's bulk seemed molded to the chair in which he sat. His face was dark with some unfathomable displeasure. What was he doing here? Keefe stared at the oak logs stacked cleanly by the fireplace. Just pick one up and bash the old prick, then finish him off with a pillow, like a mercy killing. But what if he was driven here? What if the G had seen him come in? He'd be doing them a favor, but he doubted they'd see it like that. The ungrateful bastards.

Magic reached behind him and pulled out a gun. Keefe yelped, backed himself to the wall. He cringed, waiting for the blast. Magic pointed and the television came on. Mister Rogers, his sweater, the neighborhood. The fucking remote.

"There something wrong inside your head?" Magic glared up at him.

Keefe stretched his arms back, playing it off. Just a little tic.

"C'mere." Magic motioned him over.

Keefe sat on the ottoman at Magic's feet. He felt ridiculous, like a kid. Magic grabbed him by the back of the head as if he was pulling a whore's head down for a blow job. He leaned in close and caught a strong whiff of garlic and bad medicine. Magic's skin was clammy. Magic whispered in his ear like a lover. "How much can your fat friend really hurt us?"

"Enough."

"I don't like that answer."

"Tommy, what can I say?"

"Somebody tried to shoot him the other night. You got any idea where he might be? This fat rat fuck."

"Can't say I do."

"I got some more guys you need to take into the union for me."

"Guys?"

"Yeah, more of them Russians."

"Russians? Tommy, this is a bad time. The election and all."

"Fuck cares? You get them in there. I got two in particular I want as shop stewards."

"Shop stewards? Tommy, the books are closed. I open them up now, it's gonna look awful bad."

Magic pulled back and slapped him, heavy-handed, across the face. Keefe's head turned halfway around and his ear rang from the blow. He was stunned.

"That's enough outta you. That union is mine! You do what the fuck I tell you to, or so help me, I'll hurt you like nobody's ever been hurt. And this fucking kid, you take care of that too. You hear me?" Magic stood. "Tell my sister to call."

Keefe rubbed his face and watched Magic go, the humiliation washing over him like a blast from a fire hose. He wished he had the balls to kill the old greaseball. Tell him about his sister first. Rub it in. He knew now he had to kill him. Russians. What the hell was this with the goddamn Russians? And what the hell was he going to do about Jimmy Dolan?

Tara dreamt that she and Jimmy were on a honeymoon cruise. They were on the deck of a grand ocean liner at night making good speed, when it began to dawn on them that they were alone. The decks were abandoned, and as they searched anxiously through the decks, it became obvious that they were on a ghost ship, a doomed vessel. She awoke frightened, her breath quick and shallow, the air charged with menace. Then it came to her where she was. She thought she heard something, or was it an echo from her fading dream? She listened hard in the dark, tight air of the hold. She made out Punchy's snoring, that was all. She relaxed, but then heard it again. A footstep? She felt the boat shift. Somebody was up there.

She rolled off the bunk and picked up the pistol Liam had left for her. She crawled through the hold to the next berth. The smell of Punchy, seeping booze, halitosis, was asphyxiating. She gagged as her bile began to rise. She nudged him. He did not respond, so she jabbed him hard in the neck with the pistol. Finally he came to. She clamped a hand across his mouth and whispered in his ear. "They're here. Come with me. Be quiet." She felt his body quiver, the fear surging through him like electricity.

She considered her options. She saw the deck above her splintering and realized somebody was walking along and shooting through the deck, heavy-caliber fat balls of lead from a silenced weapon. She could feel the rounds, thwack, thwack, thwack, hitting with impact, sending tremors through the frame of the boat. There was a precision to the barrage, a calculation. The shooter was methodical and practiced. She considered firing back through the ceiling, but no, that would give up their position and she had to believe they were outgunned. She wanted to get Punchy off the boat first.

She led the way to the rear hatch, hugging close to the wall. She snapped open the latch and pulled the door wide. The air was chilled by the water. "Stay right here."

She ran back and retrieved two life jackets from the locker. She forced one down over Punchy's head and ears, pulled it tight, then nudged him toward the hatch. "Just slide out into the water."

"It's cold. Too cold."

He spoke with a girlish whine, and she fought the urge to slap him. Tara wished he could see the look on her face. "You rather be cold or dead?"

"I can't swim."

"You don't have to. Just float, you're fat enough. Now go!" She shoved his head down to the hatch.

"Oh, for the love of God."

As Punchy started for the water, she scuttled along the hold, firing randomly through the deck above her head. She heard and felt movement and, in response to her shots, the bullets coming down hard and fast, rock and roll, somebody on full automatic. She scurried with her hand over her head as if it might make a difference. When she reached the stern she hit the toggle switches to illuminate the deck. She heard cursing, a staccato language rough and thick in the throat. Russian? She ran back, zigzagging, praying the bullets would not find her. As she neared the stern, she heard someone pull open the deck door and drop something down. She considered a dive into the water but instead flipped a table over and knelt behind it, dropping her forehead to the floor. A terrible light and noise filled the cabin and she felt the force of the concussion grenade against her ad hoc barricade. Her head rang from the blast and she felt disoriented. For a moment she forgot where she was. Her head cleared, and she slapped a new clip into her pistol and trained her fire on the ladder leading down. She emptied the clip and tossed the weapon aside. She took the boat's flare gun and slipped out of the hatch.

The water hit her with a shock, icy. The pain clamped like a vise on her bones. Her clothes weighed her down. Her chest tightened from the frigid river. She caught her breath, calmed herself. There were shooters running along the dock. She leaned her head back and pointed the gun straight up into the Manhattan night and squeezed the trigger. The flare shot up over the river and bathed them in a pink hot light.

She found Punchy clinging to a cleat on the side of the boat. She moved behind him and slid her arm around him, then leaned back, thankful for her summers of lifeguarding in Rockaway. She stayed close to the boat, determined not to get out of the water until she saw the NYPD. The wind whistled through her head and she wondered if the grenade had ruptured an eardrum. Punchy shivered in her arms, a huge, sobbing baby. "Maybe you should listen to Jimmy," she said.

He choked out a response. "I will, I will, I will."

She heard the sirens, but waited until she saw the strobe of the cherry tops before hauling her charge toward shore.

Jimmy sat on the stage beside Lou Condo as Rosen worked his retirees into a lather. He was a surprisingly effective speaker, and his indignation rose as he attacked Keefe's mishandling of the pension funds. He punched the air with his forefinger and thundered, "Biggest bull market in history and this—this—this horse's ass! is losing our—*your* money. You might ask why. You might ask how. I'll tell you how. This creep is in bed with the sewer rats, the gangster element, the racket boys. He's a bum!"

The retiree committee had rented the Theatre at Madison Square Garden for their annual convention. Up and down the aisles Jimmy saw banners proclaiming him the leader. Some of the attendees were in their nineties, others had recently stopped working and were still full of vigor. He watched a man in a wheelchair he had met earlier wave a small American flag. He was the last man alive who had worked on the Empire State Building.

Jimmy tried to keep focused, but the shooting at the boat the previous night had him spooked. In the aftermath, Punchy had become more determined not to inform, more scared. For now, that did not matter. He would worry about Punchy and everything else after the election.

Now Rosen was pillorying the executive board. Jimmy's fear of physical harm had morphed into an edgy numbness. He had no choice. He was not going to be intimidated. He was going ahead with the election no matter what, so he tried to keep everything in perspective. He would stay on his toes, but he refused to hide. He was surprised he had not heard back from Roth. But that was another thing he could not control, so he decided to put it aside. If he won, Roth, Punchy, Keefe, they would all be less important to his life. He listened as Rosen hit a fever pitch, and twisted to indicate Jimmy with his gnarled right hand. "And now, brothers and sisters, I bring to you the next president of Local 383, Jimmy Dolan."

Condo nudged him and Jimmy rose from his seat as the room exploded into cheers. He took the podium with the applause persisting. He felt it down through his body, in his chest, to his toes. He stared up into the reaches of the room, flags waved, men hooted and hollered for him. He had never felt anything like this before. He waited until the noise subsided and started by saying, "I want to dedicate this campaign to my father, who, like all of you here, was a great Teamster. This one's for Mike Dolan." And once again, the applause rose until it was thunderous.

The vote was held at a Teamster hall on Fourteenth Street, and the turnout astounded everyone. Jimmy stood with Liam and Lou Condo and Sol Rosen beside a truck that was providing coffee and doughnuts for the men. Jimmy had the vehicle draped in American flags and "Vote Dolan" posters. He had arrived at 7 a.m. and now, just past 10, Frankie Keefe was finally showing up. Jimmy noticed that Cronin was nowhere to be seen and wondered what had happened to him. Keefe hurried past them without as a nod, but he lacked his usual strut. His eyes were glued to the back of the bodyguard he followed into the hall.

Rosen watched and said, "The man reeks of defeat."

Jimmy passed out his campaign literature and greeted Teamsters as they pulled up in their trucks to vote. The men climbed down from their rigs and most met Jimmy with enthusiasm. As the day wore on, Jimmy's nerves calmed a bit and he began to feel he had things in hand. It was just after three o'clock when Keefe came out with a half dozen of his men and, after giving Jimmy the finger, roared off in his Cadillac. Soon after that, word came out that Keefe had conceded the election. A cheer went up, and men came over, slapping Jimmy on the back. An impromptu celebration broke out on the sidewalk, with Lou Condo producing a case of champagne. After a while they moved the party across the street to O'Hanlon's Bar.

"You believe it?"

Liam was by his side, a bottle of Bud in each hand. "Yeah, Jimbo. I knew it all along. I gotta say thanks for saving me from a murder rap. Because, not for nothing, I would've put that piece of shit in the ground, you lost. Least I could do."

"All right then."

Jimmy stayed till late in the evening, surrounded by Teamsters, accepting backslaps and congratulations. But as the party wore on, a sadness was welling up inside of him. This was the one thing his father had fought for his whole adult life. He began to feel detached from the celebration around him. Since getting wrapped up in the election, he hardly had time to deal with his father's death. Condo was beside him, but Jimmy ignored him. He tipped his beer in a silent toast to his father. This one's for you, Dad.

Then he turned back to Lou Condo and to all the others who were toasting his success and smiled, letting a look of triumph wash over his face. Condo held up a ring of keys. "Here you go, kid. Keys to the union office." And everyone cheered.

Roth took the call from the Teamster hall, nodded, and hung up. Pacing, he stopped in front of the windows overlooking Broadway. Traffic was at a standstill and the braying of car horns rose from the street, shattering the solitude of his office.

It was time to pull Frankie Keefe off the street. He would place a call to the U.S. Attorney's office and execute as many arrests as possible. As long as Keefe went along he might wrap things up nicely. Then he would meet again with Jimmy Dolan. He sat at his desk and picked up his phone.

Liam was getting a little sick of all the backslapping. He figured there was still a lot to worry about with or without Keefe. There was still that Mafia guy. Jimmy brushed off his suggestion to leave, so he slipped out of the bar for some fresh air. He walked around the corner to a deli for a soda and a *Post*. He paid and walked back toward his truck, which was parked just down the street from the bar. He sat on the hood and read the *Post*, cursing at the Rangers' poor performance, then dropped it through the window onto the driver's seat. He glanced at his watch. He wanted to get home. He idly surveyed the traffic, mostly yellow cabs and delivery trucks. He watched a dark sedan pull to a stop. There were two men in the front seat. When the passenger turned to him, Liam said, "Holy fuck." That was a face he would never forget. He reached into the pickup and grabbed his pistol from his gym bag.

Gregov's cousin never tired of complaining about American women. Gregov nodded, but he had to disagree. He loved everything about America. Where else was there so much to steal and such weak policing? He looked in his rearview mirror and saw a cop on a scooter advancing slowly toward them. He was glancing at registration stickers, looking for an easy ticket. Gregov cursed. He did not want anyone to remember seeing them. He had hoped the son of the man they killed would have come out by now, so they could get the job done. His boss was becoming impatient with all the botched killings. They looked bad, unprofessional, like amateurs. All this shooting. He would prefer to use some of the tricks he had learned in the mountain villages of Afghanistan. They would kidnap rebel leaders, peel the skin off the bodies, flay them alive. Then leave them to die slowly. Here it is all bang-bang. A woman could do it.

He watched the cop stop at a Mercedes half a block away and flip open his ticket book, then dismount. Gregov checked the bar door. Nothing happening. His cousin lit another cigarette, his hands shaking. The boy had been in Grozny for the big defeat. They say it was worse there. Doing the bad things to your own people. The cop finished writing, tore the ticket from the book, then climbed back on his scooter and moved toward them again. Gregov dropped the transmission into drive and took his foot off the brake. He would have to chance going around the block again. It was then that his cousin started shouting.

Liam stuck the gun in his waistband and moved for the car. He looked around quickly and saw the cop at the end of the block. He contemplated yelling for him, but with the noise and the crowd and the traffic, he might not be heard. He saw the car with the shooter start to pull away from the curb and he sprinted toward it, trying to stay in the blind spot. He caught the car and while jogging alongside it swung a hard punch into the face of the shooter. The man screamed in surprise, and Liam threw two more hard shots, both glancing off the man's face. He reached for the door handle, but it was locked. He was about to go for his pistol when the shooter grabbed his arm and yanked it into the car just as it accelerated up the street. Liam grunted as the man bit down hard on his wrist. He tried to swing his other arm into the car, but the vehicle picked up speed and it was all he could do to run fast enough to keep from being dragged. The driver jumped the curb and they sped down the sidewalk toward Eighth Avenue, scattering spectators, who dove for cover.

Liam ran along as fast as he could in the awkward position. When he could no longer keep up the pace, they started to drag him along, his feet scraping the sidewalk, his knees banging on the car door. He ducked his head and made a desperate dive, following his arm into the car. He came face to face with the Russian who had killed Mike Dolan, could feel the man's hot breath in his face. For a moment, shocked, they looked into each other's eyes. Liam could smell him, a thick bad stench. Then the driver started hitting him in the face, and Liam lunged and bit hard into the shooter's cheek. The car bounced off the wall of a bar, and the two men were screaming and trying to beat Liam. The front fender clipped a hot-dog cart and sent it spinning into a trio of tourists, knocking them to the ground. The driver managed to turn onto the avenue, cutting wildly into uptown traffic. Liam's body sideswiped a UPS truck and a bone in his thigh snapped. The pain was dizzying. He bit harder, tried to throw some punches. The driver pulled a pistol from beneath his seat. Liam saw the gun and let go of the passenger's cheek. Now Liam watched as the gun was raised to his face. He bucked his body up and away, trying to throw himself out of the careening vehicle. His head hit the roof of the car, and when he was coming back down the driver drove the pistol into his face, cackled, said, "Goodbye, asshole," and pulled the trigger.

The car sped up the avenue and the Russians yanked Liam

through the window and dumped him on the back seat. They drove on, blood-drenched and determined, new Americans.

Jimmy rolled out of bed to the insistent ringing of the telephone. He glanced at the clock and saw it was just after 8 a.m. His head was heavy from the previous night's drinking. The triumph of the election was a vague memory.

"Jimmy, God. I'm glad you're home. It's Punchy. I'm down at MCC. I've been arrested. You have to help me. I'm not gonna make it down here."

Jimmy was not sure how he could help. "What's your bail?"

"Bail? A million dollars, these bastards. I didn't hurt anyone, I'm not a killer. A million goddamn dollars. The creeps dragged me out of my bed at dawn. They had guns, lots of guns."

"You have that kind of money?"

"Money? No. Property, some things, my houses. Money, no. I can't buy a ham sandwich at this point." Jimmy heard a commotion, and the phone dropping, banging off the wall, then Punchy yelling, "I'm on the fucking phone!" Then Punchy was saying, "You would not believe the degenerates down here."

Jimmy said, "Punchy, what do you want from me? You want me to try and put your bail together? You have a lawyer?"

"No. Jimmy, I can't be on the street. I'll be dead in six seconds. I'm going for protective custody. You have to help me here, kid, please. Talk to that twisted fuck Roth. Please. Do something, cut a deal. Make the guy happy enough to get me probation. You're in the driver's seat now."

Jimmy agreed to see what he might do and hung up. Tara rolled over and was running her hand across his chest. "Your uncle?"

"Yeah?"

"He wants?"

"He wants me to help him get a deal from the Feds."

"How can you do that?"

Jimmy sat up. "I don't know, exactly. He wants me to talk to Roth. He thinks I can help him."

Tara sat beside him. "Jimmy, don't do anything that's going to hurt you. He might be your uncle, but he had every chance to help you out and failed."

Jimmy shook his head. "I know." He stood to dress. "But he's still family."

"Yeah, right. When it's beneficial to him."

"We all have our crosses to bear. Come on, I want to see if we got any coverage."

They moved into the living room and Jimmy flipped on the television. NY1 was on and the reporter was going through his daily summary of top stories from the local papers. Jimmy moved into the kitchen to make a pot of coffee, but when he heard the word "Teamster," he came back into the room. He stood with the pot of water in one hand and turned up the volume. The reporter was not commenting on his victory at all. To Jimmy's shock there was a picture of Keefe being escorted by beefy men in suits and scowls into a federal building downtown. What the hell?

Jimmy sat on the coffee table and peered at the set as if he were trying to look right through it. The report lasted less than thirty seconds. Evidently, Keefe had turned state's evidence and was being put in the federal witness protection program. He wondered why Punchy had failed to mention that. He had probably not heard. The reporter said that arrests were being executed all over the metropolitan area. The only mention of the election was to say that Keefe had recently been voted out of office. Recently? There was a shot of a federal agent praising Keefe for his courage and cooperation in helping to loosen organized crime's grip on construction in New York. The agent described the indictments coming down as a deathblow. The anchor moved on to a story on a domestic shooting, a sloppy homicide born of love. Jimmy hit the mute and sat down. Tara put her arm around him.

He considered what this might all mean. Keefe goes from disgraced labor leader to hero overnight. He slammed the pot down on the coffee table.

"What did you expect?"

"What do you mean?"

"Jimmy, you think these people will stop at anything to get what they want? You put yourself in the middle of two groups that fight dirtier than anyone. Get serious."

"Thanks for the encouragement."

"I'm not criticizing you."

"I ran a clean campaign."

"What did Chickie say? That and a buck fifty . . ."

"Will get me to Canarsie. I better get hold of Liam. He took off last night without saying goodbye." He rang Liam. He was starting to fear for his friend.

"Not home?" Tara asked.

"No. I'm really worried. His mother is hysterical. Liam has never not called to let her know he was gonna be out all night."

"Do you remember him leaving the bar?"

Jimmy shook his head. He had been caught up in the moment and figured Liam had just slipped out for a minute. It was not unlike him. Not coming home was another story. Jimmy began to entertain horrible thoughts. "He wanted me to leave, but I felt I needed to stay, thank all the guys. It was their campaign too."

Tara's voice was thick with worry. "What do we do?"

Jimmy slumped in his chair. "I don't know." He had ignored Liam's concern, had chosen to stay and party with Condo and the others. Now he was scared.

The phone rang and he snatched it, hoping Liam was on the line. He heard Roth say, "You better come see me. We have a good idea what happened to your friend."

Jimmy slammed the phone off the wall. Tara came and stood before him, placing her hands on his shoulders. "Jimmy, now you have to hang tough. No matter what happens, I'm with you a thousand percent on this, all right? Whatever he threatens you with, we're together on this."

He shook his head and embraced her. Then he dressed and went to see the duplicitous Fed, knowing that his best friend, like his father, was now dead.

Tommy Magic went out to his garden and counted off the steps to where he had buried his loot. He was going to dig up a million dollars and put a contract out on his weasel of a brother-in-law. He had received a phone call at dawn describing Keefe's defection, and was surprised that no one had come for him yet. Maybe the Irish prick was not giving him up. Still, a rat was a rat, and he had to go. He just wondered who he should send out. All of a sudden the goddamn Russians did not seem capable of killing a fucking cockroach.

He was on his knees in the middle of his tomato patch digging at a steady pace, his heart beating a mad tattoo in his chest. Cold, sour sweat poured from him. He had dreamt again of being buried alive, of a horrible, suffocating death, of life being crushed slowly out of him. He thought he heard something and looked up into a dazzling sun and was temporarily blinded. Nothing.

He bent harder to his task and had almost reached his strongbox when he saw a shadow crawl across his garden. He looked up, and there before him, blocking out the mean sun, was a figure dressed in black, faceless from the backlight. Magic spotted the pistol in the man's hand. He felt the fear come over him. He heard a voice, thick with gutter Russian, say, "Good night, Magic man." He lunged for the man's ankles, but he was too slow, too old, too weak. Thomas Vamonte's time had come. The bullets entered his brain, three quick shots from a silenced .22 pistol, and scrambled around the inside of his skull, tearing him from this life.

Jimmy could swear he saw a hint of a smile in the Fed's eyes, like a flash of heat lightning. Roth had just described the car that was found abandoned in Queens with Liam's gun and a pool of blood they were checking for a DNA match. Jimmy had prepared himself for the worst on the ride downtown. He fought to keep grief off his face.

"So what do you want from me now?"

"I think we are in a position to help each other out."

Jimmy shook his head. "Is that right? What the fuck can you do for me?"

"For one thing, I can keep your uncle out of prison, a place I don't think he will fare very well in."

Jimmy shrugged. He had a hard time feeling very concerned for Punchy right now. He was becoming convinced that Punchy had helped put him in this horrible spot.

"Second, I can help you get rid of the Russians."

"Russians?"

"Yes. Russians. They killed your father and it now looks like they killed your friend too."

Jimmy wondered at Roth's knowledge. "You mean, I can help you get rid of them."

"If that's how you choose to see it."

"So you come out on top—as always. The great civil servant, a model of integrity."

"I think you'd better realize what you're up against. These people are quite capable of killing everyone you know, with impunity."

"Oh, really? Looks like you're a little behind the curve on this one."

Roth studied him with detachment. "Well, do you want to be next? There is only one way to fight them. That's to let them think you're on board. I'm the only friend you have, Dolan. We can both get what we want. You offer up a bit of your soul, you still get to be the new dynamic labor leader. You help me, I'll help you."

"Why the hell should I?"

Roth smiled. "Let's run down my list. As I said, your uncle ends up with fines and probation. Two, this never happens." Roth slid a Justice Department press release over to him. Jimmy quickly perused it. It described Liam Brady as an arms trafficker linked to organized crime. Jimmy handed it back. He considered strangling the asshole, breaking every bone in his body. It was just the two of them.

"And you know if that happens, we will have no trouble bringing charges against you under the consent decree for association. You won't be in office for a month. If you think I can't make that happen today, tomorrow, or yesterday, then you are not only naive, you're stupid."

Jimmy glared at Roth. A beating and walk away from it all. Simple.

"Now, you might think, What's in it for me? We start with you keeping your position."

Jimmy stood up. "You're a scumbag, Roth."

"Scumbag? The world's an ugly place, Dolan. People like me keep the real scumbags at bay."

"I don't need any of this."

"Fine, we'll put a trustee in charge of the local. Someone with little regard for your members or the rights of labor."

Jimmy shrugged. "I still have those tapes, asshole."

Roth laughed. "Really? I hope for your members' sake you can bluff better at the bargaining table. I don't think you have any more tapes. And if you do, I'll wager they don't have much on them." Roth smirked. "And." He stood. "We'll press the case against your girlfriend. Do our best to see she not only loses her job but gets prison time." Roth let this sink in, then smiled and said, "Starting to wish you had taken that job offer, I bet."

Jimmy kicked the side of Roth's desk. "You know something, you smug prick? Someday all this is going to come back and bite you in the ass. And I'm going to be there to see it happen."

Roth pursed his lips. "We can all dream, can't we? I'll be in touch. And, oh, congratulations on your victory. However Pyrrhic it may be."

Jimmy slammed the door as hard as he could. Behind him, he heard Roth's laughter again. He fought the urge to go back and kick him till he begged for his life.

He walked up Broadway, seething, as the day began to turn hot. It was a freak early heat wave and he was sweating by the time he reached Canal Street. His head swam with conflicting emotions, and he changed his mind every few blocks. One moment he was determined to take office and do his best to fight the Russians and Roth; the next he wanted to walk away from it all, get on a train and ride it to the end of the line.

He wove through the thick pedestrian traffic and went down the list of consequences his running might have. The worst was Tara, although he wondered how much the department would go after her if she left the job. She had already raised quitting as a distinct possibility and was contemplating law school. As for Punchy, he could rot for all the shit he had caused. He made his way west. He could not believe Liam was dead, could not imagine it. He worried about Mrs. Brady. Liam being portrayed as a criminal might hurt her, but Jimmy figured with her antigovernment leanings it would be easy to convince her that Liam was being smeared. Fuck it, he thought. It was time to be realistic. He had a friend to bury. Enough people he cared about had died. He was no match for these murderous Russians. And dealing with Roth would only sully him further. He stopped at a pay phone and rang Tara, wanted her approval. No answer.

Jimmy stood on the corner of Fourteenth Street and Eighth Avenue. He watched as a caravan of four concrete trucks passed, their agitators turning slowly. Jimmy contemplated his commitment to the members of Local 383. He had taken up their cause and promised men like Condo and Rosen that he was ready for whatever anybody might throw at him. That he was dedicated and worthy of their support, that he would fight for them. Now he was on the brink of abandoning them. He waited for the light and headed up Eighth Avenue. If he was leaving he had one stop to make.

Jimmy pushed into the Blarney Stone and found Condo on his usual stool, watching the television. Jimmy sat down and Condo held up a hand to hush him. The reporter detailed that morning's execution of Thomas Vamonte in his backyard in Queens. The reporter finished the breaking story by quoting confidential sources that linked Magic's murder to the indictments of forty-two in a construction industry rackets case.

Condo sipped his Johnnie Black and motioned for the bartender to turn down the sound on the TV. He said to Jimmy, "You don't look too good."

"Yeah, well, it looks like they killed Liam." He related Roth's description of the car, the Russian involvement, and his threats.

Condo was silent for a moment. "I'm sorry to hear that. I really am."

Jimmy declined the offer of a drink. "I don't think I can go through with it."

"That means?"

Jimmy exhaled. "Listen, I'm . . . I'm gonna take a pass."

"Is that so?" Condo looked at his hands. "You know, it's all right to be scared."

Jimmy swiveled on his stool, determined to at least look Condo in the eye.

Condo stared straight ahead. His voice was soft with disappointment. Jimmy had to lean in to hear him. "You came to me, after your father was killed. Do you remember what I told you?"

"Yeah. How if I won, people would come after me."

"Did you believe me? Or did you think I was jerking your chain?"

"I believed you."

"What else did I say?"

"Nothing's on the level."

"Good. Now, I'm going to walk back there and I'm going to take a leak. I want you to think this over hard. I want you to think about the fifty-five hundred members of Local 383. I want you to think about the retirees that worked for you, that believed in you. I want you to think about the families of all these men. Then I want you to think about your uncle and your girlfriend. But most of all, I want you to think about your dead father and your dead pal."

Condo pushed away from the bar. "And when I come out of the head, I want to see one of two things. I want to see this stool empty or I want to see it with you on it. Now, listen to me closely. If you're gone, and I mean this sincerely, I won't really blame you. 'Cause it's gonna take some mighty big balls to stay and play this one out. And I'm not the guy to judge you, you want to take off. Just remember this is now a hell of a lot bigger than Jimmy Dolan and what might be good for him. But remember this too. You're not alone. We'll help you every way we can. They don't call it a brotherhood for nothing." Condo stood. "I'll be back."

Jimmy sucked in a breath as Condo made his way through the

nearly empty bar to the bathroom. The bar cat rose up, sniffed for prey, then nestled down again. The air was still. Sunlight, softened by the dingy windows, splashed along the worn and oiled wood bar. The only other patrons, two old men whose vitality had long ago been leached from them, stared at nothing at all. The steam table smelled of cabbage and burnt onion. For a moment nothing moved and an unnatural hush fell about the place. Jimmy felt the odd sensation of the world grabbing on its axis, snagged. Time stopping. He looked at the door. It was less than ten feet away. One version of his life was out there, another started where he sat. It came to him with force that he had a minute to make the most important decision of his life.

He stood. He might walk away, but he would never live it down. He knew that for the rest of his years he would live with the sting of cowardice, like a combat vet who folded on himself when the shit hit the fan. Understandable but inexcusable. But mostly he was certain he could not live with his ghosts. He could not abandon his father and Liam. What they had believed in. Condo was right.

He knew Tara wanted him to stick it out, and as long as she was with him, he would never be alone. He turned and watched the city life rush past outside. People hustled along, caught up in their lives, shoulders hunched forward, determined. He looked at a picture on the wall. It was of a street scene right outside the window taken many decades ago. He wondered how many of those captured in the black-and-white shot went to their graves feeling they had done the right thing in life. He sat back down.

He heard the flush of the toilet and the running water. The door of the bathroom flung open and Condo emerged, taking several steps before he looked up to find Jimmy waiting for him. Jimmy watched the old Teamster come toward him. He shrugged, and Condo's face lit with a warm smile. He shook Jimmy's hand and said, "Welcome to the big time, kid."

"Yeah, Louie. How's it go? In for a penny, in for a pound."

"You got that right, Jimmy. And remember . . ."

Jimmy beat him to it. "Nothing's on the level."

Acknowledgments

I'd like to thank my agents, Nat Sobel and Judith Weber, and my editor, Paul Elie, all of whom made *The Rackets* a better book.